2028

© 2020 *The Hill*

2028

A Novel by David H. Robbins

"We have met the enemy and he is us."
Attributed to Walt Kelly
From a "Pogo" comic strip, 1970

DH
ROBBINS

—Dedication—

For the preservation of Democracy.

—Acknowledgements—

Thanks to all of you who encouraged me to go ahead on this, sometimes against my wishes. You led me to believe that this story should be told. This includes but is in no means limited to: Bonnie G., Kara L., Chris M., Norm G., my writing comrades and students, and many based media outlets based in the truth and the First Amendment , who presented the facts to give me the incentive.

Other novels by D.H. Robbins
The Tu-Tone DeSoto
The Reverend
The Weight of Indifference
Boxing with Hemingway

Prologue

January 8th, 2026

Four more journalists were publicly executed last month to honor Premier Alexander Kenton's eightieth birthday. One of them had been with what used to be CNN. He had met his fate less than eight hours after bloodhounds and a small flock of drones tracked him down until he was discovered in a bayou cabin southwest of Baton Rouge. He was publicly hung for treason after appearing for fifteen minutes before a back county kangaroo court. He had editorialized on truth and common sense up until a few years back, just before the major news outlet went "rusty"—its signal reduced to a crackle of static and snow on one of the few remaining underground UHF European networks left.

The other three journalists were from an AM radio station set up in an abandoned MTA station under Boylston Street in Boston. It was literally underground so as avoid detection by the "censor/sensor" drones. The station broadcasted excerpts from the outlawed U.S. Constitution—and subsequent violations of it— from 8:PM til midnight. For their sins, the three were shot by a hail of AR-15 and Soviet AK-47 bullets from firing squad in Fort Worth. They had awaited sentencing for over a year in Unqutuck, a tundra gulag 300 miles northeast of Fairbanks. Even that frigid tundra place may have been better than the stifling, overcrowded gulags in Guantanamo, or Delaxuma, in the Arizona desert run by the infamous eighty-eight-year-old "Sheriff Jeff" Lupera and his grandson Zach. Usually no one was ever released from Unqutuck, or any gulag, but in this case the optics of a public execution were important to celebrate what the Regime had accomplished in such a short time. And, of course, to honor the Premier on his birthday.

Both executions had been ceremoniously televised on the ubiquitous Kenton/Fox News and Entertainment Network, now the only television network broadcast available. The citizens of Real-America had been compelled to stop and watch, nearly as a requirement, as though they would be tested on it.

There had been no free elections since 2020, when President Kenton took full autocratic control, before anointing himself Premier. The Electoral College, with the aid and endorsement of the New Soviet Republic, also won that one, as they had the election in 2016. The popular vote in 2020 was never even considered, because then President Kenton had lost this by over seven million votes, so they didn't count. The emasculated, reigning Repubs had painted Democratic Candidate Marcia Lewis as an outcast, because she was a woman of color with a "forged birth certificate"—faked and filed by President Kenton's staff. For the sin of challenging the president, Ms. Lewis had long since been sent to a cushy minimum-security gulag on St. John's Island in the Caribbean. It was once the estate of one of the Premier's many seedy "friends," who had hung himself under never disclosed circumstances.

1

The Bronze Star

January 8th, 2026

"Death Before Dishonor"

The brand on my forearm plagued me every time I saw it, but I needed the reminder. I had it needled into me back in 2006, inspired by my resolve that I'd stay in the army forever to complete my life as a Real Man.

That was a week before that morning in 2016 in Jaghatu, twenty miles south of Kabul. I had been sitting in the back of our Hum-Vee and was the one least hurt when it trundled over an IED. The explosion left the driver and my two buddies trapped not-quite-dead in the vehicle. A shot of adrenaline surged through me, and I managed to pull the driver and one of my buddies to safety before the Hum-Vee blew. My reaction had not been as delayed as the second explosion from an RPG fired from a craggy rock knoll above, followed a stream of bullets from AK 47s fired by at least two Taliban goons from some ruins on the side of the road. For that I got a Bronze Star. From the shrapnel in my thigh, I got a Purple Heart. The Bronze Star made me a temporary hero; the Purple Heart prevented me from re-upping to continue as a Real-Man-in-The-Army.

There were a lot of Bronze Stars awarded back in the day. Up until 2022, my award got me invited to an annual district Congressional Breakfast. I hardly attended it after 2010, after I'd married Tricia to settle down into a fat life in the burbs of New York

City. I worked in the city as an ad exec, convincing kids to eat their Wheaties, and housewives to douse themselves daily in Oil of Olay to feel twenty years younger. During those times I had recurring visions—and nightmares—of my remaining buddy's body twitching and juddering as he was pumped with AK47 shots from the fucking ruins on at the roadside in fucking Jaghatu. No amount of Pretty in Pink Bubble Bath could sud that image away.

The Bronze Star Congressional Breakfast invites ended in 2023, because that was when Premier Kenton ended Congress and then the Senate. Shut them right down because they weren't part of his plan for the authoritarian regime, he'd renamed Real-America, like some sort of pet project.

After 2020, the prospect of making choices had turned me to stone since that one I'd made to vote a second term for President Alexander Kenton. I wondered how I could have ever allowed myself to contribute, even in a small way, to the diminishment of what had once been a democratic America.

I glanced through our dining room door toward the living room mantle and the display case housing my Bronze Star. While he was shutting down Congress, and then the Senate, Kenton started revoking licenses for the newspapers and TV networks, those carriers of the blights of "fake news" and "alternative facts"—except for his own Kenton/Fox News and Entertainment Network. That's when, while looking over at my medal, l tried to stifle my regret. What had I sacrificed for it? And my Army buddy shot up in Jaghatu? He'd sacrificed his life for a now dead ideal that once used to be worth the invaluable parchment The U.S. Constitution had been printed on.

Now it had all hit closer to home. Through a recent Regime edict, a culling of seven-year-old children had become crucial for stocking the premier's newly formed BlueShirt Youth Brigade. Yesterday was our youngest child's birthday—his seventh. A week before, we found we'd been one of the lottery-selected families to receive the dreaded hand-delivered "Greetings, Real-American!" message, stating that they would be taking away my son for training to serve the greater good of the Kenton Regime in the BlueShirt Youth Brigade. The Regime had outlawed the public Internet in 2025; leaving us no chance for us to contest this, as protesting any of their edicts was illegal. What did that even mean? Kenton had gutted the Department of Justice to stack it with his personal choices back in 2020. Now there was no law except the impulsive directives imposed by the Premier at his whim— "Serving at the Pleasure of the Premier" he had called it. The stock message printed on the postcard had only announced some BlueShirt officials would be showing up at our door sometime on Tuesday—today—a date penned in on a fill-in-the-blank line. We weren't told what time they would be coming by, so we'd waited around all day listening to the ticking from our grandfather clock in the hallway—each like another tick on a time-bomb.

We knew what would happen from what some other families in our neighborhood who now had one less child had told us. The BlueShirt guards would be taking the entire family to the district processing center two towns away, in Bridgeport. Once there, the Public Reform and Immigration Control Enforcement (PRICE) agents would take and examine our child to be "acquired."

Tricia and I knew that Steven, our seven-year-old wouldn't be the one of our three kids acquired. He was on the spectrum of being mentally under-developed, and if PRICE deemed the child "deficient" or "sub-standard," it became the solemn duty of the parents to choose which of their remaining children would be chosen. It was the most dreadful choice I could imagine, and I'd come to feel there was nowhere else to turn but into the darkness of solitude to drink my helplessness away after Tricia and the kids had gone to bed.

They never showed on Tuesday, but Tricia and I knew that didn't mean they'd forgotten. The PRICE-controlled BlueShirts never forgot their duty; they just used it as a bludgeon. The cost of my drinking well past midnight into Wednesday was a wicked, surging hangover. I sipped my grapefruit juice and cringed back another hot wave of headache. "You know there is nothing we can do," I croaked dryly to Tricia, knowing it was just about the dumbest thing I could say. "Just like that?"

The tone of her voice jabbed me into a cringe. "You think *I* want to go through with this, Trish?"

"I know you don't *want* to, Robert. It's just you've seemed to've given up your will to fight this anymore."

"...anymore," I echoed. I thought back on that scene in Jaghatu over twenty years before and had that same helpless feeling now. Just as I would have sacrificed my life for my buddy then I would have sacrificed it for Tricia and our kids now. But, like then, I had felt powerless against the grinding Machine of fate.

The scrape of the knife was deafening through the silence Tricia buttered a slice of toast. "They are going to take one of our children from us, Robert," she enunciated pointedly.

I felt numbed beyond words. The only defense I could afford to offer was my solemn silence.

"Well, *I* won't let them, God damnit!" she said. "Certainly not because that sloppy, Big-Mac-eating, fat fuck lounging on his gold-plated palanquin like some sort of Nero in his tower on Fifth Avenue says I have to."

The chill that our place may have been bugged momentarily seized me. Four months back, one of the interns of a partner in my neighbor Bill Davis' law firm was reported saying leftist things during lunch in the building's cafeteria. That afternoon, the PRICE took him—hopefully not to one of the twenty or so gulags Kenton's PRICE people had set up in the nation's most inhospitable regions. No one or *no-thing* could be trusted anymore; not even the potted plastic plants bolted strategically on corporate lunchroom tables.

And even at home. I'd been suspicious since that plumber showed up to monitor our water pressure two months before. I wondered if a mic could have been placed behind one of the display plates hanging on the wall behind me. But then what if I did find a mic? I couldn't exactly report it, because the cops were all accountable to PRICE, and many of them were themselves agents.

"Christ, Trish. Don't even *say* that kind of shit."

"What, Robert? You afraid they're gonna hear us and come drag us away? Maybe put us in some gulag up in the Alaskan wasteland?" She turned the sink faucet on to full. "There!" She shouted over the sound of running water. "You happy they won't hear us now?" Concerned the stream would run over from the sink already filled with dishwater, she turned it off. "Jeee-zus…You are so paranoid."

"It's the way times are, Trish."

"Well, they don't have to be, and we have to do something."

"Like what? Take the kids and leave the country? Leave what's left of my job and live somewhere else like a family of ex-pats?"

"Well, why not? We could go somewhere else and live a normal life."

"Like where? Canada?"

"Too cold, and too close."

"Where, then? Where would we go?"

"Oh, I don't know, Robert. Maybe Australia?"

"No, Trish. Neither Canada nor Australia. You know as well as I that we have those tense moments even at the border stations even when we drive from Connecticut into Massachusetts— and that's not getting any easier. We'd never be cleared to leave Real-America."

"Ameri-*CA*, you mean, Robert." She glanced at a hanging plate. "'Make America Great Again', my bony ass!" she scoffed at the invisible mic. "We were great to begin with twelve years ago, before that dickhead pledged to 'Drain the Swamp'."

"Tricia, please...shhh!"

"Don't go shush-ing me, Robert! I don't care *who* the fuck is listening."

I sighed with the Naugahyde cushion of my dinette chair as I settled back and listened to the cartoons Steven was watching in the living room. They were old Eisenhower-era reruns of Popeye the Sailor, and Mickey Mouse. But no Betty Boop—she was too controversial and subliminal-liberal for developing minds.

I took another sip of my grapefruit juice and savored its bitter taste as I dreaded our appointment with destiny at the processing center. Then came the knock on the door. It sounded hospitable enough. I peeked through the window. Parked in our driveway was their black Hum-Vee with a a yellow P.R.I.C.E logo emblazoned on its driver's door and hood. My numbness turned to paralysis. It had come two hours earlier than we expected most likely to catch us off guard and un-prepared.

I remembered that the center was once an unemployment office. It now smelled of the stale sweat, tears, and the lost hopes it held captive within its colorless, chipped plaster walls. I counted five guards, each armed with a military-grade Real-American or Soviet-made assault weapon and a 45-caliber side arm. Although they stood at relaxed attention, they were poised to put down any scuffle that might erupt in this spring-loaded environment.

On the facing walls to my right and left hung an oversized full-length portrait of the Premier. In the one on the right wall, he poses on the golf course of his West Palm Beach Florida resort. Dressed in some loose-fitting golfing togs to make him look thinner than we all knew him to be, he smiles smugly. In the portrait on the left wall, he poses resolutely squint-eyed next to his helicopter. In this one he is slightly stooped, looking sinister in that black winter overcoat he always wears, like an aged crow sprouting a grey-blond mop of a toupee. Both portraits were meant to command respect, but instead oozed something to be feared from within the dark character of the subject.

The number on the tote board in front was 05. We were 07-th. I stared at the TV screen hanging over the bank of customer windows up front. It was tuned, as were all of the TVs in public places, to the Kenton/Fox News and Entertainment Network. The clip was an often-played re-run from the previous month. Alexander Kenton Jr., the heir-apparent to his father's throne, was bestowing some gaudy piece of bling hanging from a ribbon around an infamous free-form cage fighter's neck. It was as if he was knighting him to go forth on a crusade to advance the cause of the Kenton Regime.

I then took what I knew might be a last look at my complete family. To my left, wound tight in her tension, was feisty, misbegotten Tricia, 38 to my 45 years. She still shimmered in the same beauty as in those days back in the halcyon pre-Kenton years. To my right and leaning close enough for me to feel his quickened heartbeat, like that of a bird, was my compromised and befuddled 7-year-old Steven. He was too unaware to be frightened, thanks to the morning's dose-and-a-half of Ativan. Next to him was Michael;

strong, tall, and spry as any token-perfect 13-year-old, and just chosen as a second stringer outfielder for his school's district-winning baseball team. And then there was Emily, our flaxen-haired daughter. About to turn 16, she was as Tricia-pretty as she was pent-up. Exhibiting what our being here portended, she anxiously worked a wad of tear-moistened tissue in her hands. I could only wonder what was truly going on in all their minds. All I knew was that I had possibly never loved them more than at that moment.

A voice scraped through the static on the P.A. system: "Number seventy-five, please. Seventy-five."

"Here we go," I groaned as I stood. My kids rose sequentially. Emily was shaking. Michael tried to act proud. Steven stared vacantly ahead. Tricia remained resolutely seated; her lips drawn into a thin, bloodless line. "Come on, Trish. This will be over soon."

She closed her eyes and heaved an un-even sigh. "I never wanted it to begin."

"I know. Neither did I."

"Really, Robert?" She stole a heated glance toward one of the guards, then glared back at me as she stood.

The PRICE lieutenant sitting across from the five of us at the little conference table seemed officiously kind enough, even beneath his stern eagle-like glower. A red-haired nurse: a woman in her mid-thirties with a hard expression belying her soft features sat next to him, neat and starched. Standing off in the corner was a frail, stone-countenanced kid; a BlueShirt youth barely older than Michael. He was armed as ominously as those out in the waiting area, yet without projecting their threat.

The lieutenant glanced intently at a form in front of him. "Ah, Mr. Bryant. I see here you voted twice for President Kenton." Then he jolted at over what he read next. "Oh, outstanding! You're a Bronze Star and a Purple heart recipient. Saved two of your comrades from a burning vehicle. The Premier and myself thank and applaud you for your support and service." Despite his practiced show of enthusiasm, it was a canned response delivered from the routine of boredom.

"Just doing his duty," Tricia blurted facetiously.

The nurse glared at her.

"Shh, Trish," I nervously warned her under my breath.

"And you, Mrs. Bryant..." he glanced again at the form, "did not vote for the Premier when he was elected President."

"Just doing my duty," she whispered acerbically.

He wrote something in the margin, and then clicked on a small digital recorder on his desk. Tricia's voice was diminished to a squawk through its thimble-sized speaker: *...sloppy, Big-Mac-eating, fat fuck lounging on his gold-plated palanquin like some sort of Nero in his tower on Fifth Avenue says I have to...*

"You fucking bastard!" Tricia seethed.

"Oh, and there's more. He clicked the button again: *What, Robert? You afraid they're gonna hear us and come drag us away? Maybe put us in some gulag up in the Alaskan wasteland?* He clicked the little recorder off. "Well, as you know, Mrs. Bryant, that is not beyond the realm of what we can do."

"I hope you burn in hell for this, Sir fucking BlueShirt."

"I'm not a BlueShirt, so I'd advise you, Mrs. Bryant, against threatening a PRICE officer," he answered with a cocky smile that turned easier as he directed his attention toward Steven. "And you must be Steven. You're a lucky boy because you just had your seventh birthday."

A low moan rose from Stephan's chest as he huddled closer to me, and I drew my fingers against his temple to calm him down.

The lieutenant signaled the nurse. She nodded, then stood up and came toward us. Steven's moaning grew into a mournful keen as he began to shake. I noticed a wet bloom in the crotch of his khakis. "It's okay, Stevie," I tried to assure him, but the closer the woman came, the louder and higher became his cry until it was shrill.

The nurse drew back and looked back at the lieutenant for advice. "What's the matter with him?" he grumbled as he must had realized we were delivering defective goods.

"He's compromised, and scared of the nurse, " Tricia said.

"Okay," the lieutenant replied, as he looked passively at Emily. "So you've probably had plenty of time to decide which of your other children will have the honor of serving in The BlueShirt Youth Brigade..." he offered a surreal, benign smile, "at the pleasure of your Premier. Doesn't that sound exciting, kids?"

"None of them," Tricia said. "We're taking all of them back home with us."

"Now, Mrs. Bryant. You know that's not possible. You know you must let us have one," the lieutenant oozed in a threat. "It's a requirement."

"Well, sir. What you think is not possible is absolutely probable for me. I am not leaving this place without all my children."

Tricia's response breathed a new conviction into me. My fear quickly willed out when I saw the lieutenant's expression harden. "Trish. Will you please just be quiet? We have to— "

"No! We don't have to do *shit*, Robert," she snapped at me as she stood.

I sensed the guard moving toward us. Out of the corner of my eye, I saw he'd moved his hand toward his side arm. I grasped Tricia's wrist and she snapped it away.

"Ma'am, I'd advise you to do as your husband tells you," the lieutenant warned.

She allowed herself a moment to shake his chauvinistic comment away. "If you think, *sir*, for one moment, I will surrender any of my children to serve that fat— "

"Patricia! Sit down!"

She glared at me. "No, Robert. I will *not*." I drew my attention to the national flag hanging flaccidly near the stock head and shoulders portrait of Kenton with that smug grimace of his. The flag was a graphic design abomination, consisting of six alternating light grey and deep blue horizontal bars where the red and white ones had once been. The stars and bars of the confederate flag had replaced the star-field of blue.

"In that case, Mrs. Bryant, we'll just have to make the choice for you."

"I'll go!" Michael said as he abruptly stood.

"No, you will *not*!" Tricia scolded. "Now, sit down, Michael."

"No, mom, really. I *want* to go."

"That's very noble of you, son. But your mother's right. A minor cannot make that decision." The lieutenant said as he looked at Emily. Tears streamed down her cheeks. He then signaled something to the guard, and I froze as I felt the butt of his assault rifle rub against my upper arm. "Nurse Johnson. Please take this young woman to the next room for an examination."

"NO!" Tricia screamed.

Then all went strangely silent as the nurse approached Emily and, before Tricia could grab Emily's arm, the nurse took it and gently led her away.

"No!" Emily suddenly cried. "*No!*"

"What the hell are you doing?" Michael said.

Tricia could only gasp through her shock.

Steven's wail became louder and eerily mournful.

"Now see here, lieutenant!" I began, then felt the weight of the guard's assault rifle gunstock bear deeper into my bicep.

The lieutenant soon rose to follow behind Emily and the nurse once they were in the side office. He carried his clipboard to make it all look official.

Tricia burst into tears. "Do something, Robert. Please!" she cried.

"Take *me!*" I said as I rose in defiance of the push of the gunstock into my arm.

"You're too old," the lieutenant said frostily, then closed the door behind him, the nurse, and Emily.

"That fucking *bastard!*" Tricia seethed.

This was followed by a stunned silence of dis-belief, until it was broken a minute later by Emily's managing to fling open the door with the burst of a teary scream. I noticed the top three buttons of her blouse had been undone. She rushed sobbing into Tricia's arms. The lieutenant and the nurse lunged into the room. "You get back in here now, young lady! *Now!*" he commanded.

The rest happened quickly as in a perfect storm of serendipitous events. I felt a surge of headache as my legs weakened and I fell back against the guard as I tried rushing toward Tricia and Emily. The kid lost his footing, and I heard his sidearm skitter away. Some sort of protective instinct took over as I unslung the assault weapon with a brutal grab from his frail shoulders. This all couldn't have even taken three seconds, but adrenaline is a powerful force. I quickly stood, then aimed the gun into the room. I hadn't held a weapon for nearly twenty-five years, but I felt overcome with a pay-back feeling of power and control.

I kicked the boy's sidearm away to the other side of the room as he tried to reach for it, and then clamped his hand to the floor with my foot. The lieutenant and nurse held their stand as I aimed the weapon at them.

The lieutenant held up his hands, palms out. "Now take it easy with that weapon, Bryant. You've just put yourself in a shitload of trouble."

I noticed an exit sign over a door open to daylight in the room behind him. "There's a side exit right behind you, Trish. Take the kids and go! *Now!* Now *go!*"

She gathered Steven, now screaming uncontrollably, into the arms. Her cheeks were dampened with tears. She mouthed *I love you* to me, and then hastened our kids from the room.

For some reason, maybe due to shock, It took the nurse more than several minutes to ease toward the alarm to sound it. Plenty of time for Tricia and the kids to get away, before I felt clouted hard from behind in the backs of my knees.

The image of a burning Hum-Vee came back to me as I crumpled down to a dusty road in Jaghatu. I then recalled the muscular feeling of firing an automatic M-16 into the ruins and taking down the three Iraqis who'd blown up the Hum-Vee and killed my friend. I found out later that one of those I'd killed was a thirteen-year-old kid.

Now, as I lay with no feeling below my knees on a hard carpet, I looked up at the lieutenant, arms crossed, looking down at me. Through my blurred vision, I caught a glimpse of my tattoo: *Death Before Dishonor*.

2

Leverage

December 22, 2027

I received only a two-year maximum sentence in a detainment center—a former Marriott over-looking I-95. Though it might have once been an upscale hotel, this one had been converted to a minimum-security lock up. The detainment chambers had the ambiance of hotel room, complete with an un-stocked mini-fridge, and a Keurig coffee maker—and even a balcony. But there was no TV set; along with with no doubt that the rooms were cells with triple bolt locks. There were daily inspections along with monthly shakedowns and strip downs by the BlueShirt guards. The balcony overlooking the throughway was encased in story-height chain link fencing, and the view was dismal.

The traffic along the highway, so dense and gridlocked eight years before, was now sparse. The steel treads of the mighty, high-speed Kenton Tanks, built in and imported from the massive industrial complexes of the New Soviet Republic, had gouged and pocked the interstate beyond drivability. Adding to that, since Premier Kenton's executive order to fully nationalize Real-America's oil production in 2022, reserves had become depleted. The unemployment level was up to over 20 percent, so not many could afford having a car, even If they could afford the $16.00 per gallon gas prices. The economy had turned around and weakened, as the Dow now hovered back down in the pre-2008 territory at

8,500 due to the failure of the still-imposed tariffs. Welcome to Real-America.

I reasoned that it might have turned out a lot worse for me if it hadn't been for my having voted for President Kenton in the sham 2020 Presidential election, along with my Bronze Star and Purple Heart. Holding a PRICE agent, especially an officer, at gunpoint was a treasonous charge that could have had me sent off to a gulag to die. Yet my simply voting for Kenton and hero-status couldn't have been the only reason I'd been awarded such a cushy berth here in this beauty spot of West Haven, Connecticut.

I'd had a good defense attorney in Bill Davis's partner, Frank Crown. He made a convincing case before a mainly female jury of my love of family and a moment of irrationality in my wanting to protect them. But I believe the closer came with the private testimony of Nurse Johnson, who'd witnessed that the lieutenant had attempted to rape my fifteen-year-old daughter. That, if it ever got out, would be bad optics. It was already rumored in silence that that inner circle was starting to groan under the weight of its bleak potential. A day after the softened jury deliberation and the chambered testimony of Nurse Johnson, the judge offered up my lightened two-year sentence.

I had served nearly three-quarters of it when that annoying buzz of my door alarm signaled a guard entrance. I figured it was another unannounced inspection and stood back in an overly bright corner of my room as was the protocol.

"No inspection today, Bryant," the guard said as he approached me to slip on the Mylar cuffs. "There's someone here to see you down in the meeting block."

I knew better than to ask whom and to risk another black mark on my behavior tally. The guard's keys jangled loud as my heartbeat against the barrel of his closely held assault rifle as I followed him to the elevator.

The so-called meeting blocks set up in the chilled lobby consisted of a row of partitioned desks divided down the middle by a thick plexiglass plate. I saw Bill Davis sitting anxiously in a padded office chair in the visitor's side of one of them. I took my seat in the metal folding chair on the prisoner's side of the glass and lifted the handset receiver. "Bill," I said into it.

He offered thin smile as his eyes darted suspiciously to the partitions on either side of the. Then he settled his gaze upon me. "I have what you might think of as good news, Bob."

"I need some of that."

"They're springing you out today."

I caught my breath. "No shit? Why"

"Because they love you here."

"I think if that was true, they'd want to keep me."

"Go up and gather your things, buddy. I'll wait for you here— well, not here-here, but over in the lobby coffee shop."

"Why just *might* I think of this as good news, Bill?"

"I'll tell you when we meet."

His expression was not all that comforting. I felt the stun of a shiver through me as I thought about Tricia and the kids, and what might have happened to them.

I leaned back into the blessed comfort of the passenger seat of Bill's Buick once he'd parked at his yacht club in New Haven. Not that a private marina was immune from the reach of PRICE, but he rationalized it was one of those sacred territories where we'd be safe from prying ears. It was really nothing more than a security blanket.

I gazed at the green Starbucks logo on my grande-sized paper cup, and marveled at how something so simple, once separated by time that had stood still for almost two years, could be so meaningful. I closed my eyes to meditate on the patter of the rain turning to sleet falling like little pebbles against the car's roof and windows. I was free...but what of my family?

"Was there something you wanted to tell me, Bill? Some sort of 'but' to my being freed after serving three-quarters of my time?"

He remained silent as he measured out his response. "PRICE must have realized they didn't need you anymore."

I canted my head toward him from where I'd relaxed it against the headrest. "Need me for what?"

He sipped his coffee. "I don't know. Maybe leverage."

I scoffed a laugh. "Maybe they wanted to give me a Christmas present."

Another pensive silence, then: "Bob. I have news about Tricia and the kids."

I glared at him. "Where are they? Are...are they okay?" I went sullen. "I mean, are they...They're alive, right, Bill?"

"As far as I know. Listen, I didn't want to tell you this while you were in trial or lock-up, okay?"

My relative ease tensed into suspicion. "Tell me what?"

"And Trish didn't want you to know any of this, until a time when you were in the clear and out of whatever place they might lock you up for threatening that lieutenant PRICE guy."

"What, for Christ's sake?"

"Nothing really. It's just that after she and the kids managed to get away and clear of that processing center in Bridgeport, she managed to catch a cab to my office. It was the wisest thing she could do, because she knew if she'd gone home, she'd probably run into a nest of salivating PRICE goons."

"Yeah, that would make sense. Why didn't she and you want me to know that?"

He stared out ahead, toward the marina docks disappearing into the fog misting the Long Island sound. "She was concerned that if you knew, then word might get out among the people at the lock-up. If PRICE got news that we helped her out, then both of you would be compromised. She also feared that lately you'd shown yourself to crack under pressure. I don't have any opinion on the cracking under pressure part, but I had to agree we'd put you at risk if you knew. Sorry Bob, we didn't want to leave anything to chance with PRICE, especially anything that could result in them catching to her and the kids."

It made a weird sense to me. "Okay, Bill. So, what happened after she showed up at your office?"

He sipped his cold coffee and made a face at it. He opened his window and flung the cup's contents out onto the pavement. "After she told me what happened, I made a few connections to help her get as far away as possible. Even out of the country. You've probably seen how determined those fucking PRICE agents can be when they're on the scent. I'm surprised they and their little BlueShirts were so asleep at the wheel when Trish and the kids gave them the slip back at the processing center. I'm pretty sure some heads rolled after that."

"What Connections?"

"Pardon"

"What connections did you make to help her out?"

"Oh. Later on that, Bob. Anyway, they managed to get them to Miami and out of the country. Later I found out that they'd made it to Havana a few days after."

"Havana? Cuba?"

He huffed out a nervous chuckle as he leaned back against his seat. "Yeah. Havana's still in Cuba, as far as I remember."

"How do you know all this?"

"I'll get to that in a minute. Anyway, they made it to Havana to catch passage to Brazil. Rio. Then they...fell off our radar." I was too stunned to say anything, so I waited for him to go on. "We think they might have been duped about the passage, or turned in, because PRICE found them before they could leave."

"Oh, shit! Goddammit, Bob."

"We think they sent the kids to different locations, because that's how PRICE operates."

I felt as though a boulder had tumbled down my throat and weighted my ass in place on the seat. "Where? Where are my kids?"

"We don't know. They have some sort of holding facility there for special needs kids in Texas outside Midland. Probably Steven was sent there."

"That same one where they imprisoned all those migrant kids they separated from their parents?"

"I'm guessing that's it. We don't know where Michael and Emily are."

"Fuckin' Christ!" I sighed. "Who's 'we'?"

"Hunh?"

"This 'we' you keep referring to? Who are 'we', Bill?"

"Give me a minute about that. Now we *do* know where Tricia is."

I felt my heart go numb. "Where?"

Bill bit his lip. His empty coffee cup was shaking his hands. "Uh... north of Tucson," he replied defeatedly. "Sheriff Jeff Lupera's compound in the desert."

"Fuck shit!"

"I'm sorry, Bob."

I was seized by the hard grip of lost hope. My mind went dark, as if its power had been shut off. "Take me home. I need to adjust to all this."

"Yeah, well, about that. You no longer have a home. PRICE acquired it." My hand tightened into a fist which, crushing my cup, forced out its contents. I didn't feel the coffee all over my lap. "At the pleasure of the Premier," he added facetiously.

I could think of nothing to say, except: "Where am I going to stay? Can I stay at your place?"

He shook his head. "Too risky. I've gotten you a hotel room."

"Another hotel room."

"Well, this one's plush. It's the best I could get for you...just for a few days until you can get back on your feet."

"Plush, hunh? Is it the Grand Hyatt or something?"

"You wouldn't like it there. The Hyatt's been reconditioned for a BlueShirt headquarters." He conjured up a wan smile. "No. I got you a room at the safest place in town for you."

I felt a tingling wave of suspicion flow through my shoulders. "And where might that be?"

He picked at something in the steering wheel. "Uh...I got you a suite here in New Haven…at the Kenton Tower Hotel."

I jolted forward. A few minutes before, Bill had been my savior. Now I wanted to ring his fucking neck. I went through a full range of emotions. "Kenton Tower. You're joking, right Bill? Are you fuckin' *crazy*?"

"Like I said. It's the safest place in town for you. Probably bugged, but loosely, and not so crawling with BlueShirts or PRICE agents."

"Why do I have to worry about BlueShirts? Am I a fugitive or something? I thought you got me out."

"Well, we did. But no one who's done any sort of time is exactly free in this fucking jungle."

"Okay, sure. So, I can just waltz into the fucking Kenton Tower Hotel and ask for a room key. With my rap sheet." I've never smoked, but if I did, I'd crave a cigarette about now.

"What rap sheet?" He flashed a Cheshire Cat smile. "Though you may not be free, your crime has been expunged. The only things left on your rap sheet are probably a couple of parking tickets."

I now felt a smooth release of tension in my chest. "Really? When did this happen?"

"My firm's been working hard toward it. I just found out late last night, so this morning's when I could finally get you out of that shithole you've been staying in."

"Thanks. Really."

"Your attorney, Frank Crown, was the one who did all the heavy lifting on that. You can thank him."

"Why all this interest in getting me out of there? I mean the only thing you've owed me was that dinner we took you to..." I choked up on the memory, "when...Trish...and I... I've gotta know, Bill."

"What?"

"About how you know all that about what happened to my wife and kids."

"Which part?"

"Let's start with the beginning. With getting them to Havana; the passage to Brazil—that part."

He stared out at the gleaming web of cold rain in the windshield. "We did that. Got her out of the country and made the arrangements for Brazil. I only found out a few weeks ago about them being detained the February before last by PRICE and what happened next through some connections I have."

"You? *You* found out?"

"We."

"Okay, now. Who is 'we'?"

"'We' are some people I'd like you to meet."

I squinted at him as I let this all sink in. "Can 'we' get Trish out?"

"We can try, but there are some other things you need to know before we do."

I meditated again on the sizzle of the sleet and the whir of the car's heater and emptied my mind to regain some of the adrenaline I thought I'd lost. My family had been scattered around God knew where in Kenton's PRICE gulags. I feared nothing, anymore. "Then, Bill. I want to meet these people."

"We hoped you would."

3

Jillian's Brew Hah-Hah

December 23

Back in the 1950's, movie theaters would boast of air conditioning with banners hung beneath their marquees. Now in that same spirit, certain coffee shops and bistros displayed subtle signage in their windows advertising that they were "Bug-Free Zones." Jillian's, a latte and cappuccino cafe was one of these places. It was set innocuously on a tree-lined street north of the Yale campus in the New Haven arts district. Because the cafe was close enough to the university, it was a relatively safe gathering place for free-thinkers and students. Just inside, it was adorned with the trappings of a Gay-Nineties ice cream parlor. But beneath this cheerful camouflage seditious campaigns were discussed in a stone-walled room off the storage area in the basement. It was often referred to as the "stoned room," for all the weed freely imbibed there.

Bill first led me into Jillian's late one afternoon just before Christmas, and I indulged briefly in a few happier memories conjured through the fragrances of sweet, warm pastries and rich-brewed roasted coffee. The glazed facets in the shop glistened in the scattering of afternoon harsh winter sunlight through the two front plate glass windows emblazoned with the white script logo: "Jillian's Brew Hah-Hah." I settled back into listening to the stream of nineteen-fifties Birdland-era jazz through the speakers. It was nearly as it might have been back in the day and reminded me of how normal things had once been.

Those times had been blissfully naive by today's post-Kentonian standards, and the more the milieu reminded me of the past, the more I realized how hopeless the present seemed. Tricia and I had had our first date at an author-friend's reading in a bistro such as this. It was an historical fiction novel about romance in the *Belle Epoch*, Trish's specialties: *Belle Epoch* and romance. How could I not have fallen so head-over-heels for her? Today, as yesterday, and the day before, I had churned back my grief over my loneliness, especially now so near to Christmas. At night, I lay awake in between those recurring nightmares about the war, now plagued by others about my treatment in lock-up, and, worse, what brutality Tricia and the kids must be enduring at their gulags. All the nightmares were cushioned in the puffy comfort of my suite at the New Haven Kenton Tower Hotel. My uncertainties about being there had been swallowed up by frequent thoughts of suicide over all I'd lost, most likely forever. But then again, I didn't want to give that bastard any satisfaction over offing myself in one of his hotel's rooms. Even through all my depression, I was better than that.

Bill's tone was sickeningly chipper. "Best coffee in town, Bob! And the fresh croissants—to die for!" He chuckled nervously as I cringed over his choice of words. "Let's make sure you have one." He turned to the Gillian; a forty-something-year-old woman, grizzled before her time, but with a fine complexion. Her apron was dusted in flour. "Hey, Jill. We'll have two large lattes and two of your raspberry croissants."

"Sure, Bill," she turned to pass on the order to her barista. "The croissants, you want 'em warmed, like before?"

"*Un petit peu*," he said. "As usual."

"You see our new Christmas ornament over there in the corner?"

"Yeah. I did. Nice, but be careful with that."

"Always," she said. "We throw a sheet over him most the time."

I looked over my shoulder and noticed a half-sized likeness of Kenton set away from the window. He was a chubby-cheeked, porcine figure in a Santa suit. Beneath his red hat was an overweight fob of yellow-white hair with an exaggerated forelock sticking out like a ship's prow. In his chubby hand he held a warrant, presenting it as if it was a gift. Scrawled in red upon it was *"Happy Christmas from Premier Kenton! Ho-Ho-Ho!"*

"Why are we here, Bill? Are we getting together with these people you want me meet over lattes?"

He conjured a wan smile, and another skittish chuckle. "More like *under* the lattes, Bob. You'll find out soon enough." He turned back to Gillian. "Are we the first here, Jill?"

She passed us our croissants and coffees, then motioned toward the door to the basement. "More like the last. Piet, Paula and Rafe have been here for a half-hour already. Piet's acting grumpy today."

Bill devoured his croissant along the way as we carried our coffee and pastry down to the basement. There was a scant splay of light from beneath a rickety door off in a corner. The light scent of marijuana permeated the otherwise musty-damp smell of the penumbral storage cellar. The door creaked as Bill opened it and ushered me in.

A gaunt man in his mid-thirties sporting an unkempt goatee peered at us through the smudged, magnifying lenses of his prince Nez glasses. In another life, over a hundred years before, he might have been a starving Raskolnikov. His voice was as frail as his features. "You must be Robert Bryant. I am Piet VanDeroos."

He was either all business, or afflicted with a communicable disease, for he made a point of not extending his hand. "Yes, I am. Nice to meet you." It might have come out sounding like a question, but I was more confused than curious. "You wanted to meet with me?"

He nodded curtly. "*William,* here wanted us to meet you. You are familiar with what we do—who we are?"

"No. I don't think— "

Piet glared accusingly at Bill. "You didn't tell him?"

"No, I thought I'd let you cover that with him, Piet."

"So, William. You brought Mr. Bryant here without explaining to him why. What if he is a—"

"He isn't," Bill interrupted. "I've known him for years. You know that. Bob has a vested interest, for sure."

Piet shivered against the chill in the room, then looked at me. "Yes. I gathered." He nodded curtly and efficiently at me. "Your wife and family. Taken by PRICE agents as they waited in Cuba for a transport to South America."

"Fuckin' bastards!" A woman mumbled from a darkened corner. She took a sharp jab on her reefer, then coughed.

"They've been getting away with that shit for far too long," a young man slouching near her against the wall, added.

"Indeed," Piet agreed. "So, Mr. Bryant. Have you heard of the Neo-Publica?"

I had. "The revolutionaries?" I glanced at Bill, then back at Piet. "Is that who you are?"

"Revolutionaries," the girl smoking weed in the corner scoffed. "How romantic."

"Yeah. *Viva Che,*" the man added fecklessly.

"Rafe and Paula, there, are two of my students. I am their professor."

"Associate professor, Piet," Rafe corrected.

"Whatever," Piet said. "In this room we are all equals. Including William." He glowered at me. "Maybe including you."

"So you are members of the Neo-Publica ," I said.

"To be determined. As I just said...we are all equals. Now tell us about you. We heard you were locked up for pulling a gun on a PRICE officer a few years back?"

"Good for you, man!" Rafe spouted.

Piet shuffled over toward Paula and indicated for her to hand him the joint for a toke. He inhaled deeply. "You pulled a rifle off of a BlueShirt Youth guard?" His voice was tightened by the smoke heating is throat. He coughed, then handed the reefer back to Paula, who inhaled on it more expertly than he had. "Aimed it at the guy?"

"He was trying to split up my family. It was a moment of need."

"Would you do it again?"

"For my family? Of course," I said. "Absolutely."

"You would be more inclined to do it again now? After you'd been arrested and held for nearly two years?"

"Absolutely," I enforced.

"PRICE could do more than arrest you if you pulled a gun on them a second time. How did you get off so lightly? With just two years?"

I looked over at Bill. "I had a good lawyer."

"Why, thank you, Bob."

"And a sympathetic jury and judge." I thought it best not to mention my Bronze Star.

"Well, thank you, again, Bob," Bill said. "I think."

"I know. Also, I know about your medal for heroism. Impressive," Piet said. "We advised and helped William to get your wife and children out of Real-America."

"You did that? Thank you."

"It is the sort of thing we do," Piet said. "They would have easily been tracked down and caught if we had not. But I am sorry things turned out as they did. We have much less pull outside of the country. Especially in places like Cuba."

"So. You *are* Neo-Publica," I said.

Piet beckoned toward Paula for another puff, and she handed the remains of the joint to him. He held it between his thumb and forefinger and examined it. "You voted for Kenton for President," he said in mild accusation before he took the last available toke. "Twice."

"Not something I'm proud of, now."

He cast a searing look at me. "You have no allegiance to him anymore?"

"His agents took my wife and kids. What do you think?"

"No Mr. Bryant. What do *you* think? Would you take up a gun again, less in a passionate anger than for a purpose?"

"If it meant getting my family back? Sure?"

"Yeah. I get that. But what about for a deeper reason?" He dropped the joint to the floor and crushed it out with the toe of his boot. "What about if it meant saving other families from the same fate as yours?"

"Absolutely. What is happening now is atrocious. No family should have to be subjected to this new status quo."

"Another hypothetical question, then, Mr. Bryant. What if you could not reunite your family? Would you act against the Kenton regime for the sake of others?"

This stopped my line of thinking short, as I considered what he'd asked.

He stepped from the somber shadows engulfing Paula and Rafe and into the shaft of harsh light above the table in the middle of the room. He placed his hands on the table's surface and leaned toward me. "It's a simple question, Mr. Bryant. Let me ask another way: would you be willing to take up arms and fight against the Kenton dictatorship to restore our democracy back to what it should be?"

"I—I wouldn't even know how to begin."

"You can start by answering my question to you."

I was glad I wasn't one of his students. I remembered how Tricia had wanted so desperately to see Kenton's Real-America as the America it once had been. To "make America America, again," as she'd often said to me. Then I again remembered the night we met; how things had been so normal then—as normal as the coffee shop above us. "I would. If I knew how."

"And you have no remaining allegiance to this Premier Kenton sitting at the top of Real-America?"

"No...I hate the man."

"Why? Because you think he is the one who split up your family? Or because what he and his people have destroyed to bring us to the point we are at?"

"Both, Mr. VanDeroos. One because of the other. I miss what we once had as much as I miss my family."

Piet offered up a crooked smile, garnished with a look of minuscule appreciation. "You might be interested to know what became of the officer you threatened. He was dismissed and sent away...probably to an outpost or a gulag, somewhere. That weapon you brandished? They don't give loaded weapons to BlueShirt Youth guards—they are nothing more than weighted-down toys. More for effect than to do damage."

"Fucking guns," Rafe said. "They're just lethal toys—testosterone for the Second Amendment at the expense of the First."

"Rafe is a journalism grad student," Piet said.

"Yeah...and with no means left to express the truth, anymore." He gazed down at the floor as though in shame. "When I first came to Yale, there was a *Washington Post*, *New York Times*, *L.A. Times*, and a CNN. Where are they now, while we journalists are being executed for holding onto the truth?"

"Guns are a necessary evil for all of us, now," Paula said. "Our little guns against their huge ones."

"Well, *I'm* now thoroughly depressed," Bill quipped.

Piet relaxed in his stance as he folded his arm across his chest. "Only now?" he chided.

"Congress should have never softened their stance against impeaching the bastard back in twenty-nineteen," Paula said, as she drew another reefer to her lips. "That was our last chance." She lit up.

"Yeah," Rafe laughed sadly. "Now look. No more Congress."

"It all happened too quickly after that for anyone to stop him," I said.

"You voted for him in Twenty-twenty," Piet reminded me.

"Admittedly an act of blind acceptance," I said. "After that, *everything* was just too late to change."

"It's never too late, Mr. Bryant," Piet told him. "Maybe now you can make up for it. Actually, the fact that you voting for him twice, and your war record may work to our advantage. You have their faith in your pocket."

"Meaning?"

"When William brought you into the Kenton Tower hotel a few days ago, did you have any trouble registering?"

I listened to the thrumming of the furnace kicking on, as the trembling of the floor sent up a warm shiver through my body. "Uh, no," I finally said. "Should there have been? Except maybe that I'm an ex-con."

"Expunged, Bob. Totally expunged," Bill reminded me.

"No problem, then," I said. "They just wanted my money for a room. A signature, a few hundred dollars, and that was it."

Piet tightened in lips into a semblance of a smile. "Actually, it was William's money, but there was no problem. Why? Because they have you on record for supporting Kenton. You passed the test."

I looked over at Bill with suspicion. "Is that why you checked me into that place, you freaking scoundrel? As a test to see that I wasn't arrested again?"

"Absolutely not, Bob." He glanced at Piet. "Isn't that right, Piet?"

"Tell me something, Mr. Bryant," Piet said as he locked me down with his gaze. "You want to get your family back."

"More than anything, but I don't know how I—"

"And you are willing to work for it?"

"Yes of course."

"Okay, then. You've answered several questions for me and thank you." He finally extended his hand. His smile broadened into a genuine one as he shook my hand. His grasp was fulsome and firm for such a slight man. "Welcome to the New Haven chapter of Neo-Publica, Robert."

"Really? Then thank you, uh, Piet." I realized I now had a purpose, and a means to get my family back. "Let me know how I can help."

"Well, thank Zeus!" Bill gasped enthusiastically. "I was about to think you were never gonna tell him."

"Yeah, welcome to the shit, man," Rafe said tiredly.

Paula held out her joint. "Here, old man. You want a celebratory toke?"

"Uh, no thanks," I told her. "I don't smoke. Besides, it might lead me to stronger stuff—like Marlboro's and Winston's."

She scoffed out a laugh. "Yeah, right. If you can afford the eighteen dollars a pack."

Bill lit up a cigarette for himself. Lawyers could afford to smoke. "So, Piet," he asked, "have you heard anything about Sylvia, yet?"

Piet glanced at me. "Sylvia Morales was a philosophy professor at Yale until a few years ago. Big in the movement—a legend, in fact. She helped to found this chapter back in twenty-four. Then she was dragged away in a midnight PRICE raid on campus three years ago." He scissored his fingers for a drag off Bill's cigarette. He took in a languorous inhale. "All we know is that she's up in that Unqutuck gulag. We're still working on it."

Piet's comment seemed dismissive. I sensed he knew more than what he was willing to tell us.

"Well, my job's done here, and I've got some cases on deadline," Bill said. "So, I should get going." He shook my hand. "Again, welcome to Neo-Publica, Bob. Really, I was hoping you'd come around."

4

The Tundra

January 20, 2028

Devon Jackson stood in front of the half-track Snow-Cat and shivered beneath the puffed-up bulk of layers of outerwear. He blew into his thickly-mittened hands, as though that would have done any good. The bracing rigidity of the cold hauled in by the hard blasts from Chloya Lake bit in like the teeth of a pit-bull, even through the layers of fur and down lining his parka. Why anyone would ever choose to go this far north in Alaska was beyond his ken. But then this setting was a perfectly desolate hell to put the Unqutuk Gulag, housing ex-journalists, philosophers, and other dissentients.

It was also the perfect place to put them to work deep below-ground in the dark, damp chill to chip away at the shale used for extraction of fuel for the Real-American military. Nothing was richer than Alaskan shale, and the deeper it was mined, the more precious it was. And who better to do this than these inmates who'd questioned and rebelled against all the good the Kenton Administration had done for Real-America?

Daylight was finally breaking through a sliver of orange beneath a heavy depth of grey clouds out toward Dawson City. Down further south—much further down—the sun would be full up by now. Devon would be comfortably drinking his 9:30 a.m. coffee behind his timeworn oak desk at Ryan Airfield ten miles southwest of Tucson. There, he'd be beginning a day of training suburbanites how to operate one of the flight school's Pipers. The open Alaskan tundra was as far a cry from the southern Arizona desert as it was from the craggy, inhospitable northern Afghan terrain where he'd flown surveillance during the endless war back when he was twenty. Had it been only twelve years since those treacherously high-adrenaline, low-level recon psy-op missions over the Hindu Kush in his re-vamped Cessna?

Before he'd layered up against the sub-zero cold back at camp two hours ago, he'd noticed some wiry clusters of grey in his sideburns—made more apparent against his mahogany-brown skin. Only thirty-two years old; and already going grey. He feared that soon he'd be too aged and demented to fly. Misjudging distance. Losing reaction time. Confusing a two-minute turn with a sixty-degree, Dutch-spiral-inducing bank. Mixing up the altimeter with the airspeed indicator. It could happen. Devon's dad had started to lose it in his late thirties through an early onset of Alzheimer's—a Jackson family trait.

The operator of the Perry Mining snowcat that had brought him here slid effortlessly from the cab. "Be careful where you set foot, there, Jackson," he said over the deep gurgling of the cat's engine. "They say the crust here has been thinned by all the mining's been goin' on below. We wouldn't want you falling down a two-mile-deep shaft, now, would we?" All Devon could see from far within the fur of the operator's parka hood was the glint of his sun-goggles, the reddened bulb of his nose, and the gleam of his white-white teeth as he grinned. The timbre his voice was as grating as a rusty chain saw.

"No shit?"

"Well, partly no shit. We have been known to lose a man or two. Usually 'cause they get drunk enough to wander from the path. So, mind where the pine boughs are lined and stay between 'em as you walk out to your airplane yonder." He unzipped the layers of flys in trousers as he went off to take a leak.

"I don't see any pine boughs. I can't see crap in this darkness."

"Yeah," the operator scoffed over his shoulder as he pissed in the snow. "The Real-American Yukon. She's a bitch, ain't she?"

"Aren't you afraid you're gonna freeze your pizzle off, peeing away like that in all this fucking cold?"

He curtly zipped up. Wouldn't be the first time. I 'member one, two months back ago, ol' Dumb Arnie back in the camp got hisself a case of frostbite on his pecker. He ain't been the same since."

"I wouldn't think so."

"Yessir," the operator said through a chortle. "His voice's a coupla tones higher now." He expertly hopped back in though the open cab door of the cat and onto his seat. He tapped his boot on the accelerator and the cat's engine trembled the ground as it grated harshly. "Good luck to ya, Jackson, then!" he shouted over the noise. "If you squint really hard through alla snow, you can spot your plane over there! Parked next to that old mine entrance I tolt you 'bout! Now, again: mind where ya step!" The cab door groaned from the cold like a donkey's bray as he closed it.

"Mind where I step," Devon muttered after the cat had left. The snow had started falling with the consistency of Times Square New Year's confetti. He swept the beam of his hooded-lens flashlight for the pine boughs marking his path. By now, most of them were merely discernible beneath snow-covered mounds. He carefully trudged the five hundred feet toward the dim glint of lamplight marking the little ski-plane he was supposed to fly out of here.

Or to fly *her* out of here. His purpose on this trip was to collect Sylvia Morales and fly her to an outpost near Fort Yukon, then to

Fairbanks, and finally with her to Boston where she'd be met by some other Neo-Publicas who would drive her back to New Haven.

This was all assuming she'd been successfully sprung from the gulag and was now waiting behind the forgotten old entrance to the mine. By design, Devon had no knowledge as to whether she had been freed, or why her extraction was so important. He was just the pilot, and, as back in Afghanistan, the less he knew about his mission, the better. But he was certainly no rookie, and, to his mind, Sylvia's escape had been too hastily and carelessly arranged. Adding to it all, the snow had now started to fall in a full thickness—maybe pretty for a New England Christmas card, but hell for low-level flying. Such a snowfall wasn't so common this far north in the tundra, as the frigid air kept heavy storms at bay in favor of constant, lighter accumulations. So far, the prediction of a storm had held true, and the earlier lighter precipitation now had developed into a curtain of snow.

Brad Schneider had been waiting by the light plane for forty-five minutes until he noticed the pilot coalescing through the thick haze of falling snow. Brad opened the plane's cowling and lifted out the carburetor heater. He held the little device near to the hood of his parka like a lantern to feel its warmth upon his exposed cheeks, even at the risk of frostbite. He knew how to treat frostbite, usually through a stiff, medicinal bolt of Jack Daniel's Black.

"You're the pilot?" he called out as he lowered the heater on the ground.

"I hope so," Devon said breathlessly as approached. "Devon Jackson. I'd shake your hand, but I think my arm's frozen to my side."

"Yeah, tell me about it," Brad scoffed. "I'm Brad Schneider."

Devon brushed a blast of snow away like it was a swarm of mosquitoes. He then awkwardly adjusted his snow goggles closer to his face and took a hard look at the ski-plane. "It's a Maule-Seven," he said sounding disappointed. He squinted back over his shoulder out through the falling snow and saw only more falling snow.

"You ever flown one of these?" He heard Brad ask.

"Only the MX-Seven. How much clearance you giving me?"

Brad looked out where Devon had trained his gaze. "About five-hundred feet. That should do it. Even in this muck. Maybe."

"Maybe, you say?"

"You'll be carrying a little more weight than you mighta thought."

"Shit. How much more?"

"Two more passengers. About two-fifty—three hundred pounds. Plus a hundred in baggage."

"Oh for Christ's sake. We're already at about two-seventy. Now another four hundred? The max load in a plane like this is only eight-fifty, with fuel. No way I'll get her off the ground with that much weight."

"You should be okay. I drained your tanks down to a quarter full. Besides, it's only, like, forty kliks to Fort Yukon."

Devon looked back at the plane. "I'll be flying low and slow, Brad. At full rich, I'm gonna need more fuel than that."

Brad clamped closed the cowling and stroked it like a pet. "Believe me. This baby will fly on fumes alone."

Devon looked more closely at the landing gear—two skis placed on either side of two wheels with tundra tires, plus a swivel tail wheel for turning; also equipped its own little ski. He regarded the snow's consistency. It was corn snow, pretty to look at, but this wet, gloppy stuff could only produce more drag for the skis and for the tires to get any traction. It was enough to add almost thirty percent more to the runway he needed. The plane being a taildragger could add more to the equation. "With all that drag from the skis? Can you at least give me more runway?"

"I could—a little—but you'd never clear them two-hundred-foot-tall trees at the end. What I've given you is the safest."

Devon opened the cockpit door and sighed as he brushed his mittened hand along the old, coffee—or possibly worse—stained sheepskin cover. He groaned as he climbed in. The seat complained in a creak as he lowered himself into it. All the bunting of his clothing restricted his movement, and he yearned for those warmer days in Afghanistan, when he dressed light in jeans and t-shirts. He lifted his goggles and strained to look at the frosted-over instruments, then shook his head. He slipped off his mittens and thumped the gauges with a forefinger. "You got a topo-map? I wanna see this runway you made for me."

Brad reached into a pocket deep in his parka and drew out a crumpled note of instructions and a laminated map. Devon opened the map and flattened it in front of him and against the control yoke. He noticed the Maule's position marked with a grease pencil. The plane was facing north toward a narrow but clear apron, marked at its end with a grouping of short pines. Too fucking short. He noticed a longer, seven-hundred-foot path fifteen degrees to the left, which ended in a denser clump of trees. "See?" Brad said, his voice tightened by the cockpit enclosure as he poked his head in. "Not much choice."

Devon ran his finger up the longer path. "This longer run. That's the one with the tall trees?"

"You mean the ones you'd end up crashing into?"

"Yeah. Those." He folded the map and slid it between to seats. He abruptly flicked on the master and battery switches, and then the magneto. He flicked on the pitot heat, nudged up the throttle lever a little, and the mixture lever all the way to full. He gripped the ignition key between a thumb and forefinger. "Stand clear, my man, unless you want a mouthful of prop. I'm gonna aim this baby fifteen degrees left toward those trees you think I'll fly into."

Brad stepped away and glanced out to his left. "Yeah, right. Them trees I can't see for shit in this snow."

Devon turned the ignition key and the engine coughed to life. "Yeah! Neither can I! You let me worry about it that!" He shouted over the high reverberation of the engine. He unset the parking brake, depressed the left rudder pedal, and the Maule swiveled slowly toward the west. He felt the clattering shudder from the skis dragging against the crystallized snow. The brakes squeaked when he stopped the plane, now aimed where he wanted.

"Ther're instructions about where to land. They cleared a strip about twelve kliks east of Fort Yukon," Brad called at him. "They'll flick on a torch when they hear you coming. A cat will meet you to take you and your cargo to the airport. Oh yeah. I don't care how much it's soup out there, keep your lights off. As soon as they hear you take off, then find those three missing, and if the weather clears a little, they'll be sending sensor chase drones out after you. So fly low of any radar!"

"Right!"

"Okay! I'll go fetch your cargo, now. And don't forget. No lights here on the ground or in the air! You'll be flying dead-stick blind."

"Right!" Devon flicked him a thumbs-up and shut the cockpit hatch as he tweaked a smile. He ran his fingers over the roughened plastic grip of the yoke and let the trembling reverb of the Maule's engine warm his body. For a moment, he imagined himself back in Kush flying by the seat of his pants. Those were the days.

Until now, he hadn't realized how much he'd missed them.

5

Sylvia Six Flags

January 20

Protected by only a fleece-lined windbreaker over the loose clothing of her work-camp uniform, Sylvia Morales shivered away the frigid darkness behind the abandoned entrance to the shale mine. Huddled next to her were three men in their mid-forties; two of them suffered from late-stage two and three cancers brought on by the carcinogens of all the shale they'd all been mining for over three years.

Behind, them one of the shift managers aimed the dim beam of his flashlight along the rugged, sharp-stone floor of the mine. The feeble light set the four of them off from the mire of darkness. By now, the 10 a.m. shift was underway, and they heard the thin echoing of feeble scrapings of shale being mined in distant shafts by other inmates working otherwise in silence. Noises carried. Voices carried. Their two-hour wait had been accentuated by their occasional hushed whispers and the restrained, dry coughs and light groans of pain from the two men suffering from cancer.

So far, they'd heard none of the shrill whistle alarms signifying a break, so they were safe. But it was only a short matter of time before their absences would show up through the worker's roll call.

One of the two sick men was Hugh Blanc, Sylvia's former associate and adjunct professor back in the philosophy department at Yale. The other one, Mitch Krane, had been an investigative journalist for the Washington Post until the Kenton Regime shut it down back in 2022. Having been in the Unqutuck Gulag for four years, Mitch was one of its veteran inmates, and after mining all those years, his cancer had advanced the farthest. His cloth mittens were stained and clotted hard with two months of the blood he had coughed up through his fetid, toothless mouth.

Dave Harleson, the shift manager who had guided them here and waited with them for their transport, provided three rucksacks piled near the door containing their scant belongings. In spite of the danger they were in, Dave risked the worst punishment. If he was caught in aiding their release, and wasn't executed, he would be publicly whipped, then sent shirtless with his open sores into the mine with the other inmates. He'd be lucky to survive two months. In his mind, it would have been worth it as his contribution to the cause, and the importance of releasing Sylvia to carry out her grand plan.

The amputated third and fourth fingers of her right hand—sawed off recklessly after an onslaught of frostbite and gangrene two years before by the camp doctor, seared with stabs of hot pain as she flexed them. She clutched a ragged manilla envelope close to her chest as though she was protecting the child she regarded it to be. In it were pieces of notes, written with soft-lead nibs and hardened charcoal upon whatever paper could be gathered. Anything to write on was considered as criminal a possession as a weapon, so possession of paper was punishable as a whipping offense. Sylvia had had her back bared twice for flogging, because bits and pieces of blank, note-sized paper had twice been discovered in her pockets. The notes she now carried, written in code and shorthand, had been strategically scattered about within her, Mitch's, and Hugh's cells. Once sequestered under the protection of academia on the Yale campus, the three of them planned to put all their scribblings together as a Neo-Publica Manifesto. Her grand plan had been to advance its message though a massive public demonstration in front of the Kenton Tower offices in mid-Manhattan.

She heard a scuffle of footsteps in the snow. "I think they're here, Dave," she whispered breathlessly to her rescuer.

She stepped aside as he shouldered the door open a crack and aimed the beam of his torch down onto the snow. "Yeah. It's them. Finally," he said, as Brad pulled open the old door. "'Bout time y'all got here, Brad,"

"Well, what can I say, Dave? We been waitin' on the weather." He peered over Dave's shoulder. "Sylvia Morales. Great to finally meet you."

She chortled ruefully that his greeting sounded like one at a faculty cocktail party. Then tears came to her eyes. She smiled for the first time in three years in the realization that simple remembrances like that had come to mean so much. "I can't tell you how happy I am to see you."

He extended his hand. "Your plane is waiting for you. You ready to go home, now?"

"More than ever," she said, choked up by tears. She grasped his arm and he pulled her out from the moist darkness and into the free world—for what it was.

Dave ushered Hugh and Mitch up from behind where he remained in the shaft. "Sure you don't want out too, Dave?" Brad asked. "I can Cat you back to Birch Creek."

"I can do more here. 'Sides, it might only add to more suspicion at camp if I turned up missin' alla sudden. Who the hell knows? I might-can help later on to get some more people outta this hell-hole of a icebox."

Brad smiled at him. "Well, at least let me come back with a quart of J.D. Black for ya."

"Thanks, brother! I'll never turn down a free toot from anyone. Y'all let me get back now...time to show up for work."

Sylvia huddled Hugh and Mitch close to her to keep them all warm. "Aw, Dave, I could kiss you if I weren't so fuckin' frozen out here. Thanks for everything."

She saw his mittened hand wave though the shaft's murk. "You can pay me back with a kiss once you get done what you're out there to do."

She smiled back at him. "Well, you'll have to meet me in New York City for that."

"With pleasure."

"A steak at Gallagher's"

"With ab-so-*lute* pleasure, hon! Y'all just get that stuff of yours out there, y'all hear me?"

"With pleasure," she said before he closed and sealed the door, perhaps for another three years. He knew where all twelve of the ancient and nearly forgotten entrances were—each one waiting for a new cache of released inmates.

Devon was not quite as enamored to meet Sylvia as Brad had been. His only concern was the ponderous weight she'd brought abroad with the two extra passengers. Knowing nothing about their circumstances, he worried that he might catch something from Mitch's coughing spates, and then saw the blood covering his mittens. He looked over toward Sylvia crammed into the undersized right front seat next to his. "He okay?" Right away he knew it was a dumb question.

She looked over her shoulder at the two men now wrapped in quilted blankets and filling the little back bench seat as one big bundle. "You okay, guys? We're going home!"

"I'll celebrate once we're outta here and on our flight from Fairbanks, Syl," Hugh called weakly over the growing high rumble of the engine and the tinny rattle of the cockpit as Devon opened the throttle to half while braking to hold the plane back.

"Not me. I'll wait til we're in San Francisco—" Mitch said, then broke into a spate of coughing. "Better yet, when we land in Boston."

Sylvia trained her gaze out the windshield into the snowfall misting the fully realized high dawn, then looked at Devon. "I can't see any runway. Can you see anything?"

"Nope."

"Well, Devon. *That* certainly is a cause for confidence." How ironic it would be if she'd come all these years—with all her sketched-out revelations—only to have it dashed in a plane crash on take-off two hundred yards from the prison that had silenced her for four years. Then she heard something else above the groan of the Maule's engine—a higher tone, like the bleeping of a fire engine.

"Oh, shit!" Mitch coughed.

The snow intermittently glittered from the distant sweep of the searchlights.

"Get us outta here!" she said to Devon. "They've found we're missing!"

Hoping that the engine was fully warmed, Devon set the mixture to rich, and jammed the throttle forward to full. He released the parking and foot brakes, and the Maule, her fuselage rattling and trembling, lurched into motion.

"Christ! Here we fucking go!" Hugh said, his voice tightened with concern.

The snowfall had now started to lift, providing more visibility of the departing plane.

The plane wobbled to get traction, accelerated to ten miles per hour—the skis chattered against the welts of the snow cover—twenty—the snow became dense as a deep foggy curtain; pattering as crystalline pellets against the windshield and fuselage—thirty—the skis juddered furiously on the snow—forty—almost there; but still no tail lift as the rear wheel skid was drawn down by the softening wet snow. The rotation speed for take off with a load such as this was around sixty-five. Forty-five—the tall tree line coalesced dimly through the snowfall as if under their own power, as they came toward them, they became clearer—

"Shit, Devon!" Sylvia cried. "Are we gonna hit those trees?"

The trees came closer as a forgone conclusion. Devon quickly throttled back a little as he adjusted his left foot on the toe and rudder pedal. "When I tell you all—lean far to your right!"

"What?" someone asked.

"Your *right*! Lean to your *right*! NOW!" Devon shouted as he jammed his foot down hard on the left rudder-brake pedal. The plane tilted as though on only its left ski as the horizon listed and swiveled around and the Maule turned ninety degrees left to face south. The plane now had only the edge of the left ski in the snow, and the left wingtip was nearly hitting the ground. The weight had to be counterbalanced, as the plane waddled ahead. "LEAN! MORE!" Devon shouted.

Finally, the Maule righted with a soft bang as the right ski hit back upon the snow, and Devon took his foot off the pedal and jammed the throttle to full as they wobbled ahead east—away from the wind. They'd lost some forward momentum in the runway-turn: thirty-five— skis again chattering in complaint against the snow—forty-five— Devon applied a notch of down-flap—fifty-two—the trees at the other end of the clearing came closer into view in the diminishing snow as the tail finally lifted—sixty—another notch of flaps; now to half —sixty-five—rotation speed for takeoff and a point of no return. Devon yanked back on the yoke then furiously cranked the elevator trim handle to offset the climb away from a possible engine stall. The Maule took to the air at a thirty-five-degree pitch. He thought he heard and felt the tip of one of the right skis catch on a treetop as they barely cleared it.

Sylvia let out a heavy sigh as her head went buoyant, and she felt her chest fall weightless toward her rising stomach in the g-force. Devon leveled out the flight at 750 feet, and she settled back down into one piece. "Jesus! That that was...interesting. I haven't had that much fun since my last trip to Six Flags."

"You don't seem like the Six Flags type to me," Devon said as he settled back into his seat, then flicked the flaps back up to neutral. "When was that?"

"When I was twelve, Devon. And you don't have to question me any further on that." She looked behind her at Mitch and Hugh bunted up in their quilts in the backseat. She smiled, realizing how yellowed and browned her teeth might have become. Vanity was just another luxurious little devil. "You guys having fun?"

"I'm too busy back here puking up nothing," Hugh said.

Mitch waved his acknowledgement through another clasp of coughing.

"Well, *that* happened," Devon said relieved as he fondly recalled his flying days during the war. He reached into a pocket for his pack of cigarettes and noticed Sylvia leering longingly at it. "You want one?"

"Oh yeah. But after three years, I think I forgot how. I was just remembering how much I'd enjoyed it."

"Here. Take one then. A late Merry Christmas to you, Sylvia,"

"Thanks." She took the mitten off her left hand—intact with all its fingers, took the Marlboro in her shaking hand, and regarded it longingly as a relic. Devon lit his, then hers. She coughed.

Devon offered up a smile. "Take it easy, cowgirl." He looked ahead into the thinning snow and the brightening silver-clouded grey sky. He banked the Maule north toward Fort Yukon. "Looks like we're losing our cover. We'll need to stay low outta the radar." He said more to himself as he throttled to half to bring the plane down from fifteen hundred to a thousand feet and below the radar tracking from below.

"What the fuck was that?" Mitch gasped.

"What?" Devon said, as a sliver glimmer caught his eye. "Well, it's a tracking drone."

"Shit," Hugh muttered. "Are we *ever* gonna get out of that fucking place?"

"Yes!" Sylvia assured him. Then to Devon: "Right?"

Devon bit his chapped lower lip in the sudden realization that if the PRICE goons ever tracked them down, he, too wold end up chipping shale in the bowels of hell for the rest of his days. "Not if *I* can fuckin' help it," he said, as the drone leveled itself with the right landing gear. "Keep an eye on that thing, Sylvia, and tell me if it moves from where it is."

"Can you do something?"

He peered at a dense copse of high trees a few miles ahead of them. He remembered a tactic he'd used back in the shit when an RPG tracked onto his plane. But then, his twin-engine Cessna had twice the speed, power, maneuverability, and body strength of this little Maule-7. "Maybe." He lowered the throttle to one-quarter, then jammed down the right rudder pedal, while pulling left on the yoke for a tight, synchronized quarter-turn. He heard the clanking impact of the drone against the right ski-strut.

"You crashed into the drone," Sylvia duly told him.

"Yeah. That's what I wanted to do."

Sylvia heard the light clattering of the drone's two fore-props against the tip of the ski. She took a jab on her cigarette. "Well now their tracking drone is stuck to us."

"Right." The whooshing of the cold air filled the cockpit as Devon opened the window vent on his side to flick his cigarette out through it and left it open to air out the stench of body-smells. He lowered his flaps a notch and cranked down the elevator trim to slow and lower the plane. Eight hundred feet—the plane shuddered and yawed against the wind. Five hundred feet—once again trees loomed upon them, a hundred yards ahead. He flicked on the landing lights. Three hundred—almost at treetop level as they passed over the first line of them; he idled the throttle and the plane wiggled into a low-powered glide. Two hundred—Devon picked out one of the taller trees and banked toward it. It lightly scraped the bottom the plane, and the landing gear, dislodging the ruined drone, and along with it, the ski, which had been already loosened upon take off. He then immediately throttled up full and pulled back on the yoke as he added another notch of flaps for altitude.

"The ski fell off," Sylvia warned him. She seemed more excited than scared. "Did you want that to happen, too?"

"We still have a wheel."

"Well, that's comforting, I guess."

"Do me a favor, Sylvia, and flick on that map light to your right." She did.

Once they were back up to 1,000 feet and flying level, he lifted the map from between the seats. "Take up your yoke, Sylvia, and keep us level, while I look at this map."

"You want me to fly this thing?"

"Oh, Jeeezuzz," Hugh complained from the back. He remembered riding with her when she drove her Volkswagen back in the day. "Syl flying a plane?"

"Shut up, Hugh," she chortled as she grasped the yoke in both hands.

The Maule juddered a little as Devon throttled back to half. He spied the glimmer of the Yukon River in the distance, then spread out the map on his lap and saw where they were to land on the ice-covered river almost ten miles east of the Fort Yukon airport. He only hoped the air-temp was less than ten degrees out there. If the snow was too soft on landing—if the temperature was any higher than ten degrees—a wheel without a ski would sink in, causing a spin-out and a sudden foreword tilt. If the ice were thin, as it could be even in January, and if the river was too shallow, the nose weight could crack the ice, especially if the prop was still powered up as it should be on such a landing. The torque of the prop could chop a hole in the ice and collapse them into the frigid water.

He squinted ahead and saw the pinpoint glimmers of flame light marking their landing path on the river. "There's our spot, Sylvia. Ten degrees to the right. See it?"

She swiped off her watch cap. Devon noticed her ragged hair was a deep chestnut color, bordering on black. Bundled up as she was, he hardly imagined a person within the garb. "I think so."

"Aim us there, turn the yoke toward the right, just a little."

"You really *do* want me to fly this thing?"

Devon was confident he could even teach an elephant to fly. Acting the part of an instructor calmed him down. "Just ease her toward the right. Good. Stop there. Now do you see those marker lights?"

"Yeah. I think."

"That's your point. Keep us going there. Now, lower the nose a little. Push in on the yoke. Not so hard! Just ease it in." The altimeter showed they were descending slowly at ten degrees below the horizon at a rate of six hundred feet a minute. "Good, Sylvia. Hold us just like this." He throttled down a little more and applied a second notch of flaps, as the flickering runway lamps seemed to be rising up upon them more than the actuality of them coming closer to the lamps. After a minute of watching Sylvia relax her concentration, he reached for his controls. "Okay, I'll take it from here. Good job, and welcome back to the real world,"

She choked up and felt as though she could kiss him, but she was afraid of the fright she would cause from her breath. Instead, she opened her vent window and flicked out her cigarette as Devon had done. Somehow the rushing air smelled fresher than she could ever remember.

Devon had landed on one wheel before, and this landing was not as difficult as he was concerned it might be. It was merely a matter of applying more left aileron and tapping the brakes. The Maule skittered into an easy stop on the hardened ice.

A grey half-track was waiting to take them to the Fort Yukon airport, where Devon would fly them on to Fairbanks in a tour plane as if the extractees from Unqutuck gulag were just three moose hunters on a jaunt.

Finally in Fort Yukon, Hugh and Mitch were secured into place in the spacious, warmed passenger cabin. Washed up and somewhat more groomed and dressed in civilian clothing and a clean, white parka, Sylvia savored the fresh, mint taste of toothpaste in her mouth. She stood at the base of the ladder to climb into the big Cessna, as she hugged her precious envelope closer to her chest. She still wore a mitten to hide the ugly, cauliflowered tips of her brutally amputated fingers. She leaned her head back to bask in the sun as if it was something she'd waited to do for four years. "Thank you so much, Devon," she said as he stepped up beside her. "You really are one hell of a pilot. And thanks for the flying lesson."

"You're welcome, Sylvia Six Flags. Anything more I can do for you?"

She lifted her sunglasses to harden a friendly gaze into him. "Yes, there is." He sensed an important request as he stared back into her deep brown eyes. Serious. She puckered a tight, impish smile while trying not to display her damaged teeth. "You got another cigarette you can give me?"

He smiled back and handed her his nearly full pack of Marlboros and his spare Zippo. "Keep 'em, Sylvia. You earned it."

6

Thrones

January 24

There was a time, up until 2022, when Washington DC was the seat of the American government. Now that complex of alabaster was nothing more than a neo-classical reminder of how things were before the Kenton Regime drained its swamp. Like the Acropolis in Greece, it had become a tourist destination—a whitewashed testament to an ancient Democracy. The true locus of Real-America's power now sat in mid-Manhattan, in the Kenton Tower at the corner of 56th street and what had once been Fifth Avenue, re-named Kenton Way.

Stanley Saunders gazed out the window of his fifty-sixth-floor office and concentrated on the East River and its fringe of sparsely travelled highway, the Steven K. Banton Memorial Expressway. It had been so named after his mentor's untimely death three years earlier from an extreme case of gout. Renaming the FDR Drive after Banton had just been just another way of wringing out any reference to the old Democratic Party.

Saunders wasn't very happy this morning. Nothing new there. No one had ever seen him happy except for the time he was promoted to Commissar of PRICE and given nearly unlimited control in that department. He looked sullenly down at Lexington Avenue 650 feet below and tried counting the yellow cabs in the slow-moving stream of traffic. Counting cabs was something he did to relax. His concern had turned over into intermittent fits of seething anger, as his young secretary, and part time sex-partner, Karen Fabrizio, stood by in baited apprehension on the other side of his desk.

He took a slow sip of his green tea. Slow, deliberate sips. Never a good sign. "How long ago did all this happen, again?" The tone of his voice was a low growl.

"Thursday morning, Stanley. This just came down to us from Unqutuck this morning."

"Only this morning. After Four days," he grumbled. He took another sip of tea. "And so, Karen. *Why* did we just find out this morning?"

It hadn't come out as much a question, but a quietly veiled threat. She'd come to know that tone. It was usually the harbinger of something ugly to follow. She also knew why the administration at Unqutuck waited to release the information about the escape. Other than needing time to recapture the fugitives, nobody, not even the hardened gulag Commissar and his guards, wanted to be on the angry side of Stanley Saunders. It often meant that someone's head would roll, whether that someone was innocent or not. "I have no idea."

He remained staring mesmerized out his window. "Then find out."

"I will, Stanley."

"Who was taken out?"

"Uh..." she referred to her list. "A reporter from the Washington Post— "

"*Former* Washington Post."

"...former Washington Post. A guy named Mitchell Krane."

He finally turned to look at her. The bald pate above his heavily lidded eyes glimmered in the light. He toasted his tea-mug. "I remember him, actually. He was one of the first I sent there."

Karen continued referring to her list. "Some adjunct professor at Yale, Hugh Blanc."

"I don't know him."

"And a Sylvia Morales, a former professor at Yale. Philosophy, it says here, so my guess is she and this guy, Blanc, worked together before they were sent up to Alaska."

"Shit. Sylvia Morales." Saunders mourned into his tea mug.

"Should I know about her?"

"She was one of the founders of the fucking Neo-Publica movement," he grumbled sourly. Suddenly, he glared at her. "God fucking dammit, Karen!"

"What? Stanley? It's not like *I* had anything to do with this. I'm just the messenger."

"Yeah, well, Karen. You know what a king would do to his messenger if he delivered bad news?" He drew his free hand across his throat. "Execute him!"

She stepped back. "You gonna execute me, Stanley?" she asked nervously. The glaze in his look transmitted he could actually be thinking about it. Killing someone off was Saunders's answer to everything. "Hunh? Is that what you're gonna do? I don't see what that would accom— "

"Who let this shit happen up there?"

She looked back at the sheet now trembling in her grasp. "They think a guard, and maybe one of the civilian workers who knew the layout of the mine shafts."

"Find them. And execute the guard."

"Really?"

"No. Better yet, shoot out his knees, and leave him out in the tundra to die. As for the mine employee, find him, put him in Unqutuck, then flail him." He conjured up a frail wry smile. "Have him work naked in the mine while his flog wounds fester until he dies."

"Okay, Stanley," she sighed dubiously.

"As for the escapees and anyone else who helped them. I'll come up with a way of dealing with them. Especially Sylvia Morales. I'd kill her myself, if I could." He took on a thoughtful grimace. "Morales...That's a spic name, isn't it?"

"Mexican, I think."

"A Chiquita, then—a chimichanga-Mexi-freak-fuckin'-liberal-dem radical *cunt*." He sipped his tea as he ruminated. "I would kill her myself. With my bare hands," he repeated quietly. His cell phone warbled out at twinky-sounding opening refrain of "You Can't Always Get What You Want," Premier Kenton's perpetual entrance theme. "Shit it's him. I'm sure he's found out by now." He glared again at Karen as she widened her gaze back at him. A challenge from her, perhaps? "Yes, Mr. Premier, sir."

Karen heard Premier Kenton's voice from halfway across the room. Its husky tone sounded gravelly as concrete, even over the cheap speaker of Saunders's phone. "Stan? I've got Randy in my suite. Get your ass up here now."

"Yessir. Right away," he said dispiritedly. He held his phone against his pant leg, then glowered at Karen. "You'd better suit up, 'cause my ass is grass." *Suit up* was an expression he used when he'd fight in any way he could to keep himself from blame. Especially when it came from the Premier. Karen realized she'd just become very expendable in a very bad kind of way.

The gilded glop festooning Premier Alexander Kenton's penthouse suite would be blinding to the eyes of a normal person.

But Premier Kenton was no normal person. He basked in gleaming kitsch. It was his brand, transmitted even through today's orange-gold, oversized mantle of the toupee covering that which had started to thin to baldness a decade ago. And then there was that lasting trademark; that distinctive forelock sticking out over the wildness of his brows like the visor of a ball cap. He was set out from his gilded throne behind its matching desk only by the back suit, white shirt and red tie he always wore over his flabby bulk. His "thinking countenance" was solemn and dictatorial through a graven scowl signifying the self-importance of his office as another aspect of his brand.

Across from his desk were two uncomfortably stiff chairs, designed to make those in his attendance feel equally stiff and uncomfortable. In one of these sat his Consigliere and right-hand man, Randy Montefiore, like a looking very much at ease. He had no neck, like hunched-shouldered troll, and the face of an over-sized woodchuck with rosy cheeks. His dentures seemed to have outgrown his face, adding to his jowly, rosacea-pitted features. He had a fast manner of talking, as if he had to empty an over-filling vessel, accentuating his words with an unfettered, abrupt movement of his hands. He knew his boss's game; in fact, helped him fashion it with the help of Bill Bosch, the Premier's personal marketing director.

"I've found out a few more facts about our North Korean buddy."

"Little Rocket-Man," Kenton said.

"He's subverted the South Korean elections again, and he's running another bunch of nuclear tests."

"He's always running his fucking little nuclear tests."

"Yeah," Montefiore said. "But these are closer to the southern border."

"Short-range tests. I don't think that Humpty-Dumpty's ever gonna get it right. He's just tossing stones, not missiles."

"And violating our nuclear treaty with him."

Kenton flicked the subject aside with a curt wave of his stubby hands. "So what, Randy? That's his game, and he knows we know it."

"Well yeah, but— "

"Set up another meeting with that little slant-eyed prick. Show him and others that we're concerned about his fucking nuclear tests. Maybe have him meet me at West Palm Beach. We'll play some golf and have some smiley pictures taken, for good optics. That should appease the little shit."

"Okay, Al. I'll get right on it."

Even though Montefiore was the only one of his staff he allowed to call him 'Al', Kenton cringed at the appellation. But it made his Consiglieri feel important—that they were joined at the hip as equals in some sort of bro-mance. But Alexander Kenton knew he sat in the throne of the loneliest position on earth, and he was fully aware that he wasn't joined at the hip with anyone. Not even his son and heir, Alexander Junior, who sequestered himself away in his office three blocks down, over in his TV Network, probably jacking off to porn, for all Alexander Senior was concerned.

Jeanette, Kenton's secretary of the week, showed Saunders into the office.

"Ah, Stan," Kenton called amicably enough. "Come on in. Take yourself a seat."

"Thank you, sir," Saunders said, then bobbed his head at Montefiore, "Randy." Montefiore answered his employee's acknowledgement with an abrupt nod.

"Sooo, Stan," Kenton said as the PRICE Commissar took his seat. "We've just heard some interesting news from Alaska. You wanna tell us about it?"

Saunders cleared his throat. "As far as I know, three prisoners were taken out of Unqutuck, maybe with the help of some guards."

"As far as you *know*?" Montefiore flared menacingly. "No, Stan. It fucking *happened*."

Kenton held up a hand to stop him. "Now Randy, no need to get hot under the collar." He turned to Saunders. "Who were they, Stan? Who escaped?"

He referred to the notes on his i-phone. "Uh, Mitchell Krane, a newspaper reporter, and Hugh Blanc, an adjunct philosophy professor, and..."

Kenton jarred his head and shoulders forward as he waited for the name of the third. "...And? Who else, Stan?"

"Sylvia Morales, a philosophy professor at Yale."

"Oh, holy fucking shit!" Montefiore said. "Well, there you go."

Kenton glanced at him. "Who is she? Should I know her?"

Montefiore hefted a sigh. "She was a philosophy professor at Yale. We sent her up to Unqutuck three years ago."

Kenton shrugged his shoulders. "Okay. So?"

"She founded the Neo-Publica movement," Saunders said.

"Oh, shit." Kenton said. "That's fucking *great*. What is the Neo-Publican Movement?"

Montefiore waved the question aside.

"We'll find her, sir," Saunders said.

"You'd *better* fucking find her, Stan," Montefiore threatened.

"Why did we find this out after four days, Stan? You wanna tell us why?"

Saunders balked at letting his incompetence show in front of his supervisor and the Premier of Real-America. He relaxed his shoulders in defeat. "The information was kept from me, sir."

"Really? By whom?"

Saunders looked down at his hands on his lap, so he wouldn't have to look Kenton in the eye. It was also a clue to another one of his lies. "Uh, it was my secretary, sir, Karen Fabrizio."

"Oh, *great!*" Montefiore muttered in disgust.

"So, it was someone from our own organization. You work with her every day, and didn't even have a clue about this, Stan? Nothing?"

"I'm sorry, Mr. Premier."

"That's what you get for flying too close to the flame, Saunders," Montefiore said about the relationship he knew his subordinate was having with her. "I hope she was worth it."

In Saunders's mind, up until this morning, it was.

"Can you get anything out of her?" Montefiore pressed.

"Probably not. I'm sorry about this, Mr. Premier. I really had no — "

"I don't give a flying shit about your apology, Stan!" Kenton flared. "What are you gonna do about it?"

Saunders thought for a minute. It really would hurt him to do this: "Send her off to Unqutuck, maybe?"

"At the very least, Saunders," Montefiore said.

"She can fill the slot this Sonya person left for her."

"Sylvia, Al."

"Whatever."

"She won't last long up there," Montefiore said. "Pack her off today, Stan, with a five-year sentence. And mark her as extreme, so she'll be working stripped bare in the mine. I'd be amazed if she lasts a week."

"Sounds good to me," Kenton said.

Saunders stiffened. "Yes, sir, Mr. Premiere." He grieved the loss of her; that toned, supple body with the ample breasts he loved to grasp hard during sex—soon reduced to a cut up, dingy sack of bones like a refugee, with her breasts hanging down like loose pendulums. Her perfect feet with the toes he loved to suckle—rasped to bleeding from the shards of shale and rocks of the mine bed. He would miss her so. And then his thoughts turned to Marie McGee in fiscal management, with her red-golden hair. He'd always favored red heads.

"Now get your ass moving, Stan," Montefiore ordered glumly. "You got a lot to do, all of a sudden."

Saunders stood and offered up a leaden look at Kenton. "Mr. Premier?"

Kenton looked stern-faced at him. "Thank you, Stan. You're dismissed. Just get it done, okay?" Was that a wink?

"Yes, sir, Mr. Premiere." He turned smartly on his heel and left the gleaming golden office to send his secretary to the dark frontier of the tundra.

Karen looked straight down at Lexington Avenue. How easy it might have been to fall and abruptly end it—if only the thick-paned window hadn't been solidly and hermetically sealed away from what was once the reality outside. She'd seen Saunders deal with his employees before, after he felt they'd betrayed him. Simply firing them and setting them free would be too humane, and they would know too much—and too little —to not be vindictive. Quitting the organization was not an option. Saunders would instead condemn them like prisoners to the Kenton Tower records room in the pre-historic basement. Karen could tell who they were; they would emerge twice a day like myopic moles into the gleaming light of the lobby. Doomed to such a gloomy existence, three of them had committed suicide in the past year alone.

She took one last look down at the street six-hundred-and-fifty feet below. No. She was too good for that. And she had too much pride to have been her boss's sex-toy. He had nothing to offer there anyway, except brutal foreplay and exhaustive humping that continued well after she'd been exhausted into boredom. How had she allowed that to happen, anyway? A weakness for office politics, she supposed. Well, fuck *that*!

No. No more. Instead, she hurriedly gathered her coat and would leave the building as if she were going out to Ken's Deli to buy him another liverwurst on rye. Organ meat: his usual lunch. She left a message with Saunders' sub-secretary that she had forgotten about a doctor's appointment. That would buy some time.

She needed time to disappear into the vast anonymity of the city and figure out what to do next. It would be a short matter of time, maybe by the end of the day, for Saunders to release his PRICE goons to find her. The first place they would look would be her East 79th Street apartment. Let them whip her belongings into pieces, she didn't care. The only incriminating thing they'd find would be her battery-operated dildo; a necessary implement for her to flush out the ache of another night with her ex-boss.

Carroll Gardens, Brooklyn was about as far away from Kenton Tower as Budapest, mainly because it was safe. Protected like a fortress armed by quiet intimidation, it was an old Italian neighborhood as old as the hope of the new freedom promised to their immigrant ancestors arriving on Ellis Island. Carroll Gardens was one of those districts around the boroughs where the *Cosa-Nostra* housed their aunts, uncles, cousins and daughters. The inhabitants of the modest Brooklyn community hardly had to lock their doors, but of course did so out of habit and common Brooklyn and New York City protocol.

Though the Kenton regime had angered Organized Crime many times—usually through the unbridled comments from the Premier, himself—the two dictatorships normally left one another alone. The Mafia might be accused of many things, but being anti-American was not one of them.

But anti-Americanism was not like anti-Real-Americanism. Under wraps, they craved a restoration of the Democracy that originally drew them to America. The *Cosa-Nostra* seethed over the regime's PRICE architect, Stanley Saunders' treatment of minorities, especially immigrants. To many in The Organization, he was yet another family *deficiente* under-boss who teetered on the brink of being taught a lesson, or at the very least, sent a massage.

Karen had no way of knowing any of this as she stood wavering light-headed in place in the hard shadow of a discreet brownstone on 4th Place. Again, she rang up her friend Elise Sanangelo's apartment on the second floor. She glanced at her watch; 3:45 P.M. Her absence from Kenton Tower would have long been noticed by now. She shouldn't have wasted all this time—shouldn't have veered off at the Pub Stop for one Scotch on the rocks, then another, then... It might have been four; the last few had been rapidly consumed as quick belts. All her nerves had become tightened by the fear that Saunders would track her down. "Come *on*, Elise! I know you're home. You're always home on Monday afternoons!" she cajoled in a desperate whisper. She shrugged off her annoyance with a shiver against the intensifying cold.

Finally, the squawk of a voice from Mars, and two stories up: "Yeah?"

"Elle! It's Karen! Open up. Hurry!"

"What? You gotta take a pee alla sudden or somethin'?" After a quick angry buzz and the click of the lock, Karen thrust the thick oak and glass portal open and sprang up the carpeted stairs to the second floor. Elise held her door open as her friend brushed by her. "Jeezzuz, bitch! You look like shit. What the fuck's up?"

"I quit my fuckin' job, Elle," Karen said breathlessly.

Elise hatched a cunning smile as she closed her door. "Well, that's good news. I thought people never left that Kenton Kingdom. Somethin' about, like, I dunno, repercussions?"

"Something like that. Can I stay here for a few days?"

She patted her mussed-up mop of blonde back into some semblance of shape. "Uh..."

Karen noticed her blouse had been unevenly buttoned. "Oh," she reasoned sheepishly. "I got you at a bad time."

"*All* times are fuckin' bad, nowadays."

"Your timing always sucks, Karen," Salvatore Zinnio said as he sauntered into the living room while buttoning his shirt.

"Kar's quit her job," Elise told him.

"Why's that? Saunders finally send his PRICE goombahs after ya?"

Karen froze at that possibility. She wouldn't put it past Saunders to toss her away in some gulag for the transgression of offending him. "I didn't quit. I walked out."

"Well, Kar. They ain't gonna like you much for that," Elise said.

"Whydja do that, Karen?"

She stayed silent as she composed a logical answer.

"Come on, girl. You can tell me and Sal. It ain't like we're gonna bite you in the leg, or nothin'."

"I dunno, Elle. I got scared by a really bad feeling, I guess."

"Yeah," she scoffed. "By way of a few drinks, I smell."

Karen flashed her a glare.

"What was it, Karen?" Sal asked. "Did that bastard you work for do something to you?" He narrowed his gaze. "Did he *hurt* you?"

In more ways than one, she thought. "No. Nothing like that. But I'm afraid of him."

He intensified his dark-browed look at her. "What did he say to you? Did he threaten you, hon?"

She felt like she was watching herself from some sort of netherworld. She lost her stance as she weaved off another surge of lightheadedness. "I need to sit," she gasped, then slumped into the couch. "I—I don't know if he threatened me. Maybe. I just had a feeling something bad might happen." She cuddled a throw pillow close to her chest as though it could have been a teddy-bear, as a tear streamed down her cheek. She damped it away with a corner of the pillow, then let out a mighty sigh.

Elise sat down next to her, and gently laid a hand on her shoulder. "Kar, sweetie. I don't think I ever seen you this scared. It ain't like you. Tell us. What'd that shithead say to you?"

Karen laid her head in Elise's shoulder, and Elise lightly stroked her hair, like two sisters in a tender moment. "He might have threatened to kill me."

"Seriously?" Elise gasped.

"That *fuckin'* meathead!" Sal seethed. "What'd he tell you, hon? Exactly."

Karen tried to assemble her thoughts. "He told me he could have me executed for telling him somethin' he didn't wanna hear," she sniffled.

Elle glanced up longingly at her boyfriend, then back at Karen. "What was that, baby? Wha'dya tell that bitch shithead he din't like?"

"Uh...three people were taken, or escaped, from that gulag up in Alaska."

"Where they keep the dissidents?" Sal asked. "To me, that's fuckin' good news."

"Not to him. He got pissed because, I don't know, just 'cause I fuckin' told him. Maybe 'cause they escaped last Friday and I didn't find out 'til this morning. He acted like he might have me killed about that."

"*Acted* like he might?" Elise said as she continued to stroke Karen's hair. "You said he tolt you, right?"

"...yeah. Said he could have me...have me," she sniffed, "executed. Like kings who killed their messengers for bringin' them bad news."

"Sounds like somethin' he might say," Sal muttered. "Who was sprung? You know that, hon? Who escaped?"

"I don't know, Sal. I think some newspaper reporter, and two Yale philosophy teachers there, who'd been up in Unqutuck since, like, three, four years ago, somethin',"

Sal thought this over as he tried to connect the pieces. "A Yale philosophy teacher? Do you got a name?"

"Sylvia something Mexican, Gonzalez...something like that."

"Sylvia ... Sylvia Morales, maybe?" Sal said.

"Yeah, that was it. Sylvia Morales." Karen looked hopefully at Sal. "You know her? I think she was one of the ones who started the Neo-Publica."

Elise also looked at her boyfriend. "I've heard of her."

"Hot fuckin' *damn*!" Sal said.

"Why hot fuckin' damn, Sal?" Elle asked.

"Hot fuckin' damn we could get some mojo up against these guys fuckin' up our country, is why," he said. "If Sylvia Morales's back in business, so are we!"

"Shh! Sal," Elle said as she waved an arm in the air. "Not so loud, you asshole."

"What? You think we're fuckin' bugged? No way."

"I dunno, Sal. That guy here the other day working on our fridge."

"Right, Elle. He bugged the fuckin' calzone. Not a chance. Not here in Carroll Gardens." He looked Karen in the eyes. "Karen, hon? We maybe could get to that fuckin' *deficiente,* Saunders. And maybe you can help."

"How?" Karen asked.

"I dunno, yet," he said. "We'll figure somethin' out. I gotta talk to some guys. You jus' sit tight, okay?"

"So, I can stay here?"

He glanced at Elise, who nodded back at him. " 's long you want, hon," he said. "You got my protection, here."

"Oh, *great*, Sal ," Elise scoffed. "You don' even wash the fuckin' dishes round here. Whadya mean your pro-*tec*-tion?"

"I can do, stuff, Elle. Don' worry."

"Shit, Sal. 'Don' worry's' jus' what I'm worried about," Elle said.

7

The New-Publica Manifesto

March 3

At least the stumps of Sylvia's two missing fingers weren't so ugly anymore. Their nasty-looking cauliflower tips had been removed and softened at the expense of the remaining knuckles to completely remove her right ring and little finger. Often, she would imagine the phantom of those lost two digits when her mind was distracted as she typed—as now, with her concentration directed toward compiling her manifesto. It had been an effort to locate the far right keys—the O, P, , L, and ? ones—as she diddled her aching fingers along the keyboard. This prompted the remembrance of her time in the gulag and the mine, and then the deliberately slow, hot, gnawing pain of the camp-doctor's hand-drawn saw cutting through her fingers. Her sour memories were diverted by her typing the manifesto in the chilly, darkened basement office in Yale's School of Drama, a heavenly paradise by comparison.

Her gums ached as they adjusted to the dentures replacing her natural teeth that had blackened and rotted. She kept a bottle of Listerine available for when her fetid breath —or her imagination of it—came back to haunt her like the phantom fingers.

She looked over her shoulder at Hugh who had been putting their plunder of odd notes together into some semblance of order, as they worked on the finishing touches of the manifesto's second draft. Even so, it still would take another few drafts to make It ready for printing.

"Did anyone ever talk to Abe about turning the heat up a little in here?" She was tempted to add *I feel like I'm back on the tundra*, but the demon memories would only rise up again.

"We're on oil-heat rations this month," he reminded her. "It'll probably come on at..." he referred to his watch, "four this afternoon. At least that's what the schedule said."

"Heat ration schedules." She shook her head in dismay. "I remember a time when the only schedules we looked at were class-times."

"Gone are the days."

She glanced forlornly at the smudged up, little computer screen. It was connected to a forty-year-old PC that a sixty-five-year-old techie who still understood such ancient things was able to scrounge from some dreck in the basement. He reconditioned it with DOS and that kludgy Word Perfect. At least she could type the words in and print them out, and with no internet available, she hardly needed any other functions. She thumped an index finger on the screen as though the computer might respond back, like the bygone I-pads of yore. "I suppose they really had to take all the computers," she lamented.

"By edict of *mien Führer*," Hugh said. "Computers are tools of sedition, especially on college campuses not sanctioned by his highness's little dictatorship."

"I didn't think Kenton was smart enough to come up with verbiage like that."

"Not Kenton. Stanley Saunders, with his PRICE and BlueShirt *Sturmtruppen*." He flexed his aching fingers. "We gotta get this manifesto of ours out soon, so we can end this dictatorship, Syl."

He cupped his hands and blew into them. "Even if it's just to get the damned heat turned back on."

"Yeah," she scoffed, then looked over at him concentrating on some random scraps of their notes. "How are your treatments going? You're looking a little better—even for your normal ugly self."

He offered up a blithe smile. "Why thank you, my dear...I think. I feel a little better, so maybe those doses of aldesleukin are working. Can't say the same for Mitch. He was up all night puking and coughing. I think he might have reconciled himself to some truth he's not telling us."

Sylvia was struck with a dose of rigid silence. "How long, do you think?"

Hugh heaved a sigh. "I'm thinking more weeks than months." He looked sadly at the notes. "I guess in Mitch's case, that fucking Unqutuck will have gotten what they wanted, after all."

They shrugged in unison as they heard the clink and scrape of the door being unlocked and opened. It was Mitch bearing coffee and crullers from Jillian's Brew Hah- Hah. "Good morning troops. I figured we all could use this."

"Warmth! My hero!" Sylvia said as she skittered her chair over to him to grasp a cup and a cruller. "I love you for this." She loved him for everything, but there was no sense in admitting it to him.

"Thanks, brother." Hugh said as he took his cup. "You know you shouldn't be walkin' around out there in public if you don't want the BlueShirt shit heads to tag you."

"No fear, Do-Right." He stuck a hand into his tattered overcoat pocket to pull out his fuzzy beard attachment. "I've got my handy camo."

"That thing makes you look like you're wearing a raccoon on your face, Mitchell," Sylvia told him. "You let any of those blue-shits get too close, they'll see right through it."

"Well, Syl. It's better than my back-up Groucho glasses and big eyebrows disguise. Oh yeah, sometimes I wear an old Beatles wig."

"Shit, man. You *got* one of those things? They're priceless!"

Sylvia 's enthusiasm her warm coffee was tempered by the idea that Mitch probably didn't care about much anymore as his life was draining from him with each Chemo treatment. He looked ten pounds hollower than he had the week before, once he'd gained twenty after leaving Unqutuck. His skin had returned to its color but was the consistency of dry parchment. She marveled at how chipper he'd seemed even through the filter of all the coughing and the surges of the pain he must have felt. She wondered what *she* would be thinking if it were her with the numbered days. Perhaps she would have a light humor, too; knowing she'd have her ultimate freedom from a life that had turned so grim. She loved Mitch all the more for his bravado and light-heartedness as she watched him sip his tea and churn out single little cough.

"Anyway," Mitch said. "I had a ride there and to. My treatment nurse has a crush on me, I think."

"I'm happy for you, Mitchell," Sylvia said as she returned to her murky computer screen to squint at it. "I wish someone had a crush on me."

"I do!" Hugh blurted.

"Me, too," Mitch croaked nearly simultaneously as he seated himself in the squeaky chair in front of his HAM radio set-up.

"You guys don't count." Of course, that was a white lie in Mitch's case. "You already know too much about me to be objective. Besides, you've already seen me naked."

"Yeah," Hugh said. "Covered in all that shale and prison sludge. Beauty!"

Mitch started to fiddle with the dials on his radio to try to find anyone else than that annoying guy from Toledo with the handle

"Bird-Call." For his voice, it was an appropriate one. Besides, Ohio had a history of being solid Red and he wasn't sure he could trust him. For now, it was just more squelches, squeaks, and high, vacillating hums through his radio speakers. "No top forty today, I suppose," he muttered to his set. He adjusted the tight, wool watch-cap hiding the scant clumps of hair still left like weeds in the desert of his bald head.

They all suddenly looked up as the door chuffed open against the concrete floor. "Oops. Sorry," the intruder said. At least he wasn't a BlueShirt.

"Uh, men's room's down the hall," Hugh said, then turned to Mitch. "You forgot to lock it, Mitch," he grumbled.

"My hands were full."

"Piet sent me down here," the guest said.

"Why? And who are you?" Sylvia asked suspiciously.

"Rob Bryant. Piet wanted me to remind you that there's been a surge of BlueShirt activity around campus."

"See, Groucho?" Hugh chummily accused Mitch. "You coulda been spotted... fake beard and all."

"Thanks, Rob. Message received," Sylvia said.

"He wants me to shuttle you to the safe house this afternoon."

"Are we still that popular, to have a chauffeur?" Hugh said.

"Piet couldn't come himself?" she said.

Robert twitched something between a smirk and a smile. "He's out teaching."

"Oh, yeah," Hugh remembered. "American history to elementary and middle school kids. Actual American history."

"Really?" Mitch said as he fiddled with his radio's tuner. "I heard teaching old American history was banned. Kenton calls that liberal stuff about Washington and Jefferson 'fake history'."

"Fucking jerk," Hugh grumbled.

"Now it's all about the present history, and all the wonderful things our Premier has done," Sylvia said. "Like all life in America sprang up some time back in twenty-twenty-two, like Athena from the head of Zeus."

"It's *Real-America* now," Hugh scoffed. "And it rose from the empty head of Alexander Kenton."

"Yeah, well, fuck you Hugh, you seditious twerp," she said facetiously. She added a coy wink to her comment, then looked at Robert. "Okay, just don't stand there letting all the cold in. Come on in. You want a bottle of water, or something? I don't know how frozen it is."

"No thanks," Robert said as he closed the door behind him. "What do you all do in here?"

"It's our war room," Hugh told him.

Sylvia motioned to an empty office chair next to her. "Go on. We don't bite. Sit. We were just finishing up for the morning." Robert sat in the chair. "This is the place where stuff is gonna start to happen. Didn't Pietier tell you about us?"

"Well, I know you're Sylvia Morales. And you just got out of a gulag."

"'Got out?'" Hugh said. "As if we 'got out' of school for the summer? No way, man. We were sprung by Neo- Publica."

"Really? Sounds like no everyday thing," Robert said.

Sylvia kept her gaze trained on him. "It wasn't," she said ruefully. "Anyway, it is Rob...Right? Bob? Robert?"

"Yeah, that's right, any one of those."

He had piqued her curiosity. "Bob," she decided. She'd developed a second sight for things that lay behind facial expressions—a crucial sense, for survival in the gulag. He wasn't a bad-looking sort. Beneath the wear of time and concern accented by a greying at the temples, he appeared mid-forty-ish; around as old as she. But even in this grim surrounding, where he sat partially lit in the soft fluctuation of low light from her desk lamp, he exuded a separate sadness. His sorrow hadn't come across as the general malaise that trilled like a case of tinnitus within the normal routine of gloom among the ruins. This was a deeper sorrow from someplace specific. "How'd you come to know Piet?"

Robert attempted a solemn smile. "I was introduced to him by Bill Davis."

"Bill Davis," she thought, until it soon came to her. "Ah. Our attorney. Pretty decent guy—for a lawyer, I suppose."

"He got me out of jail, before my sentence was up."

"Sorta like what we just went through," Mitch said. "Except our sentence would never be up..." he caught himself, "until we died," he muttered forlornly, then coughed.

"Yeah," Robert said. "What you went through sounds like hell on earth."

"Nothing of *this* earth, I assure you," Hugh said. "At least not the way it's supposed to be."

Sylvia lit a cigarette and vigorously shook out her match. She noticed Robert transfixed by the glow from its tip. "Um...how rude of me." She extended the pack to him, scissored between her trembling right two remaining fingers. "You want one?"

"I don't smoke, but thanks anyway."

She replaced the pack next to her computer and stared at its crumpled package. "So, Bob," she said distracted, "Piet can be a hard sell. How'd he let you into the Neo-Pubs?"

"Bill pushed for it. We were neighbors in Fairfield, so he knew me and my family. Uh, I was arrested by PRICE for a moment of madness, and my wife took the kids and ran. Bill knew they were fugitives and arranged for them to be sent by the Neo-Pubs to Cuba to be transported to relative safety in Brazil. That's where the PRICE goons caught up with her and split my family up. Sent them away to various gulags."

"Jesus," Hugh said. "That sucks."

"More than sucks," Robert said. "Tricia my wife is in that gulag in Arizona."

"Dalaxuma? That one run by Sheriff Jeff?" Sylvia said.

"Yeah," Robert said through a choke. "That one. Bill thinks you guys can help get her out."

Sylvia placed her left hand on his trembling knee and squeezed. "I'm sorry, Bob. We'll do what we can, okay? I promise."

"Thanks." Robert's voice was barely discernible though a deeper grasp. "I hate this fucking dictatorship; what they're doing to us."

"Welcome to Neo-Publica, then, man," Hugh said. "You're in the right place to hate those assholes." Some chittering sounds came from the teletype machine on the desk behind him. He anxiously rolled in his chair toward it the and took up the paper spewing out from it.

"Teletype?" Robert said.

"Yeah. And in code," Hugh told him. "Legacy forms of communication aren't as easily tapped. We use HAM shortwave radio, too. Sometimes even telegraphs. None which can be tapped."

"Anyway, Hello, there, Bob. I'm Mitch. Your ham radio operator and decipherer of ancient media."

"What's it say, Hugh?" Sylvia said.

He concentrated on the output. "It's from Chicago. Probably just a check-in. Give me a minute to decode."

Robert craned his neck to look at Sylvia's computer screen. "What are you working on?"

"Our manifesto." She swiveled in her chair to block it from his view. "You'll see it soon enough."

"The Chicago Neo-Pubs are planning a big protest down Michigan Avenue," Hugh read from the teletype.

"Really," Sylvia said. "When?"

"Early May...once their snow melts, I suppose."

"Then so will we do our protest in New York," Sylvia said. "Send them back a message that it should be a coordinated thing. Also check with Salt Lake about how their plans are going."

"You're organizing a protest?" Robert said.

"Yeah. A big one."

"Let me know what I can do to help."

"Sure. We will. What's your talent? Like, what did you do in the real world?" she said.

"Advertising and marketing with Sloane and Jacobson in New York."

"Advertising? Of course you'd say yes if I asked you if you were any good at it."

He nodded. "Assistant V.P. of marketing for about ten accounts. Was. I still do consulting for them to eat and pay rent."

"Any of those accounts for revolutionaries aiming to overthrow a dictatorship?" Hugh asked.

"Uh..." he stalled.

"Well?" Sylvia pressed.

"I was on the team who handled the advertising for the first Kenton run in 2016."

"No shit?" Mitch said, then coughed. "You were one of *them*?"

"Until he fired us half-way in, when he stole our idea and went with his own in-house agency." He smiled mirthlessly. "Stealing our creative idea is one thing. Now I really do hate the guy. He stole my family from me."

Sylvia offered up a broad smile, displaying her white-white artificial teeth. She squeezed his knee harder. "Oh, yeah, Bob. We can use you, for sure."

March 15

I didn't know when my feelings deepened for Sylvia, but it hadn't been long after I'd first met her. The real question was why I started infatuating over her while I was so intent on getting Tricia out of the Arizona gulag. Though, as far as I knew, she was still alive, I wasn't sure she'd be the same if I were ever to find her. Despite her bravado, she could be easily broken. And the kids, certainly Steven, would be shattered beyond any recovery. *Steven-Mike-Emily-Tricia.* It ran constantly through me, looping from my mind to my heart, like a hyphenated seven-syllable mantra in one conjoined name. *Steven-Mike-Emily-Trishia—Tricia-Emily-Mike-Steven. Steven-Mike-EmilyTrishia—TriciaEmilyMikeSteven.* Thinking of them was like a curse, as intense as it was painful, and more so when I was with Sylvia, as my litany served as a talisman to ward away my guilt.

Sylvia and I had been drawn together by loss, and hers was no less than mine. In her case, the three years she spent in Unqutuck gulag hollowed out her dignity, if not her independence. By the time she was rescued, nearly all she'd had left of herself were some scraps of paper, and, for her, putting them all together had been like assembling the torn pieces of her integrity. By the time I'd met her in that cave of an office in the Yale Drama School, the strong inner fabric that had once made a legend of her had been unwoven. She was still as fragile within as the paper her manifesto had been printed on. Her gutsy, wry sense of humor was only a thin veneer to keep most others out. Also, she had fallen in love with Mitchell from a distance and knew she would lose him without her ever having had the chance to tell him.

By last Friday night it had become too much for us, as the weight of our private desolations bore down upon and into us. It took no time, because we both realized we were held captive in the cargo of our grief. So what the hell?

She, Hugh, Pietier, Mitchell, and to some minor extent, me, had finished editing the manifesto.

"We should all go back to my place for some drinks to celebrate," I offered without thinking.

"All of us together? Like turkeys in a barrel? You're fuckin' daft man," Hugh said.

"Probably not a great idea," Pietier said.

"Ducks," Mitch said.

"What?"

"Ducks, Hugh. It's *ducks* in a barrel."

"Whatever."

"We could go to Jillian's," Pietier offered.

"Latte in a basement?" Sylvia said. "I don't know. That seems a little..."

"Twinkie?" Hugh said.

"Something like that," she answered. "This definitely calls for a stiff belt of something." She relaxed her gaze at me as she considered. "I'll go with you, Bob. You've got some scotch stashed away up there?"

"I don't know, Syl," Hugh said. "You really wanna go streetwise this close to campus? I mean it's one thing for Bob, but you? What if some BlueShirt recognizes you?"

"It'll be okay, Hugh. I'm a woman of many disguises."

Pietier looked at both of us, as if he might know something about Sylvia and me that I, or we, didn't, then nodded curtly. "Just be careful, Sylvia. Okay?"

"I will. I need the practice anyway if I'm going to be sneaking into Manhattan for the next few months to set all this up."

We easily made it arm-in-arm the four blocks to my apartment's high-rise behind the Schubert Theater. She looked like some had-been Swedish model in a trench coat with her strait-haired platinum wig and over-sized 1960s sunglasses. I felt her stiffen and I patted her arm as a BlueShirt passed us by. Most people with a scintilla of intelligence might see through her disguise for what it was. The doorman offered his usual easy simper and winked as he looked her over, as if to say: *Nice going, guy!*, instead he said: "How ya doin', Mr Grant?"

Once safely sealed away in my twentieth-floor apartment, she slipped off her big sunglasses with a trembling hand. I saw that her eyes were a light blue, like my daughter, Emily's; something I'd never noticed in the office-cave. "Mr. Grant?" she said softly, as though she might pique a bug somewhere in the room.

"That's my handle, here. Leonard Grant. Piet thinks I should be incognito, too, for some reason. It's working so far."

"Christ, is that what I should call you here? *'Leonard'*?" she whispered. "'Leonard' sounds like the name of some myopic kid I'd kick sand at in the third grade."

I plunked some ice-cubes in a couple of cocktail glasses. "You don't have to talk softly here. This place is totally bug-free. Piet had some of his 'air-conditioner repair guys' sweep it before I moved in." I looked over at her being captivated by the view of the Long Island Sound at night through the wall-sized picture window. The lights of the buildings glittered off to the right. "There's a pretty good view here," I said as I walked to the couch and placed our drinks on the coffee table.

"I'd forgotten how pretty," she answered from a distance. "Even if it is only New Haven." She turned to me. "This is a nice place. Who's paying for it, not us, I hope."

"Who's 'us'?"

"You, know, Bo—Leonard. Our happy little band of —uh, people."

"Sloane and Johnson pay me pretty well, I'm kind of vested, there."

"Really." She sounded suspicious.

"Yeah, my, uh…my wife's maiden name was Johnson."

"Oh."

"What'll you take, uh—Jeanette? Bourbon, Scotch, beer? I think I have some Michelob here somewhere."

"Jeanette," she scoffed in a whisper. "Never in a million years would my parents have named me that… uh, what kind of bourbon?"

"Jim Be— "

"I'll take it! Lots of ice, please," she interrupted quickly. She turned her attention back to the view.

I kept my eyes trained on her. I watched her slide her wig, and absently run a hand though her black hair, now starting to fill out to a near normal shape since it had been shorn in the gulag. She was so thin and waif-like in this light. It was then I became certain we needed each other, even if it was just for one night. I slowly lowered myself to the couch and patted the cushion next to me. "Your drink awaits."

She walked over toward me and I noticed a slight limp I hadn't seen before. More ravages of the gulag. She smiled weakly and sat next to me. She reached into her trench coat pocket and withdrew a pack of cigarettes. "Do you mind?"

"It's fine," I said, as from the side table, I swiped a plate from beneath a pot that might have once housed a plant. "You know those things are bad for you."

She lit her cigarette and glowered sourly at it. "Not nearly as bad as that shit in the shale mines. It gave Hugh and Mitchell their melanoma." She inhaled, then held the smoking cigarette away, between the remaining thumb and fore finger of her right hand. "Hugh will probably get through it, but it's ..." she pursed her hips tightly, "it's taking Mitchell away."

"How long do you think he— "

"Let's not talk about it, Bob." She brought her left hand up to my cheek and stared into my eyes. "Okay?" She laid her cigarette into the plate, picked up her bourbon, and sipped it languorously. She set it down, then stared back at me. "You know? Until now, I'd forgotten how normal things could be."

"Or were," I said. "Who ever knew that one deranged guy could make— "

She brought her damaged hand tenuously up to touch her two fingers to my lips. "Shhh. Not now."

She drew her fingers around to my cheek. I hadn't felt as tender a touch since Tricia's. Sylvia's eyes glistened with tears—like mine. For a second, I felt smothered by the conflicts of guilt and need. I couldn't breathe. I moved her hand to my lips and kissed the spot where her gone fingers had been. She then launched into a spasm of sobs and held me to her as if she never wanted to let me go. I kissed her on the lips. She tasted of bourbon and Listerine.

8

Diana

April 12

Standing isolated in the southern Arizona desert, 30 miles northeast of Tucson, a chain-link fence surrounding four tennis courts glinted in the hot blazing sun. Sheriff Jeff Lupera had a reason beyond his tennis-playing grandson's birthday to have the courts constructed at the edge of the Dalaxuma "campus." They were meant to intimate the inmates of the sprawling tent city with a reminder of normalcy, but the courts made no sense at all. Most of the emaciated refugees housed in the gulag on an eight-ounce-a-day diet of *arroz y frijoles* had never played a game of tennis in all of their formerly deprived lives. It was just another example of how the Sheriff ran his little kingdom in a surreal desolation within the greater desolation of the desert.

Taken together, Sheriff Jeff and his son, Zach, were as dumb as a dog's foot. Today, some of the inmates who still had the strength to stand watched as Zach played a match with another one of his cutie little beauties from Tucson. The copper-tanned, scantily clad powder-puff had ridden out here with him in his red Porsche. The car, not exactly one built for the rigors of the desert, was in constant need of repair. For that, there was Pepito, inmate number 2236507, who'd been a good mechanic before he left Mexico City for a better life in America back in 2017. He was swept up in one of the first PRICE raids in 2021 and had been in Dalaxuma since then. Though he'd been easily turned and was now a trustee, he was always held under guard while he worked on Zach's Porsche to hand-brush the sand from its delicate works.

Game. Set. Match. Zach let his giggling girlfriend win again, most likely for a bedtime reward later.

"Good job, Jenny! You beat me again. Now let's have some fun, eh?"

"What sorta fun, Zachie?"

He pointed out some inmates who had been watching them from a lull of tired confusion. Eight of them. "You, you, you, you, you...you, you...no, not you. Maybe let's get a few Chiquita's in the mix. You, and, uh, *you*. Come on in here. And Jenny, you come on over and stand with me on my side."

She rested her Titanium racquet coquettishly over her shoulder. "Whadya gonna do, Zachie?" she said as she walked to his end of the court

He watched the eight chosen inmates trundle and limp dutifully to the empty side of the court, as though they knew what was in store for them. "We're gonna play a little mixed-doubles, sweet-pea." He dragged a wire basket of tennis balls from the corner. "You!" He ordered one of the inmates after they'd all filed in. Make sure that gate is closed." He politely handed a ball to his girlfriend. "Ladies first, Jenny. Take a few practice serves and make 'em strong."

She squinted at the assembled inmates. "Really? Do I have to?"

"Well, yeah, babe. I noticed your serve was a little weak. You need to strengthen it. Go ahead, don't worry about them. They *love* this." He looked at the ragged inmates herded across the court like the sheepish refugees the gulag had made of them.

Jenny knew better than to cross him. She lobbed a soft serve into the opposite court without hitting anyone.

"Unh-unh. Still too weak, babe. Ya gotta put some *umph* behind it. He picked out a ball and served it hard, hitting one of the older men in the cheek and drawing blood. "Like that. See?"

"I really don't like this game, Zachie."

"Ah, c'mon, sweet pea," he cajoled, then picked out another ball and served it hard, as some of the inmates scattered from it. Then another, and another. A fourth serve hit one of the old women as she stumbled and struggled to get up. His fifth hard serve caused them all to scramble about the court. "Hah! Look at 'em run!"

"Please stop this, Zach! Please. Come on, baby let's go back to Tucson, now. I'll make it worth your while."

"This is too much fun, Jenny." He served another, felling one of the men who was too exhausted to stand back up.

"You're *hurting* them!"

"No, Babe...they *love* this shit! HEY!" he called over to them. "Don't y'all just love this shit?" He was answered with an assortment of grumbles. "See. Jen? What'd I tell you?" He served another and hit the same woman as before, who remained standing resolutely.

Jenny placed a hand on his service arm before he was able to launch another ball. "Come on, baby...let's go." She whispered: "I'll shave myself down there for you. You can watch. Even do it for me, if you want."

He lowered his arms and looked down at her. "Really?"

"Oh, yeah, hon. Really."

He let his racquet and ball drop to the court. "Okay, y'all! Game's over for today! You can now all get the fuck outta here!"

April 18

The musty, hot air enveloped her into near breathlessness. She sniffed in the lingering vapors from the damp old canvas, rank with the musk of sweat and old sperm. A serrated beam of sunlight glared through a ragged rip in her tent wall, making all else seem that much darker. The harsh shaft of light caused her to squint in defense of it, but she was lucky to have a tent at all. Many of the rest of the refugee-inmates lived their lives beneath a scrap of canvas or thin blue tarp supported above them by four sticks. The coverings rustled and crackled in the buffeting of desert winds which provided nothing but more wafts of heat. She adjusted herself on her infested blanket and held a hand into the light.

Her hair been rudely shorn into a yellow-white clump. A few years back, she might have gone to Marlene's Body Shoppe to have her hair done, and her nails shaped, colored and buffed. Now three of them were nothing but remnants; yellowed scraps from nails torn long ago from her fingers as punishment for some minor infraction she no longer remembered—any more than she remembered Marlene's Body Shoppe.

She'd been moderately well preserved and fed double rations of undercooked *arroz y frijoles* to remain barely fit for the senior BlueShirts and junior PRICE officers to enjoy at their pleasure. Another tight ache flowed up through her chest from the stiff locus of her groin where she had been ravaged the night before. This morning she hadn't remembered or cared who or how many there had been last night as she had lain wasted as a corpse beneath them. Having become anesthetized to the act, she felt...nothing.

Drained of any emotion, dignity, or hope, she'd nearly forgotten who she once was. She had been humiliated and stripped any identity beyond the constant reminder that she was a woman. Now known only as a pronoun, she hadn't even an inmate number. As one of the few white women held captive among the brown and black-skinned inmates, she was a rarity. She had been known as

Diana—a classy white woman's name—as a point of reference for the men who had her.

On whatever day this was, she lay insentient on her blanket; like her, smudged and camouflaged by dirt. The slight, reddened welts of the whip-marks on her back occasionally stung out their reminders every time she sweat. Surrounded by a dry cacophony of Spanish, Creole, and Chicano from outside her tent, she felt oddly at ease. At least there were still signs of life out there. She huddled into her blanket and shivered through another surge of fever.

The ebbs and flows of her memory, diminished over time, vaguely reminded her of a family she once might have had—especially her three children. They were gone, too, she remembered—thrust away into places like this. She'd tried desperately to forget their names and faces, as to not associate them with this and what she had become—someone wrung out dry into what remained of her soul. She'd forgotten about the man who may have been her husband. She'd refused to let herself remember. She had stopped crying about them all months back; her tears having long since dried up—they were as useless as her memories.

The rasp of Spanglish crashed with another sudden splash of light though her flung open tent-flap. "Line up! Outside! Now!" she wondered if those dreaded four words were the only ones that guard knew. "NOW! Outside! Line up!"

She unfolded herself in aching stages and dutifully stood as the sand floor of her tent prickled into the bared, sore soles of her sore feet. *Line up. Outside. Now*—another PRICE officer, or two, maybe more, would make their choices from the line-up of woman. She had been one of the lucky ones because she and only one other older woman in the lineup were Caucasian, as were most of the PRICE officers into the camp.

She stepped out into line where other women stood in wait like slaves at an auction. To be rejected two times in a row resulted in a public whipping. This had happened to Diana only twice. Once, in the beginning, she was too sick with fever to stand. The second time was when a large detachment of favored Brazilian "dignitaries" had arrived with a thirst for Mexicali women. One of them had requested a twelve-year-old Nicaraguan boy. His choice had served up a demerit for the women, because he hadn't chosen one of them.

Diana stared down the line of ten women wavering in the heat of blazing sunlight and filmy clouds of sand-dust. Garbed in the same colorless rags as she, they remained perfectly silent unless spoken to, and, as directed, tried to conjure up a welcoming smile. The smiles that grazed many of their fatigued faces were lifeless; some of them sneers garnished with a hatred in the eyes. Not Diana's—she was too drained to remember how to hate, or love. While others patted the short straggles of their hair into place, a few of the women tried to appear enticing by exposing their weather-ravaged breasts. Diana heaved a tired-out sigh as another reminder that she was still, unfortunately, among the living.

After standing for twenty minutes in the searing heat, now rankling the whip-sores on her back, she saw four men approaching from the distance of the far end of the line. One was the "Line-up-Outside-Now" BlueShirt guard on horseback, who gripped a whip just in case any of the women got ornery. The other three were PRICE agents, who took their time regarding, poking and prodding the women. They lifted the hems of their dresses with the sticks they carried. One of the agents raised the upper lips of a few of them to examine their teeth, as if he was picking out a horse.

Once the three of them got to Diana, one of them stared heatedly at her with a special interest. He might have seemed familiar, if she had the ability to remember anything. She gazed at him, trying to smile, then her smile fell, as if there was something about his expression that eventually came through the fog of her remembrance. "No," she whispered lightly. "No!" No sooner than she said this did she feel the harsh sting of the tip of the "Line-up-Outside-Now" guard's whip upon her cheek. She staggered back.

"No talking, whore!" He *did* know some other words, after all.

"No. I can't! I *won't!*" she proclaimed in a vague rasp to both the guard and the PRICE Lieutenant looking her over.

Out of the corner of her eye she saw the guard's whip bow up again in earnest. She saw its tail arc toward her face—her eyes— just as the PRICE agent grabbed it away from striking her.

"I want this one," he told the guard.

The sound of his voice reminded her fully. "Take... another ...Not me," she gasped, then coughed.

"Why you want this one, senor? She talks against she not supposed to."

"*Why?*" he said more to Diana than the guard, as he glared more deeply into her. "Because of *her*…because of *you,* woman…I ended up at this shit-hole in the first place," the PRICE Lieutenant said. He turned to the guard. "I want this one." He glanced at his watch. "Have her prepare herself for me in an hour."

The "Line-up-Outside-Now" guard rolled up his whip as his horse nickered and pawed the sand with his hoof. "You heard him, whore. Now *go!*"

"Yes," the Lieutenant added. "You owe me. Now go and make yourself look pretty."

9

A Protest Grows in Brooklyn

April 20

Since Sylvia and I had clung to one another during those few weeks, my thoughts turned to Tricia more than I could have realized. I *needed* to think about her; to remember how it had been. It was a paradox that it was for her sake. I held Sylvia to me; although with Tricia in my imagination. For that same reason, Sylvia clung to me over her feelings for Mitch.

Not knowing what Tricia might be going through, or even if she had survived, only led me to miss her more. And Michael, Emily, and little Steven—where were they? Would I ever see any of them again? Would I ever stop my anguished weeping within over how my family might be gone forever? I missed them so deeply it was beyond description, but not beyond tears, so I held on that much tighter to Sylvia. We harbored no secrets about the why of what we were doing. She and I had become necessary evils for one-another's sanity.

She knew Mitch would soon be gone. "It's as if he's taking parts of me with him as he crumbles away," she'd reticently told me. "Every day I see him deteriorate I feel that much weaker. And I'm coming apart over my remembrances of Unqutuck and those pitch-black shale mines. Hold me tighter. Hold me together, Bob."

And I would. It was as if we could justify our actions and soften the guilt. Yet, for me, it wasn't working. It would have been irrational for me to stop wondering about Tricia and the kids, and if there was a scintilla of possibility of bringing them back.

Thinking about the up-coming Neo-Publica protest in New York kept us both from drowning in the sorrow and uncertainty hanging over our personal losses. We talked about the demonstration often—we *had* to talk about it, to try to persuade one-another that there was a greater purpose than our paltry emotions. That, too, was either an excuse or a lie.

The teletype machine in the Neo-Publica office had been clattering so much in the last hour I had to throw a blanket over it to muffle the sound. We knew there were more BlueShirts checking the campus, and we never knew when one of them might stumble upon our operation in the forgotten bowels of the Drama School. So far, we'd been lucky.

This morning, dispatches from our charter groups in Denver, Boston, Miami, Norfolk, and Salt Lake came rattling through the teletype. The plans for the Chicago Neo-Publica protests had been hacked and tagged. Our compatriots there were frantically shredding any evidence before shutting down.

"They got too fuckin' careless!" Hugh groused. "That Chicago network is just too damn porous."

"We should never have set this all up for May first," Pietier said. "Too soon, and too obvious. May Day. Communism. Revolution. Of *course* PRICE is going to step up their efforts to check us such a symbolic day."

"At least Kenton won't be anywhere around," I said. "He's been invited by Premier Vladovkov to the May Day parade in Moscow,".

"Yeah, fuck." Hugh scoffed. "All those big Soviet Toys and a parade to boot? He'll be like a kid at Christmas."

Sylvia lit another cigarette. "Probably more so with this added gift of the Chicago bust." She tore another dispatch from the teletype, read it, balled it up, and then tossed it in the trashcan for burning.

"What are we gonna do?" I asked her.

"We're still going ahead with it. Just not on May first. I never liked the idea of having this on a Monday, anyway." She referred to the wall calendar. "Let's move it to Sunday the fourteenth. In the morning, like at nine."

"While everyone's at church?" Pietier asked.

"Well at least Kenton won't be," Hugh said. "God doesn't have to go to church."

I offered up a half-smile. "Taking his communion of bread and wine from a box of Big Fries and a vanilla Thickie shake."

"Yeah. Nice" Hugh chortled. "'I'll have some self-absolution with a side of cholesterol, please.'"

"Okay?" Sylvia said. "Are we agreed? Is it the fourteenth, then?"

"Don't see why not," Pietier said as we all nodded in agreement.

"Okay, then. Hugh, you message Denver, Boston, Salt Lake, Norfolk, and D.C. We'll re-coordinate for May fourteenth at nine, our time."

"It'll be six a.m. out west, Syl," Hugh reminded her.

"All the better, Grasshopper. The earlier it is, the more shocking the surprise."

"Remember Pearl Harbor." I said, then had to search my memory. "That did happen sometime around six in the morning, didn't it?"

"Something like that," Pietier said.

"Yeah, but they had only one shot at it," Mitch said before another cough. His cancer had diminished his voice to a hoarse, breathy whisper. He fiddled the radio dial from chatter though static to more chatter. He stopped and squinted at the dial and held up a finger. "Hugh," he said and then pointed to it. "Boston."

Hugh stepped over to the set, and snatched up the mic, and keyed it. "KBN078, this is KNH640...over."

A tiny female voice crackled through the speaker box: "Yeah, hey Eli, it's Beans."

"Hi there, Beans," Hugh said close into the mic. "What's up?"

"We hear Cheryl got sick."

"Yeah, a head cold. They fear it might be a virus going around."

"Is she gonna see a doctor about it? Is she gonna be okay?"

"Nope. No doctor house-call or anything like that. She may be laid up in bed for a few weeks."

"Oh, crap. That long? Is it contagious?"

"Like I said, Beans. Could be a virus going around. Enough to take precautions."

"Okay, I'll stay off the street until I hear she gets better."

"Good idea. Oh, yeah, Beans. I meant to tell you. Due to the bad weather, the ball game's been moved up a few weeks. The Yankees'll now be playing on the fourteenth. Be sure to bring your breakfast."

"Okay, Eli. Thanks for the heads up. KBN078. Out,"

Hugh placed the mic back down on the desk. "Okay. Boston's got the message. I'll let the others know."

"You're a dear, Hugh," Sylvia said as she laid her hand lightly and reassuringly on Mitch's bony shoulder.

"I know, Syl. Like my mother used to tell me."

She turned to me. "Pack a bag, Bob. You and I need to go to New York."

"Why?" Pietier asked.

She lit up another cigarette. "I need to meet with Barbara and then walk the route firsthand."

"Really, Syl? You wanna get that close to Kenton headquarters?"

"S'okay, Hugh. I'll wear my blond fuzzy wig and big sunglasses."

"Oh, Jeeze, Sylvia," I said. "Not those things. They just scream out: 'Disguise!' and besides, you look ridiculous in them."

"Yeah, Bob. Like you're a real fashion plate," she chided.

She was good at the art of friendly banter outside of our private times. Prattling around like that was the only means to filter out our helplessness and to keep us afloat and "normal" within our tight band of reformists. We felt caught between worlds; neither of them sane.

April 24

We'd been into New York City twice before and knew the drill. Once on the commuter train speeding—and then mostly inching—down the eighty-mile track route toward Grand Central Station, Sylvia and I would settle into our seats, and she would rest against me. While she feigned a deep sleep, I'd hand our tickets and well-counterfeited I.D.s to the conductor. He was often a BlueShirt in training or near retirement who seemed as disinterested as a teaspoon of salt. He would merely glance at our two cards, punch the ticket, hand them back to us, then move on. On our last trip, the train had stopped dead for twenty minutes with no explanation. The passengers glanced around in trepidation, fearing someone, maybe a Neo-Pub, had been found out, and the conductors dispatched to re-check I.D.s more thoroughly. Finally, the train jolted back into motion. Later we found out there had been another suicide-by-train on our route. There had been more of those lately.

The crowds of Grand Central were flecked with BlueShirts and PRICE agents, but it never seemed to be a problem for us, as we were well-protected by the crowds of people. Just like they had adapted to the heavily armed soldiers and cops milling around Grand Central after 9-11, most of the throng took it all in stride as another piece in the chaos of life in Manhattan.

The subway trains were running at a third of the force it had been back in 2020, and the dingy cars were heavily packed with people who couldn't move. We were suffocated by the heat, and the stench of sweat and piss. It was as though the car hadn't been cleaned since 2021. Once we got off at Grand Army Plaza in Brooklyn it was like being released from a sweaty warren into bright sunlight and open air.

We'd be staying for a while in a brownstone apartment near Prospect Park and Seventh Avenue. For nearly the past year, it had been occupied by fellow Neo-Pub, Barbara Rivera, who'd been campaigning for Sylvia to take the apartment's next two-year occupancy after her rotation was up. Sylvia seemed a natural for the place. Since being rescued from Unqutuck, she had become too important a fixture remain stuck in the close, Petri-dish of Yale and New Haven. Brooklyn was a much easier place for her to get swallowed up into anonymity.

The innocuous-looking brownstone was only a block away from the David Hume Universalist Church on St. John's Street, where the furtively active Prospect Park Chapter of Neo-Publica often gathered. The chapter was also the incubator for the up-coming protest. Barbara, its founder, and Sylvia had gone way back to 2012, when Barbara was one her grad students at Yale. They were bound in a friendship based upon respect.

When we arrived, they hugged like school kids who hadn't seen one another for years, even it had been only two weeks, when Sylvia had shown up with Piet. Barbara put a finger to her lips: "Shh." She went to flick the switch on a cube the size of a child's building block sitting on the counter of the kitchen island. It emitted a soothing, high hum. She then walked across the room to turn on the TV, with the volume low. It was the Prime-Time Entertainment block on the Kenton/Fox Network. Tonight was Wednesday: three hours of "At Home with Kim and Kanye," complete with an over-zealous canned laughter and response track. It needed the over-dubbed laughs to accent all the digs that were more stupidly acerbic than funny—many of them aimed at Liberals: the ridiculed minority.

"Okay," Barbara said. Her voice was lightly garnished with a Castilian Spanish accent. "We can chat now." She gestured toward me. "Hello. Who are you?"

"He's Bob. He's been my right arm and confidante for the last month."

She cast me an amused look. "Really?"

"Uh, yeah. I guess I am," I said with an awkward chuckle.

She tweaked a smile at her old friend. "Then I'm happy for you, Syl."

Sylvia answered Barbara's smile with hers. "Thanks, Barb. What's with the hum?"

Barbara glanced at the little cube on the counter. "Oh, that's a neat little thing Aileen brought down with her from Vancouver a few weeks ago. I don't know if it works, but it's supposed to detect bugs and transmit anything they hear into static. It's kind of cool, but I still think it's only a toy." She looked at me. "Aileen likes to collect gadgets like that."

"I see," I said, wondering who Aileen might be.

"Where's she at, Barb?"

"In your bedroom, working at her desk. Who knows at what? Probably making ready for tomorrow's gathering at Hume Unitarian."

"No, I am not," said Aileen McDougal as she walked barefoot into the living room. She placed a lingering kiss on Barbara's cheek. With her loose shoulder-length curly mass of copper hair, fair-white complexion massed with freckles, and her light green eyes, Aileen lived up to the look of her Scottish heritage. By contrast, Barbara, like Sylvia was medium-dark complexioned, with rich black hair; Barbara's to below her shoulders and Sylvia's still cropped but grown out well from its gulag-shorn state.

"Hey, Syl." She sat on the couch-arm and rested her arm around Barbara's shoulders, then glanced at me. "And hello, whoever you are."

"That's Bob, Syl's muse," Barbara said.

Aileen smiled a greeting at me. "Well, we could all use one of those. Piet couldn't make it this time?"

"He's keeping the arrangements going back home, with all that happened."

"Yeah," Aileen said, "That thing about Chicago. Kind of careless of them, right?"

Sylvia inclined her head in a slight nod. "Yeah. They were hacked."

"Or someone in the chapter was tagged," Barbara said, referring to a mole in the organization. "I hope it wasn't something like that."

"What happened in Chicago makes me concerned," Sylvia said. "We really need to tighten our security. Especially now. We can't afford to be complacent."

"I wish we had the internet back," Aileen said.

"Why, sweetie?" Barbara said. "So you could go shopping? It would be so tapped, it would be useless to us."

"Well, at least we know it exists for some, so it isn't completely dead," Sylvia said. "The regime, PRICE and BlueShirts have it."

"Sure, and those who can afford it with proven loyalties enough to earn their Internet licenses," Barbara added.

"How much are those licenses going for now?" Aileen said.

"I heard near four-hundred a month," I said.

"Jesus H." Barbara said. "Who can afford that anymore?"

"Anyone who supports and contributes to Kenton," Sylvia said.

"They're probably mostly just tweeting dirty jokes to each other," I said. "And Kenton is still tweeting his usual preens."

"That man is disgusting," Barbara said.

"Disgusting isn't the least of it, " Sylvia said.

Aileen stole a quick look at me. "So, Bob. What's your story? What brings you to our happy little band?" She glanced at Sylvia. "Other than Syl's alluring charm, of course."

"Of course," I said. "Can we talk here?"

"Oh, yeah," Barbara said. "Nothing to worry about. Aileen sweeps up for bugs around the apartment every few weeks, and every time the super or some repair guy comes in to fix something. No cockroaches, so far."

"And I brought in this handy little thing that squelches out anything a mic might hear."

"Oh, yeah. That too." Barbara said. "You sure that thing actually works, honey?"

She nodded curtly but confidently. "The best technology the great Canadian Northwoods has to offer. So, yeah, you are in a safe place."

"How did you swing a trip to Canada?" I asked. "Haven't they thickened the border up there?"

She winked at me, then nestled closer to Barbara. "I've got connections. And it helps that I'm a Scottish National."

I recalled that back in 2024, the Scots became their own country by splitting with England to become sovereign. It had been one of those nations Real-America still tolerated, though tacitly, like Canada, Norway and Sweden. And Russia, of course—that one was more of a love affair.

"So, Bob," Barbara echoed Aileen. "What *does* bring you here?"

"PRICE split my family up a few years back, because my wife and I tried to defy their efforts..." I sat on the couch next to Barbara and went on to tell them bits and pieces of the story. "... now I want to do what I can to resist those best efforts of theirs. And to find and reunite with my wife and kids."

"Jesus H.," Aileen said. "She's in that fucking place in Arizona? The guy who runs that is a tyrant. Makes PRICE and Kenton look like Mary fuckin' Poppins."

"Sheriff Jeff Lupera, I know," I said ruefully.

"I'm so sorry, Bob," Barbara said. She placed her hand on my knee. "We'll do anything we can to help."

To take my mind off my renewed concerns for Tricia most likely no longer alive under Sheriff Jeff's brutal custody, I turned my attention to the TV show. The topic there had turned to Kanye's and Kim's 10-year-old daughter, a cute-looking Nicaraguan girl they had stolen from the arms of her mother in a detainment camp when the girl was two. They spruced the kid up for reality TV and changed her name to Khloe. It was designed as an example of good will from the Kenton camp that the dictator had a heart after all, as well as a weakness for immigrate children.

Tonight's show focused on a benign disagreement between Kanye and Kim as to whether little Khloe should get her first tattoo, or should they wait a year. Kanye thought the kid should be branded as soon as possible. Only one person could solve the dispute. A low roar of cheers and applause and overall zeal arose from the TV speakers as Premier Kenton made another cameo appearance in the reality show's kitchen. He was asked his opinion. "I dunno. Where's the tattoo gonna be?" the Premier asked.

"On her arm," Kim told him. "Or her tummy."

"What's it gonna be of?"

"I was thinkin' it should be of a Real-America flag, and underneath of it: 'A Real-America is a GREAT America!'," Kanye said.

A big round of applause and cheers. The slogan "A Real-America is a GREAT America!" dissolved up into the screen as the canned applause, catcalls and cheers grew louder.

"Then tattoo it in both places!" Kenton proclaimed.

"What a fucking jerk," Barbara commented. "Is that going to be his new slogan?"

Aileen sighed and stood. "At least until he finally makes that deal of his with the Soviets to join Real-America with them into some sort of great, big union."

"You think he's actually gonna go through with that?" Barbara asked as Aileen went to the kitchen.

"What do you think he's been trying to do for the last ten years, Barb?"

"Yeah. But I don't think it would ever happen."

"I wouldn't put anything past that pig," Sylvia said. "He and Vladovkov probably share the same bed when he's over there."

"Does everyone want a drink? All we have is beer, I'm afraid," Aileen called from the kitchen.

We all said yes.

"A Real-America is a GREAT America!" I said. "Kinda has a ring to it."

"Are you crazy, Bob?" Sylvia said. "Shut up."

"No," I said. "Maybe we could get Tony the Tiger to say it: 'A Real-America is a Grrrrrreat! America!' Don't you think?"

"I agree with Syl," Barbara said. "Shut up, Bob."

Sylvia shook her head in a tsk-tsk way. "And you call yourself an Ad-Man. "No wonder you lost the Kenton account."

"Jesus, Bob!" Aileen called from then kitchen. "*You* did the ads for that guy?"

"Well, my company did. It was a long time ago in back twenty-sixteen, for about a month, before he fired us."

"A very bad career move on your part, dear," Sylvia said, then turned to Barbara. "How much time you giving me to speak at tomorrow's meeting, Barb?"

"As long as you want, sweetie. But just remember, some of those who'll be there are very good at dosing off."

10

The Flowing Tide

April 25, 2028

The guarded secret of the Neo-Publica all changed that night in April when the Prospect Park charter members gathered in a basement room in the David Hume Universalist Church. The meeting was held under the guise of a closed, church-sponsored, soul-searching, meditation, and lecture meeting—enough of a bore to keep any BlueShirt away. The low-ceilinged room was redolent in the smell of the massive amounts of morning coffee that had been consumed there, now made that more pungent by the that now popping and gurgling in the brewer. Dirty quilts, their old smell adding to the muskiness of the room, had been hung over the street-facing windows.

The church Pastor, Martin Daniels, was a sympathizer and often spoke at the Neo-Publica gatherings. Tonight, he stood by the door to graciously welcome the members as they filtered in. So far, the crowd looked unkempt and underfed like proper seditionists. Sylvia counted that twenty had shown up, as she glanced at the wall clock: 8:05 PM. The meeting had been due to start five minutes before. Aileen was making the rounds, quipping and laughing among those few seated in the folding chairs arranged in the middle of the room, and those many others who lounged about on the old, Goodwill-style couches set around the room's perimeter.

"This is it? Just twenty?" Sylvia asked Barbara.

"They'll be more, Syl. Those coming tonight represent chapters all around the city. Besides, these guys are revolutionaries, and Brooklynites—New Yorkers. Showing up late is part of their shtick. More'll start wandering in at about twenty-after."

"Back in Yale, I'd dock them a few points for showing late."

"If these people were your students back in Yale, they would stop showing at your class if you ever did that. This is not the early aught-teens, anymore, hon."

By 8:30, around forty more people had showed. Reverend Daniels closed the door and nodded toward the front for Barbara to begin the meeting. She placed both hands on the podium and leaned forward. "Tonight, friends, we have Sylvia Morales here."

Some around the room exchanged confused glances and whispers. "Wasn't she put away in some gulag, somewhere?" One of them said from where he had sunk low in a couch cushion.

I noticed Sylvia stiffen in a chill of remembrance. She probably wanted to wring the guy's neck for providing the recollection.

"She was freed," Barbara said.

"By who?" another said.

"By us. We freed her...the Neo-Publica," Barbara said, prompting more exchanges of looks, and a few whispered: "Reallys?" "Anyway, as most of you should probably know, Sylvia founded the movement while she was a philosophy professor at Yale." She conjured up a smile of recollection. "She was my teacher, and the two of us founded this Prospect Park chapter. Anyway, friends. I give you Sylvia Morales to say a few words about our protest in a few weeks."

There was some dispirited applause as Barbara motioned Sylvia to the podium. I felt her concern from where I sat behind her as she stepped up behind the lectern. She organized her notes, then scanned the room. A couple dozen stared indolently back at her.

Many of them were young, as young-looking as college freshmen out for some sort of lark. Some of them looked to be in their thirties. There were some others who looked to be in their forties and fifties.

"Hi," she said shyly. "Uh, and welcome to this Prospect Park Neo-Publica gathering."

"Louder!" someone shouted from the back.

"In case you haven't heard, yet" she said more loudly, "our protest date's been moved to Sunday, May fourteenth, and we'll be meeting at eight-AM in the program room in the Fifth Avenue Presbyterian Church on fifty-fifth street. We'll start out at nine. Sorry about the late notice, but you might have heard about what happened in Chicago last weekend. So, we had to change it."

There were some perplexed glances exchanged among the crowd.

"Anyway," she said as she slipped on her reading glasses. She glanced at her notes, then looked back out at the audience. She lightly rolled her shoulders like a fighter going into the ring. "Once the U.S. Constitution had been hammered out in Philadelphia's Independence Hall in seventeen-eighty-seven, an inquiring woman asked Benjamin Franklin: 'What do we have, sir, a republic or a monarchy?' He replied: 'A republic, madam, if you can keep it.' With that began what Jefferson later referred to as an 'experiment' —the experiment of American Democracy. It was based upon freedoms brought up from a foundation of trust and truth and codified into law through the Constitution.

"Well...I believe that, in what we see now, that Great American Experiment may have failed. Failed our country. Failed us. We—or more precisely *they*—have not kept up the promise of the spirit that founded this republic. Franklin's glib comment was prescient. Over the last twelve years, we have lost what *had* kept America great, through a workable, if not perfect, system of checks and balances. Now, that system has dissolved into a perverted aberration known as 'Real-America.' And there is nothing *real* about it—it is based on a foundation of feathers —a foundation of lies, dis-information, and alternative facts. This has got to end!" She slammed her fist down on the podium: "Now!

"In an eighteen-fifty-eight campaign speech, two years before he was to become the first Republican President, Lincoln said: 'A house divided against itself cannot stand.' Then went on; 'I believe this government cannot endure, permanently half slave and half free.' He was of course referring to the contrasting ideologies about slavery. But I ask here now: Who are the enslaved today?

"Fifty years before Lincoln said that, Alexis de Tocqueville warned that Americans could easily become prey to the freedoms described in Democracy. I quote from his treatise, 'Democracy in America,' published in eighteen-thirty-eight..." she held her notes in her trembling hands:

"*'Tyranny in democratic republics... ignores the body and goes straight for the soul.*

"*'...everybody feels the evil, but no one has courage or energy enough to seek the cure.*"

"He even had something to say in answer to that time-worn slogan about making America great...Again? Really?:

"*'America is great because she is good.'* de Tocqueville wrote. *'If America ceases to be good, America will cease to be great.'*

"And finally, this about those who have sworn a blind allegiance to the dictatorship in power, which has snuck up on us like a cat-burglar:

" *... the time will come when men are carried away and lose all self-restraint. ...It is not necessary to do violence to such a people in order to strip them of the rights they enjoy; they themselves willingly loosen their* *hold. ... they neglect their chief business which is to remain their own masters."*

I sipped my water and looked out at the attendees—some of them mesmerized.

Sylvia put her notes back down and removed her glasses. "In a broader sense, De Tocqueville has alluded those freedoms and democracy could enslave and divide us, if we don't work for them. Today we have proof that is just what has happened. We are living it. We, the thinking, creative men and women who had hope for this Democracy, have been subjugated to a narcissist bully who runs our country like some Mafia godfather. This has got to end..." another pounding of her fist. I noticed her clenched hand was blushing deep in pain. It didn't seem to faze her—she had found her groove.

"Now!"

There were rejoinders of "Now!" along with cheers and applause from the audience as some of them stood. "Now!"

"The teaching of American history and the thinking of those such as De Tocqueville, Jefferson, and Lincoln has been banned. The natural resources we use have been rationed. Water, some of it non-potable, is available to us for twelve hours a day. It's especially poisonous in factory cities like Flint, Pittsburg, Wheeling, and most of New Jersey. Climate control is no longer an issue because it was allowed to get so out of hand. Just look at those beautiful sunsets over New Jersey. They aren't natural. That's the red, setting sunlight hitting all the particulates of pollution and smog in the air. The raw resources for heating and fuel must be mined from what's left in the ground; coal in Eastern Kentucky and..." here she stalled and heaved a weary sigh, "and shale from mines in Alaska. All the fracking that ended two years ago has left the ground so unstable that even places that never expected them before are prone to earthquakes. Remember that six-point-two quake three years ago that nearly leveled that town outside of Tulsa? That was due to too much fracking—after Kenton's Commissar of Natural Resources said we had to force one final drop of oil from the ground.

"Also, electric power has been rationed to eighteen hours a day; less in some places. Petroleum is now so costly that there is no point in having a car, which would be too expensive to buy anyway. This has restricted where we can go—kept us stationary as shut ins. And even if we could go anywhere, we'd be risking our lives to an unstable infrastructure of roadways. Phone service: forget it—three hours a day if you can find a land-line phone that works. It wouldn't do much good, anyway, because the lines are all tapped. Like many of our apartments are. And the Internet—remember the Internet? —for that you need a license; an impossible-to-get-license—and a proven allegiance to the regime being run from up high in Kenton Tower. The most distressing loss of all is our pathway to information, now under regime control and surveillance. Water, gas, electricity, information; all rationed and apportioned for the good of those whom have usurped our country, who, by the way, may access all of these resources freely."

Boos and groans around the room

She held up her hand with the missing fingers. "*We* have been rationed, people. Our ideals have been smothered. If they don't like what we believe, they send us to gulags to waste away in our dreams of what might have been." She held her hand higher and rotated it for all to see. "I can attest to that. We cannot be broken! We *will* not be broken!

"This has got to end! Now!"

The whole audience stood and approved. "Now! ...Now!"

Sylvia stood before them; her lips tightened in pride. She lowered her hand to calm the enthusiasm. "It's been said that the first casualty of war is the truth. And this casualty has been openly mounting in heaps for the last twelve years. This is not the new normal, guys.! This is nothing more than Alexander Kenton's Real-America, and we *can* beat it!"

More applause and cheers as people rose from their seats. "Now!" They shouted.

I noticed Sylvia's cheeks had dampened with tears. "This has *got* to end...!"

"Now!" the crowd responded loudly, some with their fists raised.

It took the room five minutes to quiet down. "This regime has muzzled the press, because the press, with all its faults, also brought us a truth strong enough to flourish through some of its own surrounding weeds and petty conjectures. There was never anything 'fake' about it. The press is not 'The Enemy of The People!' The press is our link to the truth! Okay? "

Cries of agreement with a rejoinders of "Okay!'s" and one "You go , Girl!" I wasn't quite sure, but that might have come from Aileen, who sat in the first row.

"Okay. Before I quit this podium, I'd like to read a passage from a letter, Thomas Jefferson wrote to George Washington's son, John, in eighteen-oh-four." she readjusted her glasses and concentrated on her notes:

"No experiment can be more interesting than that we are now trying, and which we trust will end in establishing the fact, that man may be governed by reason and truth. Our first object should therefore be, to leave open to him all the avenues to truth. The most effectual hitherto found, is the freedom of the press. It is therefore, the first shut up by those who fear the investigation of their actions.'"

She looked out at the audience and grinned "Sound familiar? The truth has been stolen from us. And we want it back! Okay?"

"Okay!"

"Good! Now show up on the fourteenth and we'll take it to that son of a bitch in his tower!"

The room thundered with applause and "Yays!" as she made her way back to her seat next to mine. Right then I loved her so much more for the flame of her conviction. I grasped her hand and held it tight. She must have seen the tears forming in my eyes, because she grasped my hand as hard and shook it. She kissed my cheek as the audience still applauded. I think that was when I truly came to realize that there really was a cause even greater than the personal one that had blinded me to the truth.

We lay by candlelight huddled close in the narrow mattress of the pullout bed in Barbara's den. I felt her shudder in a waft of chill through the leaky windowpanes as I listened to the pattering sizzle of the rain against them. I concentrated on the dim lights across Seventh Avenue and how the light webbed on the high panes and refracted through the runny beads of rain. Sylvia's comments from earlier resonated in my mind like an echo in a cave. Then I worried if we would survive this resistance; at least emotionally. I knew there would be arrests at the protests, perhaps even Sylvia's, once they realized she had emerged from hiding. Then I wondered who "they" really were. Would we be forced up against the wall of something we only thought we knew how to fight?

I felt her shiver again and nestle closer to me; fitting herself into me as though to make us one. I ran my fingertips down the naked curve of her side, feeling the smooth, and, in places, the roughened textures of her skin worn so by her ordeals. I inched my fingers back up to the smoother areas and kept them there, moving them around in a light, little circular motion. So smooth. How I had missed the feeling of a woman next to me before Sylvia reminded me that a loving touch was still possible. She had brought my senses back to life by degrees over the past four months. Through what she had said tonight, and how she made me feel, I felt completed as a person. The fire of her conviction had ignited my own.

Over the last six months, since Bill Davis had told me that he'd found out Tricia was still alive, but probably barely so, I had resigned myself that by now she had mostly likely died. Also, my fragile Emily and Steven could not have had the strength to survive two years of gulag rigors. I could only hope that Michael, always the protector, had been sent into BlueShirt training. Though his mind may have been conditioned into forgetting he ever had a family other than the *esprit de corps* of the BlueShirt camaraderie, at least he would still be alive.

I moved my fingers down to Sylvia's back, and she again shuddered at my touch, though by now I knew she could sleep through a marching band clomping through the room. Leaders must sleep lightly, so she, as inspiring as her message was, I knew would always be a follower. I felt the branches of ridges and scars left by the whip upon her back, some of them hardened solid. My breath stuttered at the feel of them, and the pain she must have endured for three years. Her convictions, and those scraps of her manifesto that she must had known no one would see, must had sustained her through all the torture.

Then I noticed a filigree of discoloration on her back—a small tattoo, maybe. I lifted the candle from the bedside table and squinted to read what it was:

"There will be storms."

11

Xander

April 20, and 27

Xander Stenopolis never knew what he had done or said that was overheard, but whatever it was resulted in two PRICE agents dragging him from his bed after midnight. The whole operation had been very silent, and Xander, a light sleeper, wondered how the agents managed to get into his apartment without making a sound.

They gagged and hooded him, forced him out into the street, into their squad car, and drove him five blocks up to their West Side station. They shoved him into an interrogation room and pushed him down hard into an equally hard seat, then strapped his wrists and ankles to the arms and legs of a creaky chair.

He was left hooded, and all he could feel was how cold the room was—not just chilly; but cold. It must have dark, because all he saw through the tight fibers of the hood was a thin, but distinct, beam of light in front of him. As he stiffened himself against the room's climate, he felt a hard blow register like an electric shock into his right cheek, and then felt another hard punch sink into his stomach. He wretched up his dinner, but because of the gag, bile and chunks of vomit welled up in his mouth. Some of it seeped out into the inside of the hood and under his nose. The sour stench filled his nostrils to a point where he felt he was choking. His breathing was labored, and he was light-headed—the prelude to one of his diabetic seizures. Then again: a blow to his left cheek, this time, then another to the same spot in his stomach. Finally, they left the room, leaving him to sit alone in the cold, breathing heavily as he tried to ward off an attack from within his body.

Finally, after what seemed hours later to him, but was probably about ten minutes, another person entered the room. Xander heard the accessories on his duty belt clatter metallically against one another. He fought the urge to slump against the pain in his stomach. He heard the searing scrape of wooden chair legs against rough concrete, as the one he assumed to be his interrogator took his seat across from him. He heard the rustling of paper, then what he perceived as an organizing tap of the little stack upon what must be a table between them.

For another infinite moment, he heard nothing at all, rather than the presence of another being in the room. If this silence was an interrogation tactic, it worked. Xander felt more helpless than his being bound to a chair and unable to move. The silence had its way in devolving him to nothing. He couldn't even wonder why he was here anymore, as he continued to fight for breath. He tried to swallow the remains of the bile in his mouth.

At last the agent spoke in a rusty, hoarse voice. It sounded as if it were coming from miles across the room, while inches from his ear at the same time. "Neo-Pubs," the voice scoffed. "Why do you even fucking try?" Xander felt a surge of perspiration along with an abrupt swell of fever—another sure sign of a coming diabetic attack. "Oh, never mind. I know why. You want to take down the government, don't you? You think it's undemocratic...and *unconstitutional*... and blah, blah, blah. We've heard it all before, and you all don't stand a chance of anything except being shipped away to a gulag for all your efforts. All of those so-called 'beliefs' of yours about restoring this country to the shithole it was. That is, before Premier Kenton came along and fixed it. So, yeah, Mr. Xander Stenopolis, I've heard it all. So, is that what you want to tell me? That Real-America is not a *Great* America? That little people like you have been denied your little rights? Hunh? Is that what you wanted to tell me?" Even if Xander wanted to answer, he couldn't, trussed up and out of breath as he was."... Hunh?...I'm waiting...Hunh? ... TELL me, God damnit! Nod your fucking head or something!"

His lightheadedness seemed complete as a sure warning of a seizure and he felt a warm flow in his crotch as he pissed his pants. He was losing control of his body. Without insulin he might die, but now he wondered if that would not be a gift. His body relaxed, then began to shake. He heard the scrape of his chair's legs against the concrete floor as it shook with him.

"What the fuck is the matter with you, asshole?"

His shaking became more violent as the rusty-voiced man squawked out for a guard. Xander felt the hood snatched away. Air! Cold as it was, it was air! He saw his inquisitor as a blur though the heat of his vision—not as tall as Xander had imagined. He groaned and grunted through the gag as he waved his hands as though wanting to say something. His tremors died down only a little, as he thought he heard another person rush into the room.

"Take the gag off. I think he's telling me he wants to talk. Jesus, he's shaking up a storm, there. He's pissed his fucking pants!"

The other guard unwound the gag and took the stuffing soaked with vomit from Xander's mouth.

"Speak up, boy. What the fuck's wrong with you?"

He slumped down as far as his bonds would allow. "Insulin!" He gasped. "I need insulin!"

The inquisitor looked at the guard. "Shit! He's one of those. Christ almighty! Doesn't Harris take that stuff?"

"Yeah, I think so," the guard said.

"Go get it, before this one craps out on me. Fuckin' Neo-Pubs," he muttered sourly. He looked over at the guard as he was leaving the room. "Henley!"

The guard stopped. "Yessir?"

"Get Harris to bring whatever that shit is he takes in here, stat. You go get some tags and a wire to suit this guy up for surveillance."

"Yessir."

" '...*The most effectual hitherto found, is the freedom of the press. It is therefore, the first shut up by those who fear the investigation of their actions.*'

"Sound familiar?"

Xander watched helplessly as Sylvia had grinned out her pride at Thursday night's meeting in Prospect Park.

"The truth has been stolen from us. And we want it back! Okay?"

"Okay!"

"Good! Now show up on the fourteenth and we'll take it to that son of a bitch in his tower!"

Xander hated himself but had no other choice. It was either this or at least five years in Unqutuck Gulag, his inquisitor had warned him. Through his gripping fear of ending up in a gulag, and for the payment of the remaining two-thirds of his insulin dosage that had been withheld, Xander agreed.

Like the thief he'd become, he snuck from his seat in the back row of the Universalist Church and out the door to the waiting un-marked squad car across the street. It would be another night in his cell, until tomorrow morning when he had to confirm what had gone on, and to answer any lingering questions.

Xander sat fidgeting uneasily in the overstuffed chair across from Stanley Saunders' desk. His inquisitor relaxed in the chair next to his. Saunders sat glumly behind his desk and read PRICE inquisitor's report. Finally, his lips curled into a cruel smile. "Good work, Danzig."

"Thank you, sir."

"We have enough. You can go, now."

Danzig glanced at Xander. "And what about our informant, here?"

Saunders looked back at Danzig as though Xander wasn't in the room. "Ah' let's see...hmmm. Put him back in his cell. We'll take good care of him until we decide later today what to do with him."

"Yessir," Danzig said as he motioned for Xander to rise, then led him toward the door.

"Oh, hey you there...informant!" Saunders called. Danzig turned Xander around to face the Commissar of PRICE. "I just wanted to thank you for all your help to Real-America, and I'm sure Premier Kenton will be very pleased with your efforts toward his service." He looked back down at the report. "You can go now."

Randy Montefiore telegraphed his angst by repeatedly tapping a pencil he held in one hand against the wrist of the other. Saunders knew this to be a sign he was planning something. The more rapidly the tapping, the grander his plan. He relaxed when his superior finally laid the distracting pencil back down on his desk. He held up the report and batted the air with it. "This is outstanding intel, Stan."

"Thanks, Randy."

"Absolutely fucking outstanding," he enforced. "Not only do we know when and where those assholes are gonna rally, we finally found that bitch, Selina Gonzales."

"Sylvia Morales," Saunders corrected.

"Whatever. We got her, and we'll grab her once she's there bloviating away at our front door. When that happens, we are gonna do her something terrible."

"Like what, Randy?"

Montefiore leaned back in his chair and locked his hands behind his head. He stared vacantly up at the ceiling. "I don't know, yet. But we're not gonna kill her, or anything. I want her to suffer through her pain. At the very least, I'm gonna send her back to that gulag."

At the least? Saunders wondered. "What could be worse than that place?"

"Silence her somehow. I'll figure something out."

"What, Randy? Like cut out her tongue? Chop off all her fingers so she can't write anything; like some sort of manifesto?"

Montefiore leveled his gaze at Saunders. "Cut out her tongue? Cut off her hands? How barbaric—how...Middle Eastern. I *love* it!"

Even Saunders wouldn't have come up with something as extreme as that; though he just did. "You can't be serious, Randy. That's...that's too..."

Montefiore's expression brightened. "Barbaric? We need to send a message to those Neo-Publica dickheads, Stan. What's a better way to set an example than torturing her publicly, then silencing her forever? Maybe we can have her to tongue preserved and framed. You can hang it in your office." Saunders shrugged his shoulders in a "whatever" way. "And forget just the fingers. I really like your idea of cutting off her hands. She can mine that fucking shale with her fucking teeth."

Saunders sipped his chilling green tea. He returned Montefiore's glance with his usual heavily lidded, leaden expression of fatigue. "Well, Randy. We gotta catch her first."

"I'm sure she'll be leading that protest. When is it...?" He scanned the report. "May fourteenth, at nine AM?" He laid down the report, then picked up his pencil and began batting it against his wrist again—this time more rapidly than before. He was on an orgasmic roll.

"What do you think you wanna do about the protesters? All those Neo-Pub activists. There'll probably be a lot of them."

"Probably so. Whatever we do will involve at least a show of force. We'll have 'em pissing in their pants." Montefiore looked thoughtfully back up at the ceiling. "One thing. I plan on making a lot of arrests. Fill up our gulags in Guantanamo and Alaska." He smiled, vaguely. "Fire and ice—that's what we'll call the operation: 'Fire and Ice'. It's got a nice poetic ring to it. I'm sure the Premier will love that name."

"What about our informant?"

"Where is he now?"

"In a holding cell at our PRICE Station on the Upper West Side."

Montefiore considered this for a moment, then decided. "Well, we owe him something for his cooperation. Let him sit in the dark in his cell for a couple of days. Give him the total silent treatment to let him think about what comes next."

"What does come next?"

"We ship him up to Unqutuck to take Morales' place."

"So, what's the payoff for his cooperation?"

Montefiore stared back down at the paperwork. "That we don't ship him up there today."

"You think the Premier will sign off on this?"

Montefiore brightened. "You kidding? He'll fucking *love* it!"

"Using those ISIL tactics? Like torturing Morales and cutting out her tongue and shit? Cutting off her hands?"

He jostled forward and stared into Saunders's eyes for confidentially. "Stan? He...will...fuckin' ...*love* ...it. Why? Because Kenton will do just about any fucking thing I tell him."

Saunders already knew that Kenton was like Silly Putty when he was under Montefiore's power. He drew his lips tight, then nodded. "Okay. You know, Randy? I like that idea of hanging her tongue in my office."

Montefiore tweaked a proud half-smile at him. "Then you shall have it, Stanley—bronzed and mounted."

12

Fire and Ice

May 14

I never knew how many, but it seemed like over five-hundred Neo-Pub activists showed up at the Presbyterian Church. Above us, Sunday services were going on as usual, as thunderous hollow-sounding organ music and the singing, echoing from the choir, seeped down through the ceiling. Good. That would serve to drown out our noises.

Some of us who had showed up before seven AM had been crafting their signs and posters: "Kenton Must GO!"; "Peace is Power!"; "Restore the Truth"; "Take AMERICA back!"; "Give us back our First Amendment!" and the like. There were a couple of "Kenton SUCKS!" signs. Some few of the protesters had constructed a straw effigy of the man, with a huge bush of straw to define his crop of overly died blond hair. It was a pretty remarkable resemblance, complete with the black suit and red tie he'd been wearing at least since 2014.

Just before game-time, at about quarter to nine, Silvia took to the podium.

"What a crowd! Thank you all for showing up." Her voice had become hoarse from having issued stage directions for the last few hours. "This morning we will be exercising our rights to assemble and speak: our First Amendment rights that seemed to have been shredded and thrown away.

"Well, all, we are not about to let these rights die! "

Cheers from the audience, and one: "You GO, girl!"—Aileen's mantra from the first row.

"This is the first Neo Publica appearance out in the open. This is what we've been preparing for! And we have the numbers to prove it!" She paused to take a sip of water.

More cheers and a "Whoot! Whoot!" from Aileen as she fisted the air. Barbara sitting next to her cast an annoyed look. "What?"

"Hell, Leenie, I don't know, just: Shhh!"

Sylvia rolled and relaxed her shoulders into her teaching mode and went on. "And it's not only us. Denver, Salt Lake, Miami, Boston, Norfolk, Atlanta, and Washington DC are also joining us in their cities. Neo Pub is out in force, today!" Resounding cheers. "Hopefully we will come upon Kenton Tower by surprise, and hopefully, this early in the morning, they will not have mustered any resistance. But if they have, there will be injuries among us...but never forget what we are here for. Nothing good can be accomplished without a fight. And we are here to fight for our right to be here!" The applause was scattered this time, as some may had not considered the part about getting injured. "We will have one another's backs. We will hold one another up!" Now more cheers. "Okay?"

There were restrained *Okay!'s* throughout the crowd. I noticed her bracing herself forward holding the edges of the lectern. Her knuckles were white. She was holding on hard.

"Now I must tell you why we are really marching today—who we are doing all this for."

"Neo-Publica!" Someone shouted from the middle of the audience.

"Neo-Publica, yes," she said. "But who is Neo-Publica *for*? We are for the right to speak out, and for the suppression of lies from the Kenton Regime. Hear me on this. For every one of us there are tens of thousands of people in this country who just want to live their lives. To go to work. Send their kids off to school," she glanced quickly at me and twitched a wry smile. "To make love, and to love one another. Most of them have become inured to what decisions are being made up in that tower. *They* are the followers who deserve the truth. *They* are our nation; a county once called America, founded on the principle that all men...and women...are created equal, and yet today are not regarded as equal. We march for *them* people, not us. We march for them—our nation, and for the truth!" She heaved a breath as the crowd loudly cheered. I knew Sylvia was never "mine" to begin with, but today, she belonged to them. There were more surges of cheers and fist-pumping, as I caught my breath and felt a warmth in my lungs.

She held her hand high to silence the acclamation. "Now. Before we leave. It's best you say nothing—no chants until we're in front of Kenton's Building. And remember above all else: this is a peaceful demonstration." She nodded curtly at the crowd. "Okay. Single file, now. Ready? ...Let's go."

Montefiore had ordered West Fifty-Seventh closed off from Madison Avenue nearly down to Carnegie Hall. A semi-truck was parked with a chain link gate open to detain the protesters to be carted way. Two armed and bored junior level PRICE agents sat inside to keep the peace among the dozens of protesters Saunders had promised would be detained and scattered around to the ten gulags within his control. No trial was necessary for treason. With any luck, they'd all be processed by this time the next day.

Two stories up from the junction of 5th Avenue and Central Park South, Saunders and Montefiore stood, wearing hard hats, 35 feet above the street in a Con Ed truck's raised bucket. They stared down 57th street at an imposing sight.

Hidden from the view of Fifth Avenue and the Kenton Tower, a full company of BlueShirts and a number of tan-shirted armed PRICE agents was mustered. Behind them were eight mounted PRICE Horse Guards. On the prompt of two horn-honks from the truck, they were to advance forward, then down 5th Avenue to meet the activists head on.

"This is fucking great, Randy!" Saunders said. "How we set this whole thing up in only a week. Fucking *great*."

Montefiore nodded pridefully. "That it is, my friend."

The drizzle had swollen into a light rain as we mobilized from 55th Street for the one-block march to Kenton Tower. Fifth Avenue, known to some, but never to us, as "Kenton's Way" was unusually and frighteningly dormant, as though it had been lying in wait. I wondered if Sylvia was affected as I about this. Of course not, she was up in front of the sluggish and strangely quiet crowd, powered by her conviction. We began to move.

I lightly swept some rain-damp from my forehead and by mistake bumped the marcher to my right with my elbow. "Oops. Sorry. I didn't mean to bump you like that."

"S'okay." she responded in a soft, muffled, voice, "Shit like that happens all the time with me. Usually it's me who's the fuckin' klutz."

Intrigued as to the buffer in her voice, I looked at her. She wore a green bandana covering the lower part of her face, making her appear done up more for a Wild West train robbery than a protest march. She warmed her hands in the front pouch of her sweatshirt—probably not the best choice of attire for a two-hour protest in the rain. "Interesting get-up you've got there."

"I don't exactly wanna be recognized."

"Why? Are you famous?"

"More like infamous. I used to work for the assholes up in that tower. I left my job. If they see me, I'm concerned they'll ship me off to one of their gulags."

I huffed out a laugh. "Aren't we all? I'm Bob Bryant."

As she glanced back at me, I noticed her light blue eyes were set in a look of childish astonishment. Her skin was smooth; seeming not ravaged by time. She didn't look to be much older than my daughter, Emily, but of course she was." I'm Karen Fabrizio."

"Been with us long?"

"A few weeks. I was at that Prospect Park meeting, and heard what Sylvia Morales had to say."

For some reason, Sylvia raised her arm, signaling us to stop, and we held our position. She may had sensed something was a peculiarly off, as I had. Maybe it was the empty street without even any sidewalk traffic. Definitely weird for 5th Avenue, even on a Sunday morning.

"God. I tell you, the crap that's been going on up there in that tower needs thinking like hers to blow it all away. I hope I get to meet her. Wasn't she just fuckin' great?" "

"Yeah, that she is, Karen. She really is terrific." I hoped Karen had been vetted for Neo Publica. One couldn't just walk in on a meeting on a whim. "So, what did you do up there...for them? What was your job?"

She gazed up at Kenton Tower. "I worked for the PRICE Commissar, Stanley Saunders," she replied distantly. "He threatened to send me off to a gulag, just because he could. That time I knew he meant it, so I walked off."

"How did you know he meant it?"

She considered her answer. "We were a thing for six months. He seemed evil—*was* evil. He drinks a lot, and sometimes he'd get drunk and tell me stuff during ... well, he'd just tell me stuff. That's why I wanna talk to Sylvia Morales. I know what goes on up there. It was my job."

I certainly would have her meet Sylvia after the protest. "You will, Karen. I'll introduce you, myself."

"Really? You know her? Like personally?"

"Uh, yeah you might say we're, like you said, a 'thing'."

"Holy crap, that's great! He I am standing next to Sylvia Morales' 'thing' guy!"

"Okay. You could say that, I suppose. Anyway, I'll introduce you when this is over."

We began to inch forward in caution. It was then I heard a guttural rumble of motorcycle engines behind us. I could see little over my shoulder, but I caught fragmented glances of several hogs spread the width of 5th Avenue and the sidewalks coming up on our rear as though to force us ahead. The street trembled beneath my feet in the sheer weight of their sounds. I knew something ugly was about to happen as I felt a rolling surge of electricity down my spine. Several of the bikers revved up their engines into banshee-like roars. Then I heard two long bleats from a truck's air horn from ahead on 57th Street. My breath quickened as I looked to my right and saw we were almost in front of Kenton Tower.

"Oh, *shit!* Oh fucking SHIT!" Karen gasped in response to what was coming toward us.

I instinctively wended my way forward to try to protect Sylvia from whatever was about to happen, and to get a closer view of what it was. Spanning the width of 5th Avenue ahead was a regiment of armed BlueShirts, flanked by two rows of PRICE Horse Guards. All, even the motorcycles, seemed eerily quiet right then. All I thought I could hear was the approaching echoing clatter of their armament and accessories against their bodies as they moved toward us.

"Everybody! Scatter! Find a place to hide! Protect yourselves!" Sylvia shouted to those who hadn't already started to do so, starting a flare of pandemonium among us. I put my arm around Sylvia's shoulders and ushered her roughly toward a sidewalk and maybe the protection of a building alcove. She stood her ground as a commander should, then relented as we hunched off into a group of protesters to the side.

I swept a glance behind as I heard the resumed revving of the motorcycle's engines as they moved toward our rear, trapping us, and herding us closer together. Some bikes disbursed and took single file to the sidewalks. They edged us closer into one another and toward the approaching front of BlueShirts and the PRICE calvary behind them.

As we all milled, desperate to escape, the BlueShirts poised their weapons and disbursed into our crowd to drag away whoever they could. The bikers closed in on us from the sides. I saw a that several of demonstrators were able to escape through the lines and run back toward the relative freedom of 56th Street. Otherwise, it was as if we gathered like fish caught up in a net.

Shouts and cries rose. Fists flew. Gun butts struck. People fell bleeding. Many of them were brutally dragged. Horses whinnied and reared up. Some of circulated and wheeled among us. More people fell. More shouts of orders from the PRICE Horse Guards.

Then I heard the first gunshot, followed by another. More shots were fired, and I saw two fall dead. Others writhed in pain on the street. Out of the corner of my eye, I noticed about ten of us had been gathered as captives under guard under the golden-gilded front entrance of Kenton Tower. I looked up and imagined Premier Kenton up there in his office, surveying us as a general would stand on a hilltop and watch his troops in battle.

More shots were fired, as dozens of police sirens wailed behind us. I rushed to Sylvia, pushed her to the ground, and protected her body under mine. She had a stupefied look on her face—a helpless expression of: *Why?* As if I had attacked her, she anxiously tried to push me away, then managed to scramble out from beneath me.

She ran in a hunch over to Barbara and Aileen who'd been marching by her side. She stumbled as she rose and then attempted to push them away and toward the sidewalk, perhaps hoping it was a means of escape. I rushed to the three of them, and tried to shepherd them toward the rear, away from the Horse Guards, the BlueShirts and their guns. At least the motorcycles, now zig-zagging behind us, and the cop cars behind them, were safer than what lay ahead of us.

"You there, HALT!" a BlueShirt shouted at our backs.

Holding Sylvia close, I felt her trembling run through me. She looked down to her feet and saw the dead body of one of the protestors. Blood was still pulsing from the gunshot in her chest.

"Stay RIGHT where you stand!"

Sylvia's lips tightened to a thin white line. She heaved a breath, maybe thinking it was her last. She then turned to face the BlueShirt trooper with his pistol drawn. He couldn't have been much older than Michael.

"All of you, come with me! NOW!" he shouted over-loud in a hoarse voice tinged by the older side of puberty.

Sylvia stared him deliberately in the eye. "Fuck...you."

He raised his gun two feet from her forehead. "Don't think I won't, lady!" he threatened.

"Go ahead, you fucking turd!" she seethed.

I cringed with my back still toward him, thinking those words were not very noble for what could be her last.

"I will! I'll pull this trigger!"

I whipped around to pull her to the ground as he fired and missed. Next I heard Aileen scream. I quickly twisted my head around and saw her kneeling over Barbara's body. Possibly emboldened by one kill, perhaps his first, the BlueShirt aimed again at Sylvia and me where we crouched at his feet. The look in his eyes flared as I saw, or maybe felt, his finger tighten on the trigger as he took a bead on us.

Then I saw him fall, clutching his neck. Blood sprouted through his fingers, then welled ferociously. I didn't have time to wonder what happened, as I looked up and saw that girl, Karen, in her bandana. Even through the thin shadow cast by the now drawn-up hood of her sweatshirt, I could see her eyes squinted tight in hate. In her right hand she held the bloody-bladed dirk she had hidden in the pouch of her sweatshirt. She quickly, and calmly, slipped it back into where she'd kept it.

"Karen!" I gasped.

Nobody had seen the kill in the melee. "In the jugular," she said as though from a trance. "Instant kill."

I could tell she had practice. "You...?"

She grasped my arm a pulled me up as I grabbed on to Silvia's arm. Karen glanced at the Kenton Building across from us. "C'mon with me. I can get us outta here!"

Karen led us, half-hunched in tow toward a shadowed, closed-off alleyway on the side of the building. She found a door. "I hope this thing still fuckin' works," she muttered as she drew a plastic card from her jeans pocket and held it up to a key box. It beeped. "It works," she said calmly, then punched some numbers on the keypad. It beeped twice again. She flung the door open, rushed us in, then closed it behind us.

"Who are y—? How did you do that?" Sylvia gasped in a faraway voice.

"Later," Karen hushed us as she led us down a short, dark corridor.

"That's Karen," I told Sylvia in an undertone.

"Oh. Karen," Sylvia whispered. Adrenaline and trauma must had tapped into her acerbic humor. "Well, Bob, now it all now makes perfect sense."

Karen led us to an empty, dimmed out employee kitchen. I made out a colorless array of some rickety-looking folding chairs around an antique Formica dinette table. The room smelled of stale cigars. "Janitor's lounge," she said more to herself, perhaps trying get her bearings to remember a way out. I saw through the penumbral murk of darkness that she'd kept her bandana on, and her hood drawn.

"Where are we?" Sylvia said.

"Believe me, Sylvia, you don't want to know."

"You know me?"

"Shit. Who doesn't? Now, please follow me. And keep your mouths shut. We need to be quiet," She urged us forward down a ramp and into a deeper darkness. We must had been in a sub-basement. It was dark enough, and had those loose, funky smells of a cellar: dead rodents, pipe insulation, and furnace heat. Finally, after what seemed like five minutes of fits and starts through a labyrinth, she found what she'd been looking for. She held up her entry card to a receptor, and it beeped. She squinted close to the keypad and punched in some code.

After two more beeps, then a metallic click, she thrust open a door to the cool, rainy air, distant police sirens, and the scant traffic sounds of Madison Avenue. I took in the misty, wet scent of fresh air as we relaxed our pace. Karen swept back her hood, then pulled down the bandana to make it a scarf around her neck. She slithered out of her bloody sweatshirt, turned it inside-out, then put it back on again. The knife clattered to the sidewalk in the process. Calmly, she stooped to pick it up, then reached under her shirt to replace it in the sweatshirt pouch.

I heard the not-too-distant sounds of sirens, shouts, and frenzy from 5th Avenue. The gunshots seemed to have stopped. I looked over at Karen. "Where were we?"

"In the Kenton Tower's basement."

"Shit!" Sylvia grumbled thinly.

"Not to worry. We're safe now. Don't think I wasn't fuckin' scared shitless in there, too."

I kind of doubted that, after having seen the routine ease with which she'd just killed someone.

"H—How did you get us in there?" Sylvia slurred slowly, as if she were drunk. Her faint, trembling voice didn't sound like her own.

"I used to work at that place. I was the PRICE Commissar's secretary and part time bed warmer." She held her entry card up for us to see, "He must have forgotten he'd given me a copy of his key. I used to need it to 'work late', if you get my drift." She tucked the card back into her jeans pocket. She stared uptown. "I had to kill that fuckin' BlueShirt kid, or he was gonna kill you."

"What? Who?" Sylvia said aghast and traumatized.

"Karen told me she heard your speech the other night and wanted to meet you. Said she might be able to help us."

Karen looked over at Sylvia. "I worked for that asshole for, I don't know, maybe three years? I picked up a lot of information. Also, he told me a lot of inside stuff when he was drunk. And Stanley Saunders drank a lot." She tweaked a dry smile.

Whatever had happened over the period of the last hour or so hadn't had enough time to sink in. It was as if I were operating on a second power of some sort. Karen was different. She was calmly in control. I did remember how she handled her knife—her lack of concern over killing that BlueShirt. She'd had practice. Suddenly, she frightened the hell out of me.

Sylvia relaxed a little back to an alternative normal for her. "Let's go back to Barbara's apartment to shake all this out with a drink. Or two." I cringed, as I remembered seeing Barbara dead, and wondered if Sylvia had processed that yet.

"Is it okay if I tagged along to your place?" Karen asked. "I might be able to tell you some things I know. It might help."

Sylvia offered her a weak smile. "I was going to ask you." She turned to me. "I'm pretty sure Barb and Aileen are making it home okay by now." No. She hadn't processed it.

I listened to the clamor back on 5th Avenue dissipate behind us. Barbara had been killed, and probably Aileen had been arrested to be shipped out to a gulag. "I'm sure they are," I said, trying to act reassuring.

The mercy of instinct was all I had going for me as I blandly tagged behind them as we all made our way to the 51st Street subway station to catch the 4-Train down to Brooklyn.

13

The Morning After

May 15

knew my bad back would be killing me in the morning, as the hard parquet floor of apartment's spare bedroom seemed to grip my spine. Sylvia was now finally sleeping soundly in the flimsy couch bed we'd usually sleep in together. But this night I felt it best she'd have it to herself, so I slept on the floor. I heard the soft wheezes of Karen's snores through the door opened to the living room where she slept hard on the couch.

I concentrated on the sounds of passing traffic on 7th Avenue through the sizzling, thin spatter of rain on the windows, as I found it to be a tonic while I tried to recount the past few hours. The carnage that had happened earlier was still beyond my comprehension as I yearned to keep it all simple.

Aileen had managed to stumble it past the bikers and the PRICE guards. She brought home the news of Barbara's death. Upon hearing this, Sylvia went eerily quiet and stood frozen in the middle of the room. We all watched her until a minute later, she screamed: "SHIT!" then burst suddenly, unabashed into tears. I stood stupidly watching, while Aileen, also in tears, rushed to embrace her.

Karen, now visibly shaken as the two women embraced, turned to me. "I need to stay with you all tonight," she announced, her voice trembling. I noticed a tear rolling down her cheek.

"Of course," I responded.

Aileen, for sure, couldn't sleep, as I heard her pacing in her bedroom, then taking breaks to go to the kitchen while trying to piece together what had happened. That was what we all were doing—stitching together the why to the how. We were a house in mourning.

It had been promptly aired earlier over the the Kenton/Fox News and Entertainment Network, with its particular spin of victory. The heroic BlueShirt/PRICE forces had taken down an attempt at a revolt against not only the Kenton Administration, but the Real-American people. At least forty "would-be assassins of the truth that had made Real-America great" were arrested—most likely to be tortured, then sent to gulags. There had been fifteen killed, and raw footage showing their bodies lying contorted in death in front of the Kenton Tower, was looped. The footage had been spiced with close-ups of the dying expressions on each their blood-smeared faces; most in wide-eyed fear, others seemingly in peace. Barbara's face was one of those in peace. All of us were partly traumatized. Alcohol hadn't helped; coffee and tea hadn't helped. It was a stalemate, and all we had left was each other, and that did help.

It had been too emotionally devastating and lurid for us to watch all this, but as shattered as we were, we were drawn to it. The more devastating the image, the more we had been compelled to watch in wait for some sort of retaliation.

Sylvia awoke before I did, and Karen was nowhere in sight. She and Aileen sat at the kitchen bar sipping on their coffees; cups held in trembling hands. Sleep may have reduced their shock, but not their seething angers. This was no longer a time to mourn, but a time to act, and quickly. The question was how, and how quickly.

I went to Sylvia and placed a reassuring touch on her shoulder, and she placed her hand upon mine; warm on cold. I kissed the top of her head and then glanced toward the window. It was a beautiful bright and warm May morning—as ironic as it was pleasing, and a mockery to our suppressed grief.

"Coffee, Bob? It's fresh, and there're some corn muffins, too."

Routine chatter seemed so surreal in our feckless attempts to play house, like all was normal. "Yeah. I guess I will."

"Sleep well?"

"Of course not. And neither did you."

"Was I thrashing?"

"You were," I answered as I poured some coffee into a mug that needed to be washed. "Between that and Karen's snoring, and everything else..."

"Karen?" Sylvia wondered. "Karen who?"

"You don't remember?"

"You know, Syl," Aileen said. "Karen. She's the one that got you and Bob out of all that mess. She snuck you out through the Kenton Tower basement."

"I don't remember...I was in too much shock," Sylvia said as she pondered the coffee in her cup. "Yeah. Vaguely. She works for the Kenton organization, something like that."

"Worked," I corrected. "For Stanley Saunders. But he threatened her nearly six months back, and she walked off the job. She's with us now."

"We'll see about that," Sylvia said. "If she worked for the Kenton Regime..."

"She saved your life, hon," I said.

"She did?"

"You don't remember?" Aileen asked, choking back tears over her remembrance of watching Barbara die. She had had only time enough to kiss her lover's forehead before escaping the battalion of Kenton's BlueShirt forces.

I was then startled by the front door opening abruptly as I choked in fear that PRICE had found us. It was Karen, still wearing her inside-out sweatshirt and some running shorts Aileen had lent her. "Nothing like a morning run to clear a girl's mind up," she said cheerily.

"Karen," Sylvia said.

"That's me." She put the bottle of Perrier she'd been carrying down on the counter and spanked the house keys next to it. "Thanks for the loan of these, Aileen."

"You stayed the night," Sylvia pressed.

"I did. We needed to be together." Karen assumed nothing, as everything seemed to be a foregone conclusion with her. "That was some pretty bad shit that went down on us yesterday."

"It was more than just 'bad shit,' Karen," Aileen said. "It was devastating."

Karen pursed her lips as she went around us to the kitchen to make herself some tea. "I'm sorry. That sounded impersonal. I really didn't mean it that way."

"It's okay," Sylvia said. "We're all a little shaken today. So. Karen. You used to work for the PRICE Commissar?"

"More than that. I slept with the bastard for nearly three years. Saunders is also Randy Montefiore's assistant, so he's like Kenton's third hand man—the hand he uses to jack off with." I suppressed a chortle. She relaxed her shoulders as she poured the hot water into a mug for her tea, then turned to face us as she leaned against the kitchen counter, dipping her teabag. "Look. I know what you all are thinking: 'Who's this bitch suddenly showing up among us who used to work with the Kenton people, while fucking the PRICE Commissar?' I get it, really. But I also must tell you that that asshole wanted to kill me, because I told him...I told him the news..." She sipped her tea thoughtfully, then stared at Sylvia. "I delivered the news about you being sprung from that Unqutuck gulag. I was just the messenger. He wanted you, Sylvia, in the worst way...like he was going to make you his mission. Instead, he threatened to send me up there to die as a surrogate for you. Again, only because I told him the news. He and Montefiore probably arranged that whole thing that happened yesterday, because someone ratted you and the protest out."

"Who?" Sylvia asked.

"I don't work for him anymore, so I wouldn't know. But I do think this: he probably had PRICE find and arrest someone—a weak link in the Neo-Publica chain—then torture him." She took another sip of tea, walked to the end of the bar and eased herself on a stool. "They then most likely planted that person as a mole at your speech in the Unitarian church—which I loved, by the way. I think they would have tagged and wired whoever it was to sit in the audience. That's the way they work."

Sylvia squared an accusing look into Karen's eyes. "Okay. You worked for him. How do I know *you're* not tagged as a plant?"

"That's a fair assessment. Operative word: 'Worked'. Listen, Sylvia, I'm on with you guys. One hundred percent. One...hundred...percent," she enunciated. "I am, and always have been, a Constitutionalist. And your speech struck such a cord in me, I went home and cried. And I don't cry easily. Not since I left that shit-hole organization. Me? I take it personally. I want to see that Saunders son of a bitch disappeared. And I know others who do, too...other than you guys. "

"I think she's serious, Sylvia," I said. "I watched her kill a BlueShirt yesterday."

"Really? When?"

"When she saved your life from a bullet aimed for your head...and mine, too I suppose," I said.

"So, you took a gun to a peace rally," Sylvia charged, as if she was more concerned about that than all the other things. "It was a *peace* rally, for God's sake." She fumbled around the counter for her pack of cigarettes. Took one out in a trembling hand. Lit it.

Karen offered up a wry smile. "Actually, it was a knife. And aren't you glad I did?"

"What others, Karen? Who are the others that aim to resist the regime? Neo-Pubs?" Aleen asked.

She took a long sip of tea. "Hardly, and it's not the regime they're after. It's Saunders. They don't exactly agree with his immigration policies, and the way he treated me. They've been teaching me things. Working with me."

"Working with you?" Sylvia pressed.

"Yeah. Working with me." She picked a piece of lint off her sweatshirt, even though that was the least of the things that soiled it. She held it to the light and contemplated it. "Listen, Sylvia. I think you know I'm serious." She held out up her hand. "Do you want me to prove it with a blood pact by cutting my palm? I will." She looked over at me with cunning smile. "You know I'm pretty handy with a knife. Right?"

"Uh, yeah," I said. I looked closely at her palm and saw a thin, lightly reddened scar: a prior cut.

Aileen must have seen it, too. "You live in Brooklyn, Karen?"

"Yeah."

"Where?"

"Carroll Gardens, down to the left, beyond those two big bridges."

"Ah," Aileen said. "Carroll Gardens. Now I get it."

Karen offered a smug smile and a curt nod at her. "Yeah. Right?"

"What does that mean?" Sylvia asked.

"That means you can trust her, sweetie," Aileen answered. "We need her."

"Okay, yeah. You do need me. And here's why. I know guys who know other guys who can, uh...do things. Plus, I know the inside of the Tower and what goes on there. *And* I know a few secret service guys who don't like that bitch they're protecting, and they could be turned. Maybe already have been. I'm just sayin'." She reached her cup back to the sink, then turned to face us as she leaned against the refrigerator. "So, anyway, I'm out jogging this morning and I usually grab a bottle of water when I'm done. I pop into this deli, and they've got the TV on. Looks like Kenton is gaming this thing he did yesterday. He's planing a big rally next week on the spot where the fifteen—he calls them terrorists— were gunned down. Says he can get a million people to show up, but I doubt that. Anyway, he's, like, enshrining that place as his own. He's gaming the Neo-Publica cause, maybe to taunt us out of hiding, or something."

"You're kidding," Aileen said as she shot an inflamed look at Sylvia. "We gotta do something, hon."

"I think we do nothing for a month, then go large," I said.

"What does that mean, Bob?" Sylvia challenged.

I never smoked, but under the circumstances, I reached for Sylvia's pack of cigarettes. She benignly slapped my hand away as she shook her head: *unh-unh.* I held the hand that had fended mine away. "Just a thought. I'm thinking we come out public and use who we are to our advantage, like Kenton is doing. We look at Neo-Publica as a product."

Aileen gulped her coffee. "A *product*? Are you fucking *nuts*?

"Hold on, 'leen ," Sylvia told her. "Bob used to be in advertising. He knows about this."

Karen folded her arms as she relaxed her stance against the refrigerator. "Neo-Pub. A product. Like Maxwell House coffee."

"Yeah, sort of," I said. "Maybe we should announce ourselves through an advertising campaign. Come out of the shadows, nationally and in force. Show them we're not gonna take this lying down. Show everybody we're prepared to do some heavy lifting, and recruit who we can. We have chapters all over the country, right. And they marched like we did, right?"

"By the way," Aileen said. "Anyone hear about how that went? Jesus. I only pray they didn't meet any forces like we did."

"I don't know," Sylvia said. "News blackout. Hugh back in New Haven probably got some reports, but I haven't reached him yet. Anyway, Bob. You've got my attention. What's your plan?"

"I'm sort of making this up as I go along, but I'm thinking we should pull all the chapters together. Have a recruitment drive using slick Mad-Ave-type posters with a slogan. It will be underground, of course, but out in the open. Under the Kenton Regime's noses."

"What 'underground but out in the open'?" Karen asked. "How's that supposed to work?"

"Recruitment will be anonymous, but our message will be clearly out there for all to see. We can even make up the numbers we recruit to draw in more. We need to show Kenton we can be bigger than them. Sylvia, before we marched you said the although there may be a few of us, there are hundreds of thousands of Real-Americans—"

"Americans," Aileen reminded me. "We're all still Americans."

"Of course. Hundreds of thousands of Americans who harbor the same kind of sentiments Neo-Publica is espousing. We need to reach them. Then hold a Kenton-style mass rally somewhere in, I don't know, some big stadium, maybe. Kenton/Fox News will naturally want to cover that, and we can show them how strong we would have grown."

"Sure, like Yankee Stadium," Karen said.

"No. Not in New York. Somewhere central in the country, like Denver."

"You don't think PRICE will go there and gun us all down?" Aileen asked.

"Maybe not if we do this right," Sylvia said. "The time for peaceful protest is over. If yesterday didn't prove that..."

"We fight force with force," Karen said.

"More like fighting brand with brand," I said. "Kenton's image is also his Achilles heel. We get him there, it'll hurt more than any bullet."

"Good point, if we want to gnaw away at him, but we'll need something more," Aileen said. "So, Karen, what did you mean, force against force? How do we do that?"

"Like I said, sweets. I know people who know people who know other people that can get something like this done. We need, how you say...equipment? I can help there, too."

Sylvia smiled for the first time in two days. "Karen? Welcome to Neo-Publica."

Karen burst through the door of Elise's, Carroll Garden apartment. "Sal! Come out here!"

Elise rushed from the bedroom disheveled by her "afternoon nap" with Sal. "Shut up, bitch. Sal's resting he's had a hard day." She went to the cooler behind the makeshift bar in the living room. "You wanna beer?"

"Sure, yeah. I'm sure he's had a hard day, girl. Thanks to you."

"What the hell? Keeps us in shape."

"SAL!" Karen cried. "Get out here! I've got some ... I need to tell you something." She looked amusedly stern at Elise, "and I'm not going in there to get him. I've had enough shock since yesterday."

"Jesus, Karen!" Sal sputtered as he came from the bedroom, this time fully dressed for a change.

"You're all dressed up. Goin' somewheres?" Karen said. "Anyway, grab a beer and take a seat." She looked at Elise. "Have you been watching the news the last few days?"

"We never watch that shit," Sal said. "You know that."

"What? You guys lock yourselves up in that bedroom all the time? Shit, sometimes I wonder if you do anything else but boff each other alla time."

"Shut up, bitch," Elise told her as she walked from the bar, two beers in hand. "Here's your goddam beer."

"Wha'dya do, Karen?" Sal said as he leaned against the wall with his arms folded. "Wake us up to tell me somethin' I already know?"

"Sal..." she sipped her beer. "I killed a guy. A BlueShirt."

This jarred him. "What? C'mon', Kar. The fuck you did."

"I did and slipped away through the crowd. I gotta tell you all about it." Sal listened in rapt concern, while Elise concentrated on doing her nails—her go-to stress reliever— while Karen told them about demonstration, how Saunders might have set the whole thing up, and how she saved Sylvia Morales from being killed.

"Holy fuckin' *shit*!" Sal said. "You saved Silvia Morales' life? An' you kilt a guy to do it? Holy shit!"

"Sylvia Morales?" Elise asked as she busied herself with a nail file. "You mean that one who started the whole Neo-Publica thing?"

"Yeah," Karen said, "her."

"And you stabbed a BlueShirt." Sal stated.

"Right in that place in the jugular where you guys taught me to."

"No one saw you, Kar? No one can finger you? You sure?"

"Like I told you, Sal. I had my face covered and my hood up. It was sorta dark in the shadows; cloudy and rainy. Besides, with all that other shit going around? No way they could see me."

"No cameras in the area?" Elise asked.

"Not that I saw, Elle."

"Yeah, well. As long as they didn't see you."

"They didn't, hon. Not to worry. All they coulda seen was a person wearing a hoodie with a bandana covering her face. My stab was quick. They might have seen a rookie BlueShirt fall to the ground; maybe slipping on the wet street. Any cameras there were looking at a lot of other shit, anyway. I can tell you. It was total chaos."

Sal lit a cigarette and grabbed up a beer from the cooler. "So, you spent some time talking with Silvia Morales. What about?"

"About them all joining forces on a national sort of thing. Flexing our muscles and showing the Kenton-types, we're a force not to fuck with."

Elise put away her nail file. "Our? ... We? What you talkin' about, girl? You didn't go out and join them or something."

"Yeah. I did. Like I said...We need to show our strength. Together. I told them I could help...*We* could help..maybe offer up some muscle. I believe it's time, hunh? Don't you?

"Starting with Stanley Saunders," Sal mused from a distance.

Karen went to him and placed her hand on his arm. "So, Sal. You're game for this?"

He took a long thoughtful drag on his cigarette. "Maybe. To offer up some muscle, yeah. And some hardware, ammo, whatever. Meet force with force, like you say."

"You shittin' me, boy?" Elise said. "Join up with the Neo-Pubs? I thought we weren't political. We stick to our own problems."

"Elle, they killed fifteen innocent people. In cold blood."

"And that's not what *we* do? Sometimes?" Elise said.

"We never do innocent people, Elle. Not like that—out in the open. No," Sal said. "So, Kar. You think your boy Saunders was behind this?"

"He's not 'my boy', Sal. And yeah, I know he was behind it. He has wet dreams about that kind of shit. Him and Randy Montefiore."

"Not to mention that bitch, Kenton, either," Elise added.

Sal took it more into consideration. "Okay," he finally said. "I need to talk to some people first."

Elise heaved a big sigh of relent. "I guess I better call my uncle, then."

"Yeah, you should, Elle," Sal agreed. "And then, I think we should send Stanley Saunders a message."

14

The Message

June 15

Stanley Saunders concentrated on the paperwork about where the 45 arrested protesters had been confined. He had sent seven of them to Guantanamo; seven to Unqutuck; four to Arapaho, the new, smaller gulag in Montana; nine to Montehaute deep in the lower Colorado Rockies; eight to Qatapica, in the endless, featureless South Texas plains; and ten, those with names that had sounded Mexican or Hispanic in any way, to over-crowded Dalaxuma for Sheriff Jeff to deal with. Each of the gulags had their distinctive brand of abuse, and he prided himself on such a creative mix and match.

He reached absently into the Ken's Deli lunch bag delivered a few minutes minutes before and lifted out his usual liverwurst sandwich. Even if he had noticed his sandwich was a tad weightier than usual, it would have pleased him—he savored his liverwurst mounded high between the slices of rye. He marked something on one of the forms then bit wide into his lunch. He felt something soft, then hard, within the glob of meat filling his mouth. A chicken bone? Those fucking idiot Mexicans that packed the sandwiches at the deli!

He pulled back the top slice of rye to pick out any more bone that might have been left in the meat. They weren't chicken bones. They were human fingers, looking like three small, calcified turds covered with flecks of liverwurst. He choked and spit out the contents in his mouth. Horrified by the finger emerging from the regurgitated meat, he flung the sandwich down. As it hit the papers on his desk, the two other fingers and a thumb flopped out with the splatter of the liverwurst. The thick, horny nails were dull black and brown. "Fucking SHIT!" he gasped in a choke, "SHIT!" He shot desperately from his seat and backed away terrorized, staring wide-eyed at the severed digits as if they might have been rattlesnakes. "Fuck *shit*!" he shouted out.

His secretary rushed in. "Stan! What's the matt—" she shrieked when she saw the one of the fingers, then tented her hands against her face. She noticed the other two and the thumb packed into the meat and shrieked again.

"Joan!" he shouted, as though she wasn't standing just three feet away from him. "Joan!"

"What?" She shouted as loudly, also mesmerized in terror by the crusty, dry fingers dappled in liverwurst.

"Pick that up!" he ordered her. "Get rid of it!"

"Hell I *will*, Stan. Shit! I'll call maintenance."

"Who the fuck brought this thing in here?"

Joan turned her head away in disgust. "The Ken's Deli delivery kid. He's outside waiting for his tip."

"Get him in here! Now!"

Hands still tented against her nose, Joan dashed from the office. "He's gone, Stan!" she called back in. "He left."

"FUCK!" Saunders shouted. A morbid curiosity kept him from averting his eyes from the finger sandwich.

He heard Joan calling up maintenance, as his desk phone rang. He rushed to pick it up. "What!" he shouted into the receiver. "What the fuck is it?"

The voice through the handset was a threatening, low, echoing croak: "That's One...One." Then there was the click of a hang-up.

Saunders took the afternoon off, but this time it wasn't to go to Aqueduct Racetrack, or one of his usual, sleazy west side whore houses. Seized with a feeling uncommon to him—the lingering one of dread—he rushed to his apartment down the hall and locked the door. Like a kid who'd just been terrorized by a horror movie, he drew closed the slatted blinds and drapes across his windows to keep the bogeyman out. He needed a drink, maybe many, to calm his shakes.

He heaved a sigh as he laid some lines of coke on his cocktail table, rolled up a ten-dollar bill and sniffed it in. He sunk down into the deep cushions of his living room couch, then arched his head back. He then let out another trembling sigh as he lifted his glass of Scotch on the rocks.

In his bloated remembrance, that split second when his tongue touched the finger, loomed. He imagined the salty, metallic, and chalky taste—how dry and rough it felt, like a small chunk of concrete. Had the seriated old nail scraped against his tongue? Or was it against the roof of his mouth? He sensed a dull pricking in both places. He felt a hot swell of fever and tried to position himself on the couch to ward away his lightheadedness. He took another gulp of Scotch.

Surely, he'd seen worse on his trips to the gulags, where body parts abounded. Often, they were set out in the exercise yards as a reminder of what could become of an uncooperative inmate—the same way the heads of medieval brigands might be stuck on pikes on ramparts as a warning. But this hit closer to home; his sanctuary. His *mouth*. He sipped his scotch again to purge a rise of bile and the finger's after taste.

He reckoned that the threatening phone call over the secured line could have only come from somewhere inside the building. An inside job! He vowed to hunt down the son of a bitch who did this. Send him off to a gulag to be flayed to the bone. He would seek out the Ken's Deli delivery boy. He would hold Joan, his secretary, and Herman Cutter, the maintenance man who picked the mess up, to secrecy on the surety of their being sent to a gulag if they told anyone. One thing was for certain: Randy Montefiore and Premier Alexander Kenton would never find out that someone had sent him that God damned finger sandwich.

He took another hefty hit of cocaine, then a desperate pull on his drink to empty the glass. He rose to get another but took a detour to pace his living room like a cat stalking pray, while muttering incessantly about how he would satisfy his revenge. Pacing. It was what he often did to work out his frustrations. He paced for at least an hour, until, exhausted, he slumped like a rag doll to rest his back against the wall, muttering the mantra: *"That's One...One."* until he passed out into the next morning.

Claiming he had a fever and another flare-up in his intestinal tract, he avoided having to go back into his office. He went underground—spending two full days tri-angulating his usual haunts: Madame LeBrau's Palace of Womanly Delights down in Times Square; an unmarked whorehouse in the bowels of Hell's Kitchen; and Angel Ambrosia's up in West Harlem. Though the places might have been scroungy, their girls were clean.

Haunted by his visions of crusty old fingers writhing like worms, he'd let himself devolve from his own recognition. He bounced among the three whorehouses like a sluggish, meandering pinball, while interrupting his two-day binge of carnal visits with bouts of drinking anonymously in shadowy bars.

He huddled in a dank Hell's Kitchen bar, redolent in the stench piss mixed with puke. Twenty-two hours without sleep or food—just tired, wet, sloppy sex with baggy, faceless, middle-aged women. And booze. A lot of cheap booze. He'd sunk down to the level of Chianti poured carelessly from straw-wrapped bottles. He hunched over a sticky, old oak bar populated with flies as he sipped from a thickly smudged wine goblet. The wriggling fingers came through the bar mirror straight for his face to gouge out his eyes. He flung his glass at them, winging the elderly bartender in the shoulder.

"You're cut off, fellah!" he croaked angrily.

Saunders continued to stare wide-eyed at the advancing fingers. "The fuggin' fingers!" he slurred heavily. "They're coming for me…agh!" He groped around and found an ashtray to pitch at them. As he did, he lost his balance and crumpled from his stool to the filthy, chipped linoleum floor.

"Go home an' sleep it off, fuckhead!" a patron barked at him.

"I—I coul' sen' you to a gulah, for talkin' me like tha'!" he grumbled from where he lay balled-up on the floor. "You dunno who yer fuggin' wi', here, ya shid-bird!"

"Get the fuck outta my bar, asshole!" the bartender carped angrily at him. "Or I'll sen' *you* to a gulag, alright! Now, get outta here, *now!*"

"I'm *not* a snot nosed whimp!" Saunders nearly sobbed, then crawled on all fours toward the door until he was able to stand and stagger out the door to collapse in a nearby alcove.

"Tha's one…tha's one…one," he whispered dryly until he passed out.

"You okay, now, baby?"

As Saunders' vision dimmed into clarity, a rotund, worn-out, dark brown woman's face filled his view. He lowered his gaze to the wrinkled sacks of her breasts hidden partially by the drooping bodice of a filthy satin slip of no particular color. Horrified that he might have had sex with an old black woman with haggish hair, he tried to skitter himself back against the headboard, until a swell of pain raged through his body.

"No, sweetie, don't try to move." Her voice was practiced and smooth.

"Where am I?" he croaked. His jaw felt tight; his lips dry and cracked.

"Why, you're in Harlem, baby, an' mamma's here to take care of you."

"You're not my mother," he replied tightly.

"For tonight, I am." She showed him a smile. Half her yellowed teeth were missing, and her breath was fetid with the odor of sardine. "An' you need me." She reached out to touch his cheek, and he weakly swept her cold, gnarly hand away. He saw his own hand was bloodied and raw on the knuckles.

"Wha' happened?" He paused to catch his breath only to feel a tightness in his chest. "How long have I been here?"

"Why, you been here two days, hon. An' I don' *know* what happen to you. You jus' knock on my do' showin' up the way you look. Beggin' fo' help. So, momma, here, she help you, tha's all."

He looked down toward his groin, and saw his shirt was spattered with blood. "Did we...?"

She disdainfully shook her head. "Laud, no! Momma don' do them sortsa things. Not anymo'" The old bed springs complained in dry squeaks as she shifted her bulk to lumber to a stand. "You wan' somethin' ta eat, baby? I got soup cookin' on the stove.

He breathed in the thick fragrances of fried onion, hot pepper and something sweet that might have been liquorish, relieving the ubiquitous taints of kerosine, old garbage and wet socks. "No.

Thank you." He tried to shift his weight, and this time it seemed easier. He lifted his hand and touched a scab on his cheek. He cringed when he touched below his right eye, which felt tight—swollen shut. He looked out the smeared window of the place and saw it was pitch dark. The timid flame light of the three hurricane lamps ebbed and flowed, casting their timid light over bolts of cloth piled around the room, and an ancient sewing machine. The smell from the many heaps of dirty laundry lying around seemed to smother the air. Momma was in the far corner of the room stirring the soup in the stewpot as if it was a witch's brew. "What's your name? Other than 'Momma'?"

She pondered her answer as she slowed her stirring. "Why, it's Maribelle. Maribelle Washington."

"No relation to George, I assu— Agh!," he groaned in pain as he shifted his weight again.

"Now you stay put, hon, okay? You bin through too much to go hoppin' about, now."

Broken as he was, he knew he'd reached a bottom and felt too helpless to move. His inner Dante had showed him the ninth rung of hell and trapped him there. He'd realized he had taught himself enough of a lesson and vowed to get back to his apartment—his world. He'd had enough of this miserable one.

The last however many days had reduced him to powerlessness among these ruins. "I'm tired, woman," he said as he slipped back down into the comfort of the stinking bedsheets. "It's best you don't say anything, now." His only recourse now was to slide his mind into a state of nothingness until he fell into the relief of sleep.

It took him several more days to eat whatever glop Maribelle had forced upon him to feel mended enough to leave her hovel of a room. He grudgingly thanked her without deigning to offer a hug for all her efforts, then hobbled down the two flights of close, creaking stairs, and finally out onto 128th Street and the slim sanity of sunlight. He hailed a battery-powered yellow cab to take him back downtown.

He felt the heat of the battery in the trunk pulsing through the stained Naugahyde of the back seat as he calculated his excuses. He'd tell Randy Montefiore that he had rested enough in his locked apartment during his six-day absence to finally go out for a drink. He'd explain his bloated, raw, wounds off to a bar fight to defend the sublime efforts of Premier Kenton. He reasoned Montefiore would buy that because it had happened twice before. He also resigned to get away from New York, in a few days, if possible, to vacation from all he'd been through. Maybe take a tour of the gulags, starting with Dalaxuma in New Mexico. He was long overdue for a visit with Sheriff Jeff, where they would sit over tequilas and compare uproarious antidotes of prisoner torment.

He finally got back to his apartment over an hour later, as the cabbie had driven slowly to preserve the drain on the battery. He opened the door of his still-darkened apartment to a gush of air-conditioning and a damp funky, stench he didn't recognize, but assumed was some food he might left out on the kitchen counter. He stooped to pick up the pile of mail and inter-office memos and concentrated on fanning through them as he made his way across his living room to the bar. He placed the stack of mail on the bar and reached for a bottle of decent Scotch.

His stomach clenched tight at the sight of a severed foot on the marble bar top. Its grey, crusted sole facing him. Looming ever larger, it held him a captivity of horror. His hand on the stack of mail dragged it to the floor as he staggered back, then hurled out whatever Maribelle had fed him over the smoked glass top of his cocktail table.

Between his wretches and heaves, he saw a note had slipped out from the stack of mail spread out on the carpet. Written on it in a firm hand:

"That's Two...Two."

15

The Soccer Game

July 2

By the way the tennis courts at Dalaxuma Gulag were decked out with bunting and Real-America flags, it could have been Independence Day. But in Real-America it had become illegal to celebrate anything relating to the former America, and anyone found doing so risked spending a week as one of PRICE's guests in a detainment cell. But today had been a cause for celebration because the PRICE Commissar was paying one of his visits. The nets had been removed from the four courts, and soccer goals set up at either end. Armed BlueShirt guards had been posted in higher platforms on the corners of the courts. They kept a furtively watchful eye on the rest of the inmates held within the labyrinth of concertina-wire-fringed fences in the near distance flanked by the vast, open desert.

Saunders, Sheriff Jeff, his grandson, Zach, and a few other dignitaries watched from a raised dais and drank copious amounts of iced tequila in the searing heat as the soccer games were played. In the first heat, the Mexicans had taken on and defeated the Nicaraguans; and then in the next heat, the Venezuelans; then the in final one, the Guatemalans. The Mexican team proved victorious throughout, as favored. Some of the players had lost control of the ball, and collapsed in the dry, wavering, desert-summer heat.

"Man!" Saunders slurred. "This is great entertainment, Jeff. Look at the way those little brown fuckers keep passing out. I'm loving this! You sure do know how to throw a party."

"More Tequila, Stan?" The sheriff asked in his slow drawl.

"Fucking-A, right!"

Sheriff Jeff poured him another, then offered a silent toast. "I planned a special treat in your honor, Commissar. I'm pretty sure you'll like it." He took up his bullhorn from the adjoining seat, held it close to his face, and keyed it. "Congratulations to the Mexican players for winning not one, not two, but all three matches. Let's have a round of applause for them!" He repeated it in Spanish. This was answered with enthusiastic applause from the BlueShirts and lower dignitaries in the bleachers, along with scattered gratuitous clapping from the inmates. He turned to face them. "Hey! You! Louder, now!" There followed a rise of fatigued enthusiasm from the captives behind the fence. The sheriff returned his attention to the courts and keyed the bullhorn. "And to the losing teams: Thank you for your try. Now, you losing players, please gather on the court in front of us here in the bleachers. I have a special prize for you, even though you lost."

The sheriff took a slow pull from his glass of tequila as the few dozen from the defeated teams milled around before the bleachers. The sheriff nodded curtly at them. "You played well and gave us a good show. Even though you lost, you deserve a reward for trying." He aimed his bullhorn toward the guard tower. "Go ahead, now."

A shower of bullets from the guards' AR-15s rained down upon the losing players as they scrambled about, sluggish from fatigue, to avoid being hit. The sound of the bursts of rounds were accentuated by loud gasps, cries, screams and a few cheers from the bleachers. Within a minute, half of defeated players lay dead, as some wounded crawled languidly and half-alive toward any sort of protection. Sheriff Jeff raised his hand, and the gun shots fell silent.

"That was fuckin' TERRIFIC!" Saunders gushed.

"You wanna try, Stan?" From under his seat, the sheriff said produced a Soviet-made AK-47 with a white party bow tied to its stock. "My gift to you."

"My god, Jeff, *Really*? God...*damn*!" he said as he took the automatic rifle from the sheriff and admired it.

"Safety's off. All you gotta do is to step up to the fence, aim it through, and pull the trigger. Mind the kick...it's a little rough on these Soviet models, but this one packs a hell of a lot of power."

"Thanks!" Saunders gushed, then sprinted like a kid toward the fence with his new toy. He rested the slim barrel on the crook of a connection of two links, held the stock snug against his shoulder, squinted one eye to focus the other, then drew in his breath. He fired a burst at one of the crawling wounded as a test and shattered his leg. "Holee *shit*!" he muttered, then fired another short burst to finish him off. The vibration of the stock against the crook of his shoulder sent a reviving force through his body like a strike of lightning. This was just the sort of self-gratification and power he needed to feel after he'd been so eroded by his remembrance of the severed fingers and foot. He fired again and killed one of the Nicaraguans. "That's one...One," he said. Then he shot one of the Venezuelans in the back as he tried desperately to limp away. "That's two...Two." He turned and shouted back to Sheriff Jeff, who was beaming down at him from the platform above the bleachers. "This is fuckin' *great*, Jeff! Thanks!"

The sheriff waved him back up. "Okay. Now y'all come on back up here an' drink some more tequila with me, Commissar!" He waved another signal to the guards to finish off the rest of the defeated. The crowd looked on in horror, and in dumb amazement. The inmates looked vacantly at the carnage, seemingly as detached as zombies.

Once the court was bloodied and littered with dead, Sheriff Jeff called the victorious Mexican team forward. They reluctantly approached and stood, heads bowed, like a gathering of spindly gladiators before their Caesar. The sheriff congratulated them. He then ordered them to clean up the mess and bury the dead out in the desert; their reward for winning being that they hadn't been executed.

From the prisoner pen, the woman they called Diana had watched the whole incident in a catatonic state, as did the many others around her. She had been too worn down to feel anything, until she saw the PRICE Commissar take his shots, and then the guards beginning to finish off the rest. She spied her lieutenant in a guard tower with his rifle aimed down in her direction. Off to her left she saw an old Mexican woman trundle away in desperation toward the far end of the pen, only to be taken down by a shot in the back from the lieutenant's rifle. She felt her skin bristle in a surge of hate; this rare sense of emotion igniting a dim realization of who she had once been—Tricia. She whispered her name: "Tricia." The recognition urged on a resilience she'd held increasingly veiled through her years of abuse; years of conditioned silence when there was nothing worth saying.

She stood stoically in place, then turned to the one cringing next to her. Obviously a new arrival, he appeared still relatively hearty, having yet to suffer the starvation that time in the gulag would bring on. He didn't look as indigenous as the others, but more like...her— light-skinned. She spoke in a ragged voice: "My name is Tricia."

He glanced at her, his eyes glistening in tears. "Max," he said nervously. "This fucking shit is all too familiar to me."

"Fam...iliar?" she replied guardedly as if she was just learning to speak.

"A few months ago, in New York City."

She had a fragmented memory of the place. She barely mouthed the words. "New York ...City?"

There was another burst of semi-automatic gunfire into the remains few scampering players on the court. "Shit!" Max shouted out. "God DAMN!"

"You...saw this...before?"

"Fuck! Yeah. This same shit happened to the Neo-Publicas at fuckin' Kenton Tower."

"Neo...?"

To avert his gaze from the carnage, he looked askance toward her. "Neo-Publica. The resisters..." He noticed her perplexed look. "To the fucking Kenton Regime."

"Kenton?"

He hardened his gaze at her, probably thinking she was mentally challenged, or more likely brainwashed. "Yeah. Kenton. The Premier of Real-Amer— oh never mind," he dismissed. A final burst of fire shattered the air, finishing the remaining defenseless soccer players. "*Fuck!*" he said as he swiftly turned away, "I'm getting the fuck outta here!"

"No!" She reached to grasp his sleeve. "No... don't show them... your weakness." She canted her head toward the old woman who'd tried to run but now lay dead. "They will...they will...shoot you...like her."

"Why? How can these mother fuckers get away with that shit?"

"They shoot anyone...anyone...who tries to...run." She felt his tension soften as he bowed his head to not look at what had just gone on. "You came here...when?"

"I don't know...maybe a month ago? I don't really remember."

Tricia knew what he meant. The first loss an inmate sensed at Dalaxuma was time. There was nothing to relate it to. "Me? More than...two years, I think. Maybe...I can...help you. And maybe...maybe you can...help me."

Tricia spent the next week milling around the camp, while hoping for a chance encounter with Max. She wanted to know more about this resistance movement he'd mentioned just before they were herded back into the gulag complex by the BlueShirt guards. Her memory of her children had come slothfully back to plague her, along with the scant recollection of her identity. Maybe this Max, with his connection to that neo-resistance group he mentioned, could find out about them.

Max may have not been hard to locate as one of the few white skins among the scores of brown and black, but it was he who found her as she toted a bucket of sand from one part of the compound to another. It was just one more nonsensical duty, like the others which defined the gulag as a work camp.

"Hey, you. Tricia," he called softly at her from where he hunkered near one of the men-worker's barracks tents. He had already started to show the typical signs of wear: his soiled grey uniform; hoarse voice; work-worn hands; dry, heat-blistered skin; a developing "thousand-yard-stare" into nothingness—those beginning signs of no longer caring, even enough to care.

She looked down at him, then shyly away. "No. They call..call me...Diana, here."

"Sit and talk with me?"

Conversation had become something foreign to her as she'd conditioned herself to suffer in silence over the last years. She glanced around to see if any BlueShirts were watching and saw them to be off in the distance. "Max...are you... alright?"

"What the fuck do *you* think?"

"No."

"No," he agreed. "Back home, a few months ago, I was an I.T. person at a bank."

"I.T.?"

He shook off her query. "That doesn't mean anything, anymore. Now all I do is rake sand out in the fuckin' desert. What the fuck is *that* all about? It's a big God-dammed desert."

"That is what they...do." She offered a forlorn smile, overturned her bucket, then sat on it. "I have to...carry sand. From over there..." She motioned in a general direction away, "to over there. I ...empty it out...then go back and fill it...do it again."

"That's stupid."

She huffed a sigh meant to be a gentle laugh. "Stupid. Yes." For a few moments they sat in silence, as though sharing a precious moment. "You said something ... about... Neo...Neo...?

"Neo-Publica. A resistance movement, yeah. But after what happened in New York, I doubt if it exists anymore."

"No?"

"The Kenton Dictatorship. It's too strong."

There was that name again. "Kenton is...again?"

"An asshole. The guy who runs the country."

She had another flash of recognition. "Yes. He *is*...an...asshole. Right?"

He smiled a little at the the ground. "That's the least of it."

"We need a resistance...here."

 "Good luck with that," he scoffed.

"I am… nothing but a..." she looked down at her soiled bare feet. "A whore...to them. I...I don't want to...want to...live anymore." She gazed back up at him, feeling relief in the comfort at his returned look of concern. "But I don't…want to...die, either."

"What have they done to you, Tricia?" he whispered harshly.

"Diana."

"*Tricia*," he enforced. "That's who you are, no matter what they call you, here. What have they done to you, hunh?"

She let out a ragged sigh and turned her back to him. She lifted her shift to reveal her whip-scars.

"Oh, *fuck*! Those sons of fucking bitches!" She let the hem of her shift fall back down. He must had surmised from the softness of her skin around the the scars, and something in her shy demeanor, that she probably hadn't been plucked from the depravity of the streets to end up here. "What did you do to get thrown into this place? What were you before they put you in here?"

"What...was I?"

"Yeah. What did you do, before? Where were you from?"

"I have a hard time...remembering. My memories...They come and go. I was...married. I think. And I know I had…children ...Three, I think. When they...took me, they took...them. My children."

"Took them?"

"To a place like...this. I can't remember...where."

"Fucking Kenton! Fucking PRICE!" he muttered.

"Yes...fucking Kenton and...fucking PRICE. Can you...can you help to...to get me out? Find my...children? Maybe do a Neo...Neo—?"

"Neo-Publica."

"Yes. Neo-Publica...here?"

He smiled weakly. "No, Tricia."

"Shh!" warned a nearby voice. "Not so loud!"

Max looked toward where the voice had come from, and vaguely recognized one of those who'd been arrested with him in New York. He was a darker-skinned, wiry man, older than him, maybe in his mid-thirties. "You were there, in New York, at the protest?"

"I was, and I would do it again. If I could. But no, not here."

"No?" Tricia said, her tone now energized into a challenge. "Why not?...why not?"

He moved closer and hunkered down, forearms on knees. "Because there's no Sylvia Morales here."

"Shit, yeah," Max remembered. "Man, she was great. I wonder if she got out?"

"Not that I saw. Even if she did, PRICE would have found her by now."

"Sylvia...?"

"Yeah," Max told her, "a leader with a vision." He turned to the silhouette of the other man and squinted into the sun at him. "This is my friend, Tricia. And I'm Max Salerno."

"I'm Sardo Garcia. You're Italian? Your name sounds Italian."

"It is," Max said. "My family's from, like the name says, Salerno."

"And they put you in here? With all us other *vaqueros*?"

"What the fuck do they know? If your name ends with a vowel or a 'z', they probably figure you belong here. Did you know Sylvia?"

"By her speeches, and I did meet her once after one of them. Her boyfriend, a guy named Bob, introduced us."

"Her speeches?" Tricia said. "What are they...are they about?"

"America," Sardo told her. "What it was...what it could never be again."

Max shook his head forlornly as he drew a finger through the sand. "It's a lost cause, Tricia. There's nothing here to start any resistance."

She looked at Sardo. "Did you see what...what happened back then? The shootings...shootings in the soccer game?"

"Yeah," he said dourly. "I did." He glanced over at Max. "It's worth a try."

"What? A fuckin' resistance? Sure. If you wanna get killed."

Sardo waved his hand on the general direction of a cluster of emaciated Mexican inmates. "These are my people, Max, which makes them *our* people. We risked our lives in New York for a cause, and while we have our health, and some strength, we should try. Unless you wanna end up getting shot on the Sheriff's tennis courts."

Max considered his Sardo's comment. "Are there any more of us from New York here?"

"I know about eight of us are."

Max heaved a sigh. "Okay, Sardo, see if you can get them together. My tent is right here. We can talk about...whatever...tomorrow night after our portion of rice and beans."

"Me too."

"You too, Tricia."

"Uh...we don't have to," Sardo said.

"What do you mean?"

"I mean, get together in your tent."

"Why not?" Max said.

Sardo shifted his weight, then compiled his thoughts. He glanced around for any BlueShirts. "Do you shoot dice? Like, craps?"

Max cast him a sideways look. "I'm more of a blackjack fan, myself."

"Well, I think you'll like our craps game, Max. Some of us who came in from New York have been running a game two tents down every other night. Ya know? There's a lot of strategy in craps. And we've, uh, added a lot of players over the last three weeks."

Max picked up on his drift. "No shit?"

"Yeah. We're way ahead of you. The stakes might get high. You want in?"

"Shit, yeah!"

Sardo looked up at Tricia. "Women are welcome in the game, too."

"I...uh...I don't play....dice games."

"Yes, she does," Max answered for her.

Be as discreet as though your ass hung on this, Max. Right?"

Max stared off at some inmates, then out toward the desert he and the others would be raking tomorrow. "Always."

August 4

The mechanic, Pepito, the trustee known among the dice players as Number 26—the second and fourth numbers of his seven-digit inmate number—squatted among them and watched Number 32 roll the makeshift dice. A two and a six. Number 88, the Nicaraguan with a crescent birthmark on his cheek, then rolled a seven. The other Nicaraguans in the group cheered as Number 88 gathered up the central pile of pebbles for himself.

Tricia stood behind the cluster of men and a few women bantering quietly away in Spanish, wondering what the sense of the game was. The pebbles won were nothing but a metaphor, like the game; yet perhaps one that took them all away from her for the few hours played. The seven former Neo-Pubs—as even she called them, now—from New York sat off to themselves and talked calmly in low tones of rebellion as if they were comparing Yankee batting averages.

She watched as Pepito turned his attention back to his whetstone to sharpen the point, then the edge of a metal shard. The discards from the abandoned pickup truck sitting outside the tent where he worked under guard on Zach's Porsche had proved valuable as shanks. He held his handiwork up to the flickering lamplight, then rotated it like a treasure for one final inspection before he placed it in the pile with the dozen others he'd fashioned over the last few weeks.

Tricia turned her attention to Number 47, a swarthy Venezuelan, and a relatively new arrival. He manufactured smaller shanks from prongs taken from the rakes used to tend the desert. By looping the middle of the tine around a bunk post, he used a short bar and a pair of pilfered pliers to twist it around itself like yarn, then to a point. This was an arduous process, but Number 47 had once belonged to a street gang in Caracas, where they'd fashioned and used such weapons with ease. They were small, easily concealed, and, in the right hands, quick and lethal.

Her nostrils twitched at the stench wafting in through the barracks tent door, from where some stooges boiled up some yucca root to extract their juice. The juice would react with human bile to create a strong sedative, which, once inhaled went straight to the nervous system to immediately relax the body into near helplessness. The collection of bile might have been a problem, but in this case, not. When the victorious Mexican soccer team went out to bury the slaughtered Guatemalan, Nicaraguan and Venezuelan defeated in the desert three weeks before, they harvested the bile from their stomachs. This highly vicious yellowish-green substance was brought back to the indigenous Mayan spirit-healers to mix with the yucca root extract into the concoction the Mexicans called "Tonto Juice." Strips of the dead's clothing lay in small stacks near the cooking kettles, to later be soaked with the mixture.

"We're ready now," Guardo Rodriquez, Number 82, said to Sardo, Number 48. "I think we should try something tomorrow. Like a test."

Sardo nodded. "Make sure it's quiet. And remote."

"Who's gonna do it? We need someone with, you know, experience," Max, Number 36, said.

Guardo glanced around the tent, and fixed his eyes on Number 47, as he finished wrapping another rake tine into a chiv. "Him," he said. "I've talked to him. He was with M-Thirteen in Caracas, and he's killed before. Told me one of the murdered Venezuelans hung with him back in the day. He's got a grudge and there ain't noting worse than someone from M-Thirteen with a grudge."

Sardo looked over to him. "Yo, Number Forty-Seven," he called to him in Spanish.

Number 47 looked over. "Yeah, what?"

"Come on over here."

He nodded, then flicked his product off the bunk post and onto a towel with the other ones. He pushed the wrapped chivs under the bunk and crammed his blanket over them.

"Twenty-six, you too. Got a minute?"

Pepito wrapped up his small pile of larger knives and stuffed the bundle into a torn pillow. He labored to stand, as Rodriguez went to fetch one of the Mayan healers.

They hunkered around in a small group pretending to watch the dice game. Sardo worked his aching fingers as though warming up to play piano—a nervous habit. "We're gonna move tomorrow," he whispered in Spanish, while Guardo translated into English for the other Neo-Pubs. "Forty-Seven, you're our triggerman with one of your chivs. You know what to do, right?"

"I know where to stick the knife, yeah. But the rest of it...?"

Sardo glanced at Pepito, who drove the inmates out into the desert in the camp transport, a grey, twenty-five-year-old school bus. "You can drop forty-seven off on you last stop, the farther out the better."

"I will do that, yes."

He turned to the Mayan. "You can have the Tonto juice ready before dawn?"

He nodded.

"Tell Forty-Seven what he needs to do."

"Yes. What I will do is give you some rags soaked with Tonto. Be sure you cover your nose to keep from smelling it, otherwise you will fall."

"I'll be wearing my kerchief over my nose and mouth, as usual."

"Good. Carry the Tonto rag away from your face." the Mayan said. "When the time is right, you will bring the rag from behind to the guard's face like this." He brought his hand up to cover his nose and mouth. "And hold it tight until he weakens. My mixture will be strong so it will not take long... probably less than fifteen seconds. You will know when to do what you do next. You understand?"

"Yeah, I get it," Number 47 said.

Sardo looked at Pepito. "So, Twenty-Six, you can pack some extra shovels in the bus with the rakes. You can find some extra tarps?"

"Yes. I have some."

"Pack them, to wrap and bury the body."

"And the Tonto rag," the Mayan said.

"No." Sardo said. "Bury that and the chiv separately, far apart. Oh, yeah—and don't forget to lift his weapon."

"I can wrap it and any others in an oiled cloth and bury them in the dirt underneath my salvage truck," Pepito said.

"Good," Guardo told them. "We can start an arsenal."

"I'm keeping my chiv," Number 47 insisted. "I'll keep it hidden tight."

"Just remember to say your prayers tonight that this works," Sardo said.

"*Cinco cero!*" A stooge called from where he mixed the yucca-root "tea" in his kettle over the cook-fire.

"BlueShirts!" Guardo whispered tightly. "Let's pack it up and play dice."

The BlueShirt guard stationed to watch over Number 47's dessert raking crew never showed up in the return trip on Pepito's bus the next day. At first, the other BlueShirts reasoned he might have wandered off to take a piss and got bit by a rattlesnake. Such things had been rumored to happen. The PRICE guards were not all that concerned because the inmate count held steady, and that was what mattered. Besides, some of those BlueShirts were as stupid as a dead buzzard, and it would be just like them to get bit in the pizzle by a rattlesnake.

Sardo was stoically pleased that the plan worked. He had number 47 work with training several other Venezuelans to be quick and quiet with the Tonto juice and knife as the growing resistance's hit-men—and woman, as Tricia, volunteered for training. She had a revenge of her own to carry out and was reminded of this with each searing hot pain in her groin from the PRICE lieutenant's abuse of her.

16

The Window Washers

August 19

"I wish you wouldn't keep doing that, Randy," Kenton groused.

"What?"

Kenton pointed to his wrist. "That. All that tapping."

Montefiore glanced down at how he was batting his pen against his wrist again. "Ah. Nervous habit. Something I've done since I was a teenager."

"Well, my friend, you've been doing it a lot more of it lately." Kenton sipped his chilled black coffee, made a face, and sipped it again. "Anyway, it's fucking annoying. Are you nervous about something?"

In either an act of compliance or ridicule, Montefiore made a point of placing the pen on Kenton's desk. "Okay. Done and done. And yes, Al, I am a little concerned." He narrowed his gaze at the Premier. "It's about Saunders. He's been acting...distracted, lately. Not concentrating on his work."

"'course he is. He just got back from one of his tours of the gulags." Kenton took another sip of his coffee, made another sour face, then took another sip. "He's perfectly doing his job. Look at all those Neo-Publican shitheads he shipped off in May. He did an outstanding thing, there. Outstanding. Don't you think. Randy?"

"Okay, yeah, Al. But lately? Not so much. He's been walking around in some sort of funk. Totally distracted. He hardly ever shows up in his office anymore." He picked up the pen again and poised it against his wrist. "He's locked himself away in his suite. His secretary hasn't seen him in a week." He started to flick the plunger on his pen: click-*click*...click-*click*. "I saw him in the hall two days ago walking around like some sorta zombie. Looked like he hadn't 't shaved in a week."

"Sure, of course. He's probably preparing a report on his gulag visits. You know how fucking thorough he can be."

Montefiore had to admit, Saunders could be anal retentive about his reports. "But, still, I'm worried for him. He could become a liability."

Kenton stared annoyed at Montefiore's clicking away on his pen. "Look, maybe he's just tired. Why don't I send him for a week at my place in West Palm Beach? He can play a little golf, then come back to us in perfect shape."

"He doesn't play golf."

"That's fine. I've got some of the best pros in the business who'll work with him."

Montefiore stared briefly at the cleanliness of Kenton's desktop—the sign of one who chose to do no work. He mused over how easy the Premier's job was. And he would know; he did most of his boss's work. "Saunders once told me once. He doesn't want to learn golf," he glanced back up at Kenton to make his point, "he hates golf." He knew that would cut Kenton to the quick.

The Premier glared at him. "He'll like it if I tell him to."

"Look, Al, why don't you send him on a long sabbatical? I can fill in as PRICE Commissar for a while."

Kenton's glare turned moderately challenging. "You'd like that, wouldn't you, Randy? But no. I need you here with me, and I need Stan where he is. He's good at it."

Montefiore's vision was sideswiped by a window washer's platform being lowered from the roof. "And I wouldn't be good at it?" he said, distractedly.

"I don't know, Randy. But you're better at being my legal counsel. I need you for that."

The two window-washers expertly waved their squeegees against the window. Montefiore became quiet; entranced with the way the soapy water oozed down the glass.

"Let's get Stan up here, Randy. Let him explain. Maybe it'll put your thoughts at ease."

As Kenton dialed up his PRICE Commissar, Montefiore noticed the window washers were Mexicans—or something like that. He wondered how nice it would have been to open the window and push them off into a 58-story fall. He started batting the pen against his wrist.

———————————————————————

Maybe it was because Saunders had recently watched a re-run of the movie, but in a nightmare, he'd imagined he woke up next to his own severed foot, like the horse's head in "The Godfather." Then, in waking, he became clumsy, as if he had lacked a foot —bumping into furniture, dropping things. Drinking more, he'd become increasingly vacant from his office, as he sequestered himself away in his apartment. His lingering image of old Maribelle, the once-upon-a-time whore who had nursed him back from his bottom almost two months before, also plagued his nightmares. It had been enough even to keep him away from his whores.

He'd also kept his distance from Randy Montefiore, to whom he'd become persona-non-grata. Every meeting Montefiore had alone with Premier Kenton was another clench to the heart of his chronic paranoia. *One more day away from all the other shit on the outside,* he'd convinced himself. *Just one more day.* Then, tomorrow: *Just one more day.*

He allowed another moment of silence until his inter office cell squawked out "You can't always get what you want..."; that ring tone from Premier Kenton's office. He put the phone to his ear but said nothing.

After a second or two, Kenton spoke: "Stan? Are you there?"

"Yes, sir," Saunders croaked dryly; barely audible.

"Can you come on up here for a minute?"

This bolted him with a wave of dread. He never wanted Kenton to see him this way—so self-demolished. "Yes, sir. I'll be right up."

He straightened his tie and moved heavily toward his front door. His vision was caught by a card that must had been slipped through the mail slot while he was cowering away within his thoughts. It was a kid's birthday card with a dancing pink and blue hippo on its cover. "What the fuck?" he muttered as he picked it up. He opened it and immediately recognized the innocuous block printing:

"Three...Soon...Three."

Saunders shuffled into Kenton's office as he tried to retain a semblance of professional demeanor. Montefiore noticed his color had drained. His forehead was dampened in sweat. His eyes were bloodshot. His hands trembled at his sides. All of this was proof to his point that the Commissar had come undone.

"Have a seat, Stan," the Premier invited.

"Is it okay if I stand, sir?"

"Well, sure. If you want. Now, Randy tells me you've been acting a little out of touch, lately. Is everything okay?"

"I...think so, sir," he replied weakly.

Montefiore gloated over Saunders' show of weakness.

"Okay," Kenton said. "I thought so." He glanced at Montefiore. "*We* thought so. See, Randy? All is good."

Montefiore saw that certainly, it wasn't. Saunders was cracking—or maybe already cracked.

"How are your reports from your gulag tours coming along, Stan?" Kenton pressed. "Anything new? Any suggestions on how we can make our inmates any more..." he suffused a chuckle, "comfortable?"

"As if they weren't comfortable enough. Right, Stan?" Montefiore said.

Saunders tried on a fleeting grimace of a smile. "Sure, Randy. Yeah."

"Anyway," Kenton said, "we think that because you've done such a great job, you deserve some time off. Maybe take a few weeks off in West Palm. Maybe learn a little golf. There's nothing like some holes of golf to ease your mind. Isn't that right, Randy?"

"Oh, yeah. Right. It really relaxes me." Montefiore said lack-lustered.

"Would you like that, Stan?"

"I would, sir. But now I think my time is best spent here."

"Ah!" Kenton said. "See that, Randy? Total dedication, that's what's needed around here." He turned his attention back to Saunders. "So, Stan. You're good?"

"I'm good, sir."

"Well, then. That settles it. If you're good; we're all good. Right, Randy?"

Montefiore had become distracted by the squeaking of the squeegees against the glass. It annoyed him to all else, and he would like nothing more than to push those illegals off their platform to stop the noise.

"Randy?"

"Yeah, Al?"

"Are we good, now?"

"Yeah. Super-good," he answered distantly with a rueful smile. "Real good."

"Okay, then, Stan. You can get back to your reports. Can I have them by Friday?"

"Of course, Mr. Premier."

"Okay, then, you can go."

Montefiore stopped Saunders as he turned to leave. "Uh, Stan?"

"Yeah, Randy?"

"You, uh...you pissed yourself."

Saunders looked down at the wet bloom in his pants-front and blushed from white to red. "Oh. Sorry," he replied ashamedly, then sauntered back out of the office, with his hands fanned over the stain to hide it.

"So, Al. You still think he's okay?"

Kenton regarded his answer. "Well, Randy? He's been going though a lot, lately."

"Uh-Hunh," Montefiore said facetiously. "He has."

17

The Third Move

August 23

Saunders was off the liverwurst, or any other organ meats. Now he was into salads—healthier, if not all that tasty. He'd missed his diet of pure meat but could still not imagine biting into it without that sense he was chomping into a dead finger or two. He stabbed a chickpea with his fork and gazed out through the rain-drooled view at Lincoln Center across the way. That was one name Premier Kenton did not cover up with his own. Back during the first times, in 2021, he'd likened himself to the 16th American President, perhaps not to so much that he had freed the slaves but defined them more precisely as illegal immigrants. Or it might have been because Lincoln was the first Republican—the party that had propelled Kenton into power—and the party he'd weakened enough to manipulate into being his loyal subject. So, Lincoln Center, Lincoln Memorial, Lincoln, Missouri, Lincoln cars, and all other things Lincoln kept their names. Washington, as in Washington DC, was okay, too, because it was a Museum City, and George Washington was a curiosity like a museum artifact, such as the dreaded —now shredded—U.S. Constitution.

Saunders shifted his gaze out toward the street. Primary-colored spatters and glitters from the neon lights at the confluence of Broadway and Columbus Avenue webbed the window, as pedestrians huddled beneath their gleaming black umbrellas rushed past. He glanced again at the lone chickpea stuck on the tines of his fork. *What the hell?* he told himself and plunked his fork back down upon the salad. He called the server over to order the drink he needed more than a salad.

As he waited, his cell phone buzzed. At least his time it wasn't Kenton or Montefiore summoning him up for another meaningless meeting. But who else would have his private, inter-office number?

"Hello?" he said guardedly into the annoying silence on the other end. "Hello? This is Saunders." More silence, and a hint of rustling. "Fuck it," he muttered as he began to put his phone away.

"Stanley?" The voice sounded as timid and distant as it did vaguely familiar.

"Yeah?"

"Stanley? It's...it's Karen."

"Karen?"

"Fabrizio. Karen Fabrizio? Your old secretary?"

He relaxed his shoulders. "Karen! Of course! How the fuck *are* you? *Where* are you?"

"I'm...I'm really sorry I left the job like I did, Stanley." He heard her sniffle. Twice. "Can you ever forgive me?"

He thought he could use a little of her right now, and her timing was a gift from God. "Oh, sure, honey. That's all in the past now. You sound a little rattled. Is everything okay?"

"I'm scared, Stanley. I need to talk to you soon."

The server placed his bourbon before him. He took a quick sip. "What's the matter, Karen. You're okay, right?"

This was met with more silence. "I...I don't know," she finally said. Then more silence. "I've been getting these, like, messages? from some very bad people. I think it has something to do with when we...you know."

"Oh, yeah, I remember. And I've really missed it."

Sniffle. "Me, too, Stanley. Really." Sniffle. "But these people, they scare me. I don't know what they want. The things they send me... I need to talk to you."

He calculated her obvious fear. "What sorta things, Karen? What are they sending you?"

He heard her sigh unevenly in resignation. "Weird shit. They're ...they're like...body parts. And they're, like, numbered; One, Two, like that."

He froze with his drink held halfway to his mouth. His mind became suddenly void. "Body parts?"

"Yeah. Like fingers and toes. The last note said something like: "'We know all about you and the PRICE Commissar. We're watching.'"

At least her notes said more than the ones he had gotten. "Fuck yes, Karen, we need to talk. I've been getting the same shit sent to me."

"Really? Can we meet somewhere?"

"Yeah. I'm at the..." he referred to the menus on his table "The Prince of Monaco, a French place on Columbus Avenue, across from Lincoln Center. I'll wait. You can meet me here."

"I'm scared, Stanley. I don't want to take a subway. Someone one might see me."

"I'll send a cab, then. Where are y—?"

"No don't even do that. You meet can me here in Brooklyn, okay?"

"Brooklyn? I though you lived up on—"

"I got so scared moved to Flatbush. I'll wait for you on the corner of Flatbush and Fulton Street."

"Fulton Street?"

"Yeah. You'll see me standing on the corner in my yellow slicker. Please, honey...hurry. I need you."

Before he could say "Okay," she cut the conversation. "Fuck!" he said, downed his drink, slapped a fifty on the table, and then rushed out to hail a cab.

Karen felt fixed into the darkness. She clasped the collar of her slicker jacket close around her neck, then glanced down Flatbush Avenue. One carload of teens out on a midweek joyride had already stopped to look her over. She flipped them off and they drove away. One of the kids in the backseat stuck his arm out the window to return her Brooklyn salute. She backed into the sanctuary of the shadows and waited. Finally, she saw a yellow New York City cab slow its approach to the curb. Its brakes squeaked when it stopped. Saunders' bulk huddled out of it and she went to him.

He tried to embrace her, but she benignly pushed him away. She looked around. "Not here, Stanley."

"No?"

She patted his cheek. "You ever know who might be watching."

"So what?"

"So plenty." She rolled her shoulders in a shiver. "Let's go someplace warm...and dry."

He offered a sinister smile. "That's okay with me."

"I meant that bar over there." She motioned toward a lonely-looking glow of red neon next to a darkened construction site across the street. "It's a lot less grungy inside than it looks on the outside."

Some forty-year-old headbanger hit—a cacophony of clangs, percussion, and meaningless screams—clattered out from a jukebox twice as old. Karen sipped her wine while Saunders stared dubiously at his smudged glass of bourbon. Karen leaned a little closer to him from across their table. She realized it wasn't such a big deal to see him again, after all. Not that she expected anything new. "So how have you been, Stanley?" she said passively. She wanted to get this meeting out of the way and go onto the next thing. She wanted it *all* to be over with.

"Shitty. You sounded desperate over the phone."

"Oh, yeah. I was. I am," she said as if she'd suddenly remembered. "Yeah, really. I've been getting these creepy things dropped off in my apartment. Bits and pieces of ...things. I don't know how they got in, and I don't know why they're doing it. Just that note about them knowing about us."

He decided not to chance drinking from the glass and placed it down on the table. Stared at her. "The note. You have it with you?" She nodded. "Let me see."

She reached into her slicker pocket and fumbled around for the note. Headed it to him. She could see him tense up as he held it. "You've been getting them, too?"

"I recognize the writing. 'We know about you and Saunders. We are watching you. This is Two...Two.'" he read. He handed it back to her with a trembling hand—trembling enough to telegraph his vulnerability. "Did anything come with his?"

"Two toes," she replied as she slipped the note back in her pocket. "So gross. I couldn't sleep all night, so I had to call you. Stanley? Have you gotten the same sort of things?"

"Uh, yeah."

"What does it mean?"

"I don't know. We're being watched for some reason. It's like someone is trying to put the screws to us," he said morosely. "Fucking shit."

She chugged the rest of her beer, shuddered her shoulders, and looked suspiciously around the place. "Now I suddenly got the creeps. Let's get outta here. My place is two blocks down Flatbush. Let's go there. I feel safer there." She slid out from the booth then slipped up her slicker hood. "You pay," she told him, then made her way toward the exit.

––

Saunders drew the collar of his trench coat up over his ears. He glanced around at the muted structures on Flatbush Avenue as they made their way past a construction site. She hated herself for the arm-in-arm way she'd insisted they walk. As if there was still something between them. She pursed her lips in anger and apprehension before her next move.

"I've missed you, Stanley," she said.

"Me, too," he replied through a quiver of his body against the rain.

"Well, it's good to see you again."

She hoped he hadn't noticed how wooden and impersonal her comment had sounded. Probably not. She'd come to know him too well. He had most likely become too intent on getting her into the sack at her apartment, like two desperate souls sharing a need for one another. It was something worth playing into.

"I'm so scared," she muttered. Off to the side she noticed an alleyway between the construction and an abandoned apartment building which looked to have been built back during the Irish immigration times. It could have even been an orphanage, like something out of an old Pat O'Brian movie. She had to squint to spot the black panel truck parked in the far shadows with its engine idling.

"Kiss me, Stanley," she said, while clenching his arm tighter. He drew her into a sloppy embrace and crushed his mouth onto hers. She swiveled him off the street and into the darkness of the alley.

She felt choked, not so much by his rigid kiss, but by the memory of it all. But there was no time to delve into that. She drove her hand into her slicker pocket and clenched the shaft of her dirk. She swiped it out quickly, then jammed it deep into his neck. He held his lips to hers, as she felt them quiver. Then they collapsed to the muddy ground. as he labored for breath. She gazed fire into his widened eyes.

"That's three..." she seethed. She jammed the knife in deeper. "Three." She withdrew the knife. His slowed breathing had diminished to gurgling. She held the knife up. "And this is for Neo-Publica!" She gasped, then drove the blade of the dirk deep into his right eye and into his brain.

Three of Sal's goombahs rushed from the panel truck to drag Saunders' writhing body with the knife still stuck in his eye into the bay of the truck.

Karen flung off her bloodied slicker and threw it in with the body. "I'm done here," she said, then left for the bar to order another wine for herself.

Randy Montefiore rarely made it over to Brooklyn, but there was a place down in the Heights called Guigliano's that he liked. Also, it had been a while since he'd met his older brother, Guaco, for dinner.

Guaco shoveled a forkful of penne and calamari into his ample mouth. "Ma says you never call anymore," he said as he chomped away.

Montefiore sipped his red wine. "Yeah. Always the typical Italian family lament. Of course I do. I called her last week."

"Yeah. Well, she's gettin' old, Randall."

Montefiore swirled a little spaghetti onto his fork. "*We're*, gettin' old, Guaco...so *she's* getting old. Fuckin' cycle of life." He reserved his professional-speak for the office. When with his family, he'd assimilate into their causal way of talk.

"She's forgettin' things, you know?"

"She needs a home—you know; one of those places where they're supposed to take care of people like Ma."

Guaco dug into his fork into his penne and lifted a hearty glop.

"You're never gonna fit all that shit in you, Guaco." Montefiore said. "You shouldn't be eating all them carbs anyway. Your heart."

"Yeah, well, fuck the heart. Long's it's still tickin'." He shoved the food into his mouth.

"Keep that up and it won't be for long."

Guaco was too busy chewing to answer.

"Anyway. About Ma. I found one of those places for her on the Jersey Shore. Nice town. Spring Lake."

His brother chewed the last of the penne, then swallowed with difficulty. "Forget it, Randall," he said, his voice tightened. "You'll never get her outta Carroll Gardens."

"'Least we could take her down there to see it."

"She wouldn't leave them peonies of hers for a day. Her back plot looks like the fuckin' Botanical Gardens. She couldn't do somethin' like that at some old-person's home.

"Fuck, Guaco...she's fuckin' eighty-something!"

"Yeah, well don't tell *her* that."

Montefiore worried over twirling another fork load of spaghetti around in the bowl of a spoon. "So. About the family. How's my favorite second niece doin'?"

"Elise? She's fine."

"She married yet? What's the guy's name? Salvatore?"

"Elise? Married? You've forgotten who she is, Randall. The day she marries anyone is the day hippos fly."

"So, she's keeping herself busy, then, Guaco. I mean, I haven't seen my...associate around the office for a few days, now."

Guaco concentrated pensively on his next move with the penne, then speared a tentacle of calamari. "Yeah. It's been handled."

"How?"

"You don' need to know, Randall." He popped the tentacle into his mouth.

"Okay," Montefiore said. " 'long's its been handled, I'm okay with that. And thanks."

"Don' mention it."

He looked at his brother and pointed to the corner of his lip. "Uh, you've got some...I dunno, sauce or something."

Guardo daubed the speck of tomato sauce on his upper lip. "Thanks, brother. Sometimes I don't know what I'd do without you telling me shit like I got a tomato stain on my mouth. I dunno how I could ever go out in public without you to tell me how."

Montefiore half-grinned at him. "Yeah, I love you, too, asshole."

18

There Will be Storms

Sept 12

Mitch's condition had turned a hard corner three weeks before, and he was now lying catatonic in wait for the more conclusive inevitability. Sylvia had pretended not to let his state get to her. But it had, and it showed in the way she clung so tightly to me. I could only embrace her back, as I'd given up all faith on Tricia's survival, and could only hope that Michael's, Steven's and Emily's captors had gone easy on them. To anyone else but me, they were just kids, and though I couldn't trust their dim-witted guards, I could only continue to hope they would have considered that.

Anyway, sometimes denial works best. I'd been kept too busy with Neo-Publica to become any more shrouded in my deeper concerns. Sylvia knew how I had shielded my lingering apprehension, as I knew how torn up she was about Mitch. Our only recourses had been to keep ourselves in a state of perpetual motion over The Cause.

Working with my new assistant, Marcy, a former Sloane and Johnson art director, we'd come up with quick and dirty campaign. She and I had spent our days and well into the night in our makeshift office at a small printing house down in Manhattan's Lower East Side. Our poster had the look of a 1960's magazine ad. Simple black and white. "Flex Your True Belief.", the headline read, with a graphic of the former American flag superimposed on a background of the U.S. Constitution, with all but "We The People of The United States..." and the flag faded out. The tag line at the bottom read: "Neo-Publica Remembers...WE *Are* the People" in block type to reflect the headline.

Aileen had flown out to and around the west to distribute them, while Piet, now spending most of his time in Boston, had cartons of them shipped to him to distribute for posting out around New England. We'd placed them as ads in Neo-Publica's national underground paper, *The True American,* printed and sent out from London, Ontario, where the Neo-Publica Manifesto would be finally printed in a few weeks. Karen had used her mysterious connections in New York City, New Jersey, Pennsylvania, Denver, and oddly enough, Atlanta, to place the posters. "The less you know, the better," she'd tell us, which gave us a pretty good idea who her connections might have been.

So the word was out, and the results clattered in through the teletype Hugh had set up next to the ham radio clustered away in the walk-in closet off of Sylvia's and my bedroom. He came into the living room to announce: "Well, guys, we're making an impact." We hushed him as the news was breaking over the Kenton/Fox News and Entertainment Network. "What's up?"

"Looks like our PRICE Commissar has turned up missing," I said.

"What do you mean?"

"No one's heard from him in over two weeks," Aileen said. "They think he's been kidnapped."

Karen yawned and went to get herself another coffee.

"Kenton's about to make a public announcement about it," Aileen said.

The newscast broke into another one of those two-minute-long commercials about some blood pressure medication called Sondex.

Most of it was devoted to listing all the caveats about when you shouldn't take it; not the least of which was that if not taken properly, it could kill you.

Then the scene broke to our stern-looking Premier standing behind a lectern festooned with mics—even though they served only one news outlet—but the set-up did look impressive. Hunched next to him like a mediaeval troll, and sporting his usual somber expression, was Randy Montefiore. Television had never been one of Kenton's preferred venues. He was more of a live rally type of person. From those, he could pull his juice from the electricity of his cheering audience. Here, he appeared drawn, distracted, even fearful, as though he was facing a firing squad rather than one of his Kenton/Fox News cameras. His voice slurred as if he'd been drugged.

"My devoted Real-Americans," he began.

"That's not me," Hugh heckled, then flung a grape at the TV screen.

"Wish you wouldn't do that, Hugh," Aileen said. "Now I gotta go clean it after."

"I can't help myself. He is so fucking grape-worthy."

"Shh!" Sylvia scolded.

As Kenton's eyes darted from side to side —yes; he was definitely on something—he continued: "Yesterday I got some horrible news. Stanley Saunders, our wonderful Commissar of PRICE—those great soldiers holding Real-America together as one of the world's best countries—has gone missing. Last night I found out he was abducted—kidnapped."

"We know what 'abducted' means, asshole," Hugh groused.

"Shh!"

"And we know who did this awful thing," Kenton said.

"Was there a ransom note?" Aileen said. "I'd love to know what that said."

Sylvia, transfixed by the image on TV, held up the two fingers of her right hand. "Come on, Allie. Let's watch this."

Karen stood fecklessly behind the kitchen island, concentrating on slowly stirring Half n' Half into her coffee.

"Right," Kenton went on. "We know who kidnapped our terrific PRICE Commissar. We know these awful people to be members of a terrorist organization..." he referred to his notes, "determined to take down all we have done to make Real-America great. They want to bring us back to the past, to a time when the Real-America's people had no say in how to best change our country." He shuffled some papers on his lectern. "I will read the note we got sent to our offices last night..."

"I'm surprised that shithead finally learned how to read," Hugh said.

"See?" Aileen said. "A ransom note. There *had* to be a ransom note."

The Premier slipped on some glasses that no one had seen him wear before. They made him look officious and studious but were nothing more than another one of his props. He began to read: "'Mr. Premier —We have your PRICE agent, Stanley Saunders, in a cell at our headquarters. For now, we are keeping good care of him, but we cannot guarantee this for tomorrow. As an agent for your cause, Mr. Saunders has, like the rest of you, violated—'" here he cringed; another of his brand tidbits, "' the Constitution of the United States; put forth by this nation's founders.' " He flashed a glare at the camera to show his anger to be beyond words. Then he went back to reading. "'We could release Mr. Saunders, Premier Kenton, with your guarantee that *you* will release your control through a free election that allows for the chance of restoring,'"—another cringe, accented by the gritting of his teeth, "'*America* to the Nation she was designed to be two-hundred-and-fifty years ago.' "

"Man!" I mused. "That's fuckin' *brilliant*!"

Sylvia rested her hand upon mine to quiet me.

"Until that time when you reach out to us, we will continue to hold Mr. Saunders, your PRICE Commissar. Beyond that, as we said, we can make no guarantees for his safety or his life.'" He folded up the note and started at the camera—eye to eye. "Signed: The Neo Publicans."

"What the FUCK!" Hugh gushed. "Shit, he didn't even get our *name* right."

"Because we didn't write it," Sylvia said.

"Shit, Bob! That was a great note!" Aileen blurted "Did you write that?"

The Premier went on: "Well, you Neo Publicans, we have a message for you. And you will hear it very soon," he threatened. "Some of you out there may not know who these Neo-Publican people are. They are the ones who, last May, tried and failed to take down the wonderful Real-America's government that I have been chosen—by you, and by God—to establish. This will not stand. *They* will not stand! I have authorized PRICE to double down on finding all and every one of these Neo-Publicans and take them down." He held up the ad that Marcy and I had put together and waved it in front of the camera. "You may not know this, but we see you. It says on this terrible ad now being shown all around. It says right here: 'Neo-Publica Remembers...WE *Are* the People'. To you I say: No, you Neo-Publcans, you are NOT the people. The only real people are the Real-American people, those who, under my guidance, are making this country great, as it was always *meant* to be great. Good night."

"Shut that fucking thing off," Karen grumbled from where she leaned against the island.

"Right, I agree," Sylvia said, and shut off the TV. She turned to the rest of us. "I am not scared by this," she announced.

"I'm not either," Hugh said. "But just in case, maybe we should move our operation to the basement and lay low for a while."

I felt wrapped by a surge of pride. "What are you talking about, Hugh? We couldn't *buy* publicity like this!"

"If I were a weaker woman, I'd be worried about this," Karen said. She approached us, then eased down to sit cross-legged on the floor. "But. Then, I am not a weaker woman."

"Yeah. We know," Sylvia said. "If anything, we're prepared now to go more public. I propose that rally we've been talking about. A big national one."

"Where?" I asked.

"Denver!" Aileen responded quickly. "They've been talking about a Neo Pub rally for months now."

"Yeah, what are we gonna do?" Hugh said." Spring for renting out a fifty-thousand seat stadium? How we gonna do that?"

"They've done it." Aileen said.

"Who's done what?" I asked.

Aileen toasted us with her beer. "The management at Mile-High Stadium. Last time I was out there, I talked to the guy who runs it. He and the city government are supporters—by silent proxy of course. But they're in for a rally."

"When?" Hugh said. "During halftime at a Bronco's game?"

"Why not?" Aileen said. "If they can spin it that way."

"And you didn't tell us this, why, Allie?" Sylvia asked.

Aileen answered with a flicker of a triumphant smile.

"No," I said. "Not after a football game. Too chancy. It would have to be a stand-alone event."

"It would," Sylvia agreed.

"Then you agree, Syl? We should do this?" Aileen said.

"Sure. Why not? This is the kind of message we've been wanting to send out."

"Christ, Sylvia," Hugh said. "You just heard the bastard on TV. He's doubling down on us, and last I heard, they're a lot of cowboys in Colorado. They like Mr. Shithead and they've got the guns to prove it."

"Hugh, honey. I've said this before, and I'll say it's again. You want something bad enough that you believe in, There Will be Storms."

I leaned against the arm of the couch and turned to Karen, who remained staring at the blank television screen. She took a slow, deliberate sip from her coffee mug. "You've been pretty quiet, Karen," I said. "What's on your mind? You up for this?"

"I don't know about a rally, but I do know that Neo-Publica didn't kidnap that son of a bitch. Or write any note."

Hugh lit a cigarette. "Yeah. I think we all know that." Sylvia scissored her index and forefinger together beckoning for a drag. He handed her his cigarette.

"And I know he's not kidnapped. Period. He's just fuckin' ...*gone*." Karen announced with such conviction we waited for her to say more.

"Okay, Karen," Aileen finally said. "And you know this, how?"

She stared down into her mug to avoid answering. "It's almost noon. Time to switch to beer, right?"

"Karen," Aileen pressed. "Do you know something you're not telling us?"

"I don't know. It could be one of those things that, as I say, the less you know, the better."

"Oh, shit, Kar!" Hugh said. "Don't tell me—"

"Okay, then I won't," she interrupted, then turned her gaze back to me, and then to Aileen. "Allie. Did you say you might be going to Colorado again, soon?"

"No. But yeah, I was thinking about it."

She made her way toward the kitchen to switch out her emptied coffee mug for a full bottle of Budweiser. "You mind if I tag along? I need to check with some friends of mine in Boulder to pick something up."

"Sure," Aileen said.

I was surprised she didn't add a comment like, "I could use your company...as a bodyguard." But that would have been too glib. We all shared the belief that, after knowing what Karen was could be capable of, it was best not to mess to question her. Especially at times like these when she was distracted away into some other world.

Sept 18

It had been an intensely packed two weeks since Kenton's TV address. His threats against Neo-Publica's presumed treachery had sent our cause tumbling into its own inertia. The rising rebellion no longer belonged to Sylvia, and by extension, to us alone, but to everyone in it.

Since morning, nothing seemed of any consequence to her, anyway, as she suffered in silence. Mitch had died the day before. She trembled in my arms as she searched for a tranquil answer, and I could provide none. She might have been crying in silence, but that didn't seem to matter. Like me, Sylvia had hollowed herself out of this world to occupy one of her own. Whether it was more from Mitch's passing, or that she hadn't been able to hold him as he departed, I wouldn't know. But she held me tighter, as if I was all that was left for her to grasp onto as we tried to sleep. I listened for the dim hum of the Ham radio; the light crackling of the teletype, and the clacking of the telegraph key from our closet. The sounds would lull me to sleep like the breezes sloughing through the trees I'd remembered from when I was a kid.

But there was none of that reassuring din tonight. Hugh and his equipment had taken a room attached to Pastor Daniel's place near the Universalist Church. He paid the Pastor back by acting as the sexton, tending to the trash, and the little park behind the church. It was safe. PRICE and their BlueShirts tread lightly around churches as if they feared stepping on the toes of God and incurring His wrath. Such a superstitious lot, they were!

News had come across Hugh's equipment that scores of us in the New York area had been arrested and sent off without trial to gulags. The higher up their position in Neo-Publica, the more dire the punishment. The worst offenders had been sent off to Dalaxuma or Unqutuck, both of which were now groaning under the pressure of their enlarging populations.

Plagued by another one of many her nightmares, Sylvia clenched my arm as she wriggled and whimpered in her sleep. I stroked her hair and wondered if what love I'd felt for her had reached its critical mass. It had been convenient enough for me to have convinced myself that Tricia was dead. From the dispatches we'd received about Sheriff Jeff's hair-triggered executions and the treatment and malnutrition of the Dalaxuma inmates, she could not have survived. She just couldn't have.

Sylvia shivered herself awake and cuddled closer to me. "Have we fallen in love?" she whispered dryly, as if having read my mind. It had been an unlikely question from her, and I reasoned it had come more through her need than a conviction.

"Have we?" I responded rhetorically.

She thought it over for a few full seconds. "I don't know."

Now I was convinced that her feelings for me had been those left over from Mitch. "You did love him very much, didn't you, Syl?"

She huffed out a sad laugh. "Probably more than anyone could understand. Especially me." She laid her hand on my chest to feel for my heartbeat—to feel if anything in her life was still alive. "When we were at Unqutuck, we were bound by something deeper than any feeling I could describe. Something more desperate. It was a need from the gut, and we required one another, like food, to survive."

I shifted my position to lie closer into an embrace. "I know what you mean, Syl. I've felt that way. I don't think I can ever fathom the love I feel for my children. It's not the same as for a wife."

"No?"

"It isn't. It's a deeper sort of...connection. You have kids, and your blood flows through them. I loved Trish, of course, but when you have kids, it isn't a matter of loving more. It's a love out of necessity."

"Interesting," she whispered. "I mean, you mention your wife in the past tense: you loved her; but your children in the present."

I took her hand in mine and stroked it; traced the smooth hollow where her fingers had been. "I'm certain Trish is gone."

She sighed deeply. "And your children?"

"They'll never be gone. Not to me."

"Neither will Mitchell be, for me."

"Then we're just nothing more than two empty needs looking for a purpose, you and I."

She nestled closer. "It doesn't have to be that way, does it?"

It was a simple question which, at that moment, I found as perplexing as Einstein's relativity theory. "I don't know what you're—"

"Maybe we should get married, Bob. Hold together what we now have."

He suggestion drove into me like one of Karen's knives. But oddly enough, I felt no pain. It was enough to arouse a chortle. "You mean like to make an honest woman of you?"

Through the light flickering in from the street, I saw her lips bloom into the first smile I'd seen from her in weeks. "If that's what it takes, why not? My mind is just soggy enough to want to go through with this. We can't go on living alone within ourselves like this, at least I can't."

She might as well had told me neither one of us had a choice anymore, and that getting married was the only logical thing left for us to do. The realization made me understand just how lonely I'd become. "Then, well maybe I can't either."

"Okay."

"What do we do next about this, Syl? Talk to Pastor Daniels?"

"I don't know. You're the one who's been married before. You tell me."

I remembered the Holy Catholic ceremony that Tricia and her parents had foisted upon me. It wasn't much of a tonic for an agnostic such as myself, but at least Marty Daniels was a Unitarian. "I'll talk to him," I said.

"Good. That's happened, then." Often, whenever Sylvia became uncomfortable with a personal subject—whenever it filled the moment to the brim—she would abruptly change the topic. "We, uh, heard from Aileen this afternoon."

I shook my head to wend away the subject of a marriage. I realized for now that was what it was: *a* marriage—not yet *our* marriage. "Everything okay?"

"Actually, yeah. Apparently, her friends at that big stadium in Denver really had been working behind the scenes to set up a Neo-

Publica rally. Planning one of their own. Anyway, it's all set up for the end of October—Sunday the twenty-second."

"A month from now? So soon?"

"Now's the best time to act. Your ad campaign has taken hold, and after Kenton gave us such a big endorsement on national TV...so yeah, sure."

"You're ready?

She kissed my cheek. "Now I am"

It was good to see her so re-motivated. I smiled back at her. "It's good to have you back."

She fidgeted her fingers through my hair. "It's good to *be* back," she said, then kissed me again.

19

The Forces of Nature

Sept 22

It would be another month or more before the dry greens of late summer would blaze out into the yellow-golds of autumn. But already the leaves had begun to fall and skitter wind-blown upon the paving stones of the little park behind the church. As I grew bored with waiting for Pastor Daniels to join me, I picked a leaf up and twirled it by its stem between my thumb and index finger. It wasn't like Marty Daniels to be late. I reckoned he must have run unexpectedly into a soul that needed saving. *No.* I rebuked myself, *that wasn't fair.* I vaguely concentrated on the leaf and wondered what might be keeping him.

I held the leaf up to the light for a closer look, and then glanced up at the tree from which it had fallen. I turned my sight back at the leaf. The stem and veins of the leaf seemed a smaller replication of the trunk and branches of its parent. Another one of those little details in God's plan. Well, it might have been if there had actually been a God to have a plan. Maybe it was my being at a church that led me to sink into such thoughts.

Trees and their leaves—parents and their kids. Are children such replications of their parents, like the leaf from the tree? How much of the parent is mirrored in the child? Over one hundred percent? I couldn't help but to think—or hope—that my own kids would have been a more productive version of myself; more loving; more giving; more understanding. If they were even still alive under the lash of abuse from Kenton's prison BlueShirt guards and PRICE agents. I hated myself for thinking that way. I let the leaf flutter back to the ground and watched as it blew away on a breeze like it wanted nothing more to do with me.

"Sorry, Robert," Marty interrupted my inner journey as he sat next to me on the bench. "I allowed myself to be sidetracked."

"Church stuff, Marty?"

A smile flickered across his face. "Isn't it always, though? At least if you have to sit outside and wait, it's a nice day for it."

"Yeah."

I'd rolled up my sleeves, and noticed he was transfixed by the tattoo on my forearm. "'*Death Before Dishonor*,'" he read. "You were a Marine?"

I had to think about my answer, as though I'd forgotten, "Army. Iraq, two thousand three, back in those 'Shock and awe' days." I sequestered a sad smile behind a little sigh. "Guess I've had almost too much of that lately. You never get used to it."

"Shock and awe are just two more of the many building blocks of life, I suppose."

"Yeah," I said to the ground and then looked searchingly at him. "You're not gonna go all churchy on me now, are you, Marty?"

"Sorry, Robert. Occupational hazard. But don't forget, that's why you came to see me, right?" Another breeze sloughed through the trees, and a leaf flittered down to the bench-seat. I picked it up as I had the one before. "You want to marry Sylvia," he stated.

"Yeah, Marty, I do." I said to the leaf.

His silence weighted down my own thoughts. "You're convinced of this, Robert?"

"I am. We need each other. Unless we can have our closures, we're like some sort of unanswered question."

"A rhetorical question?"

I looked from my leaf over to him. "Meaning what?"

"You said you need one another. Have you confused 'need' with the convenience of wanting something for the moment? Confusing the torments of the heart with that little gremlin telling you what's in your head?"

"We do need each other, yeah. Trish is gone, Marty. Probably dead. Sylvia's lost Mitch, a man she loves beyond all else."

"More than she might love you?"

I turned the leaf as I tried to look into it. "It was different between them," I defended. "They held themselves together through something we can never imagine." The drill of his look into me defeated my accusing glare at him, and I relaxed. "Something worse than hell, I imagine."

He scoffed. "I don't hold with all that 'hell' crap."

"Then you can't believe in heaven, Marty," I said back to the leaf. "You're not doing your job." I chuckled nervously. "Shame on you, you hypocrite, " I chided.

"I suppose I've been accused of worse." He rested his elbows on the edge of the bench back and relaxed against it. "Did I ever tell you I used to fly my own little plane?"

"I'm surprised you could afford one a preacher's salary, but no."

"Probably not something on the top of my list to tell my congregation. And, anyway, it was my father's plane...uh, my biological father."

"Right. I wouldn't think the Spiritual One would have much use for a Piper Cub."

Marty chortled. "Well, I would suppose not. Anyway, my father's was a Cessna…and I wasn't very good at flying it."

I leaned against the seat back just as he had. We must have looked like twins. "Then remind me not to fly with you, Marty." I arched my head back and looked up into the leaf-shedding tree above me.

"No problem there, Robert. So, the first time my dad took me up—I must have been about twelve—he brought the plane to three thousand feet and turned the yoke over to me. That was probably frightening enough, but then he told me to pull back to bring the plane into a twenty-degree climb to maybe another thousand feet. I remembered feeling really confident that I could fly for that moment. I had visions of doing loop-de-loops and hammerheads. Then, as the plane was still climbing, he did the unthinkable. He cut the engine."

"That would have scared the shit outta me."

"As it did me. I was sure we were gonna crash, so, as a gut reaction, I pulled back further on the yoke to regain some sort of control. He pulled my sweating hands from the yoke and told me not to touch it—to be patient. Sure enough, without any of my control, the plane arced downward. I remember looking at him. He had a confident smile on his face, almost proud, as I was certain my father had gone crazy and was out to kill us both. Looking out through the windshield, I saw the ground coming closer: four-thousand-two-hundred; three thousand-eight hundred feet. But then, without my helping it, the plane climbed back up little, then down and so on until it leveled off in a gentle and non-threatening downward glide. Finally, my father increased the throttle again for straight and level flight." Marty smiled in remembrance. "I asked him how it happened and he told me: 'lift, weight, thrust, and drag, son. The forces of nature. You have to trust them.' If I'd relied on my instincts and tried to regain control by pulling back on the yoke into more of a climb, the plane would have reached an angle to flip backward. We would have gone into a death spiral and crashed, because I had panicked and pulled back on the yoke too much. That was when I realized that I had to turn death-defying situations over to the forces of nature. To have faith." He looked at me. "Faith, Robert," he said pointedly, then leaned back to look up into the tree dappling its shadows upon us. "Anyway, I think that's when I decided to become a pastor—when I realized there was a power beyond than my own, and I could do *nada* about that. Unless, by trying to take my own full control of things, by losing faith in the forces of nature."

"Faith," I echoed. "Like a faith in God."

"Robert, I'm going to tell you something that I'd never tell another one of my congregants. But a faith in God alone doesn't mean squat."

I leaned forward and relaxed my forearms on my knees. "Maybe then you should reconsider your career decision, Marty, if you believe that."

"You can travel around the world a million times. Go to the moon and back. But the longest and most treacherous journey a person can take is that eighteen-inch one from the fear that lives in here, " he tapped his forehead, "to the faith that lives in here." He placed his hands on his heart. So, Robert—I believe in the heart.

"You cannot have faith in any greater power," he went on, "unless you have faith in yourself. Otherwise, a belief in God has no ground." He glanced at my tattoo. "'*Death Before Dishonor*'. Dishonor to what, Robert? Your country? Well, that may have been what you thought when you branded yourself." He rolled up the sleeve of his denim shirt to show his tattoo. "That's what I thought, too."

He showed me his tattoo of a Marine insignia, above an American flag. I read the inscription. "'*Semper-Fi*'—you were a Marine?"

He rolled his sleeve back down. "Two tours in Afghanistan—two-thousand-nine and ten. The Marines did their best to teach me to, well…do my job, but after the second time I killed, I no longer had the heart to do what I had been trained to."

"You killed two Afghans? Maybe they were Taliban—bad guys."

"I killed two human beings, Robert. It may be on my record, but it's not on my resume, for sure." He tapped his temple. "But it's in here. And if I let what's in here control me, I will crash just as soon as if I'd tried to control that little Cessna."

His point melted in to render me speechless. I picked up the fallen leaf again.

"So, my friend. I ask you again: 'Death before Dishonor' of what? Certainly not Kenton's Real-America, we Neo-Publicas know that. Dishonor to The Cause we believe in? No. To yourself? I don't think so, that would never last. Who, then? You tell me."

My reluctance to say it scoured my tongue like hot pepper, as I stared deeper into the leaf. Trying to count its veins. "To God." I told him, pissed of that he'd gotten to me enough even to answer him.

"Believe it or not, no, Robert. Not even God. Faith—you must honor *faith*."

"In myself?"

"And everything. Including making the right choice in marrying Sylvia. The right choice for both of you. Marriage is no antidote for vulnerability or even loneliness. Okay?"

"Yeah. I hear you. But we need each other."

"Well, then, enough said…for now." His voice tightened. "Listen, friend. You came here to see me, but I was gonna call you this morning, anyway."

"Yeah? Why? To talk about faith?"

"You read my mind, Robert."

"Well, you've spent the last few minutes setting up the subject."

He conjured up a childish smirk. "Touché. Well, anyway. Can I show you an example? Of the power of faith?"

"I get it, Marty," I answered sourly. "You've made your point."

He put his hand on my knee. "Oh, I think you'll like this one, Robert." He looked over toward the opened door to his vestry. "You can come out now, Karen!" he said.

What? I jolted. *He's bringing* Karen *it on this? What the hell?* I jolted again as I rushed to stand. She cautiously approached with a smirk on her face, a tremble in her lip, and a glisten in her eyes, which was far removed from the Karen I'd come to know, and at times fear. But that wasn't the true feature of what I saw. The true feature was the roughened-up, cropped-blonde-haired teenager clinging to her arm as she might have to Tricia's ten years before. "

I gasped, as I felt a rush of tears to my eyes.

"Hi, dad?" She replied raggedy, as though she'd had trouble finding those two most wonderful words I'd ever heard in my life. My joy was tempered by a wave of seething anger when I noticed a brutal scar on my daughter's cheek, and her stare into nothingness—the gaze of the blind. But she wasn't blind. She tried to smile but couldn't. She reached up with trembling fingers to touch my cheek. "Dad?" This time her tone was more decisive. I knew better than to frighten her with the hug I yearned so deeply to give. Instead, she fell into me with her own embrace, tenuous, but grasping. She felt so weightless in my arms. I could feel every blade of bone in her scrawny frame.

"I *told* you I had to stop off in boulder to pick something up," Karen said, her voice trembling as she tried to hold back her own emotions.

I held Emily's head close to my shoulder, never, ever, to let go of her again, as I could no longer restrain my tears. Her newly softened hair smelled of Ivory Soap. I unclenched the leaf in my hand. It fluttered to the ground to be picked up by a breeze to join the other one I'd dropped moments and a decade before, when I had felt little hope except the tenuous one I shared with Sylvia.

"You see, Robert?" Marty told me. "Faith."

Emily huddled close to Karen as we made the three-block the trek from the church to our apartment. Stepping rigidly and cautiously—automaton-like—Emily moved as if she'd been sacked by a linebacker. It would have been ignorant of me to wonder what had happened to the daughter I once knew. The ragged, thick, red scar running in an arc from the edge of her right eye to the corner of her mouth told me everything. If I hadn't learned to detest PRICE enough already, I hated them now enough to kill.

Upon her arrival home from Denver earlier that day, Aileen had prepared Sylvia for my daughter. As for the rest, Karen had engineered Emily's release, and taken her usual 'The less you know, the better' attitude. After seeing the effects of the gulag upon this child, Sylvia started to weep as she remembered her time at Unqutuck. Emily cringed in Sylvia's fragile embrace. She was not only my daughter to her, but—more so—an innocent, eighteen-year-old girl ravaged by forces authorized by Kenton's Regime. Sylvia gently ushered her to the couch then tucked some blankets tight around her. She brought her some warm tea and a lightly buttered slice of wheat-bread toast. She mothered her. Stroked her hair. Whispered some underweight banters of confidence. She tried to do what she could to reassure her. She kissed her lightly on the crown of her head, and then turned to look at me. A few tears ran down her cheeks, and she daubed them away. There was nothing for her to say, but her look told me: *Those fucking bastards!* She knew it all from her nightmares.

Even rest had been taxing for my daughter, as she lay tucked away on the living room couch. Instead of thrashing around or even whimpering as a girl her age might, she lay rigid, eyes open, arms stiff at her sides. Her scant recognition of me had passed, and though those few words: "Hi, Dad." had been so welcome to me, I'd started to wonder if they hadn't been rehearsed. Her second recognition of me: "Dad!" and her hug—they seemed real. After that, she spoke no more. Words had become another source of her pain.

Karen sat on the edge of the couch. Emily reached weakly to touch the khaki sleeve of her savior, while keeping her eyes trained on the ceiling. As though having finally come across someone stronger than she, Karen, with a show tender respect, lovingly stroked her hair.

"Maybe its time you and Allie should take Bob to Slade's Place, now, Syl," she whispered, then kissed my daughter on the forehead. "I'll see Emily to sleep. It'll be fine." This was an entirely new Karen from the street-smart, no-nonsense broad—her words not mine—we'd come to know her to be.

"Sure, Kar," Sylvia said. "You think your guy'll be waiting for us?"

"Far's I know. He'll be in the safe room in the back, across the hall from the restrooms. He'll know you." She caressed Emily's hair again.

"Who's the guy?" I wondered.

A gentle smile graced Karen's face as she looked from Emily at me. "His name's Tom Roebling. Other than that, for now at least, the less you know—"

"Yeah...the better. I get it."

It was a wide enough couch for Karen to halfway lie on it next to my frail daughter. "And, hon, definitely don't worry about Emily tonight. Nothing's gonna harm to her, long's I'm around." She beamed another little smile at her. I noticed her lips quiver as if she might cry. She stroked Emily's cheek. "She's my angel." I recalled what Marty had told me about the forces of nature. It didn't take much more than that scene to convince me that, for that night, Karen maybe needed Emily as much as Emily needed her.

20

Slade's Place

Sept 24

Slade's Place was marked by a subtle neon glow on the corner of Hicks and Montague Streets in Brooklyn Heights. Streetlight slanted through the window into the penumbra of darkness tracing the forms of people pensively relaxing over their food and drink. The place had the look and feel of a millennial yuppie fern bar. The waiters in their waistcoats and fezzes seemed picked out of central casting for Rick's American Cafe in *Casablanca* They would have not been so shocked—shocked! — to find out if there were gambling going in the back rooms.

Slade's Place was also the kind of establishment that was above the pay grade of most BlueShirts, though there could have been some under-cover PRICE agents there. I was of such a "fuck-it" kind of attitude, anyway, that if a PRICE goon came up to me, I'd have run him through with a Slade's Place steak knife. Sylvia must have sensed my anxiety though the tension of my silence. "Calm down, honey," she soothed as she took my arm. "You're still kind of new to all this, and like we would say: *your slip is showing*. I promise we *will* do something."

Aileen led us into the plush, oak and leather safe room. It smelled of cultured leather, brandy, and cigars. A husky blond man in a business suit—strictly Ivy League—rose from his chair behind a rich-looking desk. The desk chair was like something he'd picked up from the gilded age a hundred and fifty years before. He acted like he owned the place, which he did. He smiled amicably and extended a beefy hand to me. "You must be Bob Bryant. I'm Tom Roebling."

"Okay," I said cautiously as I shook his hand. His grasp was dry and tight.

"He works with Karen. Sort of," Aileen told me as she closed the door.

I stole another look at him. "Of course he does."

"And you're Silvia Morales? I've heard a lot about you." She looked nervously at Aileen who shrugged her shoulders, then back at this Roebling fellow. "S'okay," he assured her. "This is my cafe, and it isn't bugged, or tagged." He looked around at all of us. "You're safe in every square inch of Slade's Place." Sylvia smiled a nervous acknowledgment. "And, Aileen, of course I know you." He looked the two of us over, and then motioned for us to sink down into the office couch and easy chair. "Aileen and I had a nice chat during our four-hour flight back from Denver."

"Okay, Tom," Sylvia said as she eased down next to me on the couch. She looked with no little apprehension at Aileen. "So. You know who *we* are. Who are *you*?"

He looked at Aileen. "You haven't told them anything about all this?"

"There hasn't been a hell of a lot of time, Tom. And we've been a little busy."

He relaxed forward, and then lit a cigar. "Fair question, then. And don't be too shocked by my answer, but I'm a believer in getting to the point." He took a languorous draw on his cigar. He leveled a glance at me. "Oh. My manners, sorry. You want one of these?"

"I don't smoke," I passed.

"I'll take one," Sylvia said.

"No shit? Really?"

"Really, Tom. No shit," she answered him.

He took one from his humidor, handed it to her, and then pushed his heavy desk lighter forward. "Anyway, I do like to get to the point. I'm one of Premier Kenton's chief security men."

"What the *fuck*!" I gasped, thinking Karen had made us.

Sylvia held the cigar in halfway to her lips and glared at Aileen who stared dumb founded ahead. "God dammit, Allie! What have you done?"

"Now, calm down, just calm down," Tom said. "I'm with you guys, okay?"

"How? How do I know you're not with PRICE?" Sylvia challenged.

He let a poignant silence weigh down the moment, and then looked at me again. "Well, for one thing, I arranged for the release of your daughter."

"How? How and why the fuck would some Kentonite do that?" Sylvia challenged.

"Okay. Let's get this straight. I am not a Kentonite, as you say. I am an American—a constitutionalist through and through—and former CIA, so I know the score. That guy in his tower just happens to pay my check, and like you, I'm fed up with the son of a bitch. As to the how..." another pause as he stared me down, not in a challenge, but oddly reassuringly. "The how, Bob?" He sighed. "I bought her."

Now it was our turn to cast out a silence. "You *what*?" I seethed.

Aileen leaned forward and placed her hand on my knee. "Hear him out, Bob. It sounds horrible, but it isn't. "

"How could it be worse?" I said.

"It could have been," Tom said. "Much, believe me."

"I don't think I can trust you enough to believe anything you tell me, *agent* Roebling," Sylvia said.

"I'm not a Kenton regime agent," he insisted. "I'm Neo-Pub. Have been practically since you first helped start it, Sylvia, so don't go bullshitting me around with your legendary self-righteous platitudes, okay? I get it. Now, is that clear enough?"

Sylvia pursed her lips as she tried hiding her anger.

"Okay. I and some others are ready to mobilize the Cause."

"Others?" Sylva said. "Other Kenton guards, you mean."

"Right. Other former CIA. I've worked closely with them since I graduated Yale in oh-nine. The first thing we learned was to trust one another with our lives. So, yeah, there are three of us. May not sound like enough, but with us three you've got a hole to the inside. A big, silent, hole."

"So, Tom," I said. "Now you want me to buy my daughter back from you? Is that it?"

"No, Bob. You've paid plenty enough, already. And forget all that about me buying her, it's just kind of a matter of expression."

"It's a pretty wicked one."

"I'll tell you about it later." He took another draw from his cigar and slowly exhaled as he leaned back in his chair. "But now, let me tell you about how these gulags handle their young women inmates."

I definitely did not want to hear that. "It's okay, Tom. I have my daughter back, that's enough for now."

Aileen took my hand and squeezed it. "No Bob, there's more you need to know, because it won't all be fine by the time you wake up tomorrow. Really. So, hon, you need to hear Tom out. As much as it might hurt you to listen to it, it's for Emily's own good. And yours. She's been through so much, and you need to know this to help her."

Sylvia squeezed my other hand and smiled the kind of smile meant to defend against tears. "Allie and Karen told me some things you have to know, Bob. You can only imagine how damaged she must be. Our life together just turned around today, and this can only help us all to mend."

At least Sylvia hadn't reminded about the gulag hell she went through, but she didn't exactly keep it to herself, either. I had seen it through the way she would toss in her sleep and wake up sweating from yet another nightmare. I let that sink in for a moment—long enough to realize how hellish it all might have been in the mind of a seventeen-year-old girl who'd been in a gulag for over two years. I reluctantly reasoned it was more than only fair for me to know. I squeezed their hands. They didn't let go. "Okay," I said.

"You should be proud, Bob," Tom said. "You've got one tough kid, there. She's been through more than any of us can imagine, so here's what I know..." He told us about how when a young girl, especially a pretty teenager, is sent to a gulag, she is examined, then—depending on how pretty and unviolated she is—sent to a higher-up PRICE official in the camp. Virgins, of course, were considered premium."

I remembered how the nurse, and then that fucking PRICE Lieutenant, took Emily into that office when he had chosen her. The look of panic and fear on my then fifteen-year-old daughter's face when she escaped that office continued to carry my nightmares over into cold sweats.

Tom Roebling went on about how once the higher PRICE official was done with her, the girl might be sent down the line. If there was a bright side to this, the teen, now probably eighty-percent broken, was never sent out to work the fields, mines, whatever. Nothing to scar her body, which was the only thing keeping her alive. One of three things might have happened: the girl would have developed a sort of mind-out-of-body Stockholm Syndrome. In that case, she might have been toughened into expecting her sexual treatment, as might a whore. The lower guards liked this, and could be as rough as they wanted with them. Or, most likely, the girl would have committed suicide. Suicide rates among teens at gulags hovered around seventy-percent. Here, Tom broke for a minute as my imagination sizzled again over how my Emily might have been treated. By now, in a real world, she would have been a high-school senior coming home from cheerleading practice; dating the first—and of course, only—love of her life; going to the prom; experimenting with liquor, God forbid, no drugs; and choosing what college to go to. She may or may not have remained a virgin, but Tricia and I would have been the last to know. That might have been in the real world—a long-ago place, and Real-America was far from the real world.

"I could use a drink," Tom announced. "Anyone else?"

Of course we all could, and he placed an inter-club call to the bartender. The drinks were delivered within ten minutes, and Tom lit up his second cigar. Sylvia, her face ashen, glanced sourly at the end of hers and tamped it out.

"Working as I did in Kenton's upper echelon security, I could gain access to certain inmate records. Karen told me last July about your situation and had me look it up. In Emily's case..." he sketched out how she was first sent to Qatapica, in south Texas. She hadn't been passed too far down the chain of command until six months later, when she was, uh..." —he stopped short of saying "sold"— "transferred to Arapaho in Montana. She was there for about a year and was worn down fully by the time she was sent to Montehaute in Southern Colorado, from where she finally had been rescued a week before. Tom let out another sigh as he looked toward me, then leaned forward. "As you can imagine, Bob, Emily was nearly broken by then...useless to even the BlueShirts. When the girls reach that point, they usually put them up for auction."

"Auction," I said in a croak.

"Uh, yeah. To the highest bidder, be shanghaied to places like Saudi Arabia, China, or Iran. The ones who retained some balance of beauty, usually those who'd developed those whorish attitudes, would be sent to the Soviets, as Kenton's 'gifts' to his good friend Premier Vladovkov to do with as he pleases."

I remained numbed as I looked toward Sylvia, who had pursed her lips against crying. She abruptly turned to me, buried her head into the crook of my shoulder, and burst into tears. "Those FUCKING sons of bitches!" she sobbed. "Oh, God, Bob! I'm sorry. So sorry."

All I could do was woodenly embrace her back.

"About a two weeks ago, Karen found out through her —lets call them what they are: mafia connections—that there was going to be an auction at Montehaute, where I knew your daughter been sent. Through no less nefarious channels than Karen's—that would be Kenton's—I found out that Emily was up for being auctioned. I flew out there immediately on the excuse of going to a security convention in Boulder. Karen met me there and we had a Neo-Pub bush pilot out of Tucson fly us south to Salida, where I went to Montehaute for the auction. Then, as I told you, I made the highest offer in a bidding war between some Saudi and myself. I did what I could, and bid high. I got Emily out of there and we flew back here. All the way home, she clung to Karen. I knew she was in good hands. Protected."

"How did you know who to find in the first place?" I asked.

"The gulag's admin keeps lousy records," he said. "But the inmates they keep for sale are a commodity, so Emily had been on file since she got to Qatapica two years ago. She's been easy to track by following the money."

Now I found it hard to choke back my own tears. "Thank you, Tom, thank you. I take back all that stuff I said earlier."

"No problem."

I felt Sylvia's quick stir. "Bush pilot? Out of Tucson?" she said. "Do you remember his name?"

"Oh, yeah. It was a guy named Denton...Devon."

"Jackson?" Sylvia said. Her voice was shaking as though she'd heard a ghost. "Devon Jackson?"

"Yeah, that was it. A black guy. Hell of a pilot."

Sylvia let out an opened-mouth sigh. "That, he is."

Her reaction had been abrupt enough to even draw me from my funk. "You know this pilot, Syl?" I said.

She smiled broadly. "Good old Devon Jackson!"

"Who the hell is he?" I pressed.

"He flew me out of Unqutuck." She let out a little laugh. "Then he taught me how to fly."

"Well, he got you all back to Denver to meet me, sure enough," Aileen quipped. "Just in time. We damn near missed our flight back home."

Tom let another silence soak in as he took a slow puff off his cigar. "You, uh...any more questions for me? Like about my loyalty to the Neo-Publica? Any more doubts?"

It took a moment for me to remember my next obvious question. "You found out about Emily, Tom. Did you find out anything about my wife, Tricia, and my other two kids, Steven and Michael? Uh, Steven's on the mental disability spectrum, he's a special case." Sylvia softened her hold on me on my mention of Tricia.

"I have a pretty good idea where he might be, Bob, at least I know where they put defective kids. The regime calls it a 'storage facility,' like some sorta warehouse. I've got to tell you. On that one, there might not be much hope. As far as all of it, though, I'll try to look into it."

"Would you?"

"Sure. Have you got anything I can go on? A photo, maybe?"

"Yeah," I said, then rummaged through my wallet for the snapshot I'd carried around. I hadn't looked at the photo of Tricia and the kids since around February—too painful. I fished out the ceased, folded photo I'd taken of my family back in 2024, when we were in St. Martin, and handed it to him.

He glanced at it. "Okay, I'll try, Bob."

"Thanks," I said.

"Oh, yeah, another thing," Tom said. "Emily does not know her name is Emily anymore. What I bought was a number. What they do is, they change the girls' names each time they're sent to another gulag, until they become just a number, with no other identity. By then, they don't remember who they were. So don't be surprised if she doesn't respond to her name."

"What can we do about all this, Tom?" Aileen asked. "How can we bring these people down?"

"We'll talk about that later, Allie," Sylvia hushed, and then sniffled away the last of her tears as she held closer on to me again.

"Listen," Tom said with a new type of gravitas. "I know about that rally you've been planning in Denver. Maybe not the best idea, but a necessary one for a show of force. But I gotta tell you. The Kenton shitheads know about it, too. And there will be a big PRICE contingent there, most of them in plain clothes, to look for you all. So, watch your backs. I've already purposed myself as the Kenton's head of security there. I made sure of that. Neo-Publica can't survive on rhetoric alone, anymore. It needs outside muscle from the inside, if you get my drift. I can do that for you."

"Yeah, Tom," Sylvia said. "Absolutely."

"Good. I'll take care of us. Maybe come up with some sort of excuse to keep my BlueShirts out of the rally arena at Mile High. Can't account for the PRICE assholes, though. They circulate on their own, or under Chancellor Randy Montefiore's bidding, now that Stan Saunders has been disappeared. But I might be able to spot them out."

"Thanks, Tom," Aileen said. "Is that what you think? That Saunders has been 'disappeared'?"

"I know so, on the best authority. Kenton couldn't have asked for a better means as an excuse to go after Neo-Publica. Anyway, " he said toward Aileen, "don't thank me, Allie. Thank Karen. You've got yourselves a true trooper, there."

"We know." Sylva said. She took another one of his cigars. "For the road."

He smiled. "Why not? Oh yeah, and as if your brains haven't been addled enough, there are a couple of more things."

"Okay," I said.

"Well, first. Consider this place absolutely safe if you want to meet here. I'll have Fred, my bartender, make you up a key to this office, because I'm not here all the time, as you can well imagine. And with Kenton cracking down on us, and all. Well, you know."

"Jesus, thanks, Tom," Sylvia said.

"Just doing my duty...as an American. And Bob—one more thing for you to know. *I* didn't buy Emily's freedom. I have a big expense account in the organization, so money was no object. I can write it off to a couple of RPG's or some such I bought at the so-called convention I went to. So, I leave you with this irony." His mouth bloomed into another smile. "It was Kenton organization money that freed your daughter."

He waved us to stand. "Okay. It's getting late you all, and I'm sure, Bob, you want to be with Emily. Just handle her carefully, but like I said in the beginning, you should be proud. You have one tough kid, there.

"I'll leave whatever messages I have with Fred at the bar, and you can reach me through him. He's one of us, too. I'll keep you posted. And, oh yeah, your drinks are on the house, but any dinners are on you. I gotta make *some* sorta profit, here. I recommend the lamb.

"Now get outta here. All this makes me want to go home and hug my own daughter."

21

El Diablo del Desierto

Sept 28

The knot of fluff on Tricia's blanket was the only solace in her world now, which was anywhere else but within the cloud of this stench. The relentlessly hot New Mexican sun-bake had not made things any easier, and that little tuft on the blanket had come to mean everything to her. Within it churned a deep network of fibers, molecules, atoms, electrons—the hum of life. Tricia's spiritual mentor, Jesus—not the biblical one, but "hey-Zeus" from Guanajuato—had taught her well about how to take herself away into a grain of sand.

Soon, yet slowly, the surrounding banter brought her back into the unwashed world of Dalaxuma. Though she couldn't completely understand the mixed dialects of Spanish encircling her in fits and starts, she knew what the women attending to the rips and holes in their blankets were prattling on about. The previous day, another BlueShirt guard had vanished in the desert, yet the group of inmates who had been under his charge returned in full to the camp. That had made four guards this week, maybe sixteen in all since the undetected lightweight resistance campaign had begun a month before. The rumor was that the PRICE officials who'd managed the camp would be doubling up on the BlueShirts overseeing the work-gangs.

Tricia looked around for guards and saw none. She drew back her blanket and lifted a large Yucca banana and one of the chivs Number 47 had made for her. The others around their blankets warily followed her lead, lifting up their own Yucca bananas and chivs.

Number 47 had told her that the skin and meat of a fully ripened Yucca banana closely replicated that of the human neck. "*Reloj*—watch." She said as she held up the Yucca fruit and the chiv by its looped, taped handle. They all followed along as she demonstrated. "*Cuello*—neck," she pointed to her own neck. "*Sostener*—hold," she held her neck in a demonstrative choke-hold from behind, then dropped her lightened grasp to position the chiv's point on the right side of the banana.

"*Halal*—pull," she drew the sharpened point of the chiv laterally across the fruit, and then pointed it down against its left side. She quickly jabbed its point down in. "*Jab EURO*—jab HARD." She conveyed a suffused, muted smile. "*Bueno!*" She rested the point back against the right side of the marred fruit. She looked around for any more guards, then turned to Consuela, one of the newcomers from Tijuana. "Translate, please...Consuela: Always...from behind. Never from the...front." Consuela translated.

Tricia's pidgin Spanish had come more easily for her than her native English, even though she'd become better at stringing her words together. "You...can not let the...the guard see you coming...at...at him. Sneak up behind and wrap your arm around...around his chest." She demonstrated by holding her arm up and across her chest, while glancing off to her side, as might the guard. "Try to turn...away to not to let him see... see you...or else he will kill you first." She crooked her arm around her face and neck. "Then hold tight...like this. *Sostener.* Then: *Halal...Jab...EURO!* With your chiv-knife. And...quickly. Hold your...chiv-knife in deep, until he... he falls."

Consuelo finished translating, and then added: "*Siempre zemore desde atras. Nunc desde el frente.*" Always from behind. Never from the front.

"*Siempre zemore desde atras. Nunc desde el frente.*" The six women said in roughened unison. "*Cuello. Sostener. Halal. Jab EURO! ...Siempre zemore desde atras. Nunc desde el frente.*"

Ahora de nuevo— Now. Again."

"*Cuello. Sostener. Halal. Jab EURO!*" The women recited along with the actions.

"*Bueno. Ahora de nuevo...*"

One of them had a question. "*Y si no Murder?*...uh, what if he does not die?

"Then, stab your...your knife deep into his...his eye; into his...his brain. And hold it there until...until he dies."

Consuela translated as she pointed to her eye.

A round of *Ah, si!* 's filtered around the blankets, accompanied by some shallow nods of understanding.

Tricia conjured up a tiny feline smile over the progress her class of six women had made over the last week. "*Ahora de nuevo...Cuello. Sostener. Halal. Jab EURO!*" they recited one again.

Tricia's quiet satisfaction was promptly interrupted by an anguished "*Cinco cero!*" She glanced over her shoulder and spied a BlueShirt meandering distractedly toward them. "*Bien. Vamos a poner esto de nuevo, por ahora.*" Then as a reminder to herself: "Let's put these...away for now." But they had already hidden their chivs and scarred-up Yucca bananas under their blankets as they went back to their pretend mending.

October 4

There had been four more BlueShirt guard disappearances. But this time one of the victims had been a lower PRICE officer who'd happened upon a work gang taking down one of their guards. He, too, was dispatched, or so the inmates thought. The officer had had just enough strength to crawl from the lightly covered pit his body had been thrown into four hours earlier. A morning patrol of BlueShirts, being driven around by a PRICE Under-Lieutenant, discovered his body in the desert. The patrol followed its track to the corpse-filled pit of BlueShirt guards. They had found *El Diablo del Desierto*'s —The Desert Devil's—burying ground.

Bells and gongs clanged and sirens wailed throughout the camp, and the BlueShirts brutally assembled the prisoners. Four of them were executed, along with the directive that four more would be chosen and shot each day until the BlueShirt murderers showed themselves.

There were seven one-hundred-prisoner barracks tents with two rows of low-slung canvas bunks lining the opened, long walls within each one of them. Each of the barracks housed a range of personalities, resulting in squabbles and fights within. Though the occupants of each of these loosely held tribes silently and tacitly agreed with the idea of a rebellion, there was a muddle of understanding on principle. They cared nothing about the U.S. Constitution like the Neo-Publica organizers had. They just wanted out to vanish into the Real-American population. Maybe find a job to support the families from which they'd been separated and had little hope of finding. Or maybe they would drop their past to start a whole new family—the flesh of hope.

The prisoners had clustered over their dice game in a different barracks tent every other night. By now they were over sixty strong—enough to gather around an important game of craps, but also enough to arouse suspicions among the guards. Some of the guards even insisted on joining in the game, substituting the pebbles of inmate currency with cash and high interest payback rates. Their joining in would shut down any further conversations about whatever rebellion the inmates had planned. Tonight, they were free to talk.

"They execute four of our men every day to their one," Max said to Number 47 as he fashioned another chiv from a metal rake-tine.

"And there are about fifty of us to every one of theirs," Number 47 responded and then pulled the spiraled coil like an accordion out to a sharp tip.

"That's my point. We need to move ahead."

"I don't think we're ready," Sardo said from where he hunkered down in the fringes, blithely watching the dice game.

"No, Sardo," Max said. "We are. With every four they kill, they're getting closer to us. It's a fucking miracle no one has talked, yet. We have to act—and soon."

Sardo picked at an insect creature-of-the-night crawling on his pant leg. "You can get whipped 'til your bones show as you rake the desert for no reason, or you can get shot and die quick to cash in your ticket to paradise. To a lot of these people, it's a pretty cut and dried decision. They're not gonna betray us. They feel there's no real hope for them. Besides they're too weak to fight."

"You can't know that, Sardo. But say you're right? What if you're the next one about to be shot? You wouldn't fight back?"

"I might, because I don't believe there's any sort of paradise. I guess you'd say that gives me a reason to live."

"And to hope?" Number 47 asked.

Sardo found a wan smile from within his depression. "I don't believe in hope, either. Not today, at least."

"Then I feel sorry for you, Sardo," Max said. "Maybe if we got our plan off the ground and mobilized, you'd find something to hope in. And yeah, we're ready. I think we need to do this. The night after tomorrow." He looked around at the eight other Neo Publicas doused in the shadows of twilight. Tricia stood off with some other women—her students—milling around to watch the dice game. She nodded solemnly at Max, as though granting her approval. "Then," Max said. "I put it to you. Do we go ahead in two nights? Let's say at ten, right after the watch has changed?"

Seven of them grumbled their acknowledgments. Sardo, the holdout, shook his head, and then stared vacantly at the dice on the blanket.

Max looked out through the rolled-up tent walls. "Then," he said reservedly out to the dots of mesquite fires punctuating the falling desert darkness. "Let's get the word out tomorrow, then light up the night after that."

22

The Dalaxuma Rebellion

October 7

Frenzied shouts filled the air. Flames licked up the night sky. The gulag grounds smelled like an omnipresent barbecue, but whether it was the odor of burning flesh or the sweet fragrance of mesquite was hard to tell—most likely it was both. Separate flares from countless torches fed the fires billowing up from the guard and PRICE barracks. A few BlueShirts with their uniforms aflame ran blindly amuck throughout the melee. Others, both BlueShirts and PRICE officers, cowered beneath flays and swings of the inmates' makeshift knives, machetes and chivs. Several of them already lay dead. A number of trustees, organizing inmates, and with those who'd rolled high enough in dice to carry arms taken from the killed BlusShirt guards, fired their weapons into the air and at anyone who looked like a guard.

Dumbfounded over the sudden burst of a riot, the guards had taken several minutes to grasp what had happened. Then they fired back at ranges so close they may have taken out a rioter with one of their own. Finally, they stepped away enough to get their bearings, and fired into the torch-wielding clusters of rampagers. The whooping of sirens accented the commotion, as camp police and patrol vehicles inched their ways through. Some of the guards outside the mass hurled tear gas. Rings of other guards and PRICE operatives soon roughly contained the rioters.

Sardo, smothered in sweat and fumes, looked from the corner of his eye and saw Sheriff Jeff's grandson speeding away in his Porsche, as if not to soil its fire engine red finish. Then he felt a bolt to his back and fell gasping for breath. He was beaten until he died.

The guards closed in, and more rioters crumpled to the ground. Two stubby eight-wheeled tanker trucks mounted with a platform on which stood a guard poised with a thick water hose, nosed through the mass of people like two sluggish rhinos. Several mounted price guards wheeled and reared their horses menacingly within the closing clutch of rioters. Max managed to crawl on fours through the crowd, and beneath the clouds of gas and curtains of sprayed water until he'd found a small, vacant tent.

Catching his breath, he had some latent visions of the Neo-Publica demonstration in Manhattan three months back, as he leaned against one of the tent's stanchions. Dimly protected by shadow, he was able to glance through the open tent flap. There he saw Tricia jam a chiv into a BlueShirt's neck. Another snuck up on her with his piece drawn. Max stepped quickly into the light and fired his purloined weapon, taking down her would-be attacker. He reached out long and grabbed her by the arm to pull her into his his shadowy sanctuary. She seemed no longer the distracted, shy Tricia he'd come to know. There was a fire in her wide-eyed gaze. As if not thinking, she drew him into a hard kiss on the lips. "Thank you, Max!" she breathed, broke from his grasp, then hugged him again. "I...can't," she sighed into his shoulder. "I just need...to get away...even just until...morning."

He held her head close to his breast. He felt the same as she. No words were necessary—only the feeling they shared.

"To get away, but not...alone," she said.

"Shhh, Tricia...shhhh," he soothed, and then drew her further into the shadows, toward a cot. No. They would not lie in it. Max turned the cot on its side to serve as a barricade to hide them away. The chaos roiling around outside their tent disappeared somewhere else as they embraced, wrapping one another into a cold comfort, until morning.

In the end, the great riot of Dalaxuma had lasted less than twenty minutes. When the smoke cleared, forty inmates lay dead. And nine BlueShirts, along with one PRICE Lieutenant with a chiv lodged into his clavicle and hollow sockets where his eyes had been.

October 10

The asphalt surface of the tennis courts had been stained indelibly brown by the blood shed from the soccer massacre. The reminder served its purpose as a threat, and a harbinger of what was to follow this afternoon. Tricia felt her entire body clench under the grip of terror. A mere sensation of fear would have been too much of a luxury. And terror was all that was left beyond the desire to die.

The BlueShirt guards had clumped the swollen population of inmates into a tight mass. She squinted through the glare of the relentless desert sun, and she shielded her eyes with the visor she had made of her hand. She furtively arced her hand down to hide the view before her. A passing BlueShirt slapped the hand away. "No. Must watch!" he grumbled menacingly. Everyone had to watch the example soon to be shown as an experience in terror.

The guards had spent the night hammering away as they erected mediaeval gallows on the bloodstained tennis court. Two thick beams on each end supported another long eight-inch-thick beam eight feet above a platform upon which ten stools had been placed. On these stood nine captives from the riot three nights before. Their bodies had been trussed up with thick twine like a turkey readied for the oven. Hang nooses had been looped around their necks. Some of the indigenous captives stared pleadingly up into the blank sky like Saint Sebastian stuck with arrows as they awaited a final absolution. But arrows would be too kind a fate awaiting those nine deplorables who had rebelled against the immense ego of Sheriff Jeff, and by extension to the entire Kenton ideal for Real-America.

Tricia recognized two of the captives as Neo-Publicas who had come in with Max three months before. There was one woman at the end. It was Consuela. She wore a white surgeon's mask, stained deep with a thick line of blood where her mouth would have been. Next to her; an empty space with stool below and a noose above. An empty place for…whom? At each end of the platform stood two BlueShirt executioners—one wielding a machete, and the other an axe and sword. They wore black hoods—an intriguing, theatrical, touch from the mind of Sheriff Jeff.

Another platform rose above the gallows. Here stood the tribunal of Sheriff Jeff, his grandson, Zach, and eight PRICE officials. They lounged in plush, comfortable chairs as they sipped their beers, bourbons, and tequilas, while joking and laughing among one another as though preparing to watch some sort of yacht race. They had won another one, and this was more like a celebration.

Tricia tried easing herself deep into the lingering memory of Max's tender embrace—what it had felt like to be loved in the comfort of nothing but silence. It was a new feeling for her, but perhaps not completely foreign. Had she ever felt this way before? She again remembered her faceless children, but then wondered if there had ever been children. A husband? Had she really had a life before this imprisonment she'd reconciled would never end? No. There was nothing before this: just a tease of an embrace between two people with a mutual need—and a mutual realization that no longer was there a life beyond this. Any alternative would require hope, and hope was not an option.

They had won. They always win.

Sheriff Jeff stood and hoisted a toast of his beloved tequila to his beloved doppelgänger grandson. He strode to the podium and tapped the mic. "Well!" he offered up another toast to the assembled inmates. He leaned into the mic as though he might take a bite from it. "Hello to mah pris—" A shriek of static filled the air to drown out the rest of his sentence.

Zach rose from his seat to crouched forward over the amplifier equipment to adjust the gain to stop the feedback. "Go ahead, grand-daddy," he said. He looked over toward the audio person sitting off to the side. His accusing glare telegraphed his intention to include him with the prisoners on the gallows for the crime of setting the audio too loud. Instead, Zach slunk back into his chair and sipped his drink.

"Hello y'all! Mah *favorite* prisoners!" Sheriff Jeff said out to the assembled inmates. His aviator sunglasses caught a glare from the high sun and shot it out into the crowd. "How y'all doin' today, huh?"

No response but blank stares from the terrified onlookers.

"Ah *said*: HOW Y'ALL DOIN' TODAY?"

Now there were a few lackluster responses.

"Ah did not HEAH ya…!" he chided. "Now 'less you wanna be part of our show today, I wanna *HEAH* yah LOUD! Now! HOW Y'ALL DOIN' TODAY?"

There was a louder assortment of lackluster cheers; Tricia's not among them. She just intensified her glower at the horrible man.

"Good!" he went on, smiled broadly, and took another sip of his tequila. "Good to have yah, heah. Now, ahm-a-gonna give y'all a little show today. A dee-mon-stration about how justice was done during' the Roman days." He swept his gnarly hand out toward the nine captives on the dais. "Now, these he-ah fellahs and, oh yeah, one gal did some verah, verah, bad things th' other night, so's we are gonna do what they call 'mete out the punishment to th' crime." Happy in his element, he smiled again. "Lemme show ya. Our first, uh, contestant," he turned so his grandson and smiled an aside, "Oh, yeah, ah like that! Cont-tes-tant. Don' you, Zach?"

"Oh yeah, grand-daddy," Zach nodded. "Contestant. I like that *real* good!"

He turned back to the congregation of his prisoners. "My grandson, Mister Zach, heah. He gonna run hisself a good gulag someday, eh?" He paused to listen. "I *said*: My grandson, Zach. He's a-gonna run hisself a mighty *fahn* gulag someday!"

Some gratuitous cheers. Tricia furtively looked down the line and saw Max. He had his arms crossed, remaining as stoic as she.

"Okay! Les say we get on with our little show, now. We got our first con-tes-tant, heah," he looked at his notes on the lectern. "Says heah, this first fellow, uh, Pay-dro Man-well-u-ize… ah, well, fuck the pu-nouncer-a-tion, y'all's Mexi-names, they sounds all the same ta me. Anyway, our friend Pay-dro, he raised a knife up in angrah to one our *fahn* BlueShirt guards. Well, now Caesar of Rome said 'a hand fer a hand'…" he said, ascribing Hammurabi's Code from two thousand years before Caesar never said anything of the kind. "So our buddy Pay-dro's a-gonna pay his price." He nodded over to the henchman with a machete.

The henchman wandered up to Pedro and professionally sliced his arm from his body, to Pedro's sharp scream and the horrified gasps of the audience. Tricia tried to avert her eyes but looked on with morbid curiosity over how the fingers of Perdo's severed arm continued to flex as the rest of his body bled out.

"Now, now y'all," the Sheriff said with a benign smile. "We'll have none o' that hemmin' an' hawin' out the-ah. C'mon, now y'all. Your Sheriff Jeff's jus' tryin' ta give y'all some sorta history lesson, is all. Now on to our next con-tes-tant. Mar-ciello Guitar-ez." He looked up from the notes and at the second captive. "That yo' name, boah? Reallah? Mar-ciello *Guitar*-ez? Like mah six-string ah sometimes play at night? That right?"

No answer, as a stream of piss dribbled down Marciello's leg.

"Is that *raht*, boah? That yo' name? *Guitar*-ez? Ahm tawkin' you, boah! Now you go an' answer yo' Sheriff Jeff. Now!"

"Is, *si*!" the prisoner choked.

"Well, ah know what *si* means, ah suppose. Well, now. Says here that senor Guitar poked a guard in his tummy with a knife an' kilt him. Well, back in the middle ages, there they had a wha-cha-call mete for that crime, too." He nodded to the same henchman to step in front of the captive. He lightly laid the tip of his machete against the sternum and pressed down and in toward his groin to open him up. The crowd shrieked and gasped and choked as the henchman gently pulled out his entrails as Marciello, shivering, still lived—barely. "Now. That there's called 'gutting', one o' the favorites of merry ol' England way back when."

Pedro screamed hoarsely out in pain as he recovered from his shock and realized his arm was gone. The Sheriff glanced over at the second henchman with the axe. "Will ya pleeeeze shut him up?" The second henchman swiped his axe at the legs of Pedro's stool and swiped it away, allowing Pedro to hang as he wriggled to his death.

And so on down the line. Most of the infractions had been stabbing to kill or morally wound the BlueShirt guards. As a result, a few of them were sliced in two either across their middle, or laterally split down their sternums. Two, the Neo Publcas, were beheaded by the axe. The last to die was Marciello Guitarez, with his insides hanging out.

Tricia watched in muted shock from where she stood stiffly within the growing stench of excrement, blood, and the acid brine of bile and vomit. She tried to close her eyes to remember Max's embrace. The memory became more fleeting, as a machete-man approached Consuela.

"Now," Sheriff Jeff said after a final sip from his fluted tequila glass. "We come to our woman captive, Cunt-suealla Hernandez. She is our first woman murderer. And her crime was the worst. She. SHE! Went an' *murdered* a PRICE Lieuten't. She at least had the good sense to admit it. An' y'all know wha' they used to do to people who admitted to murder?" He nodded to the henchman to tear off her bloodied surgical mask. She had no lips, just a skull's smile where her mouth had been. "They cut out their tongue!" He held up a dull, pink, six-inch blob that might have been a slug. "An' ah have it raght 'chere!" He gulped the rest of his drink, and then swung his attention toward the machete-bearer standing before Consuela. Now his tone turned as evil as his gaze. "Strip 'er down!" the guard swung his blade lightly down her rag tunic and it fell to the blood-soaked platform to reveal Consuela's writhing, plump, old body. "Whoa-hoah!" the Sheriff Jeff bellowed. "Now, she's a fat ol' sow, ain't she? Must've popped out plenty of greaser brood from tha' big fat, ol' tummy ah her's!" he looked over his shoulder at the observers, some of whom by now were looking away in revulsion. "Remin' me in th' mornin' I been feedin' my guests here too much!" Then back to the crowd: "Tomorrow, y'all's food rations 'll be cut in have for th' next three weeks—at *least*!" he nodded at the executioner. "Go 'head!"

The henchman poised his machete. "NO!" Tricia called. She rushed the fence as a BlueShirt missed in his attempt to bring her down with his rifle butt.

Sheriff Jeff held up his hand to signal his henchman to stop. "Who! Who said that?"

"I did!" Tricia screamed tearfully.

"Who're you, girl, to this old' hag?"

Tricia noticed Max step from the crowd, only to have a Blue Shirt bar him back into place. "I am her friend!"

"Were, you, cunt?" Sheriff Jeff spat, then nodded for the henchman to proceed with his quick stroke of the machete to slice Consuela's torso from her trunk.

"You fucking son of a …BITCH!" Tricia screamed.

"Now, y'all will not talk about mash mama, that' way!" the sheriff threatened back. "Bring that' shit firkin' cunt up here. She needs her punishment fir insulin' my mama an' Zach, here's, great-gramma."

Tricia came to terms with her impending death. Max tried to reach for her as she jostled past three BlueShirts. She was herded toward the bloody platform, and up its loosened, blood-slicked steps. For the first time in as long as she could remember, she felt a smile bloom in her face. Finally—*finally*—she was to be dispatched from this hell!

She willingly, though ungraciously, stepped up onto the shaky stool and allowed the noose to be slipped around her neck. "Now theah, Missy. How'd y'all feel? Comfertble?" Sheriff Jeff taunted, as the machete henchman dug the tip of his blade on her breastbone. "Strip her!" the sheriff commanded. A slice of the blade felled her tunic to the deck. The Sheriff admired her. "Ah, y'all are a pretty li'l twat, ain't cha?"

She widened a menacing smile at him. Finally! Peace! She closed her eyes, if she'd remembered how to prey, she might have done so. She felt the heat of the machete's tip stick her ribs, as the henchman awaited the sheriff's command.

"HOLD!" Zach shouted, as he approached the lectern. "Let me take this one, granddaddy."

"Whah o' course, Zach. Do 'er a good one, okay?" Sheriff Jeff said as he stepped away.

Zack seemed mesmerized by Tricia's naked body. She wasn't one of *them*. First of all, she was blonde…a Real-American, and not a terribly bad looking one at that. He then recognized her. "You're that PRICE Lieutenant's whore, ain't you?"

She didn't answer; just tightened her eyes shut and wondered what this hold-up was. She just wanted to hurry up and die.

"Hear me, woman! I asked you! You're that PRICE Lieutenant's slut? Or were. Until this bitch hangin' next to you went an' killed him?"

"Yes," she gasped loudly.

She opened her eyes and stared into the watchers at Max as he forced his way forward. "You will not harm her!"

She smiled tenderly at him, oblivious to the noose around her neck. "It's alright, Max," she whispered even though he couldn't have heard her. "I'll be fin—" then she shrieked as Max was taken down by a bullet fired by a guard in his tower above the courts.

"How, *cute!*" Zach said. "Looks like a little love thing going on there. So sorry we had to shoot that son of a bitch." He sipped on his tequila. "I know the score here, little one," he said through the P.A. system. "You wanna die, rather than spend another day in this nice hotel ours. But I'm gonna do you one worse. I'm gonna let you live." He ordered the henchman. "Turn her loose, 'n' put her in the Tin Box."

The henchman balked, and he looked to Sheriff Jeff.

"Ya heard mah son. Ya do it! NOW!"

The henchman slipped the noose off Tricia's neck. The Sheriff then nodded to the other executioner standing with his machete at the ready to strike at Consuelo. He swung it like a batter hitting a homer and sliced her in two.

Tricia collapsed in a faint.

23

The Tin Box

October 14

A low-level BlueShirt guard guarded the dreaded Tin Box. It was easy work for them; for there was no way anyone could Houdini their way out of it. Elevated upon a six-foot high platform set a half-mile away from the camp and out in the desert to conduct the sun's heat, it was like an oven set to very low. The Tin Box was an eight-by-eight-foot ironclad cell, four and a half feet high; quite less than enough room needed to stand. At the top of one of its walls there was a little six-by-two-inch slot for air, which also served as a peephole to check if its occupant had yet died. Usually, the fetid scent of death wended from the little hole as an indication the box had done its job.

The dried-out brakes of Pepito's makeshift flatbed pickup squeaked in complaint as he parked it, and then left its engine clattering away as he walked toward the platform. He reminded himself again that he should turn his talent as a mechanic toward his own truck. But then he chose not to risk being beheaded for turning his attentions away from Sheriff Jeff's son's fussy Porsche.

"HALT! Who is it?" said the rookie BlueShirt guard. He emphasized his point by cocking his weapon.

Pepito reckoned he must have been the new replacement for Tony, the usual guard. "Pepito," he said. "Tony did not tell you this station was on my rounds?"

"No, Greaser, he did not. Now you go turn tail back outta here!" he threatened, as he rose his rile to aim.

The old Mexican had had too much experience around the camp to be dusted off like this. The kid's voice had been shaky, and the rifle trembled in his hands. "First night on the job, señor?" Pepito asked calmly, as though the rifle was invisible.

"None o' your fuckin' business. So get outta here!"

Pepito stood his ground by relaxing his stance as an indication he was going nowhere. "I am here on the order of the Sheriff's grandson, Zachary."

"Bullshit you are."

Pepito lifted the ID card hanging around his neck to show the rookie. "See? I am Zachary's personal trustee. I come around here every night to check on the prisoner. Now I am sure you will not want me to go back to the sheriff's son and tell him you blocked me here,"

"Lemme see," the guard said as he lowered his weapon. He stared at the ID card. "Oh, shit. You ain't kiddin'."

"Tony should have told you."

"Okay, go ahead," the guard muttered as he motioned the barrel of his rifle toward the steps leading up to the platform.

Pepito went to the box and aimed his flashlight through the slot. Within the dim shimmer of illumination, he could see in she was barely breathing as she huddled naked with her knobby spine turned to the beam from the light. Her short hair was mussed as a desert tumbleweed. It didn't look blonde anymore, but the color of mud. There was little to discern through the darkness, itself captured like a second prisoner within the box. It, too, was the color of mud. He failed to ignore the stench coming through the slot in heated waves.

"Now *señorita*," he whispered reassuringly into the void. "This will be over soon. I know this. Soon. I will always be praying for you. God is in here with you." He waited for her to say—anything. He heard nothing but her thin, ragged, breathing. "I have two extra rations of food, given to you from me and some others." He slipped three little cling-wrapped morsels of *arroz e frijoles* through the slot. They dropped to the metal floor to join the other contributions piled there from days before. "*Per favor, señorita*. You must eat and keep your strength."

"For...what?" He thought he heard her say in a serrated husk of a whisper.

He wondered about this, too, then said: "For your freedom, *señorita*." He waited for her return comment, as though for another dim proof of life. None came. "I will pray for you, *señorita*. I will always pray for you."

"You do...that," she finally answered. Her voice sounded dead. "*Si, señorita*. I will."

The beam from Pepito's flashlight swung away and returned her to the dark void where she knew she belonged. Although she knew must have deserved it, the reason had escaped her. But no matter, and who cares? Her thoughts were as stiff and empty as her huddled body. Every night, Pepito had left her with the same reassurance: *I will pray for you*. So, what? Pray for *what*? What good would any of that do anymore? She had long forgotten when she had died away into this world where time meant nothing at all. This wasn't even hell. This was just...nothing. She huddled in closer to herself.

She bowed her head not to pray, but to sniff in the stench that had become woven into her world. The only other items in the pitch-black enclosure were an infested blanket and an open pail for shit, piss, and the inevitable vomit. The parcels of four-ounce, dimly glittering Saran-wrapped clumps of *arroz e frijoles* lay scattered about the floor of her box like so many useless turds. Yes, that was it. She was queen of her eight-by-eight-by-four-and-a-half-foot fiefdom of useless turds.

She hadn't slept, but she had imagined weird things when she still had the strength to do so. But tonight—if it was even night—there was something different. She had long before reached her bottom; low enough to feel the weight of the iron floor upon her shoulders. She felt a warm shudder, not like a heat of the desert kind of warmth, but oxymoronic cooling warmth; something like a balm from within her. Was this her soul leaving her body? No. It couldn't have been. To believe in a soul was to believe in life—to believe in God. She reminded herself she believed in nothing—she had been emptied of it all.

But believing in nothing left a vessel to be filled. It started with a vision of glowing feathers—wood shavings, maybe. Floating around on their own like big gleaming flakes of snow, until they settled on the floor of what barely remained of the void within her. Then they caught fire lit up her life. "Is this what it's ...it's like to die?" she asked the darkness. "To die a…second time? After I'm already...dead?"

She tried to turn away from the vision, but she couldn't. It was inside of her: illuminating the face of a child, a boy; then another boy; then a third, this one a teen-aged girl. Their faces were as familiar as yesterday—this time, there *was* a yesterday, and it was close. Their faces; so relaxed and innocent: Steven-7; Michael-13;

Emily-15. Her entire body beamed into a smile, and she reached out into the darkness to hold them.

And then emerged another visage—the broad face of a man, confident and strong. Protective. Her husband. His name had been Robert. She recalled herself, once again—this time determined, and resolute. She shouted: "I am Tricia!" Her voice, now strong, rang off the iron walls. "I am Tricia!" The fire within her continued to burn. No. This wasn't what it was like to die. This was what it was like to remember.

The glow she saw within her—her children; her husband; herself—a life—burned on with the energy of hope. It was enough to sustain her for might have been hours, days, and months. But finally, another—an outer one— compounded her inner light as the wall with the slot was drawn away. She squinted hard into the unfamiliar sunlight. In a blur, she saw her nameless guard, and Pepito standing next him with the power drill he'd used to unscrew the bolts that had secured her captivity.

The guard helped her out of the tin box with a gentleness more attributed to a nurse. When he could, Pepito took her other arm to help carry her to the waiting air-conditioned car. "You were in the box for six days, *señorita*," Pepito told her, as he helped her walk.

She had the strength only to nod.

"You see? I have prayed for you, *señorita*."

"I ...know," was all she could manage to croak out in a whisper, and through a smile nurtured by the glow of her remembrance.

October 21

Zach's lavish chrome and glass California-style bungalow was set off a mile from the gulag in a shadowy oasis of palms next to his father's more provincially southwestern estate. Here in his bathroom—truly a room housing only the sunken bath—Tricia sat stiff in the Jacuzzi brewing with soapsuds and surrounded by mirrors. The process of her makeover had begun after four days of rest and plumping out through steak and potatoes prepared by Zach's cook, Maria. She gazed into the mirrors and appreciated the woman she was being fashioned into, but it was not her. The only version of her she'd come to know was a scarred, bedraggled, dim-eyed, boney, sunken-cheeked, hag of a woman, years beyond her years. Yet now her body was fleshed-out and smooth. Her cropped, white-blonde hair had been softened and fluffed out into a semblance of fashion. Her nails, three of them replaced, were full and polished. Her lips were plush. Her lightly tanned skin glimmered and felt plush to the touch. The person reflected back to her was as forgotten as she was vaguely familiar.

She hadn't minded that she was being washed and fondled from behind in the surge and gurgle of warmed tub-water by a pert, naked young girl who was hardly a teen. Tricia was sentient as stone to whatever was happening to her in the world of the moment. Her world was a more was a more soothing out-of-body one that she'd found easier to visit day-by-day as she recovered. She had only to close her eyes and remember.

She eased her eyes open to gaze into the reflection of the two doorways open to her captor's bedroom. She saw her clothing laundered and pressed, stacked neatly upon the feather duvet. Well, it wasn't her clothing. It was an ensemble Zack had put together for her: a pleated, green tartan knee skirt, loose white blouse, white ankle socks, and black Mary Jane's of a Catholic schoolgirl's uniform. And the white cotton panties. Always the white panties.

Zach liked to pretend. They had experimented in this role only once, and she had emerged even colder than when she went in. During it all, she closed her eyes while Zach immersed himself in his creation of dress-up. She was a vehicle dressed, then undressed, and redressed in and out of costume as his plaything of the day. She knew that, to him, she was nothing more than another hole, and even that was okay. She cared no more for him than he had for her, and at least Zach hadn't been as bestial as the PRICE Lieutenant had been.

She started as she felt the supple young fingers from behind her wander to the inside of her thighs, then within. This startling sensation was unexpected, causing her to gasp as she widened, then relaxed her eyes. She spied the reflection of Zach sitting off in a corner and stared in weary fascination at the surging lump of his hand working vigorously beneath the loosened brim of his jeans.

24

It's Only a Little Pinch

October 22

"Okay, now, how are we gonna game this thing?" Alexander Kenton Jr. demanded of the small cluster of the Kenton/Fox News staff seated around the conference table. Sitting at its head was Alexander Kenton Junior, with his father's fob of silver-blond hair, and a body starting to chunk up; a fifty-year-old who never grew out of his thirties.

He had a sister, Madelyn. Now in her pretty, early-forties. She had Max-Factored herself into a Barbie Doll. Despite that superficiality, she had made her reputation as a hard warrior against child and animal abuse, and other honorable causes, to leverage against the more bogus ones of Alexander Jr. The world did not need any more of the amber plastic beer bottles he'd crusaded for. Alexander was a strong supporter of the rights of big-game hunters and big guns for everyone—but not Liberals, because they didn't count in his world. They were all too panty-waste pussies to handle a weapon, anyway. As his sister fought against cruelty to animals and humans, he fought for it. That was among the least of their publicly known frictions, which most people wrote off to sibling rivalry.

Madelyn was smart—she'd even graduated with a master's from Columbia Journalism—while Alexander, a grad of Passaic High, was their father's chosen heir-apparent. It was beyond a male-in-the-family thing with her. In her mind it was worse: stupidity begat ignorance. "Game *what* thing, Alex? There about five talking points going around this table at once."

Five talking points; aside from Madelyn and her brother, there were five others seated around the table. Alexander sat at the head as the bloated bully in the sandbox, puffing on his cherrywood pipe and stinking up the room with almond-smelling tobacco. To his right sat Madelyn, occasionally making a show of swiping the smoke away. Then there was Greg Palmer, the News Editorial Director—a patrician hold-out from the early years of the millennium. Next to him sat a rookie editorial assistant, Tim, trying to hide his fears from the pipe-smoking Darth Vader seated at the table's head. Seated across from Tim was the evening news anchor, Carmine, a swarthy almost-forty-year-old obsidian-eyed beauty from Valencia—and Alexander's unrequited favorite. Next to her, slouched Brian, a young street reporter who didn't give a shit, but had nothing better to do. Seated next to him was his reporter-wingman, Andy, who did give a shit, but also had nothing better to do.

Over by the window, meditating on Sixth Avenue—renamed "The Avenue of Real-America"—55 stories below, stood Randy Montefiore. He'd popped in for one of his occasional visits to Premier Kenton's media shop, now ceremoniously sipping from his paper cup of Starbuck's bold. It was important for him to be listening in today, considering all that was going on for and against the Kenton Regime.

"She's right, Alex," he said, as he turned, and strode back to his seat at the table. "What are we 'gaming,' right now?"

"I was thinking about our coverage of the December Kenton Rally in New Orleans, Randy."

"Ah, good, then," Montefiore said. "Let's start there, and then work back a little. What are your coverage plans?"

"Cameras everywhere, Randy," Alexander stated boldly. "And reporters."

"And lions, and tigers, and bears, oh my!" Madelyn quipped back at him. "The Super-dome's a big building, Alex. You can't just have cameras and reporters 'everywhere'."

"You know what I mean, Madelyn. Come on."

"I know what he means!" Tim blurted.

Brian poked Andy and shot him a smug, mocking half-smile.

"I'll map out the reporter-coverage sections," Greg said. "It's a sixty-thousand seat stadium. I think no more than eight crews should do it. Plus four rover cameras, three drones and the usual set-ups up in the fifty-yard line press boxes. I'd say four stationary angles of the Premier and keynoters. And two for the officials on the dais. That should handle it all."

"Sounds like a Hollywood production," Madelyn said.

"It is. These damn rallies are always like Hollywood blow-outs," Carmine replied furtively.

"See, Randy?" Alexander gloated. "Packed up all nice and neat."

"Okay, that's very good, Alex. Now what about that other rally?"

"Other rally? What other rally?"

"Randy's talking about the Neo-Publica one out in Denver, Alex," Madelyn reminded him. "When is that? Sometime early December?"

Carmine referred to her notes. "The second...it's a Saturday."

"And we're covering that?" Alexander asked.

"Of course you are," Montefiore said. "You haven't forgotten, right?" He began to tap his pen against his wrist.

"Uh, no, Randy. I haven't...forgotten."

"*I* remembered about that rally," Tom piped in.

"Oh, shut up," Madelyn hissed privately at him.

"It's just that, well, they're on the other side, Randy," Alexander reminded him. "Do we even *want* to cover it?"

"Yeah, Alex," Madelyn reminded him. "It's news. It's our job." She recognized his befuddlement, then turned to Montefiore. "Greg and I will arrange to send a skeleton crew out there to Mile High Field."

Montefiore returned one of his churlish grins. "Thanks, Madelyn."

"Fuck, yeah! I'll go to that one," Brian said, then looked at Andy. "You, too, Bro!"

"I don't know if—" Andy said.

"Dude! First week of December; Denver; Boulder; Aspen...Steamboat Springs. The powder should be freakin' cherry!"

"Well, okay, then!" Andy cheered up through a simpering grin. "If I absolutely have to, I will."

"Yeah!" Brian blurted.

"I decided to stick you guys with covering it, anyway," Madelyn said over the accentuation of a feral smile of the tigress she yearned to be. "Given as much as I know you guys *hate* skiing."

"Right," Montefiore said. "I'll talk some specifics with you, Madelyn. Later at the Top of The Sixes."

She leveled a tightened gaze at him. "How about a sidebar right here after this meeting?"

"Tonight. Top of The Sixes," he insisted. "Case closed."

She hated when Montefiore Shanghaied her like that. That man would never, ever, get what he truly wanted from her. That was an assurance that came with her being a lesbian. "Okay, Randy," she said to his scowl, knowing she would need back-up. "I'll bring a friend along."

Montefiore's expression fell soft.

"Now," Greg said officiously to reel the moment back into the room. "How about the Premier's trip to Helsinki in a next month to meet with Premier Vladovkov? I'll be flying with him in Real-America-One, along with a crew of two camera jockeys and four writers."

"Okay, Greg," Alexander said. "But he doesn't want that interview taped. You know that. "

"No, true, enough. But he *will* want to tell us Real-Americans what he accomplished." He considered Alexander's confused expression. "And that's why we'll need a crew," he explained.

"That's right, Alex, he will," Tim agreed.

Madelyn knew it was time for her to disentangle from this bear-trap of a meeting. It was turning—as they all did—foolish. She had a hair appointment in an hour-and-a-half up on East 77th, and anything beyond a fast cup of Yoplait for lunch had already become a non-event.

"There is one other thing," Carmine said.

"Yeah, Carmine? What is it?" Alexander said softly, trying to invite himself into her interest.

She looked up from what she'd written and primly placed down her pen. "That 'Second Child Amendment' your father signed last week. Apparently, it slipped through without anyone knowing."

"We aren't ready to discuss that yet," Montefiore said.

"Well, Commissar Montefiore," Carmine challenged. "I think we are and should."

"What?" Madelyn asked. "What is this 'Second Child Amendment?' Why haven't I heard about it?"

"Dad didn't think you needed to know, Madelyn," Alexander whispered in confidence to his sister.

"Oh, really, Alex? And why was that?"

"Well, for one thing. It doesn't involve you, because you're not married." His gaze turned accusing. "And you're not likely to be having any kids."

She answered his confidential dig with a sibling's sneer.

"I'll tell you what it says," Carmine said.

"You don't have to *do* that, Carmine," Montefiore interjected.

"Yes, Commissar, I do. Three days ago, Premier Kenten signed into the record that, after her second child, a mother can opt to have a…pro-ce-dure." She strung that word out to let it soak in.

"A procedure," Madelyn said warily as she fleshed a glare at her bother. "What kind of…pro-ce-dure, Carmine?"

"It'll be no more invasive then going to the dentist to get your teeth cleaned," Montefiore assured.

"It's only a little pinch, I'm told," Alexander said.

Tim cringed. "Ugh. I hate getting my teeth cleaned."

"Yeah. Okay, right," Carmine dismissed them. "Apparently word had gotten out that parents were planning to stand up against having their third children taken away for the BlueShirt Brigade training. So. The regime has offered the mothers an option…"

Madelyn visibly stiffened over what she feared was coming.

"That *option*," Carmine stated, "is voluntary sterilization."

"What the FUCK, Randy?" Madelyn blasted at Montefiore. "What the God-damned *fuck*! Sterilization? What is this? Nazi Germany?"

"It's only an option, Madelyn," he excused. "It's still a woman's choice. And the BlueShirt Youth Brigade is at force now, so we'll need fewer children."

"A woman's choice. Sure, Randy. She can either give up her kid or get sterilized to keep from having to do that," Madelyn said.

"I know what," Tim offered blithely. "The mother can choose an abortion of her third kid."

"Abortion is against the law, and a sin, Tim,"Alexander reminded him.

"And this sterilization thing fucking *isn't*?" Madelyn demanded.

"Well, Madelyn, it actually isn't," Alexander said dourly. "There is no mention of sterilization in the Bible."

"But there is in Hitler's playbook," Carmine said.

"Whoa, there, woman!" Montefiore seethed threateningly as he rose from his seat in confrontation. "You have gone way too deep, there...way, *way* too deep! "

For the first, maybe second, maybe third time since her father declared himself Premier in 2022, she thought that maybe he should have been removed from office back in 2020. There might have still been time, then, to keep him from going too far like this. She'd seen the warning signs of gloat in him since his reality TV show days when his power started surging. But with this Second Child Amendment meted out at his pleasure through another fucking executive order, he'd gone further out than she might had imagined.

"*Have* I dug too deep, there, Commissar?" Carmine said. "No, sir. The Real-American people need to know about this, and I've decided to announce it in my show. Tonight."

"You can't do that, Carmine. Not before Premier Kenton does," Montefiore warned.

"As head anchor, I can say whatever the hell I want in my show, if it's the truth. Right Greg?"

"Well, yeah, but Carmine? There are limits—even to the truth" the old man of the airwaves cautioned.

"The *hell* with the truth!" Montefiore shot back at her. "This is for the benefit of the administration and, by extension, the Real-American people as a whole! You say anything about this on your fucking show, and I'll have you bounced back to that the ditzy-blonde slot on The Morning Koffee Klotch."

"That's not your call, Randy," Madelyn said.

"No, Madelyn." Alexander countered. "It's mine." He looked at the inaccessible Carmine. "And I will do as the Commissar just said. So don't report it, Carmine." He grinned condescendingly at her, as if to convey: *Who's in the head chair,* now, *eh, Carmine? Hah! Touché!* He took a satisfied, meaningful pull on his now-extinguished pipe.

"I'll hold it until day after tomorrow, Alex, then we'll talk," Carmine said back to him. "By the way…" she reached down into a little "Dora the Explorer" book-pack her daughter had given her. "Did any of you know about this?" She held up a paperback book with a blue cover with a wide red stripe on its outer edge and a white star in the upper right-hand corner. Over this was emblazoned in gold: "The Neo-Publica Manifesto" and beneath that: "By Silvia Margoles."

"Holy crap!" Alexander blathered.

"Where did you get that?" Montefiore asked.

"It's an advance copy, delivered to my office first thing this morning. There's some interesting stuff in here, as you can well imagine. Including the U.S. Constitution in full in the appendix."

"That's just God Damned illegal!" Montefiore shot back. "Who published that thing? We'll shut them the fuck down."

Carmine flipped to the Copyright page. "They're out of Canada…let's see…London, Ontario. It's got a Canadian copyright. We can't touch them."

"Let me have that."

"Sorry, Commissar, I can't. It was sent to me. It's network property."

"Fuck that shit!" Montefiore said. "Let me have it!"

"No."

"Actually, Randy, Carmine's right. It was sent to her and belongs to the network," Madelyn told him.

"Then I'll take it, Carmine," Alexander said. He reached out his hand for it. "As I *am* the network."

"I won't let you have this any more than I can't let the Commissar have it, Alex. Reporter privilege. It was addressed to me. You can buy a copy once it comes out, though."

"God Damnit, Carmine! All right you can break the Second Child Amendment thing on you news report. In three days. No. On Saturday when viewership is down. Now give me the God-damned book."

"Okay, then. You all heard that."

"Yeah, I'll back you up, Carmine," Madelyn said.

Carmine handed the Manifesto to him, then looked over at Madelyn. "You want one, too? They sent others, and you may want to look at it before you go cover the Neo Publica rally. You know, homework."

"Homework. Absolutely. Thanks Carmine. I'll drop by your office later today." Madelyn replied

---

Sitting in the back of her father's limo gave Madelyn a sense she was imprisoned in a rich, leather and oak, gold appointed padded cell. It smelled so new, yet so old; used, but not used, to accommodate Premier Kenton's alleged germ-phobia. Even the germ-phobia had been just another one of his lies, as he sat across from his daughter with his ditzy, silver-tined haired bimbo of the week, dipping his fat fingers into a paper cup of McDonald's fries without fear of picking up any germs.

Madelyn felt the presence her brother next to her, wearing his black suit and long overcoat and replicating the way their father dressed. Her deeper self had been held captive far too long by these two ignoramus men. They had systematically removed her from the inner sanctum of the family, especially since the Premier's ex-wife, Alicia, had resorted to suicide four years earlier. Alicia had been her anchor, as her father and brother had now become her sinker.

For now, her prison was the Lincoln Tunnel traffic jam in her realized nightmare of helplessness. She had tunnel-phobia, anyway, and over the past fifteen minutes she had broken out in a sweat. Her breaths had shortened, and she was starting to feel suffocated. The dirty, porcelain-tiled walls seemed to be closing in on her. Opening the window would do no good this enclosure seething with carbon monoxide and the echoing cacophony of traffic noise.

She coughed lightly and called over her shoulder to the driver. "Lars, could you turn up the air-conditioning a little?"

"Yes'm," he replied, and did.

"That new hotel should make lots of money, Dad," Alexander said about the opening of the Kenton Plaza in Secaucus, where they'd just been.

"Yes," replied the Swedish bimbo, with a single abrupt nod, which bounced the cute, silver-colored bob of her hair. The action appeared to add an exclamation point to the only English word she apparently knew.

"We can hope so, Alex," Kenton replied wearily as he gazed out the window at the traffic. "My hotels always make money. You know that." He absently popped another French fry into his mouth and made a protracted ceremony out of chewing on it.

"I wish you wouldn't do that, Dad," Madelyn said.

"What? Do what?" he said as he returned his attention to them and added another fry to the visible mush in his mouth.

"Those French fries and cheeseburgers. Maybe you should cut back on all that crap. When was the last time you had your cholesterol checked? And your blood pressure? Alex and I are worried about you."

"Hey, Maddie," Alexander said. "Dad loves his Big Macs, ya know?"

"Yes," agreed Kenton's Sweedish girlfriend. She then lifted a French fry from the cup.

"I'm fine, Maddie," Kenton told her. "I'm healthy as a bull."

"According to who? That doctor in Times Square?"

Kenton nodded. "He's a perfect doctor."

Maybe for him, Madelyn surmised. *But that quack was far from perfect. He'd probably gotten his medical degree from an ad on a matchbook cover.* But no matter—he told the Premier whatever he'd wanted to hear. "Okay, Dad. Whatever." She looked worriedly out the backseat window again as she fussed with her cellular phone. No stored messages from Sarah, her on-again-off-again partner. "What *is* the holdup here?" she asked frustratedly.

"Don't know m'am," Lars the driver said.

"One of my tanks," Kenton blandly replied.

"Shit, Dad. There's someone driving a *tank* through the Lincoln Tunnel?"

"Yeah," Kenton chuckled. "Drove. Last Monday."

She remembered the the tank-in-the-Lincoln-Tunnel snippet on a sidebar in Tuesday's newscasts. She passed it off as just another stunt from one of the Regime's rich supporters, and never thought to attribute such a circus act to the Regime, itself.

"He made a bet with the Soviet Premier that he could pass one of his new tanks through the tunnel on a drive from Jersey City to Port Authority in the city," Alexander told his sister.

"So. Now a fucking tank is corking up the tunnel," Madelyn said nervously.

"Not *now*," Alexander muttered back at her. "Last Monday."

"No, it isn't, Maddie," Kenton said. "It made it through to Port Authority. And now there's still some roadwork going on in here from where the treads chopped up the pavement a little. Anyway, I won the bet."

Maddie shook her head. "Jesus, Dad! A bet with the Soviet Premier? What did you win? Estonia?"

"Aw, come on Maddie. Stop picking on Dad...Yo, Lars!" Alexander called over his shoulder "Why don't you flick on the siren and the lights? Maybe it'll get us through here faster."

Madelyn glanced around at how tightly they were trapped in. "We won't get very far, you dunce. You know? At times, Alex you can be a real idiot." *'At times' is too generous,* she said to herself.

"No. Not Estonia," Kenton told her. "Vlad tells me he has a special prize waiting for me when I get over to Helsinki next month."

Madelyn supposed it would be another white-blonde headed woman in a tunic to act as her father's slave for the week. "Well, that's nice." She looked nervously ahead, trying to will them passage through the clot of honking traffic.

"When is that, meeting, Dad?" Alexander said. "I'll need to set up a reporter pool,"

"Yeah, but you're not gonna record our meeting. It's closed, totally closed, to everyone but the Premier and me."

"I told Greg that. It's just for the after-story, and your comments."

Kenton chewed on another fry, and sipped his Coke. "It's on the fifteenth. I think I'll have a little announcement to make afterwords. Then I'll make it a bigger one at my December rally in New Orleans."

"Yes!"

"Maybe you two shouldn't talk so openly about this," Madelyn told her father, as she inclined her head toward his Swedish girlfriend. "You never know."

"What?" Kenton said. "A spy? Oh, come on, Maddie." He turned to his girlfriend. "Sveltva, dear, are you a Swedish spy?"

She nodded. "Yes!" she enthused.

"See?" Kenton replied. "Sveltva's no spy. She can't even speak English. Right, sweetie?"

"Yes!"

He offered up his cup of fries to her like a doggie-treat. "Here, dear. Have another one."

Madelyn despised the way her father demeaned women so, especially since Alicia had died. But even she hadn't been saved from his gross public innuendos and put-downs. He had a talent for diminishing anyone who posed was a threat to him. And women posed a threat. Alicia especially—until she couldn't take any more, then killed herself. This surfaced that topic that had been brimming beneath the surface of her thinking for the last two days. "Dad. What is this 'Second Child Amendment' you authorized?"

Alexander sighed out: *Oh, Jesus,* as Kenton glared across at her. He leveled the telling "Kenton Squint" at her. "How did you know about that, Madelyn?" he accused. "I wasn't gonna announce that until next week."

God. Madelyn thought. *He's gonna send me to my room without dinner.* "Carmine Valenzia's gonna cover it on her show on Saturday night."

Kenton inattentively popped another french fry into the potato field he'd made in his mouth. "What the *fuck*, Alex!" he groused at his son. "Why are you gonna let her do that, son? Fire her! Tomorrow!" Kenton blathered. His voice then suddenly tightened, and he began coughing. Alex hopped across to his father as his face was turning red. He slapped him between the shoulders and the Premier regurgitated a blob into his napkin. He heaved a sigh, caught his breath, and cleared his throat. He then took up another fry.

"I want you to go see my doctor, Dad," Madelyn said.

"Fuck that! I want to know why you are allowing that gypsy broad to preempt my policy announcement?" he barked at Alexander.

"Why announce it at all, Dad? Why even propose it?" Madelyn asked.

He thought about his answer. "Because I can, Maddie. And because I will." He turned to his son: "And your reporter will not. End of story."

"Yes!" The Swedish girlfriend nodded emphatically.

"Okay, Dad. She's gone, okay?"

"Tomorrow," Kenton pressed, then coughed twice.

"Yes, Dad. I promise." The traffic finally started inching into a crawl.

"Ah," Kenton said as he finished off the last two fries. "We're on the move." Another dry cough.

"Oh," Alexander said as he reached into his satchel. "I meant to show you this." He held up his copy of "The Neo-Publica Manifesto."

Kenton squinted at it. "What is that?"

"It's the manifesto written by to Neo-Publican people. They're having a big rally next month. I guess they wanted this out in time for that."

Kenton took the book and thumbed through it. "What's it about? Is it good?"

Madelyn simpered. "Well, it's not exactly a novel, Dad."

"It's about the old America. There's even a copy of the U.S. Constitution in the back."

"What the fuck?" Kenton sputtered. "That's illegal!"

Madelyn wondered what "Illegal" even meant anymore.

"I'm gonna fucking shut that publisher down for doing this fucking book. Alex, I want you to publicly ban this book on our news-shows."

"Yoo can't shut down the publisher, Dad" Madelyn told him.

"Why the fuck not? This is Real-America, God-damnit! I can shut down anyone want! That's the fucking business of doing business." His face had blushed red again.

"Yes!"

"Oh, quiet, Sveltva," he said. "Where is this god-damned publisher?"

"They're out of Canada, Dad. We can't shut them down."

"We can, and we will. I don't care if I have to invade those fuckin' Canuks to do it." Kenton sputtered on. "We're gonna end that book. That fucking Constitution, again! Jesus!"

"Calm down, Dad," Madelyn tried to reassure him. "You're gonna choke again." She gazed at the book cover and forgot about her tunnel claustrophobia. She's been up well into the night reading the copy Carmine had given her.

She couldn't put it down.

25

The Neo-Publica Rally

December 2

Aileen's breath steamed as she blew into her cupped hands. The hard, early December chill had hit Denver hard and the snow-faced Rockies loomed high in her view from her seat at Mile-High Field. The jagged mountains rising into the deep blue, pre-dusk western sky gave her heart that there was something greater than emotional idealism in the air. There was— seemingly for the first time—hope.

She looked down twenty or so nearly filled rows of seats to the football field. She saw Sylvia on a dais built on the fifty-yard line in the center of the field giving Piet and Hugh some instructions. She then went and sat back down in her chair as Hugh went to the podium to adjust the microphone, and Piet went off to the side to fetch something. He brought some auxiliary paperwork to her. She continued to study her keynotes as though trying to memorize them. How small she appeared; how large she loomed.

Aileen had felt for an unknown while that she had fallen in love with her. Since Barbara died, she'd had hardened the shell of her denial: to not think about it was to believe it never happened. She'd come to regard Barbara's death it as if she had merely left town, leaving the connecting thread of her love. The truth might had been too devastating. Was this love for Sylvia a rebound reaction over the loss of the one she'd absolutely loved during what had become known as the "Kenton Tower Rebellion" in May? Who would know? Feelings like love are not controlled by fate, sanity, or reason. Feelings of true love are driven by loss. She camouflaged what she thought — or feared — she had felt for Sylvia by telling her that she loved her *conviction*. That seemed to help a little to ease the frustration, but once that cleared, it only seemed to hurt more.

Robert huddled in his seat next to holding with his beer. He passed her his cup. "Here, Allie, you want a sip?"

She shivered her shoulders. "No thanks, Bob. How can you drink a cold beer on the coldest day of the year? And at this altitude? You'll be drunk in a minute."

He simpered at her. "Maybe that's the point, hon. It's a football stadium. It's November. I'm a guy who likes the Broncos. It all fits."

Right. A guy. Sylvia's guy. she thought. She seemed to forget that before reality surfaced to haunt the myth. "Well, dearie, this isn't a football game, and we're gonna need you sober for this."

"Whoa! Look there!" he said, pointing up to the jumbotron above the bleachers on the other side, and then the ones above the two end-zones. There was Sylvia studying her notes, unaware that she was on camera as it did a position check. The people, now filling up half the seats an hour before her address, cheered. Droves of others continued file in through the gates. Sylvia, wondering what the cheering was about, looked up at the screen. She smiled coyly and held her notes up to cover her face. "That's what I love about her," Robert said. "Her modesty."

Ouch! Aileen thought. But they both knew he was being facetious. "Me, too," she said softly, and meaning it.

Some more cheers rose as the image changed to a graphic: "We, the People…" scripted out as it was on the Constitution. Below that in bold san-serif type: "We ARE the People!"

Realizing she was off camera, Sylvia rose and left the stage with Hugh and Piet to go to the locker room area for last minute preparations before her address.

The 'Screemin' Deemons' rock group played out some headbanger rifts from another stage, and another world, set up in the endzone. It wasn't Karen's kind of music, and she tucked it away in the back of her mind. Equipped with a wireless headset transmitting to a Regime security R.V. outside the entrance, she stalked the ramps and walkways through the seats of people. She was put out there by Tom Roebling, who sat watching six video feeds like a TV news director in the darkened interior of the R.V. Karen had been one of only three Neo-Pub sympathizers among Roebling's twelve BlueShirts circulating through the crowd, searching for anything or anyone suspicious.

Roebling had spun the affair to his operatives in the Kenton Regime as a defensive one. Even through the sixty-thousand or so people expected to fill the stadium were Neo-Pub oriented, they were still Real-Americans until they were arrested and questioned. He added that the Kenton Regime wanted no bad press, especially on the eve of his going to meet with the Soviet Premier, followed by his big New Orleans rally. So, yeah. Be vigilant for bad guys in the stands with guns. "Everything ends peacefully. And then after, you guys can go out and drink all the Coors you want. But during the rally, stay frosty. Think of this as training for the Kenton Christmas Rally in New Orleans."

So, Roebling's men, most of them BlueShirts in plain clothes with concealed pieces, wandered the seats at ease. For them, it was a cushy job. Karen and Roebling's other Neo Pub sympathizers, Mike Hastings, and Dan Harris were more on edge, and on guard. She reached deep into her heavy windbreaker and placed her hand on her lucky dirk. Guns were no more her thing than that trashy head-banger stuff. She was strictly a knife kind of women—knives were quiet, graceful, and beautiful, like the Bach and Brahms concertos she'd come to love, especially before an operation. Karen was, above all, a complex person.

Madelyn busied herself as a producer with her crew in the Kenton/Fox News and Entertainment semi-truck trailer. Inside, the thing was as annoyingly appointed as her father's big limo. It was as though the car may have been spawned from its black leather and oak interior.

"Let's get a lock on six," she said. "Who is that?"

"Frank, one of our steady-cams," one of her crew told her.

"His camera's wavering around like he's drunk. Tell him to stand still."

Greg Palmer, the old man of the airwaves, was directing and controlling the console as well as the cameras. He spoke into his headset and told Frank to stand still. He waited for a reply, then turned to Madelyn. "He says it's too fucking cold up where he is. Verbatim."

"Jesus! Tell him to tie himself to a fucking lamppost or something."

This was Madelyn's favorite part of the job. Concentrating on producing a show took her away from the calliope of the outer world and settled her into an alpha state of relaxed attention. Governing her crew and their array monitors in the darkness gave her the feeling of being a submarine commander, with Greg as her helmsman. "Let's get a tighter shot on the podium with camera two," she said. "And draw back camera three to a two-shot of whoever will be sitting in those chairs on the stage. Okay. We are set." She glanced up at the massive LED timer above the monitors.

"Ten minutes to air. Smoke 'em if you got 'em." It had only been a manner of speech, but Greg took her literally and lit up a Marlboro. "Jesus, Greg, I never knew you smoked."

"Took it up last month, Maddie. I figure once you get to my age, a person should catch up on lost time."

"And maybe hasten up that time a little," she quipped.

"Yeah, well, I gave it up thirty years ago, and missed it all that time."

She fanned away a stray filigree of smoke. "Just don't do too much of it Greg. I need you."

A Neo Pub roadie stepped up to the podium and tapped the mic. Thump-thump. Then blew into it. "Test. Test. Test," he enunciated.

Camera Two was the one assigned to Sylvia. The roadie's ruddy, pocked, face, with a rosacea-swollen nose on Monitor Two, looked a little too far away. "Maybe tighten up on two some more?"

"Maybe that'll be a little *too* tight, Maddie?"

She realized he was right. "Okay Greg, yeah, I defer to your experience, old friend."

Another camera had been trained on Carmine, whom Madelyn had chosen to do the field reporting. She had made it though the Second Child Amendment story, because she finally deferred to Alexander. She dre the line on her journalistic integrity when it came down to threat of two years in a gulag, Probably Unqutuck, the regime's choice for subversive journalists. Carmine tongued her plush, perfect lips and brushed a windblown stray hair aside with a perfect hand. Madelyn cringed to a flow of warmth throughout her body. She only wished Carmine hadn't been such a mom and devoted to a husband—so *hetero*. "Tighten up Camera Six on Carmine," she said.

His handle was "Brick," but the lithe features of his skinny build defied that moniker. Though he'd spent a day in the stadium staking out his place, surviving in the shadows on Fritos and water, he wasn't tired. He'd been trained to counter sleep when he was on a mission. Sleep only resulted in further fatigue, and he needed to stay alert. Amphetamines would have only distracted him. SEAL training had taught him that. Despite the SEAL height and weight requirements, his talent lay in his smallness. He knew how to slip into and stay hidden in small places, such as where he lay prone on his stomach in the stadium lighting housing cage below the left end zone jumbotron.

He had other assets than his jockey-size and agility. He was called "Brick" by his cohorts Commissar Montefiore's private and newly formed and growing Real-America Coalition because his aim was rock solid, steady, and true. He had slipped in early in and taken up post here after reconnoitering for several possibilities, and this was best. He preferred to accomplish his assigned tasks from the side, such as when John F. Kennedy was shot, it allowed for more opportunities. He tested his position one more time. The flag in the stadium flicked steadily toward the southeast, so the wind was steady at with 20 mile per hour gusts from the northwest. Perfect. He raised his long-barreled precision rifle and checked the aim, even though he knew it was solid. He adjusted his windage, then trained the crosshairs on his sight toward the podium and at the roadie's head, to check. He lowered his weapon and took up another Frito. Now came the waiting for his cue from the Coalition Commander. It was all about timing for a sniper.

Most of the crowd didn't hear whatever Piet had said as he announced Sylvia. They all knew who she was by now. She stepped up to the podium to the sound of thunderous and enthusiastic cheers, catcall-whistles and applause from all around.

The crowd flickered in dots of red, blue and white as the audience waved the American flags they were given at the stadium entrance. Others held up and waved copies of the *Neo-Publica Manifesto* they'd bought as they came in. Sylvia smiled broadly, and raised her hands as she was received, often flexing her fingers to beckon more. Finally, after nearly five minutes, she lowered her hands to signal for silence.

"Hi, I'm Sylvia Morales, and we ARE the people!" she said close into the mic, then went quiet over another loud rush of cheers. "Okay…Okay," she said. "Let's leave a little time for my remarks!" The cheers died down, except for an occasional *We love you, Sylvia!* "For nearly ten years, we have been fighting to restore what had made out country great for two-hundred and fifty years. It's only taken those ten years for one man and his cohorts to tear all that down. The tear *America* down" Loud *Booos*! Echoed through the assemblage. "America may never have been perfect, but she was always great, no matter who tried to tell us otherwise. She was always *great!*" Now there were thousands of chants of: "*U.S.A.!* *U.S.A.!*" "We ARE the people…and we are all working to bring this nation back to what she was destined to be…AMERICA!" The "U.S.A.!"s were joined by another chant, and some waving signs: "*Bring America Back!*" She allowed more time for the fever to die down. "Okay. Now, you know about me as the one who has been fighting for this, but I have only been the most vocal. But I and my cohorts were not the only ones fighting for this. We *all* were fighting for it!" More cheers. "And you were fighting for it maybe even harder than I was, because what you'd believed in your hearts was suppressed by a regime who wanted to make such thinking illegal. But no more!" *No More! No More!* "We the people have been held captive by our wants our needs for our OUR nation. Not theirs…Ours!…" An eruption of cheers. "It's our Constitution that made this county what it is and has always been. Even now. And every tenet of our Constitution has been violated into a dictatorship! Two weeks ago, our Premier announced that women—mothers—could choose—choose!— to be sterilized, if they did not want to risk their third child being taken and sent out for BlueShirt indoctrination and training. I repeat: Sterilization. Another right reduced to a quid-pro-quo choice." Boos. "If we are not already there, with these gulags and sterilization, we are on our way to Nazi Germany. Maybe its more devious than that, because all this came about while we slept, and through a rule of lies. While we slept, Kenton and his people spent their time reaching into Hitler's playbook and suppress our truths with their lies. I believe we are beyond already there, and we have systematically led to believe that this is the status quo. Our teachers—as good as gone; our scientists—gone; our thinkers, authors, philosophers—gone. And why? Because they are a threat. This regime is so frightened by the enemy of intelligence, it throws it into gulags! And what remains behind? The I.Q. of a gnat! But we were not sleeping, guys; merely waiting for the right time. And that is now! There is nothing to be afraid of with them, people. Intelligence and reason, faith, and hope, have not been put away, and the will exists to fight against those who try to take away what is in our hearts and minds. I know this. Why? Because people. We are *here*! And we ARE the people!"

Chants of "We ARE the people!" thundered through the stadium, as the Jumbotrons flashed an image of the Constitution.

The sun had nearly slipped behind the mountains, and the stadium lights glared brightly. Karen first caught an unusual glint while she patrolled an upper far row of the stadium's east side. It wasn't much; almost like a camera's strobe flash coming from below the different brightness of the stadium lights in the end zone.

She blinked twice as she trained her gaze there, and the glint happened again.

One of the Neo-Pub attendees in the upper row was watching Sylvia speak through his field glasses. "Hey, there," she said to him. "Can I borrow those for a second?"

He held them down and glanced at her. He saw the security badge pinned to her windbreaker snd the ID—faked—in its plastic envelope around her neck. "What? You gonna take these from me? They're not illegal, ya know."

She tried easing her expression into a smile. "Just for a second, okay?" He grumbled something and handed her his field glasses. She aimed them toward the glint, and though it was hard to make out through the network of struts and ganglia of wires in the lighting cage, she made out a figure. She adjusted her gaze tighter and saw he was aiming a long gun. "Shit!" she said as she fumbled to bring her headset mic closer to her lips. "Tom! Tom! Are you there? It's Karen."

Tom Roeblings's voice came cracking through the headset. "Yeah, Karen?"

"Tom. I think we've got a shooter."

"Where?"

She raised the field glasses again for a better look. The barrel of the rifle sticking from the cage shifted a little. "Yeah. Up in the lights below that big TV over the north end zone. I don't know how he coulda gotten up there. What do I do?" She glanced up to the top row above her and saw some sort of lighting control shack with an open front built into the stands. She blinked into the harsh glare of spotlights beaming from it onto the field.

"Shit!" Roebling said. "Stand your ground, Karen, don't try to get up there. Anyone closer to the north end zone?"

"It's Dan Harris, Tom. I'm about ten rows down from the top. The lights are right above me."

"You see anything, Dan?"

"Can't tell from my angle. I'm going up."

Karen spied Dan fifty feet away racing toward the upper rows in the end-zone. Both of them were beneath the shooter's line of vision. She started toward the stairs leading to the top row.

"Hey! Can I have my glasses back, now?"

She knew she'd need them. She glared back at the guy. "No."

"Why not?"

"Because they're illegal," she said, and hastened up two stairs at a time.

Dan got to his position and then edged to his left for a side view of the cage. "I've got him, Tom," he whispered into his mic. "I'm maybe twenty feet away. He can't see me."

"Can you get up there?"

"There's a narrow catwalk, I think, and a ladder up to it. It looks a little creaky, like it might make some noise."

"Can you get a bead on him from where you are?"

"I think so, but it'll be tight."

"Guys," Karen said. "Don't try that. If you miss, he'll fire at Sylvia." She saw the door of the shack, and a technician in it. The spots looked as though they might swivel. "I might have an idea," she breathed into her mic as she rushed toward the shack's door.

"What?" Roebling said.

"Leave me alone, Tom," she quipped back. "Sorry. I'll get right back to you. Don't shoot now, Dan. I'll let you know."

The lighting tech jolted to a stand from behind his control panel. "What are you doing in here?"

"Security. We need these lights."

"Why?"

"Never the fuck mind, okay?" she breathed hastily. His look turned suddenly stern as he tried to protect his post. "Sorry, man. We may have a situation here. No time to explain."

"For fuck's sake," he groused as he stood aside.

"No. Stay at your control panel. Can these two end spotlight be turned?"

"Uh yeah. But I'll have to do it manually."

"Okay. Do it…please. When I tell you, I'll need you to quickly aim them at the bottom left of that lighting cluster over there, over the end zone."

He complied almost too casually as he sipped over to the end lights and pulled out the cotter pins on their stands to free them to swivel.

She brought up the glasses to get a view of the sniper. This time it was much clearer. She pulled her mic closer to her lips. "Dan?" she whispered. "You there?"

"Yeah Karen."

"You got him in your range?"

"Yeah."

She trained the glasses on Dan. He was about fifteen feet away from the lighting cage, protected from the shooter's view. He had his .45 drawn and aimed. "Okay I'm gonna try to distract him. When I do, take your shot."

"Yeah, Karen. I've got him."

"Dan?"

"I hear you, hon."

"Don't call me 'hon.' Listen. Are you sure you got a good shot at this guy?" She raised the field glasses and had a good view of the shooter wriggling himself into a what could be his shooting position.

"Yeah. Pretty sure."

"Pretty sure isn't good enough. I need to know for solid you've got a solid shot at him. You'll probably get only one. You gotta go for your first shot when I say so."

"What are you doing, Karen?" Roebling asked.

She looked over at the lighting tech. He had his hands on the levers controlling the swings of both lights. "You ready?"

"Yeah. You want me to shoot these spots over at the end zone housing."

"Right. You may have to do some adjusting. I'll tell you." She raised the glasses again and trained them steady on the sniper.

"Okay…Tom? I've got control of some spotlights, and I think we can aim them right at him. Maybe fuck up his concentration. That's when you take your shot, Dan." She saw the barrel raise through the housing as the shooter took his lock on Sylvia. "Shit! Pull those lights around hard and fast. NOW!"

He swung the light hard to glare right into where the sniper lay, hopefully right into his eyes. She saw him startle. Another roar rose from the crowd. "NOW, Dan! Take it!" She didn't hear the report of Dan's .45, but she saw the long gun tumble from the housing and on to the empty upper row of seats.

"Okay," Dan said. "Target down."

"Good work, man," Roebling said.

"Yeah, pretty fucking amazing. I guess you can call me 'hon', now."

"Thanks, hon."

She focused the field glasses. The sniper's arm dangled from the housing. It looked like a clean kill. Then she noticed the upper sleeve of his khaki shirt was wrapped in wide black armband with a diagonal white stripe. It might have been a uniform. "Hey, Tom."

"Yeah, Karen?"

"Looks like he's wearing some sorta armband. Black with a white stripe. Does that mean anything to you guys?"

"I have no idea. Wait, something's coming up out here. I gotta go."

Tom would soon find out what the black armband meant, as four bikers fronting a squad of six men afoot stormed toward the main gate. "What the fuck?" he said, as he saw they were all wearing black armbands on the upper sleeve of their khaki shirts. The armbands were emblazoned around their circumference with one, two, or three diagonal white stripes like designations of rank. The bikers rode in a zig-zag pattern as they up-ended the two kiosks where the crowd had bought their manifestos. The excess books spilled on the pavement as some troopers went to slice open the boxes to empty their contents of books. It had all happened quickly and precisely.

Tom rushed from the van and ran through the crisscrossing motorcycles to one of the troopers with two white stripes on his armband. "What the hell are you doing?"

"What's it look like? And who the hell are you?"

Some other troopers kicked the stray books into a rough pile and set fire to it.

"I'm Premier Kenton's security head for this operation."

"Okay. Fine." the trooper said blandly. "Nice to fucking meet you. We're the Real-America Coalition Army."

"Who? Who the fuck is the Real-America Coalition Army?"

"Make sure you get those books over there, sergeant!" he ordered a one-striper.

The sergeant gathered up a stack of manifestos in his arms and fed the fire. "Godamn it! Who the fuck *are* you?"

"Excuse me, there, gumshoe," the two-striper said and brushed past Roebling. Another few troopers emerged from the stadium entrance carrying some bundles of American flags from which the attendees drew as they came in. They threw them on the fire with the books, and the flames raged higher, the fire's smoke blackening from the dies in the burning cloth of the flags.

"Widen out the shot on Sylvia on Camera Two, Greg," Madelyn said. "That's a good crowd shot Camera Six." She stared closer at the Camera Six monitor. "That looks weird. Hey, Six, zoom in on those lights below that end-zone Jumbotron." Greg gave the instruction and Camera Six zoomed in on a strand of khaki hanging like a limp pennant below the light cage. She squinted at the monitor. "Is that an…?"

"Zoom in closer, Six," Greg said. There was an undercurrent of reluctance in his tone.

"Shit. That's an arm! Is that a *dead* guy in the light cage?"

"Excuse me, Miss Kenton," came a large voice from behind her.

"Now what fresh hell is this?" she asked as she saw the Coalition Army three-striper fill the tight space behind her.

"We'll take it from here, ma'm."

"The fuck you will! This is my trailer, my operation. So please…get the fuck out."

"No, sorry, Miss Kenton. "He edged his hand toward the .45 in his holster. "It isn't, anymore. Not today, at least."

"You do know who I am?"

"Of course I do, and I am under orders from your father to seize this operation."

She was too stunned to respond, *Am I on, yet*? It was a familiar voice coming from Monitor Eight. Her father's face filled the screen. It reminded her of how much she hated that man.. "What the fuck?" she said to the three-striper.

He talked quietly into the mic clipped to his collar. "Take your shot, Brick. Target's clear."

Madelyn, mouth agape, looked back at the monitors: Sylvia making her speech on Two; the dead guy's khaki clad arm on Six, then something long and shiny on the seats below; her father's face on Eight as he straightened his red tie.

"Brick? Target's clear. Take the shot! You read, Brick?"

Madelyn glowered at him and pointed harshly to Monitor Six. "This what you're looking for, Ranger Rick?" She reached for the phone wired to the security trailer.

"Shit!" the three-striper spat.

Madelyn tightened her expression into an ugly scowl. "Looks like your boy dropped his gun." She spoke into the phone's handset. "Tom? We've got a situation in our trailer....Tom? Are you there?"

The three-striper lifted his side arm from the holster and motioned its barrel toward a corner of the trailer. "Line's cut. Now, I'm sorry, Ma'm. I'm gonna have to ask you and your crew to step over there. Except you," he said to Greg.

"We can't be Americans unless we gather together!" Sylvia's voice echoed as she spoke into the microphone.

"I'm sorry, Maddie," Greg told her. "I have to." He punched up Monitor Eight and spoke into the mic transmitting to the stadium's Audio Video control room. "Okay, Eight. Let's go live," he said

26

Twenty Miles South of Pueblo

Later, December 2,

"We can't be Americans unless we bond together!" Sylvia's voice boomed throughout the stadium.

The crowd's cheers turned to gasps as the image on the four Jumbotrons dissolved into static and then Kenton's face filled the screens. "Hello, Real-Americans!" he said. He'd sounded chipper as if greeting an old friend. He was answered with a resounding round of *booos!*. "I really do hate to break in like this but believe it or not I'm on your side. I'm here to tell you the truth."

"Fucking bastard!" was all Sylvia could think to mutter, as she felt as if a bolt of lightning had frozen her in place.

"This whole Neo-Publican game is meant to bring down the country that we, as a people, under my guidance, has made great." The camera pulled out reveal Premier Kenton at his Regime podium and Commissar Montefiore hunched like Quasimodo by his side. Behind them hung the grim New America flag. Montefiore was handed a message. He shook his head as he read it. "They only want to bring us all back in time, so we had no choice but to take down your leader…"

"Huh? Take me down? What the fuck?" Sylvia gasped.

"Huh?" Kenton said incredulously off to Montefiore. "We didn't….?"

Sylvia shouted into the microphone. "No! You didn't, you son of a bitch! I'm still standing!" She raised her fist. "WE'RE still standing!" The crowd erupted into a deafening cheer. "WE'RE still standing!" she repeated. *America* is still standing!"

Kenton seemed deaf to their cries because he was—there was no reciprocal feed in his direction. He tried to hide his blustering by staring blankly into the teleprompter even though he was off-script. "No? " His voice boomed once again through the stadium speakers: "Well, I'm sorry to hear that. But, Sylvia Morales, if you can still hear me, I tell you this. I'm coming for you—there is no place for you to run."

Booos! upon *booos!*

Sylvia, drained of all her decorum, she leaned into her mic. "Come and find me, you fat dickhead!"

Resounding cheers

"We will find you, first!"

"You and your Neo Pubicans will be squashed under the righteous weight of Real-America!"

"America! AMERICA! " the crowd chanted. "U.S.A.!"

"Now I know many of you were forced to show up at this rally, and I don't want you to think I have anything against you. So, in the name of fairness, I'll allow you to turn yourselves in on the way out of the stadium. All you have to do is claim your allegiance to Real-America. And stop playing this silly game of yours. That's it. We outnumber you. And I outrank you all!"

"Fuck him!" Sylvia shouted into the mike.

"Fuck him! Fuck him!" Tunneled its way through the crowd, but with less enthusiasm as the quieted audience seemed to be weighing the option of getting arrested...or worse.

Kenton looked down to his right. "Well, now. There you are. Now I see you and you see me. You've got a big crowd, there,

Sylvia." He leaned forward and stared straight into the camera with his reptilian squint and pouty mouth. "We May have to build a few more gulags to put all your people into," he threatened. The crowd quieted nearly completely in mass-contemplation. "Ah. I see *I'm* the one who's got your attention now." Some of the attendees headed for the exits. Then more.

"Don't leave!" Sylvia said. "They're waiting to arrest you at the door! Please. Stay in the stadium!"

"Ah. Yes, we are." Kenton growled. "Anyone not claiming allegiance to New America and me will be carted away. So, you have three choices. You can stay in the football stadium, there; you can come out and be arrested; or you can come out and claim your allegiance to Real-America and go home peacefully to your families. To me, that choice is obvious."

"You will not intimidate or harm any one of the Neo-Publica followers, Mr. Premier."

"Or what, Sylvia? Here I am, standing shivering in fright."

She noticed several droves of people heading out the stadium exits. She could sympathize with them. The prospect of ending up in a gulag, perhaps to die there was terrifying. But she saw others head back to their seats in solidarity. "You can't stop us, but we can stop you."

"Oh, really? How?"

"How? Through our right to freedom. FREEDOM!" she said into the mic.

Cries of Freedom! splintered through the crowd.

"We ARE the people! And We are free! FREEDOM!" Sylvia shouted hoarsely.

Cries of "*We ARE the people! FREEDOM!*" grew through the crowd as their voices rose loud.

Kenton stood staring into the camera, looking dumb founded. Montefiore took his place behind the podium. "You can't stay in that stadium forever, people! This is your last chance to leave before we force you to. And believe me when I say we can, without even breaking a sweat. To those that remain there: We will END you!" Montefiore's sounded like a threat from hell.

But the crowd stood their ground: "*We ARE the people!*"

Sylvia quieted them. There was a tense silence through the place as one side waited for the other to make its next move: to draw first. She pursed her lips hard, then leaned into the mic to speak in her normal voice. "Let my people leave in peace, Mr. Premier. It's not them you want. Do you really want to arrest them for seizing onto an idea?"

Scattered cries of "No! "rumbled throughout the stadium.

"It's me you want. We both know that. Take me and do with me what you will."

NO! NO!

She quieted the growing cries. "This is not to say anyone has lost or won," she told them. "Let everyone here go in peace back to their lives…as Americans."

AMERICA! AMERICA! U.S.A.! U.S.A!

"No." Kenton said. "As *Real-American*s. That's the only way. Then we will take you. *If* we leave the others be."

"Premier Kenton. Everyone in this country has the power of choice. Let them make that one their own. Just not today. And to all of you here, I ask that you leave in peace. I will wait right here until I know you have all cleared. Do we have a deal, Mr. Premier? You can finally have me."

Kenton thought for a minute, then conferred with Montefiore. Finally, the Commissar nodded in acquiescence. "Very well, Sylvia."

"I have your word?" She knew his word was worth nothing, but she called on something that might. "This whole exchange has been broadcast live over your network, to your people. You have just made a public promise to me and to them. You violate that, and you may stir up some Real-Americans. So, I need your public promise right now."

"I promise, Sylvia." Kenton said.

"You promise what, Mr. Premier?"

He wet his lips. Sighed. "I promise I'll let the people in the stadium leave without arresting any of them. Unless they incite us to in any way."

"Now to the rest of you, I say. Give the guards no trouble and just go home. I expect that promise from you, as…" She stopped short of saying "Neo-Publica". "Honest and free people. Now thank you for showing tonight. I will wait. And peace be with you."

It was a solemn crowd that left the stadium over the next few hours, as Sylvia waited patiently in her chair on the stage. Aileen, Robert, Piet and Hugh sat with her in quiet solidarity. Karen was off doing something else.

After the waiting, it had all been a numbing blur to Sylvia. It was as if she'd been drugged and perhaps she was. Yes. She definitely was; her arm still hurt from the sting of the needle right after she'd had a hood drawn harshly over her head.

She remembered the tears in Aileen's eyes and on her cheek; how they accentuated her freckles. She had hugged Piet, who'd seemed to fall into her as though weakened in the knees. Then the hug with Hugh, who stood shivering and breathing hard, as though holding back his tears. Karen, maid of the mist as she'd always been, never showed. Sylvia thought fitting for her nature. She remembered how tightly she embraced Robert—for the last time—but hadn't remembered anything they'd said, though words of love farewell must had been spoken. The two security guards had to practically pry them apart before they led her alone from the stadium, like Joan d'Arc to the chopping block. She had held her head proudly, knowing her run had all been worth it.

The guards had handled her gently as they walked her to the waiting PRICE squad car. They turned her over to another angular-faced man, and they went to take their places in the driver and passenger seats. The angular-faced man was not as gentle as he cuffed her, forced her into the backseat and forced a black hood down over her head. She then felt the prick of a needle into her right bicep. The last thing she recalled seeing was the black armband with two diagonal white stripes wrapped around the arm of his khaki shirt. He smelled of sweat and Vitalis.

She heard the muscular engine of the car turn over, then felt the car take to moving slowly, then faster, as though it was on an open stretch of highway. "Where-where're we goin'?" She asked drowsily.

She felt a quick punch to her ribs from her backseat companion with the black armband. She gasped at the hard pain in her side. "Shut up, bitch!"

"Settle back m'am," said one of guards in the front seat. "It'll be a long drive. We're taking you to Arizona."

Shit! She reasoned. *Dalaxuma! Sheriff Jeff's gulag. No trial. They're just going straight for the kill.* The drugs soon caught up with her body, and she gradually passed out.

As she came into a dull wakefulness, she heard and sensed a hard thud against the outside of the backseat door. The juddering of the car and muffled shouts of a brutal struggle outside brought her more awake. Realizing she was alone in the backseat, she tried to free her hands from the plastic cuffs. All she got for that effort was a sharp, binding pain around her wrists.

Too late, no chance, she thought as the door opened again and let in a rush of hot desert air. She settled back into her seat and felt her guard take his position next to her. Her hood was swiped up over her head, and she blinked to accustom her vision the too light. Something like fresh air at last. She breathed in hard, as though she'd been underwater within the hood. She winced as felt another jab to her ribs; this one much lighter than before.

"Hey!" said the guard, who'd suddenly taken on a female's voice. "Hey, Syl!" She turned slowly to face Karen. "Hey, hon. Miss me?"

"Yes," was all Sylvia could gasp.

It had started about five minutes before. About three-and-a-half hours into the ride and twenty miles south of Pueblo, the guard on the passenger side announced he needed to take a piss. The driver found a dirt side-road leading off into a no-man's land and stopped the car. Driver and passenger got out, then swiftly opened the back door where the Real-America Coalition Army sergeant sat.

"The fuck?" he yelped as they roughed him out and forced him against the car. "You know who the fuck you're dealing with, here?" he groaned under the force of their restraint.

"Oh, yeah, dickhead," Dan Harris, the driver, told him in one ear.

"Best you shut the fuck up," Mike Hastings said into his other ear. They turned him sideways against the car, then ripped open his shirt and pulled it down.

Karen slipped from where she'd lain in wait in some bushes. She snuck up unnoticed in the confusion of the squabble and behind the Coalition sergeant. " 'Scuse me, Bucky," she said, then held a chloroform-soaked rag across his mouth. Once he relaxed into unconsciousness, Dan removed the guard's shirt and armband, while Mike relieved him of his wallet and gun. They dragged him to the edge a deep ravine, where Karen performed her trademark jab of the dirk into his neck for the kill. They rolled his body off into the shadows of the desert ravine.

"Karen?" Sylvia said fatigued, but aghast. "How did you…?"

"D'ju think for one minute I'd leave you so that fat fuck could take you down, again?" She flicked her bloodied knife blade through the plastic cuffs to release them. "Oh ye of little faith."

"Karen!" Sylvia gasped one more time and pulled her into a tearful embrace.

" 'S gonna be okay, now, Syl."

Mike and Dan slipped into the front seats, then eased the squad car into the dirt road leading back out into the CanAm Highway. "Who are these—?" she motioned to the front seat.

"Ah," Karen said as she put on the Coalition guard's shirt. "These two fine gentlemen are Dan Harris, driving, and Mike Hastings, riding shotgun." She slipped a black ball cap over her head. "They're two of Tom's guys. They're with us."

"Hey, guys. Thanks. Really." She leaned her head against Karen's shoulder.

"Any time," Mike said. "So, there's been a change in plans. You won't be going to Delaxuma, where we've been ordered to take you…

Sylvia went weightless with relief—a delayed reaction.

"Instead, we're gonna stop at a rest-stop outside of Sante Fe, and you'll be taken to a private airstrip, where our jet will fly you to Bridgeport, Connecticut. From there another car will take you back to Brooklyn," Dan said.

"And this will all work?" Sylvia said.

"It'd better," Mike said. "I'll stay with you the whole trip."

"We're not just telling all this just because to give you an itinerary, Sylvia," Dan told her. "Well, that, too, 'cause you need to know. But we just want you to know that the drivers and pilots you'll meet along your way are with us, too. Totally devoted to the cause. But just try to stay mum with them, anyway, while we work out the next steps with Tom Roebling."

"Things have been happening pretty quick over the last few hours, hon," Karen said. "We're kinda making this up as we go. Tom's in control, for now."

"Meaning?" Sylvia said suspiciously.

Karen squeezed her hand. "Well, we got the manifesto out, right? We now know the Neo Pubs are gaining strength and leverage. Tom will fill in some blanks when we see him."

"The car you catch from Connecticut won't be taking you back to your place in Brooklyn. Too risky." Dan said. "Tom's set up an apartment on the second floor of Slade's Place as a safe house. That's where you'll keep put and lay low for a while."

"Okay," Sylvia said cautiously. "Why do you have to drop me off at a rest stop? Why can't you just drive me to the jet?"

Mike lit a cigarette. "This is a PRICE car. It's tagged, and we're being tracked to stay on Route twenty-five and then to the Dalaxuma gate. We gotta bring it through the motions to make them think that happened. That means no detours."

"Can I have a cigarette, Mike?"

"Sure." He lit another and passed it to her through the cage separating the front seat.

She took a long inhale. Savored it. "You don't think they'll notice I'm not dropped off there?"

"Kenton and company put Tom in charge of getting you there. That's the sort of thing the head of security does. He arranged it by not telling Sheriff Jeff and the boys you'll be coming to visit," Dan said. "They expect nothing. Besides, its such a cluster-fuck down there, they wouldn't even know if Santa Claus came through their front gate."

"Cluster-fuck?" Sylvia said.

"Yeah," Karen said. "They don't normally know what's going on, anyway, but now the fucking place is so over-crowed it's beyond their simple minds."

"Plus," Mike added. "There was some sort of riot there a few months back. It kind of dissolved their abilities."

Sylvia took another drag. "You guys are amazing. All of you."

"No, Sylvia," Dan said. "You are. You got us here, for better or for worse. You've got a lot of support out there, and I think you're getting into Kenton's and Commissar Montefiore's heads."

"You really think so, Dan?"

"We *know* so, Sylvia," Mike said.

"Hell of a speech you gave back there," Dan said.

"We've got a long ride to Santa Fe, hon," Karen soothed. "And you've got a longer ride after that. Try to get some rest."

Sylvia tamped out her half-smoked cigarette and leaned her head further onto Karen's shoulder. She felt Karen's light, tenuous touch stroking her hair. She reckoned that maybe caring for Emily had brought out her mother-side. Karen had already gone up to Boston twice in the last few weeks to visit her in the the rehab there. Sylvia relaxed her eyes and watched the brambles and the immensity of desert slither by.

27

The Martyr

December 5

Montague Street hummed with activity two stories down. It was a different life down there, like some alien activity. All Sylvia could do was watch, as if there was nothing else to do anymore. The Neo-Publica Movement had rolled away from her under its own inertia. Reading between the lines of the Kenton/Fox News reports, she had the impression it was tightening its grip around the Kenton Regime. Ever so slowly.

She would have gone completely stir crazy without her disguised morning think walks down Montague then along\ the promenade toward the Brooklyn Bridge. There she would pause, perhaps sit, in silence and take in the screeching and squawking of seagulls and the bracing, briny air churning north with the water of the East River. She let her thoughts wander back to her childhood in the country. The peppery-sweet smell of new-mown grass. The way the wet clipping clung to the white fenceposts. Simple times. Clean memories. Refreshed, she heaved a sigh and returned to her rooms above Slade's Place to wait and contemplate on what would be next for her. She now knew she would have to leave.

Roebling had already told her, even after he'd arranged for it. After the group meeting in the cafe he'd closed for tonight, she would have one last time to say goodbye; this time for real. Tomorrow she would take another private jet out to another private airstrip in the sovereign State of California, which had finally seceded in 2025. She would settle in San Francisco with its attitude now as nascent as it was 150 years before. It was the gold rush all over again, but this time the gold was a Constitutional Democracy. California had been struggling, but it was holding its own, even though its border had been closed off solid for a year and a half. She vaguely remembered her parents telling her about the Berlin Wall, separating free Germany in the west from Communist Germany in the east. The California wall was like that...exactly like that. And people had been killed trying to escape Real-America into what was left of America. Her job here was done. She would be more needed out there.

Tuesday night , December 5

It was as if the New York was running out of power. Another blackout had happened again without notice, and we had no idea how long it would be this time. Flame light guttered through the darkened room the in the rear of Slade's Place, rendering it more like a setting for a seance than a meeting. Seven of us stood around flutteringly lit from below, with our drinks in hand; scant rations of ice watering them down. What we talked about was as meaningless as it was soon forgotten. We weren't listening to one another but were just comforted by the sounds of our voices. It was like a dirge.

I'd spent the last few days on an edge which left me struggling for breath. We had survived Denver, but Sylvia had not, and was probably now being ravaged in some gulag. Yet here we were, prattling nervously over our drinks about anything other than what happened three days earlier. Karen seemed aloof; even complacent, as she talked to the two men, Dan and Mike. They were new to our cadre, and Karen hovered around them like she knew them. Hugh, Piet, Aileen, and I were shrouded in skepticism—at least I was.

But that didn't matter tonight in this chilly, dark room. I stared into the fire in the open hearth, the room's only source of warmth. I tried to allow the oblivious flicker of the licking flames take my mind away somewhere else, maybe back in time. But my thoughts always brought me back to the dim reality of the present. Both women I loved were gone; most likely dead by now. I felt cursed. All I could do was to channel more of my love into Emily. I could feel her redeveloping love for me, even from where she was safe and rehabilitating in a Boston rehab. The day before, I'd received a short letter from her; the first since she'd left still traumatized five weeks before. The timing had been good. Her message was scrawled in an uncertain version of her handwriting:

Dad—I am fine, here. I miss you and I love you. And I will see you soon.

Really, I'm okay.

Love, Emily.

That was the sum of everything that had kept me going.

Tom Roebling made his sudden presence known as he strode boldly—confidently—into the room. How dare him.

"Sorry for this nineteenth-century environment, all. Generator crapped out his morning, and I can't get any guys in until tomorrow to fix it."

"I kinda like it, Tom," Karen said. "Has a sort of Wild West feel to it." She seemed almost chipper; she knew something the rest of us didn't.

Tom rolled his hands together to warm them as he went toward the hearth. "Okay. Let's cut to the chase. There's something some of you still need to know."

Karen offered up that smug smile of hers as she huddled in restrained giddiness closer to the two men. "Well, Tom. For Pete's sake. Don't keep us guessing." Her tone was facetious; rehearsed. She definitely knew something.

"Okay!" Tom called to the door. "You can come on in now."

Aileen huddled closer to me. I could feel she was just as stiffened with shock as I was. Confused shock, as Sylvia came into the room.

"Where have you been, Syl?" Aileen finally said, as if she'd stayed out too late.

"Oh...around, I guess," she said, then glanced at Karen.

I could find no words. I rushed to her and wrapped her into an embrace she was curiously reluctant to return. I sensed she'd been crying—there was more to the story.

Once Aileen's confusion lifted, she rushed to us and made a threesome of our hug. Hugh and Piet remained behind, dumbfounded.

"No fucking way were we gonna let let them take her off to some damn gulag," Karen proclaimed.

"We?" Aileen said through a sniffle.

"Well, yeah, Allie. Me, Tom, and Dan and Mike, here. Tom handled the extraction—her rescue."

"As head of security, I was put in charge of getting her out of Denver and down to Delaxuma," Tom explained as he sauntered over to the center table.

"Christ!" I said. "That God damned place."

"Yeah. And Damn! Somewhere along the way the incompetent guard lost the prisoner. How about that?" Tom said fecklessly as he took his seat. "And you might say Karen, and my two drivers, here, found her."

"And who are you?" I asked the one named Dan.

"Tom'll explain it all," he answered.

"Have a seat," Tom invited us. "There's a lot we need to discuss."

We took seats around the table. I sat next to Sylvia and held her hand. I wasn't letting go this time. Her squeeze back seemed flaccid.

"Our plans have hardened," Tom told us, then lit a cigar. "So, let's get to it. I may not be able to leverage my position in the Kenton regime that much longer. It's probably only a matter of time before they're on to me—on to us. I'm more convinced than ever that we Neo-Pubs have to act fast...and decisively, to cement ourselves in place. Knowing what I know about Kenton and his people, the longer we wait, the quicker they will try bringing us down." He glanced around the table. "All of us. So, here's the deal," he took a long draw on his cigar. "I'm taking the reins."

I quickly gazed at Sylvia. She sat stoic, as did Karen and the two men across from her. "What the fuck, Tom! Come on. Sylvia's back now, and she's in charge."

She squeezed my hand. "It's okay, hon," she said. "Really. Hear him out."

"Oh, yeah, sure," Piet said. "What do we know about these others, huhn? I mean, Tom's been really helpful in this, and all—more than helpful. But what do we really know about him, except he's with the Kenton regime?

I looked at Tom. "And what about these other two guys?" I said. "They're with Tom, right? In the Kenton camp? How do we know they're not part of Premier Kenton's grand plan to take us down?"

"I think I've more than shown you that I'm not," Tom replied irritated. "As far as these other two, Dan Harris and Mike Hastings, they've been with me since the beginning. We've been in the field together for twenty years."

"Okay," Hugh said. "If we're gonna go with you, it's not enough that you three know each other. How do we know we can trust you?"

"He has a plan," Sylvia said. "I trust him. So you trust him."

"Syl?" Aileen implored. "You've been through a lot. Don't be so willing to drink their Kool-aid."

"Okay," Tom said. "You want proof? Kenton and Montefiore are out for blood. So, A—if it weren't for me, Sylvia would be Delaxuma, probably dead by now. Okay. And B—my plan: I'm going to be the trigger man in taking Kenton down." He let this sink in. "I'm taking him out."

"Jesuzzz!" I gasped while the others, except Sylvia, sat in shock. "You are fucking kidding, Tom. Right?"

"No," he answered decisively, "I am not."

"Jesuzz, bitch!" Karen gasped at Tom as she forgot her manners. "You're just full of surprises! How the hell are you gonna do that?"

"If anyone can, it's me," Tom said.

Even Dan was incredulous. "You've thought this through, Tom? We're ready?"

"Yeah, Dan. Sylvia and I talked about this last night, and we decided it's the only way, and now is the time."

"You're fucking nuts, Tom," Hugh said. "How are you gonna do this? Walk up to him, tap him on the shoulder, say 'Excuse me, Mr. Premier' then blow his face off?"

Tom smiled grimly. "Nothing that dramatic."

"How, then?" Piet said.

"Yeah, Tom. What's your plan this time?" Karen said. "I mean is it something like: 'I'd tell you, but I'd have to kill you'?"

"Probably something like that," Mike told her.

She turned to him. "You knew about this, Mike? *Both* of you?"

"We hadn't worked out the details, but yeah, Karen. We knew," Dan said.

"Jesus wept!" she gushed. "And I thought I was the queen of: 'The less you know, the better.'" She folded her arms tight across her chest, as though she wanted nothing more to do with them.

"And *you* knew about this, Sly?" Aileen said.

"I found out last night, so yeah."

"God damnit, Syl!" Aileen blathered as she openly wept. "Why? How can you let this happen?"

"Because, Allie, and all of you," she said. "This *has* to happen. Kenton has taken this all too far. We have to stop it and…well, we just have to stop it. This is what Neo-Publica is all about."

"Killing the Premier, Syl?" Aileen said for all of us. "I never knew that was our endgame."

"No," Tom said. "But it's mine. Look, I know where he plans on talking this whole thing. I know why he's going to Helsinki in two weeks. Neo Publica must act. And soon."

"Hell, man I don't want my name on this plan, whatever it is." Hugh said. "Trying to restore Democracy is one thing. But killing the Premier just because he's an asshole?"

"A very fucking dangerous asshole," Dan said. "Dangerous to what we are as Americans—what we're fighting for."

This left a silence in its wake. As if to emphasize it, a blaze of light rose from the hearth and a log sizzled as it broke in two and crumbled into the others. Tom drew on his cigar.

"Why?" I finally said.

"Why, what?" Tom said.

"Why is he going to Helsinki? I mean we already know he's meeting with the Soviet Premier, that's nothing new. But why this time?"

"I'm sorry, Bob," Tom said. "That's a need-to-know thing."

"And killing our Premier in cold blood isn't?" Karen asked. "Listen, man. You brought us this far and look where it's gotten us? Yeah, it's need-to-know, alright. And we need to know. We risked ours and Sylvia's life for this, so fuckin-A, yeah. We need to know."

Tom looked to Mike.

"She's right, Tom," he said. "You might as well tell them."

"Can I trust you not to say anything about this?" he asked the table.

"Can you trust us to trust you as Neo-Publica?" I said. I wondered why Sylvia had remained so quiet through all of this.

"Okay," Tom sighed. "He's going to Finland to meet with Premier Vladovkov." He paused while we waited. "They're gonna firm up an alliance to have the New Soviet Republic absorb Real-America—to turn us Communist, as one alliance controlled by the Soviets...and Kenton, of course."

"Holeee Shit!" Hugh breathed.

"What the *fuck*?" Karen gasped.

"That son of a bitch!" Hugh said

Stunned, I couldn't think of anything else to say: "I knew I shouldn't have voted for him that second time," I whispered.

"You *what*?" Aileen said.

"That was a past life, Allie," Sylvia said. "That's all this would have been—all of our efforts— wasted in a past life. All of it, unless something is done now. It has to be stopped or there'll be no turning back."

"How long will it take for all this to happen?" I asked Tom. "Turning America Communist. How long?"

"Inside word says he'll be signing an executive order right after the first of the year," Mike said solemnly.

I looked at Sylvia for reassurance. She just smiled sadly and nodded back at me. There was no choice. I looked at Tom. "Okay," I said. "Do it soon—and quietly. Are we all agreed?" Hugh, Piet and Karen—she by saying "Shit!"—nodded in agreement. I knew it wasn't exactly our choice, as Tom had made up his mind.

He played along. "Okay, then thanks. But I can't guarantee how quiet it'll be."

"Okay, Tom." Piet said. "So, you kill the man. What makes you sure MonteFiore and his goons won't come after you?"

"That's a problem," Tom said. "I can't be sure."

"This totally sucks," Hugh said.

Tom simpered at him and then around the table. He stood. "More drinks?" he said. For as long as I'd known him—and would know Tom, this was the only time I'd seen him so fearful.

"Sure, Tom," I said, trying to be normal. "Bourbon—on whatever rocks there are left."

Later. December 5

Things became unusually mellow, under the circumstances of what we could not mention, even among ourselves. There was no stove, so dinner was strictly a deli-affair of chicken salad and roast beef sandwiches. Thankfully there had been a good stock of wine, and that night I would have drunk anything that would take me away from the abstract reality of it all.

Then, once we had eased a little, Tom announced another part of his plan. Something more personal. He lit another cigar and eased back in his chair. Sylvia bummed another cigarette from Mike. I knew she knew something that had saddened her.

Tom heaved a sigh to settle into another confession. "Tom drove Sylvia from Denver in a PRICE squad car, so it looked official. A little way south, they made an unscheduled stop where Karen joined the crowd after 'relieving' Montefiore's Coalition guard of his duty of guarding Sylvia."

"Coalition guard?" Piet asked. He seemed drunker than the rest of us. "Whazzat?"

"It seems as though Commissar Montefiore's started his own police force," Tom continued. "The Real-American Coalition Army, he's called it."

"A private Gestapo, maybe?" I said. "I always thought that was PRICE's job."

"No," Tom said. "Best to think of them as Storm Troopers. They were Stanley Saunder's brainchild."

"That asshole had no brain," Karen quipped.

"Anyway. Karen took care of him and put on his uniform so any cameras along the way cold pick out that there was a Coalition guard taking Sylvia —a mannequin after we transferred her to a flight from Sante Fe to here—to Delaxuma."

"Fuck, Karen!" Hugh said, "You went to that Sheriff Jeff's gulag?"

She flicked a smile. "Lovely place. Anyway, I didn't go in. We just stashed the dummy and parked an empty PRICE car at the gate. All routine. Then we left."

"You weren't worried about cameras?"

"Two security guys getting out of a squad car with a Coalition guard?" Dan said. "Purely normal."

"They weren't expecting a prisoner," Tom said. "I called them in advance to tell them a Coalition guard a two of my security men were going to be leaving a PRICE squad car there for a few days. That's it. Anyway, we flew Sylvia back here and she's been staying upstairs for a few days."

"And you didn't tell us?" I said.

"He couldn't, Bob. Even if he wanted to, I wouldn't have let him." She stroked my cheek. I felt the tremble in her touch. It felt…faraway.

"Listen," Tom said. "I know you're all gonna hate this, but it has to be done. There's no easy way to put this."

"Put what?" I asked skeptically. One zinger had been enough for the night. I braced myself.

"We're flying Sylvia out of here tomorrow morning. You won't be seeing her again."

I did nothing to hide my tears. He fucking deserved it. I was blind to the reactions of the others, but I knew they must have been similar to mine. I might have been better off believing she was in the gulag. No. I wouldn't.

"I wanted you to know she was alive and well. I did not want you believing she was at the mercy of Sheriff Jeff. And she's as dedicated to the cause as ever."

"Let me explain it from here, Tom." She scanned us with her eyes. They were glistening was deeply as my own. "You all…I love you *so* much. You must know that. And I know you love me, too." She sniffled, then wiped her injured hand across her face. "But— no: AND—I love you and I love the Neo Publica. It would have never come this far without you. But now it's beyond us. The cause has matured, and we have more of a chance now more than ever to make our dream this nation's reality. The Neo Publica cause has to do that on its own ideals, those you helped me to bring public. Remember it wasn't me. It was never just me. It was us and…" she tried on a subtle smile, " 'We ARE the people.' Okay? I have to leave all I've done to the cause."

"No," Aileen said. "You don't." Her tone had weakened. Like all of us, she knew we were defeated.

"She must, Aileen," Tom said. "As far as the regime is concerned, Sylvia is in Delaxuma, and probably dead by now. They have washed their hands of her, and, they believe, the Neo Publica. If the world believes Sylvia is… gone, it could go two ways. Neo-Publica is yesterday's news, like so many other things get spun under the rug by the Kenton Regime. Or, it could rise up stronger than ever, with your help, because the Neo-Publica would have a martyr. And a hard cause requires martyr to work. After I do what …I can, like I said, and it's a success, I, *we*, can really bring our ideals to light."

"Where are you flying her out to?" I asked. "Some non-extradition country?"

"Something like that. California."

"California?" I said. "Since it left and became sovereign, its been held together by duct tape and wires."

"And a belief in Constitutional Democracy, hon." Sylvia said as she grasped my sleeve. "A real democracy. I can do some good there—more than here. But you've got to let me go. All of you. I know you can do it. You've got this from here on with Tom at the lead."

Losing Sylvia was a hard pill for us to swallow, but we knew we had to do it. For her sake. It took us another hour to say our goodbyes. I was the last. Sylvia's face was sopped with tears. "I love you, Bob. And I will never stop. You gave me the strength…" she collapsed into my arms sobbing, "the strength to carry…carry this through. Okay?"

"Okay." I sniffed.

"There's something better waiting for you." She kissed my cheek, then left me alone with Tom, Mike and Karen.

"There's something else, Bob," Tom said to me.

"What? Another disappointment? Well, buddy. As you can no doubt tell, I'm all disappointed out for one night."

"This is not a disappointment, Bob," Karen said as he wrapped an arm lightly around my shoulder. Maybe you should sit." She guided me to a chair. I didn't care enough anymore to resist.

Tom heaved another one of his sighs—another zinger. "Bob. I want you to know. We've found Tricia…and she's alive."

"What!" I gasped. I rose from my chair, not knowing whether to finally punch him out, or hug him.

Karen turned me to her and took care of the hug. "We're gonna go get her, sweetie. You too, we need you along. And we will get her out of that fucking place."

"You sure?" I choked.

She held me away and looked into my eyes. "This is me telling you this, hon. Fuckin' A, I'm sure! Emily's well enough to travel now, and she'll be coming along, too."

"We'll need to bring you and Emily to her," Tom said. "She's damaged goods, I'm sure, so prepare yourself."

I knew. I recalled how Emily was when she was delivered to me.

"You two being there might help her to readjust. You okay with that, Bob?" Tom said.

"Of course," I whispered.

"Okay, then. Tomorrow Mike will drive you and Karen to Boston to pick up your daughter. Spend some time with her, and then the next morning, you, she Tom, and Karen. Will meet our jet at Logan to fly out to Tuscon. It's all been arranged."

I smiled. "Let me guess. On the Kenton Regime's expense account."

Tom grinned back. "Yeah. There's another 'security conference' in Tucson I've authorized Mike to go to. Your tax dollars at work."

I looked back at Karen. "I need to know this, Karen. Does Sylvia know?"

"About what?"

"About Tricia."

Karen now smirked her puckish feline smile. "The less you know the better, hon."

That gave me my answer. Sylvia knew. I recalled her last words to me: *There's something better waiting for you.*

28

Finding Snow White

December 6 and 9

'd gone up to see Emily as often as my schedule allowed, and it had been well charged for the previous five weeks. The first of my four visits was a week after Karen and I drove her to Boston. She'd arrived traumatized and dehydrated and was still connected to fluids to calm and revive her. On my second one a week later, she was talking, but not able to connect her thoughts. I didn't know if she had recognized me or not, but she had remembered Karen. They held one another's hands the whole time. By the next time I saw her, she was up and in the rehabilitation center up in Gloucester. This time she fully recognized me, held my hand, and we had light conversations. She had finally filled out to her teenage fighting weight.

I next went up a few days later and saw nothing short of a miraculous recovery. She talked daughter-to-dad to me. Talked about a crush she'd developed for a boy down then hall. She was my daughter again—or at least a subdued version of her. She wanted to know about Mom. I didn't know what to tell her. "Still waiting," I'd replied, and we left it at that. Then I left for Denver.

Now, on this visit, I could tell her. "We found Mom, she's uh, okay, and we're going up to get her."

She couldn't restrain herself, and we crushed into a tearful embrace. "We?" she sniffled.

"We," I confirmed. "You, me, and Karen. We're flying out tomorrow morning, so pack some things."

"Oh Dad! I knew you could find her! I just *knew*!"

"Sweetie, you're gonna have to know. She will probably be pretty sick. Weak. She may not even recognize us."

She remained silent for a moment, then she hugged me tighter. "Don't I know." she answered somberly. "She will recognize us Dad...Just like I recognized you. You know that, right? From the beginning I knew who you were. I just couldn't say the words."

"Thank you, sweetie. I needed to hear that."

"I love you, Dad."

"And I love you, too, Emily. So much."

I felt her giggling in my arms. "Now don't you go all sappy on me!"

We arrived at the Tucson Airport the following afternoon, and the dry dessert heat assaulted us as soon as we left the air-conditioned terminal to wait for Mike pick up the rental car. Emily still clung lightly to Karen, and I sensed she was trying hard to contain some excitement—but more so, apprehension. Most of what she'd said to me were words of reassurance. She must have sensed my apprehension as well.

Tom drove us to a small airport twenty miles away, where we were met by our pilot, Devon Jackson. He told us he'd remembered Sylvia and asked how she was. I told him we hadn't seen her in a while. I wondered if he'd detected the choke in my voice. He just nodded as though he knew.

"She's really pretty amazing," he said.

"Yeah," I agreed.

"She had a way of kicking ass," Karen said. Her use of the past tense was not lost on me.

"She did," I said.

"Who's Sylvia, Dad?" Emily hadn't remembered what I had—how Sylvia had laid next to her as she rested on our apartment couch in Brooklyn. She hadn't remembered Brooklyn at all.

"Someone I knew, honey." I said, and we left it at that as Devon herded us into his roomy twin engine Beechcraft. It was stocked with boxes anywhere there weren't seats.

We strapped in. "Okay!" Devon called back at us over the whine of the two engines. "Let's go get your wife!"

Never a fan of small planes, I held my breath as he throttled to full, and we took off shuddering toward the west. This was finally happening. I looked over at Emily, who was doing nothing to hold back her tears. My daughter's tears reminded me this would not be easy—for either of us. If anyone knew how we'd find how diminished Tricia would be, it was her.

A half-hour later, the plane wobbled into the low-setting sun, and into a jarring landing on a darkened strip in no-man's land. Mike reminded us of the instruction Tom had given us. Emily and I would have to stay on the plane and let Karen, him, and Devon handle the rest. We totally understood that we needn't get involved in freeing her. The trauma would be too much. Besides. What if things turned sloppy? "But don't worry, they won't" he assured us. "But if you two need it." He handed me some keys. "There's that car parked near the pilot hutch." He motioned to a small shack and the PRICE squad car parked in front of it.

Devon and Tom hunched out from the plane to the airstrip.

I watched them from my porthole as they met with a little Mexican who'd been waiting with his sawed-off, platformed pick-up truck. "Hey, Pepito," I heard Devon say to him.

"*Buenos nachos*, Mr. Devon."

"I brought a couple of other people along to help unload, this time."

Karen slipped on the Real-America Coalition Army khaki shirt with its armband. She drew a black ball-cap onto her head. She gave me a little kiss on the cheek, and Emily a big, lasting hug. "We'll be back in a minute...with Tricia," she said, then fumbled her way through the door to join the others.

"It's gonna be fine, sweetie," I said to Emily, more as a reassurance for myself.

She squeezed my hand. "Yes, Dad. It will."

Delaxuma

Backstory: December 4th and 7th

Despite all the layers in the situation, a simple fact led Roebling to Tricia. Throughout Delaxuma, a gulag meant to retain its inmates of color from the south, Tricia was one of two Caucasian women inmates, and the only blonde. This had been unknown to Roebling until Devon told him and sent a picture he took of her to him. The week before, Roebling made a comparison with the vacation snapshot Robert had given him, and a photo he had dug from a basement archive, all but forgotten, of a woman and three children. Her name was recorded trough a clerical error as "Patricia Dryant", seized with her family in Havana on September 22nd, 2026. She was listed as sent to Dalaxuma.

Devon was able to take his picture two weeks before on another one of his Saturday deliveries of tequila and cocaine to his provisional customer, Zach Lupera, Sheriff Jeff's son. Usually when the delivery was made, Devon would share a few tequilas with Zach in his "party tent" where, for over the past month, Zach would show off his "capture" —in this case, the only blonde Caucasian prisoner in the gulag. Zach liked and encouraged pictures of him and his "trophy", and Devon took one. Zach had even kept her in a cell in his tent, like a caged animal. He also liked to dress her up as his fantasy of the night.

After Roebling had called him, once he'd made his basement discovery, he and Devon planned the extraction. Right after, Devon called Zach to arrange for the Saturday delivery.

"You gonna have that pretty woman with you, this time, Zach?"

"Damn right. Snow White'll be there, okay."

Devon remembered that, in the Disney movie, at least, Snow White had black hair. "I meant that blonde you keep in your tent."

"Of course it's her, but I've been in a Snow White mood, as late. Always wondered what it would be like to boff her once or twice. No reason them fuckin' dwarves shoulda had all the fun."

Devon tried to make his laugh sound genuine. "Okay, man, great. For Snow White, I'll double the delivery."

"You're a fuckin' Saint, Dev, ol' buddy. I'll send out ny trustee, Pepito, to help you carry it all."

"It should tide you through for a while. Think of it as an early Christmas gift, old friend. 'Cause I won't be here for the next delivery."

"Oh yeah? Why not?"

"I meant to tell you. I'm going on vacation for the next month and a half, down to Antigua to see my sister. A couple of stand-ins will be filling in for me. Totally trustworthy. I'm bringin' them around with me show them the ropes."

"More the merrier, good buddy. See you Saturday night. I'll be waitin'. And so will Snow White."

The trap was baited and set.

Night, December 9

Tricia had been garbed in a different costume and make-over for each of her adventures with Zach. Starting with the Catholic School girl almost two months before, she had served him dressed as a nun, a "soft" dominatrix, a housemaid, a cowgirl, and other fantasies. Aside from the rough—and sometimes tender—sex, these weekly dress-ups had been humiliating, but harmless enough. Almost like a vacation after the nightly brutality she'd had to endure from the PRICE lieutenant. Tonight she was Snow White, and this time his seamstress-girlfriend in Tucson had outdone herself in the authenticity of the popular Disney version of the Brothers Grimm's *Sneewittchen*. A living cartoon, she'd been outfitted with a pert black wig adorned with a red-bowed headband, the puffy short-sleeved blue blouse with its high white cowl-collar, ankle-length yellow skirt and yellow-bowed Mary Jane shoes.

As usual, she'd been confined to her cell, like a princess waif under arrest—a sorrowful disconnect. She sat with her knees to chin, waiting for the familiar routine. Zach would breeze triumphantly into his tent as her rescuer who would ritualistically undress her to repay with often weird sexual pleasures. Tonight, she heard the rattling of Pepito's truck as it idled outside. She heard an enthused Zach calling out his orders to the trustee and to where to stock the delivered goods. So, she reasoned, the pilot, Devon, who'd flown the goods in, would be with him. She liked Devon, as he expressed his compassion and once had told Zach his charade was ridiculous. But then, she'd rather be here than back in her musty tent crawling with memories and lice. She thought she heard another man's voice from outside. And a female voice? She cringed over what her captor might have in store for her tonight.

Pepito crouched through the door of the tent dragging a hand truck stacked with four cases of tequila. "Buenos nochas, senorita," he said to her, as he usually would when he carried Zach's Saturday goods into the tent. This time, she'd noticed something different in his tone—something more detached than usual.

"Pepito," she nodded back to him.

Then he said whispered an unusual aside. "It will be fine tonight, senorita." It frightened her more.

He left back out to his truck four another load, as she listened to try to make out what the voices outside were saying. They were still too muffled and indistinct. She heard the female say: "I'll just wait out here." Her voice sounded hard.

Pepito rolled in another load of four cases and edged them next to the others. Then he did something strange. He smiled and winked at her. He brought his calloused index finger to his lips as if shush her, then reached into his pocket and handed her a chiv. This sent a wave of fear through her, as she reached beneath her blanket to hide it. "Pepito?" she breathed uneasily.

"Shhh, senorita," he whispered. "You will need it, maybe. Shhh!" He smiled benignly, then left, dragging the squeaky-wheeled hand truck behind him as he left.

The last thing she wanted to do would be to brandish a chiv to the sheriffs' son then be thrown back into the hard misery of the tin box, again—or more likely sliced in two by the sheriff's henchmen.

In less than five minutes, three men: Zach, Devon, and a beefy-muscular third person, strode into the tent. The third one glanced disbelieving at her, then hardened his gaze as though assessing her face. She furtively reached beneath her blanket for the jagged comfort of her chiv. She reminded herself: *Cuello. Sostener. Halal. Jab EURO!*

Zach swung his arm toward her as an introduction. "Do you like my Snow White?"

"That's a really good costume job, Zach," Devon said. "The best yet."

"Yeah," the third man said. "Really good." He nodded at her. "Hello."

She inclined her head dutifully back at him but detected a taint of sarcasm. She tightened her fingers around the handle of the chiv.

"Come on, y'all! It's tequila time!" Zach said, then knifed open one of the cases. He lifted out a bottle and held it up to the dimming orange glow of the sunset coming through the door.

Tricia watched dolefully as Zach cracked the bottle, poured some into paper cups and passed them among the three of them. They ignored her as they sat around and drank; Devon and the third man, nursed one drink to Zach's three. She knew when the sheriff's son got drunk enough to make his move on her. She also noticed the third man eyeing her, the more Zach got drunk, and huddled back in her cage for protection.

"You guys ever wondered what Snow White looks like naked?" Zach finally asked them as he toasted her with his cup of tequila.

"That's okay, Zach," the third man said. "We gotta get goin' anyway." He glanced pointedly at Devon.

"Oh, yeah. We've got another delivery over in Tucson." Devon said. "She's all yours." He made to leave.

"Aw c'mon y'all, stick around! Look, I'll even undress 'er for ya!" He bounded to a stand from where he'd been sitting on the cot. "Okay, honey pie, step on outta your cage and stand before me. We got a show to put on!"

The third man nodded perfunctory at Devon, and Devon furtively returned his nod in understanding, as Zach rushed over and stood behind her.

"Wait! Zach!" the third man said. "Here, let me do it!"

Tricia closed her eyes and sighed unevenly, as she waited for whatever performance Zach had planned for the two other leeches. She was surprised that Devon had turned this way. No man could be trusted, even the ones who acted nice. She held her breath and reached for the chiv she'd now slipped into the folds of her puffed-out yellow skirt.

She sensed the presence of the third man behind her and shut her eyes more tightly in anticipation. But then nothing seemed to happen as she felt Zach's hands loosen and slip away from where they had been fueling with the zipper running down the back of her medieval-style blouse. "Th' fuck!" she heard him groan raggedly. She smelled something weirdly harsh and chemical. She swung around to face the third man holding a chloroform-soaked bandana hard over her captor's face, until he collapsed to the floor.

She instinctively drew out her chiv as she glared at Zach's attacker.

"You won't need to use that on us, Tricia," he said.

"Triz? Who is…Triza?" she croaked weakly.

He stuffed the bandana away and smiled benignly. "Tricia. That's your name," he said.

"My name is …Trica!" she recalled. "Yes!"

Devon walked to her and draped his arm tenderly around her shoulders. "That's right, sweetheart. And we've come to take you home."

"H-h-home?" She knew of none other one than Dulaxuma.

He stared into her rheumy eyes. "Yes, Tricia. Home." He draped her cage blanket over her shoulders as she let the chiv fall from her fingers.

December 9

Karen took in the chilly night air, and she stood guard near the truck as Pepito smoked his cigarette. She felt the itch of the stiff khaki shirt against her bare forearms, and her vision was caught by the splash of black around its upper arm. To any gulag outsider, she appeared as just another in the growing number of Real-

America Coalition Army troopers who'd been dropping by the camp lately. She pulled the bill of her black cap lower and leaned against the truck-bed. Its hard edge dug into her lower back, and she stood to back away.

She listened to the sometimes-spirited conversation from inside the tent, as the men drank their tequila, and wished she could have one. She had to do something to relieve the boredom of her waiting. She felt a sudden craving for her weekly cigarette and bummed two and a pack of matches from Pepito.

"Thanks, man," she said hastily. "I'm gonna step away for a few minutes to smoke this."

"Si, senorita."

"Okay. Give me a shout out if anything happens, okay?"

He nodded, leaned back against the truck cab then folded his arms, and bowed his head. He appeared as though he was sleeping while standing.

She stepped away toward the lights of what she assumed was the sheriff's house—an out-of-place oak-beamed and stucco affair on a square patch of grassy turf. She lit her cigarette as she walked, then found a Joshua tree to lean against. She gazed up at the star field in the dark azure night sky. It made her feel more meaningful as she felt momentarily connected to a world beyond the usual one that sucked.

"Y'all shun't be doin' that missy," came a voice from behind her.

"What the fuck?" she vocalized as she roused back into the sucky world.

"Sorry, there. Din't mean to startle ya."

She squinted into the growing darkness at the old man she recognized as Sheriff Jeff. He was made all the more intimidating by the glittering jangle of armament strapped to his body, like he'd just stepped out of some former life of having been a rodeo circus hero. But tonight he was just another obstacle. She tried to formulate a strategy to keep him from his son's tent and wondered if was making is way there to partake in a *manage au trois*. That thought horrified her. "Shouldn't be doing what?" she asked.

"Why, smokin' a cigarette is what. That stuff can kill ya'."

She held her cigarette away and stared at it. "Not the way I smoke these things, like, once a week."

He settled back against the other side of the spiny tree trunk. *Oh, shit, a fucking conversationalist!*

"Never knew that Po-leece force o' yers had women guards attached ta it."

She smiled a bit. "Well, it's an equal opportunity employer."

"Y'all believe in alla tha' shit?"

"Well, yeah, sheriff. I'm a woman. Equal opportunity comes with the territory."

"Aw, horse-piss! Y'all bin havin' what 'che wan' all along. Cookin' and rug rats."

She wondered if she should take him out now for that kind of attitude or let him prattle on. Best to let him prattle on but change the subject. "So, you're the famous Sheriff Jeff."

"Tha' I am, missy. An' this here is mah camp. So wha'cha'll doin' here?"

She held up the cigarette to the rising moon and rolled it in her fingers as she pondered an answer. "We're making a delivery to your son. I'm just along for the ride."

"Tequila?"

"I guess so."

"Well, God bless ya, then, Missy." He shifted to a stand and took a step toward the tent. "Whyn't y'all follow me along to his tent an' we can share one?"

She stood, too, as she calculated her next move, and focused on the red Porsche parked surrealistically near Zach's pleasure palace. "Uh, maybe we shouldn't drink while we're on duty."

"For Pete's sake, Missy. A women's lib-ber, an' a goody fuckin' two shoes alike. 'The fuck's got inta ya, eh? This is *lahfe*, missy. Ya gotta live it whilst ya can!"

Says the man who systematically tortures helpless people to death. She rushed to step in front of him. "Now, hold your horses there, Buffalo Bob. I've got orders to watch over that tent."

"Really? Whah?"

" 'Cause I got them from the top. That's *whah*."

He stepped in front of her and swiveled to face her. He sported a smug, puckish look on his withered face, as clearly he was enjoying this game with this perky little filly. "Okay, there. You wanna go to mah sons's tent, ya gotta pay the toll." He stretched wide his arms. "Now, y'all come an' give yer uncle Jeff a hug."

She stood her ground. " ' th' fuck?"

"Naw, now, missy, le's not get ahead o' ourselfs. That part c'n come later, if'n yer good. C'mon, now. A hug for yer Uncle Jeff." He puckered his fat, dried out, ninety-year-old lips.

"You ain't my uncle anything, you old bag, and I ain't your Snow White." She mumbled as she eased her hand down toward the handle of the dirk held tight in her jean's right pocket.

"C'mon now, Uncle Jeff's a-waitin'!"

She stepped toward him, clear on her intention, which was certainly not his. "You're beginning to annoy me, old man," she said, and moved toward him as she grabbed onto the hilt of her knife and deftly drew it. She cringed off guard as she felt his aged, spindly arms wrap around her. She arced her knife up and then down into his neck. She knew right away it was not a killing stab.

"Shit!" she spat as he reeled back a step with his hand over his wound.

"Fuckin' Jesus! *Shit!*" he yelped as he drew his hand away and saw it covered with blood. "You l'il fuckin' cunt!" he blathered at her as he swept his hand to draw his famed six-shooter.

She saw that the wound was gushing out more blood and hoped that maybe she had hit his carotid artery; or at least nicked it enough to weaken him.

He aimed his gun at her chest. Noticed his arm was shaking. He fired. With it came a deafening, nineteenth-century, old-west-style, shoot-out-at-the-O.K.-Corral kind of bang. The bullet hit her in the upper chest; a hard thud fringed in fire. She tried reeling away, but then instinctively rushed him, with her knife held out at her side with what little control she had left of her arm. She heard the cocking of his gun for another shot, and thought she heard Pepito shouting out *"Sinorita!"* from the distance.

She fell into Sheriff Jeff's trembling body, barely still standing, and jammed the knife into his side near his lungs before his next shot, and drove it quickly and deep in, near his kidney—neither jab was a kill, but seemed to deflate him as he collapsed to the ground.

But not before he got off one last shot at her.

At first, she felt nothing, but then another searing heat from where his six-shooter bullet had drilled its way into her stomach. She staggered and fell, seeming to gasp her last, as Pepito rushed to crouch over her. "No. No, *sernorita*. Too much killing! No!" His voice sounded soothing. She opened her mouth for precious air.

"Nah…" Sheriff Jeff croaked weakly from where he lay near death. "Ah ain' done killing' ya, yet, missy…"

Pepito saw him feebly raise his gun from where he lay to aim his last shot. *"No! NO! Diablo! NO!"* he cried as he rushed him with his chiv drawn high. He crammed its point down hard into the Sheriff's left eye and into whatever he had for a brain.

Three people scurried from the tent—first Devon, and then Mike ushering Tricia huddled and wrapped in a blanket, with its edges whipping in the rising gusts of wind. "Oh shit! Oh God damned *shit!*" Mike cried as he rushed to Karen and crouched down over her. No need to ask what had happened.

She lay panting, struggling for breath. "I can't—" she said weakly.

"No, honey. Don't try to talk. You'll be fine."

"The fuck I will…" she muttered and then fell into a faint.

"Pepito! Where's the nearest town? Where's the nearest hospital?"

"Uh…uh…"

"Pepito! The nearest hospital! Where?"

"Yuma. It's about twenty miles west on Route eight," Devon said as he glanced from Karen to Sheriff Jeff's body.

"Si, Senor Mike," Pepito said. "We can get there by that dirt road, there" He pointed vaguely north.

Mike looked over at Pepito's raggedy truck and reckoned it would take an hour and a half to get there. Then he spied Zach's Porsche parked outside the tent. "Pepito. Do you know where Zach keeps the keys for his car?"

"In it, *señor*. In the ignition."

"Help me, Devon," he said, as he gently removed the khaki shirt to bind it fast to her stomach wound to stem the slowing flow of blood. They eased Karen to her feet. "Pepito, you take Devon and Tricia back to the plane, while I'll get Karen to a doctor. Don't wait for me, Devon. You take off as soon as you get Tricia on the plane."

"Yeah, okay, Mike."

They half-dragged Karen toward the Porsche. At least her legs were still moving a little.

Pepito trundled ahead and adjusted the back of the passenger seat of the Porsche so that Karen could lie relatively flat. Mike and Devon eased her in. Her eyes gradually fluttered open halfway. "Tha'...fuckin' hurz... you... dickheads!" she huffed out at them through her labored breathing.

Mike motioned Pepito to take Tricia to his truck. "Okay, now go. I've got this from here."

The truck was soon lumbering north toward the airstrip, while the Porsche spun out in a hurry toward the west, and Yuma.

29

Reunion

December 9

Rays of the lowering sun peered beneath the light charcoal-blue horizon of clouds. casting the desert in orange. Gusts from the west riled the brambles and stirred up little whirls of dry earth like fluff. We sat on over-turned milk cartons at the foot of the plane's little door, and stared, wrapped in our separate thoughts, at the blush of twilight over the desert. I glanced at Emily as she trembled against the fast onslaught of chill.

Her voice was soft—small. "I never thought it could get so cold in the desert," she said as she huddled closer to me. I adjusted the blanket she wore over her shoulders closer over her shoulders. "I mean deserts are s'posed to be hot, right?"

She rested her head against my shoulder. I stroked her dusty brown hair, which had now grown out full. "Not all the time, sweetie. Not at nights in the winter."

"Mom'll recognize who we are, right?"

"She will, like you said you recognized me."

"That was different. Kids remember things different than adults."

But she was no kid anymore. She'd experienced more evil and pain than almost any normal adult. For now, she was taking two doses of alprazolam twice a day so that she might fatigue herself away from it all—maybe, if temporarily, to hide it. She had, before her time, matured naturally into young adulthood; losing those built-in forgetters that most kids had. Soon, once the medication wore off, those ugly times in the gulags would come back to haunt her beyond her nightmares. How could they not? But Tom had been right: Emily was one tough kid.

"Really, honey. Mom will remember us," I stated hopefully. "Or you." I kissed the crown of her head. Her hair smelled lightly of wheat. "How could anyone forget you?"

"Oh, Dad!" she teased. She stared further into the distance. Perhaps she imagined Tricia would emerge from over a distant rise, like a long-gone desert wanderer finally returning home. "Would we ever want to live in the desert? Get away from all of the hassle and all the people back East? I mean, it's so quiet here. So peaceful."

I had to think about that. It was a fair question. "No. I don't think so, Sweetie. Not here at least." *Too many bad associations.*

She nestled closer. "Maybe to the mountains, then. Way high up—away from any more people?"

Her answer was packed into her question, and there was nothing I needed to say. We tried not to show one another how bound up in apprehension disguised as hope we were. We stayed silent and stared out into the night growing over the desert, wondering what had taken so long.

Then, off in the distance, approached some trembling lights. Headlights. Emily stirred and suddenly rose. She visored one hand above her eyes and clasped the folds of her blanket up to her chin with the other. "Dad! It's them!"

I could hear the rattle and clink of Pepito's make-shift pick-up truck echo lightly through the quiet of the night. I heaved an uneven sigh of relief, and then rethought Emily's question: Would Tricia remember me as I was sure her mother's instinct would remember Emily?

The dimmed, flittering lights of the truck appeared closer, and I saw Devon crouched on its wooden platform. There were two people in the darkened cab: Pepito and a dark bundle of someone next to him. I briefly wondered where Karen and Mike were, but then saw a face in the folds of the blanket wrapped around it. A woman's face. But not Tricia's—at least not from this distance. This woman had black hair. I was struck with the fear that they had rescued the wrong person.

Emily must have known better and bounded out toward the truck. Then she stopped as the truck squeaked to a stop, and Devon hopped from the bed.

"We got her," he said as he quickly passed me to step into the plane.

"Really?"

Pepito gently helped his passenger to a shaky stand from the truck's sawed-off cab. She stood close to him, as if for reassurance. She drew back the blanket from her head, then let it fall to the ground. It wasn't Tricia. This woman was dressed in some puffy-looking, off-world costume, and made over with a powder-white face, red rose-bud lips, and spots of rouge on her cheekbones, like some sort of Geisha. My God! It was Snow White!

Emily rushed toward her. "Mom!" she cried.

At first, the woman drew back, but her rosebud lips slowly blossomed into a smile I vaguely remembered as Tricia's. "Em...Emily?" Her uncertain voice hinted it might have been Tricia's. Then she swept off her black wig and opened her arms. I caught my breath hard, and I could swear I felt my heart stop. That was definitely Tricia's red-blonde hair. "Emmie? ...Dar..darling?" I was perplexed over how her voice seemed to have lost its power, as if she hadn't used it in months.

"Yes! It's me, Mom!" Emily said then, sniffed as she fell into Tricia's embrace.

"Oh...my *God!*" Tricia gasped tearfully, then tightened her embrace. "Emmie! Emmie! Sweet...sweetheart. It *is* ... It *is* you!"

Tricia hadn't looked in my direction, and if it were any other situation, I would have been gravely hurt. For now, I felt warmed by the sight I never thought I'd see again—my wife embracing my daughter.

"Ohh...Mom! Mom! You're back!" Emily sniffled deeply into her shoulder.

I cautiously stepped forward. "Trish?" I said, feeling the mention of her name fall like powder from my lips. Now that it was happening, I couldn't believe that it was. "Trish? It's me." It was the only dumb thing I could think to say. Of course it was me! "Robert." I reached out my hand to touch her cheek.

Slowly, she raised her head from where she'd buried it in Emily's shoulder. Seeing a man approaching her, she gasped and broke her embrace. She stepped backward toward Pepito's protection with her beautiful light blue eyes wide in fright. "No...No!" she whispered. She clutched Pepito's sleeve.

I stood back, confused. "Tricia, it's Robert."

"It is okay, *senor*," Pepito said. "She does not trust...other men."

That didn't help. "But I'm her hus—"

"Mom! It's Daddy!" Emily interrupted briskly as she placed her hand on Tricia's arm. "Daddy. Your husband, Robert." She eased her away from Pepito and toward me. "It's okay, Mom."

She softened her gaze. "Ro...Robert?"

"Yes," I smiled weakly. "Your husband."

"Hus...husband?"

"Yeah, Trish, honey. It's me," I said, feeling myself tremble as I reached tenuously out again.

Emily drew us closer. Tricia's eyes were glistening. Then her unsure expression transformed into a glare of near horror. She slapped me across my right cheek. Though the slap was weak, its intent was firmly earnest. She cowered back.

"Mom!" Emily gasped.

Her looked softened into one of dim remembrance. She then kissed me tenuously on my on the cheek. It felt like nothing more than a dry tickle. "That...that is...for finding...me." She wiped away a stray tear and smeared her pancake makeup. "Robert," she gasped hoarsely.

"Yes." I still hadn't come around to believing this was finally happening. I heard the crackling, stuttering grumble and whine of plane's engines starting—first one. I stroked her hair. "I love you, Trish." Then the other engine. Not knowing what to make of what I'd said, she stepped back again.

Once the engines had caught, their sounds idled down, and we heard the gulag's alarms blaring thinly in the distance. Devon stooped through the plane's door. "Come on, we gotta get outta here!"

Emily looked anxiously around. "Devon! Where's Karen? And Mike? Where are they?"

"They'll be fine! I'll fill you in along the way. Come on, Let's go!"

I looked past Tricia's shoulder and saw the glow of approaching headlights at speed from where Pepito had come.

"Shit! They're coming for us," I said.

Tricia huddled closer to Emily, as though to either protect her daughter, or herself as they hustled toward the plane. Pepito stood looking off into the distance. "Hurry, señor! They are ten minutes from here...maybe less. Hurry!"

"Come on, Pepito. You, too!" Devon called. "We're gonna get you out of here too! Come on!"

"Gracias, señor Devon, but no. I am needed here. *Por favor*, you go, now."

Tricia nodded at him. She knew what he meant. "You will...will fight, Pepito?" she called.

"Si, *Señora*. We will fight!"

She smiled weakly at him, then at Emily and, then me. "He'll stay…he'll stay and fight." We helped her into the plane.

Pepito rushed to his idling truck as Devon sealed us in and bounded to the cockpit.

Devon busied himself furiously over his instruments, and in less than five minutes we were airborne. It had been a juddering take off into the strong wind. Three hundred feet below, the two PRICE jeeps pulled up to where we'd just been. Two of the four guards aimed their weapons at us to no avail as the wind carried their bullets off. Once we were at five-hundred feet, I noticed Pepito's pick-up truck tottering north, away from the four PRICE guards and toward the camp, as though he was returning from just another camp supply delivery.

I felt a gentle touch on my sleeve; one I never thought I would feel again. "Robert," Tricia sighed. "I'm…sorry. But I…I can't…yet," she said ruefully. Piecing together what I knew about what had happened to Emily, I began to understand what she meant…and why. It would take as much time for her to trust me as it would take for me to be patient.

She settled into her seat across from me, then nestled Emily to her. She rested her head on Emily's upper arm and gradually fell asleep. Emily drew her head closer to her shoulder. They needed one another much more than they needed me. A contented and relaxed smile crossed Tricia's lips—the smile of the wife I remembered. *Patience,* I reminded myself.

December 12

I met Tom in front of Slade' s Place the following Wednesday. He tightened his Burberry muffler around his neck. "Walk with me, Bob," he said. We walked west down Montague Street, toward the promenade, as we prattled on about casual thing: the cold December; the Jets; The Giants, and those lousy Yankees.

We found a bench facing the East River and he brushed away the light dusting of snow so we could sit. He leaned back and lit a cigar. "Everything okay so far, Bob?"

"Yeah, really," I said. "Tricia's still having episodes, but Emily calms her down."

He smiled. "Like Karen calmed Emily when she got out. Everything healing in the world requires a woman's touch, right?"

"Part of the cycle of life. How is she? Karen? How's she doing?"

Tom bowed his head and concentrated on his cigar as he rolled it between his thumb and index finger. His solemn reaction told me everything I didn't want to hear. "Mike just called me this morning." He heaved a ragged sigh. "Karen didn't pull through."

Suddenly I felt twice my body weight in numb disbelief. "What? Oh, shit! Fucking god damn SHIT!" I gasped. "Tell that didn't happen, Tom."

Tom shook his head. "She bled out the morning after she got to the hospital. The first bullet that God damned sheriff fired at her angled into her heart. It bled her out faster than they could transfuse any blood into her. She held out as best she could."

I let the news of her death settle within in silence. "As tough as she was…of course."

"Of course."

"Mike just told you this today? After two days?"

"He wouldn't leave her side. Then after, he probably went out and got sufficiently drunk for a day. I guess he was drawn into her more than I thought."

"She drew us all in. She had that way about her."

He promises he'll be home by Tuesday. In time for…"

"You're gonna go through with that thing next Thursday, then?"

He blew out a heavy stream of cigar smoke. "It's the only chance we'll have. We have to take it."

"You can still back out, you know."

He reflected for a moment, then looked north. "You see that bridge, Bob?"

"Of course. The Brooklyn Bridge."

"One of the biggest achievements of mankind," he said. "Some call it the eighth wonder of the world. I believe that. Two hundred men died during its construction, doing things most people thought impossible. It was a dream that held that whole project together, every stone above and below the water; every cable and wire strand keeping it suspended, each inch of pavement laid. All by man's hand, and a dream to unite two of the largest cites in the world. Man's achievement to to good of mankind and promise of progress." He took another puff. "God! I love that bridge. Sometimes, Bob, I come out here and sit, trying to feel a part of it." He looked at me. "More and more now, I'm feeling a part of it."

"I know," I said. "It's a beautiful, magnificent bridge."

"More that that. It's the fulfillment of a dream. A reality of what people sharing a dream can do if they pull together. We don't have that anymore. Never, not even since the Civil War, has this country been so divided—now raped by the ego of a few men and their egos. And now on the fast-track to losing everything that made this fucking dream possible. So, yeah. I'm going through with it, before there's nothing left."

I knew where he was coming from, and I agreed with his solution. There was no other way. "So how *are* you gonna do it, Tom. You know you'll get killed, too, right on the spot, probably."

"I'll take that chance."

"And if you miss?"

"Then at least, I'll die trying. Maybe set an example for someone else."

"So. You're just goin' to aim at him and pull the trigger?"

He smiled. "In the words of our dear Karen Fabrizio: 'The less you know the better.' "

"…Bitch."

"Huhn?"

"'The less you know the better, *bitch.*' Sometimes, when she really likes you, she adds: 'bitch.'"

He huffed out a laugh. "Yeah. Listen, Bob. There's something else you need to know. Hearing about Karen has really messed up my thinking this morning. This was why I originally wanted to meet you today. I was holding it from you until you got Tricia back here."

I thought I knew what knew what was coming. There was a 'I'm sorry' written through his tone. "Michael and Steven," I said.

He sighed. "Yeah. I found out while I was getting the information on Tricia. Steven…uh, he didn't survive."

I let this obvious truth sink in. Hearing someone say it crushed something inside of me. "I figured that. I dreaded it, but I knew. What about Michael?"

He shut his eyes, as though there was something he couldn't do about what had become of my older son. "BlueShirts," he said. "He's a Private First Class, now, in advanced training."

"Shit!" I gasped.

"This may not make you feel any better, but it might. But he volunteered; nobody dragged him off and forced him."

Michael. The high-school freshman sports kid. Second string outfielder for the state champion ball team. Nothing would keep him from the action. Now he was on the opposing team. "That would be like him," I relented.

"I'm sorry."

"No. Tom. Don't be. You've done more than everything you could."

He looked out toward Manhattan looming up into the snow-flurried air across the river—trying to find another connection point for him through another one of man's greatest achievements. "You're taking Emily and Tricia back up to Boston, when?"

"Tomorrow," I said.

"Okay, Bob. I want you to do me and yourself a favor. Don't come back—there's nothing keeping you here. Dig in up in Boston—it's a safe place for you to get a new start."

This had been on my mind. Sloane and Jacobson, the ad and marketing agency I'd worked for in New York, and who'd served me some consulting work to tide me over since January, had a satellite office in Boston. I'd gotten a few calls to sign on as their Marketing Director. Same job; smaller stage. "I'd considered that."

"Good. I don't think you should be here after what'll be going down in New Orleans next Thursday. If they take me down, then they're gonna be all over the city, and Brooklyn, like a bad suit. There'll be a big recoil. That's why I told Mike not to come back on Tuesday, and to keep Karen in Tucson." I couldn't imagine Karen living anywhere but Brooklyn. Much less Tucson—not that she would ever really *live* there. Not her. "That's okay with Mike." He smiled at something faraway. "You know, him and her. Didn't take too long. Anyway. There could be a big recoil here either way. You, Tricia and Emily have been through enough, so stay there and take care of them."

"Then, it's best I do that, Tom."

He nodded solemnly in agreement and crushed his cigar to a frilly nib on the bottom of his shoe.

Tricia and Emily were with me. Steven was gone, and Michael had made a decision he wasn't prepared to make. And now Karen was gone. But war takes in casualties. Sylvia, too, was gone, at least from New York. I heard somewhere—probably from Tom—that she had landed in San Francisco. The Neo Publica cause was no longer ours because it now belonged to everyone. I looked at the Brooklyn Bridge—everyone who still believed in the dream.

30

A New Dawn for Real-America

December 19

Premier Kenton picked another piece of fried chicken from the bucket. This was a particularly good and spicy batch. But then, this was New Orleans where fried chicken was a specialty and it, like everything about the place, was spicy. The smell of tabasco hung in the air as crisp as the clatter of the trolleys that lumbered down the center of the Saint George Boulevard.

Randy Montefiore wasn't as impressed by the mild taint of tabasco as that of the soft weighty one of fresh paint here in the prep room of the Superdome. Something about that smell was as confining as an allergy to him. Up on the monitor screen overpowering the tight room he saw Louisiana's Governor, Frank Kennersly rambling on in his creaky high voice. He evangelized through the echo of the big stadium about how great his state had become under the regime of Premier Alexander K. Kenton...etc., etc., etc., and blah, blah, blah. Among all the state's Governors he was the one who pandered the most to the boss of Real-America.

Montefiore found it best to shut him off, as he shifted his attention toward the Premiere and his fried chicken. Normally he took the gaffs of his boss in stride, but the whole Helsinki thing with New Soviet Premier Vladovkov stuck in his craw. He fumed over the worst thing about it—that Kenton had gone ahead with it without consulting him. Well, he did tell him about it, but appeared immune to his Consigliere's advice, because he'd advised Kenton against it. In the shadow the New Soviet Premiere's relationship with the Real-American Premier, Monetefiore felt increasingly useless—emasculated.

"You're rushing into this alliance, Al," he'd warned Kenton just before he left for Helsinki. "You should think about it another year." Then the clincher: "You'll risk losing control of Real-America."

"Ah, Randy," Kenton had replied as he pat his Consigliere on the back, "but gaining control of something much bigger. This will be *huge*!"

End of story. Montefiore made no secret to to himself that an alliance with Premier Vladovkov is a fast track to making him a useless drone to the watery man who'd once had his ear. It wasn't long before—perhaps a week—that Montefiore had basked in the promise that Kenton had made to him the year before. "You're the only one I can trust, anymore, Randy," he had said. "If I ever get run over by a Mack truck, my idiot son is not prepared to step into running things. But you are."

All Montefiore could say was "Thank you, Al," but that promise became his credo. So let him go on eating all the fried foods. But this alliance would do nothing but thin him out. It would be nothing more than a corporate raid. Even he knew Vladovkov was ruthless, because he was cagey smart—beyond the tactics of Randy Montefiore.

He folded his arms and leaned against the wall in something like a sulk. He looked up at the monitor and watched Kennersly prattle on.

"...Louisiana has been made great in the light of Premier Kenton! And we will be greater still! Our state has the tenth best economy of all of the states in Real-America. Our great seaports are thriving! Why? Because of the shale coming into our processing plants. Our employment rate is up to twenty-five percent. Why?..."

"Because of Premier Kenton!" The crowd roared back.

"I can't heeeer you! Now WHY?"

"Premier KENTON!" The audience shouted back.

"That's our cue, Al," Montefiore told Kenton. "He's got them stoked."

"Show time!" Kenton said as he stood, still holding a cup of spicy fries. He greedily popped one last one into his mouth. "You want one, Randy? These are about the best fries I ever had."

Montefiore held up his hand. "No thanks, Al. I'm more of a fresh calamari type of guy."

"Okay, then!" Kenton said. "Let's get out there and let' em know!"

Tom had done his usual best in positioning his armed BlueShirts. One for each of the twenty exits; forty or so interspersed in the full house of 65,000 people; Dan to the left of the podium and him to the right. Two other Neo Publica sympathizers, Fred Marks and Sam Gilliam stood near the two stage entrances. So all of the possible positions for the plan had been placed.

He glanced out toward the left wing and saw Kenton and Montefiore in the shadows. Kenton was straightening his tie, while Montefiore stood a distance away with his head bowed in thought. Kennersly still had the podium and his little voice cracked menacingly through the immensity of the Super-dome.

" ...Our New Orleans—-" sounding like *Nawleens* "is a city of saints. They march in our Mardi Gras and live all around us. Tonight Naw-*leens* is blessed by saints. And let's not forget our ten and two Saints, whose house this is, and who will —*will*—be going to Phoenix on February fifth!" Cheers erupted here accented by calls of "Bruuu!...Bruuu!...Bruuu!" in reference to the second-year New Orleans Saints quarterback, Harlan Brubaker, out of the University of Alabama. Kennersly let the cheers die down. "Now tonight we are blessed with a man who brought this crippled nation out of the weeds and into the promised land. A land called Real-America!" Cheers, and more cheers. "He has built our strength, and —lest we forget—has given us back our guns!" More cheers. Kennersly switched to his evangelical tone: "We are the true power behind what our Premier has accomplished, because we...ARE...Real-Americans!" Thunderous cheers. "Our Premier by using the power he has vested in you, has cleared and rid Real-America of those Starbucks millennials; those latte-sucking, snowflake philosophers who prophesied about how this nation should be drawn backward and down into its muddy roots!" Booos "We now bask in the light of a new nation! A strong nation! A nation brought into it's rightful light by Premier Alexander K. Kenton!" More cheers. "I truly believe as I'm sure most of you do, that Premier Kenton is no ordinary man. He is above man because he was ordained by God himself to lead us! Ordained by God, himself!" More cheers, but a little more refined now—were carpeted by a sizzle of whispers. "God, himself! Ladies and Gentlemen...I present to you...our *true* Messiah...our *true* savior...The SECOND COMING, itself... Alexander...K...Kenton!!"

Thunderous cheers erupted as Kenton made his way—looking small in the scale of the place—to the podium as he waved to his congregation. He stepped up to the microphone, and waited hands extended in an embrace until the hoopla finally died down. He glanced behind him leveling a proud smirk at Kennersly, then turned to the audience. Tom hardened his poise as Kenton's protector, then scanned the stadium.

"Thank you, Governor Kennersly, for that modest introduction." Scattered laughter. "And hellooo, New Orleans!" Ruckus cheers, peppered with cries of Bruuu! "And hello Real-Americans! It's great to be here!" More cheers as he waited with that same smug smile pursing his lips. "And Merry Christmas. Ya know? There was a time I couldn't say that: 'Merry *Christ*-mas', because the Dems and liberals thought it was 'Politically Incorrect.' Well! I guess we showed *them*!" Another explosion of cheers. "But I am here tonight to tell you that I have saved this country that we love. I alone could do it. And I got it done!" Cheers and catcalls, as some stood and applauded. "I got it done," he repeated almost solemnly. "And I am not done yet. We can be greater...I will tell you how I have made Real-America a global nation! Yes! A *global* nation!" More applause and cheers rocked the stadium. "But first, let me remind you what has been done so far..."

Here he went into his usual soliloquy of self-congratulation and empty promises about the once raging, now deficient yet growing economy. The improving infrastructure. The quelling of liberalism. The success of law enforcement through PRICE and the BlueShirts. How voluntary enrollment in the BlueShirt Youth Brigade had risen, allowing for an even stronger system of law enforcement to crack down on immigration and "other transgressors of the state." How successful the gulags project had become. How the information Real-Americans heard was now filtered through one network—his—and not the "fake news networks" he had fully abolished. How the student test scores had risen, especially now that history was no longer taught; only the 'glimmering future' he had set forth for the nation.

Tom had started to settle into another two-hour boondoggle about his accomplishments. The man never seemed to tire, but Tom noticed he was sweating a little more than usual; taking more water breaks; breaking up the droning of his speech with an increasing number of subtle coughs. He'd notice if he had paled, but his face had been slathered in Man-Tan over the years, leaving it colored in orange. It hadn't made him look any younger, especially now that his skin had leathered. It only made him look space-alien-ish. Tom waited for his cue to move with his hand resting on his hip and near the .45 sidearm in its holster.

Kenton went on into a subject that brought Tom from his state of relaxed attention. "And this year there was that group advocating treason against Real-America, they call themselves the Neo-Publicans. They have tried to take us down." Booos! "But my security force under the leadership of Tom Roebling, the head of our security, and PRICE under the leadership of Commissar Montetiore have eradicated them completely." He glanced at me and then off to the wing where Montefiore stood. "Thank you, gentlemen. Because of you, the Neo Publicans are gone! Their manifestos have all been burned!" Through the corner of his eye, Tom thought he saw Madelyn Kenton, sitting close in the front row, tense and blush at this. Alexander Junior sat next to her looking bored, sometimes scanning the crowd, most likely for a possible girl for the night.

"And now," Kenton said. "I have a Christmas surprise for Real-America..." this was probably it. Tom edged his hand toward his pistol. "A few weeks ago, I met with the wonderful New Soviet Premier in Helsinki..." He subtly unsnapped the restraining flap on his holster. "...We had a perfect discussion..." Tom rested his hand on the wooden stock of his gun. He glanced a Dan on the over side of the podium. "...On January eighth, Premier Vladovkov will be joining me in West Palm Beach..." Dan nodded curtly at Tom, as he lowered his hand to the butt of his pistol. Locked and loaded. "... I tell you now, Real-Americans, we will be doing more than playing golf..." Tom wet his lips, the held his breath to draw. "...The Premier and I will be signing my order..." Tom nodded at Dan as he eased his weapon from the holster "...To make Real-America a..." they both drew at once and attempted to assume a firing stance.

Instead, someone screamed as there came a shot from the second row. The bullet clipped Kenton's right ear and tore it off. The Premier's eyes widened expression bloated up like that of a landed trout. The first bullet found its marked in the throat of Governor Kennersly sitting just behind Kenton. A second bullet pounded into Kennersly's forehead. "There is no other Savior than Jesus!" the assailant shouted loudly from where he continued to brandish his weapon. He was no sooner taken down by a bullet fired by the stage, then a second one.

Tom and Dan had both acted instinctively to do their jobs to protect the Premier, at any cost. Tom's shots had taken down the assailant, while Dan jumped toward the podium to shield the Premier with his body, but he was too late.

As soon as he was hit, Kenton quickly grasped his where his ear had once been, as though he were swatting a mosquito. His adrenaline pumped into action, and the blood rushed quickly to his head, diminishing the flow that his heart had been straining to pump. A globule of fat in his aorta expanded like a balloon, and he collapsed clumsily to the floor; taken down by the aneurysm plugging his right ventricle like a cork. Within moments, Kenton gasped his last. The blockage in his heart had been waiting for one more contribution from a French fry.

31

Epilogue — 2029

assachusetts was one of those few states not fully committed to the dictates of Real-America, and, for some reason, the regime looked the other way. Perhaps they tolerated the Commonwealth because it was more like a recalcitrant child and not the threat that California had posed. So Boston was a good, safe place for me, Tricia and Emily to settle during the triage of putting our life back together—minus two.

Tricia cried openly for days, and then for the next week in private over Steven's death; first because he was dead, and then because he had been so helpless when he needed his parents most. Emily took the news with pursed lipped strength, preferring not to let any anguish show. Michael? Well at least he was still alive, though most likely by now brainwashed by BlueShirt rhetoric. We knew he'd be eventually swallowed deeper into the system, that in my heart I vowed to continue to fight. However I might.

My wife and my daughter's reactions to Steven's death served up metaphors for their changed emotional states. Tricia, once so strong and committed to her commitments, would have expressed her fiery temperament through a thrown plate, or even an occasional slap on the face; all countered by a visceral passion that only a deluge may douse. Now she had turned in the opposite direction.

Emily, once so emotive and shy, given even that she was a teenager, had grown stronger from her captivity. She, not me, was

Tricia's anchor, perhaps because of their shared horrors. Of course I knew what hell she had been through, and I think she knew I knew. Some things are best left closeted away, at least that's what I thought was most convenient.

Emily had helped see Tricia through her recovery first in the hospital and then in the rehab. I was there all the time, but two doors down. There were times, in the rehab, and even now at home, I'd walk by the closed door of their room and hear them crying together; sharing their grief to strengthen their hopes into a conviction of faith in themselves. Not getting involved was the best I could do for them.

It took a few months for Tricia's voice to strengthen back to it's full timbre, and for her to knit her words together. Even so, she might break into tears over the smallest thing, and, though she was getting better, would recoil at any hint of my intimacy. I respected her wishes never to talk about what she had been through at Dalaxuma. There would be time for that on her terms. Finally, after six months, she came to the room I'd set up as my own.

"Robert?"

I looked up over the book I'd been reading myself to sleep with. I sensed her apprehension as much as my own. "Trish?"

Her tone seemed constricted. "I'm so sorry, sweetheart." *Sweetheart*—a word I hadn't heard directed from her toward me in three years. "I'm so ashamed for—well, for what I'd had allowed to happen to me back…back there."

I put the book down and sat up against the headboard. "Oh, Trish, hon, please. You don't have to be ashamed of anything."

"No, Robert," she said as she tenuously approached the bed, and sat. She took my hand. "Can I lie next to you?"

"Of course."

She lay next to me, though above the covers. "You need to know what happened. And I'm ready to tell you. You have to know." She nestled close to me.

I'd gotten to a point where I never wanted to have this conversation. She reservedly told me about it into the next few hours—probably not all of it, but enough. "So, can you see why I've been avoiding you so? It wasn't because of you; it was me. I didn't trust myself to be able to express how I really felt about you; how there was never a time when I didn't…love you." She sniffled. "You saw me through it, Robert—you, and Emily, and Michael…and…and Steven; dear, sweet, Steven. You kept me alive and gave me hope. And I felt so…filthy and ugly. I was afraid that if some miracle happened—the one that finally did—you wouldn't accept me." She looked meaningfully at me. "Can you ever forgive me?"

I stroked her hair. Kissed it. "Oh, sweetheart. Of course I can."

"Really? Robert! I love you so much!" She collapsed into my arms.

I caught my breath. I had hoped for this moment, but I wasn't prepared for it.

She positioned herself under the covers, then embraced me again. "I could lie here like this with you all night. Just holding you," she said. She sniffed some tears back. "Will you make love to me?" She smiled ruefully. "It may be awkward, but I really need this now."

I tried to find my voice. "So do I, Trish."

Turning to more superficial matters I had been able to get that marketing manager's job in the satellite office of Sloane and Jacobson in the Prudential Center. It was an easy commute from our place in Beacon Hill; a posh address filled with threadbare furniture. Tricia's uncle had once owned the brownstone townhouse when he'd been a banker in pre-Millennial Boston, and when he died, passed it down to Tricia's Dad as a white elephant. We lived in the first two floors and were able to collect a little income from renting the two above us. Life wasn't totally great, yet, but is was getting a hell of a lot better.

Emily went back to repeat her junior year in high school. She was looking to get into U-Mass or Boston College to study sociology, then to get a PhD as a psychologist working with and counseling abused women. This had become her passion. It was her way of working things out, not just for herself but, naively —in her words—for every tortured woman in the world. I believed she'd do it.

Alexander Kenton Senior's funeral had been one fit for a Tzar, with three repeat days of pomp, circumstance, services and homilies filling Madison Square Garden each time. Naturally, it was televised on the Kenton/Fox News and Entertainment Network, and naturally I didn't watch it. To me the thing had no more significance than a Skee-ball championship.

Alexander Junior's Coronation came nine months later, after Randy Montefiore found that ruling a nation was not for him. Just like his attitude about Putin controlling the failed New Soviet Republic, he preferred the roll of puppeteer over that of puppet. Alex Junior was a perfect figurehead for him, and Alex excitedly accepted the opportunity of walking in his father's footsteps, but in a much grander context. Thus, the Coronation. It was all about optics over substance. Leave that to Randy Montefiore.

Montefiore was so impressed over how Tom Roebling and Dan Hastings had done their job in trying to protect Premier Kenton at the New Orleans rally, he promoted Tom to head of PRICE. Tom knew why. PRICE had become a lost leader through their sloppy gulag management, and Montefiore wanted to build up his cherished force, the brutal and clandestine Real-American Coalition Army.

But through this, Tom had leverage. As he once told me when we got together for lunch and martinis at Tavern on the Green at Central Park, "Neo-Publica was not dead. Just resting."

Aileen smuggled some messages from Sylvia through her California channels in Canada. The Neo Publica for a New America movement she'd begun in San Francisco was had gained some momentum. "First," she'd written, "we'll mend California into the Constitutional Democracy it had wanted to be. Then, we'll fight to take it east."

Aileen told me that Sylvia would have liked to spend more time on the Cause, but she had been busy taking care of her infant daughter, Michelle, born October 8, 2029.

END

About the Author

David (D.H.) Robbins has been actively writing fiction for nearly 30 years. His first novel is a family saga centered around the 1960s, "The Tu-tone DeSoto" (2014), introduces eight teenagers growing up in Iowa during the veiled turbulence underlying The Kennedy Years (1960-63). His second novel, "The Reverend" (2019) is set in New York City in 1963-64. His third, "The Weight of Indifference," takes place in San Francisco and Vietnam during the counterculture years (1965-68). His fourth Novel, "Boxing with Hemingway" (2022), is set in Paris, Hollywood, and Vienna during the mid-1920s.

He has also created and produces a five-part lecture series, "The 1960's-Revisiting a Crucial Decade." Robbins has taught learning module design and has recently taught a fiction-writing course/workshop. He now facilitates a casual monthly online writers' group. Robbins was born in Darien, Connecticut, and currently lives in Simsbury, Connecticut where he lives with his wife, Kate, and Gypsy, his Cavalier King Charles Spaniel.